I0712880

Testament

Hal Duncan

Testament
Paperback Edition
Publication Date: October 2015
Copyright Hal Duncan

Cover Art copyright David Rix

ISBN: 978-1-908125-42-2

www.eibonvalepress.co.uk

For Felix, king amongst men.

Contents

Jordan

A Horn of Salvation

1

Since many have taken in hand to organise accounts of all that has been brought to fruition among us, as passed down by those who were witnesses and ministers of the word from the beginning, it struck me also, having followed closely from the start, to write everything in careful order, excellent lover of the sublime, so you may know the truth of what you have been taught.

What you have been taught, lover of the sublime, is a lie that made you live a lie, until one day it broke you on a cross of contradiction, sent you naked and hysterical onto the streets of Los Angeles as some meth-head in meltdown, a white saviour of Uganda's child soldiers gibbering delusions of your devil at palm trees and passing cars, all of this caught on a cameraphone, footage exploding across the internets as fast as your charity's original viral evangelism—a twist as tragic as it was ironic.

I watched it and knew it was time.

The beginning of the gospel of Joshua the anointed, then:

In the days of Herod the Great, king of Judaea, there was a priest named Zechariah of the order of Abia, and his wife was of the daughters of Aaron, and her name was Elisabeth. And in the sight of the sublime they were both upright, walking without fault in all the edicts and directives of the Worker. Still, they had no child, because Elisabeth was barren, and both were now well on in their days.

Now it came to pass that in Zechariah's service as a priest, through the deployment of his sacred class according to the custom, he was selected by lot to enter into the temple of the Worker to burn incense in the presence of the sublime. And at the hour of incense, the whole mass of the people were praying outside, when a messenger of the Worker appeared to him, standing to the right side of the altar of incense, and when Zechariah saw this, he was startled, and terror fell upon him.

Fear not, Zechariah, the messenger said to him, your petition has been heard, and your wife Elisabeth will bear you a son, and you will call him by the name John. You will have joy and jubilation, and many will rejoice over his birth, for he will be magnificent in the Worker's sight.

He will drink neither wine nor liquor, but will be filled full with the sacred inspiration even while in his mother's womb. And he will turn many of the sons of Israel back to the Worker sublime. It is he who will go forth in his sight, in the inspiration and the power of Elijah, to return the hearts of the fathers to the children, and the intransigent to the wisdom of the just, to prepare the people to make ready for the sublime.

But how can I believe this? Zechariah said to the messenger. I am an old man, and my wife is well advanced in days.

How can *anyone* believe this? I asked Joshua once.

I'd rather they didn't, he said. I'd rather they *understood.*

Twenty centuries later though, understanding is long lost. So I pin the scalpel-sliced pages of gospel to the wall, Greek and English texts. I take the highlighter from my mouth, start swiping instances of one word, haloing it in lurid pink: *angel.* A word encrusted with import of centuries, like a coral of salt shrouding some statue hurled into the Dead Sea by catastrophe, salt to be chiselled away, revealing the *messenger* beneath.

2

I am Gabriel, the messenger answered, who stands in the sight of the sublime and has been sent to speak to you, to give you this good news. And behold, because you did not trust my words, which will be fulfilled in their due season, you will be silent, incapable of speech until the day these things have come to pass.

Outside, the people waited for Zechariah, wondering that he took his time in the temple. And when he came out, he could not speak to them, but they understood, as he made gestures but remained mute, that he had seen a vision in the temple. So it came to pass that when the days of his priestly service were fulfilled, he returned to his home, and after those days, his wife Elisabeth conceived, and she concealed herself from him for five months, thinking that the Worker had done this to her in the days when he gazed on her, taking away her disgrace among men.

I wonder how long you hid the shame that shattered you, lover of the sublime, thinking the Worker had done this to you, wondering why. Was it seeded already when you sang hymns in the church at age twelve? Was it straining to burst forth in your teens as they told you tales of praying the gay away? Was it sprouting in your twenties when, as a trust fund hipster, you went biking with Fellowship friends, sons of the US missionaries in Uganda who inspired Bahati's murderous bill because it was, I quote, *too late* for such measures in America.

Then in the sixth month, Gabriel the messenger was sent by the sublime to a city in Galilee named Nazareth, to a virgin engaged to a man of the house of David whose name was Joseph; and that virgin's name was Mary.

Rejoice, you who are graced! he said on entering. The Worker!

But she was troubled greatly at his speech, confused as to what kind of salutation this could be.

Fear not, Mary, the messenger said, for you have found the grace of the sublime. And behold, you will conceive in your belly, bear a son, and you will call him by the name Joshua. He will be magnificent, and he will be called son of the highest, and the Worker sublime will give to him the throne of his father David, and he will reign over the house of Jacob for aeons, and of his realm there will be no end.

How can this be, said Mary, with me an unknowing virgin?

The sacred inspiration will come upon you, the messenger said to her, and the power of the highest will overshadow you, and so that holy begotten babe will be called scion of the sublime. Even now, behold Elisabeth, your cousin, she has even now conceived a son in her old age; even now this sixth month is with her who was called barren, for nothing shall be impossible with every word of the sublime.

Behold the handmaid of the Worker, said Mary. May it happen to me according to your word.

———

I flick through the leatherbound bible to The Song of Songs, find the inspiration I'm looking for, start typing into my MacBook, transcribing: *Let him kiss me with the kisses of his mouth, for your love is better than wine.* I picture them in a garden at night, Mary and the messenger, a sweet scent, a susurrus in the palm trees. Her hand reaches to his beard as she whispers the quote. He has Joshua's face.

Yes, she says.

3

After the messenger left her, having risen now, in those days, Mary went into the hills with haste, into a city of Judaea, into the house of Zechariah, and called a greeting to Elisabeth. And it came to pass that when Elisabeth heard Mary's greeting, the baby in her belly leaped, and Elisabeth was filled with the sacred inspiration. And she cried out with a loud voice.

You are blessed among women! she said. And blessed is the fruit of your womb! But why is this mine, that the mother of my master should come to me? For behold, the moment that the sound of your greeting reached my ears, the baby in my belly leaped for joy. And blessed is she who believed, for there will be a fulfilment of that which was told her from the Worker.

———

I watched you in your viral video, ruffling a cherub's blond hair, spelling out your holy mission to your son in terms as saccharine as they were simplistic, conjuring poor little black boys with assault rifles, and the big bad bogeyman in Africa you had to save them from, buck nigger of colonial nightmares, icon of horror, fetish of agitprop. But the video itself, the campaign, the charity, that was your child too. It was clear you saw yourself blessed by the Worker, blessed with this purpose: propagation. You spelled it out in images as slick as they were sickening.

My soul exalts the Worker, said Mary, and my breath rejoices in this spirit, my saviour, for behold, from this moment on, all generations will call me blessed, for he who is mighty has done great things to me, and holy is his name, for he has marked the lowly station of his handmaid. And from generation to generation, his mercy is on those in awe of him. He has done great works with his arm: scattered those who were too proud in the temper of their hearts; toppled tyrants from their thrones and raised up the lowly; filled up the hungry with benisons; and he has sent the rich away with empty hands. He has helped his child Israel to remember mercy, just as he spoke to our fathers, to Abraham, and to his seed for aeons.

I see Mary press Elisabeth's hand to her belly as I splice in the words of her confession: *By night on my bed, I sought him whom my soul loves. I sought him, but I found him not.* She talks of love-sick wanderings through the streets, an encounter with watchmen, how she found him in a garden, beneath an apple tree. Flowerbeds of roses of Sharon, lilies of the valley among their thorns— but it's the apple blossom I smell. Cut: *I held him, and would not let him go, until I had brought him into my mother's house, and into the chamber of her who conceived me.* Splice: *and his fruit was sweet to my taste.*

If you want redemption, lover of the sublime, it has to begin this way, with temptation in the garden, with an angel Adam, his sword unbuckled and set aside, with seduction by a serpent that was never sin, only ever life. With the coiling energies of naked flesh entwined, lost in passion. Snakebite delirium, apple juice in the mouth. No Fall, just a stumble.

I see Mary clutching Elisabeth's hand, fraught at the consequences of freedom:

Stay me with flagons, comfort me with apples, for I am sick of love.

———

And Mary stayed with her for about three months, and returned to her own home.

4

Now the time for Elisabeth to give birth was fulfilled, and she brought forth a son. Her relatives and neighbours heard how the Worker had been so merciful to her, rejoiced with her. And it came to be that on the eighth day they came to circumcise the child, and they were calling him after his father's name, Zechariah. But his mother said it was not so; rather he should be called John.

But among your kin, they said, there are none called by this name.

So they gestured to his father—how would he have him called? But having asked for a writing tablet, Zechariah wrote, astonishing all, saying, His name is John.

At once his mouth was opened then, his tongue unbound, and he spoke and celebrated the sublime. And terror came on all those who dwelt around them. And throughout the entire highlands of Judaea all these matters were talked about; all those who heard them surely stored them in their hearts, thinking, What a child is this to be? For surely the hand of the Worker was with him.

———

I saw the twitterstorm, hashtags spattering my tweetstream woven with ciphers like *#Anonymous, #Occupy, #Wikileaks.* I clicked a link to your YouTube vid, felt the vomit rising in my throat at your message: behold, a Mandingo in Uganda; spread the word; help send a hundred

US military men for the nigger hunt. John was right, I thought. Unsure if he was insane or inspired, Phil Dick or some secret self called Thomas, as he typed out his pulp prophecies for the new aeon, it was the hand of the Worker tapping keys. He was John, and he was right: The Empire never ended.

———

And his father Zechariah was filled with the sacred inspiration, and prophesied:

Blessed is the Worker sublime of Israel, he said, for he has come to aid, to accomplish the emancipation of his people. In the house of David, his child, he has raised a horn of salvation for us, just as he spoke by the mouths of his holy prophets of the aeons: salvation from our enemies, from the hand of all who hate us; mercy to our fathers; for his holy covenant to be remembered, the oath which he swore to our father Abraham, granting us, having been rescued from our enemies' hands, to tend him without fear, in holiness and rectitude in his sight, for all our days.

———

I circle the phrase *horn of salvation*, think of Gabriel's horn sounding the world's end, trumpets and vials of genocide, HIV poured out upon the queens of the earth, Wormwood wrath of Katrina, fantasies of eschaton.

———

You, child, he said, will be called the prophet of the highest, for you will go forth in the sight of the Worker to prepare his paths; to give to his people the knowledge of salvation by the forgiveness of their failings, because of the tender mercy of the sublime; whereby the dawn will come to us from on high, to give light to those who dwell in darkness and the shadow of death, to guide our feet along the paths of peace.

———

I think of epistles and apocalypses accreted over centuries, viral mutation of a taxman's lost gospel to an evangelism of blood with as much to do with the *pneuma theos*—holy *breath*, sacred *inspiration*—as a schizoid webmaster's space lizard conspiracy.

———

And the child grew and flourished in inspiration, was in the deserts till the day of his showing forth to Israel.

———

I slice the scalpel across another page of a cannibalised King James.

A Martyr of the Sublime

5

Now the birth of Joshua the anointed came about this way: his mother Mary was engaged to Joseph, but before they wed, she was found with child.

The scalpel slices another line from the Song of Songs. *My mother's children are angry with me: they made me keeper of the vineyards, but I have not kept my own.* I hesitate. There were no outraged sisters in the story Joshua told me, not even a bearded patriarch casting out this second Eve. No judge, just stubbornly supportive love.

Since her fiancé Joseph was a just man and unwilling to disgrace her publicly, he was of a mind to quietly dismiss her, but as he was pondering, behold, a messenger of the Worker appeared to him in a dream, telling him, Joseph, son of David, fear not to take Mary as your wife, for what is begotten in her is of the sacred inspiration. And she will bear a son, and you will call his name Joshua, for he will save his people from their failings. Now all this has come to pass that it might be fulfilled, as was spoken of the Worker by the prophet, saying, *Behold, the virgin womb will have a child, and will bring forth a son, and they will call his name Emmanuel*—which being translated is, the sublime with us.

I doubt you've read the cult sci-fi novel that sits on my shelf, close to hand, cracked yarn of alien divinity made flesh in a child messiah known as Manny. Even if you read it, I doubt you'd *get it*, see the truth in the trash, epiphany in the echoes: *Manny* as *manny* as *mannish* as *manlike* as simply *man*. You'd see only schizophrenia or psychedelia, delusions or drugs, or both, not the dream as doorway to and from the Æternity I've walked in.

I read it, and knew that door was opened again, finally, after two thousand years.

Then Joseph, woken from his sleep, did as the messenger of the Worker had instructed him, and took his wife, but knew her not till she brought forth her firstborn son. And that teaching which was told them as regards this child they made known abroad; and all those who heard it wondered at these things they were told. And Mary kept all these things, and brooded on them in her heart.

And behold, in those days, when Joshua was to be born in Bethlehem of Judaea, there came to Jerusalem magi from the east, saying, Where is he who is born King of the Jews? For we have seen his star in the east, and are come to adore him.

Herod Archelous ruled now in the room of his father, and when he heard these things, he was disturbed, and all Jerusalem with him. So when he had gathered all the chief priests and clerks of the people together, he demanded of them where the anointed should be born.

In Bethlehem of Judaea, they told him, for so it is written by the prophet, *And you, Bethlehem in the land of Judaea, are not the least among the princes of Judah: for out of you a governor will come, who will rule my people Israel.*

Peel back the myth of magi to the history. Picture: Archelous preparing for a trip to Rome to kneel before Augustus, beg the Empire to ratify his father's will; wise men whispering that his subjects planned an embassy sent after him to protest; arrests, interrogations, the rooting out of rival claimants.

Three thousand Pharisees executed to secure his throne.

6

Then Herod, summoning the magi, made fervent enquiries of them privately, what time the star appeared. And he sent them to Bethlehem, ordering them to go and search thoroughly for the young child.

And when you find him, he said, bring me word again, so I too may come and adore him.

And when they had heard the king, they left. And behold, the star which the magi had seen in the east went before them, till it came and stood above where the young child was. When they saw the star, they rejoiced with great jubilation; and when they were come into the house, they saw that Mary his mother was with child, and fell down to adore him; and when they had opened their treasures, they presented gifts for him—gold and frankincense and myrrh. But being warned by the sublime in a dream that they should not return to Herod, they departed into their own country another way.

Picture Archelous newly ascended to the throne of Herod the Great, his wise men deserting him as revolution brewed among the Pharisees, hearing rumours of messianic readings from the Book of Zechariah, rumours of Pharisees gathering to a leader who claimed royal lineage as legitimate as his own, this insurgent casting himself a messenger of the sublime, a Gabriel in flesh. A rebel with the charisma to seduce another man's bride or another man's realm. Picture Archelous brooding alone in his palace, a king without counsel.

When the magi were gone, when he saw that he was made a fool of by them, Herod was furious, and sent forth, and throughout Bethlehem and all the coasts thereof, he slew all the children that were of two years old and under, according to the time which he had got from the wise men with his ardent enquiries.

But behold, the messenger of the Worker appeared to Joseph in a dream.

Arise, he said, and take the child and his mother, and flee into Egypt, and stay there till I bring you word, for Herod seeks the child to destroy him.

And on awakening, Joseph took the child and his mother by night, and went into Egypt, to remain there until the death of Herod, that it might be fulfilled as was spoken by the prophet of the Worker, saying, *Out of Egypt I have called my son.*

I pin up a scene from an abandoned scripture now. Red ink scribbles out *Zechariah*, writes *the messenger* above.

Now Herod sought for Joshua, and sent officers to the messenger, saying, Where have you hidden your son?

I do not know where my son is, he said to them.

And the officers departed and told Herod all these things. And Herod was furious and said, His son is to be king over Israel. Then he sent to him again, saying, Tell me the truth. Where is your son? For you know that your blood is under my hand.

I underline *His son is to be king,* wonder at two thousand years of readers missing the blindingly obvious. Since when was John to be king? Whose father could this be but Joshua's?

And the messenger said, I am a martyr of the sublime if you shed my blood, for the Worker shall welcome my inspiration because you shed innocent blood in the forecourt of the temple of the Worker.

And about the dawning of the day the messenger was slain.

And Herod's subjects detested him, so they sent an embassy to Rome to say, We will not have this man to rule over us.

7

nd when Herod was deposed, behold, a messenger of the Worker appeared in a dream to Joseph in Egypt.

Arise, he said, and take the child and return into the land of Israel, for he who sought the child's life is dead.

So Joseph arose, and took the young child, and returned into the land of Israel, but when he heard that the Romans reigned now in Judaea in the room of his father, he dreaded to go there, so he turned aside into the region of Galilee, and came and dwelt in a city called Nazareth, that it might be fulfilled as it was spoken by the prophets, *He shall be called a Nazirite.*

And it came to be in those days, that a decree went out from Caesar Augustus that the whole Roman world should be registered in a census for taxes, the first taken when Quirinus was governor of Syria. And all went to be registered, each to his own city; and Joseph, since he was of the house and family of David, went up from Galilee, out of the city of Nazareth, into Judaea, to the city of David which is called Bethlehem, to register with Mary, his fiancée heavy with the child.

So it came to pass, while they were there, that the days for her to be delivered were fulfilled, and Mary birthed her firstborn son, and swaddled him, and laid him in a trough, since there was no room for them in the inn.

No room that they could afford, that is, Joshua told me once.

Where *did* you come from? I'd asked him in wonder, with a shake of my head at this mystery of mysteries. So he filled our wine cups, led me outside into a starlit night, and told me this, or something not too different from this. He came from the soil, he said, from the stable, from the same dust of poverty every man comes from.

Not me, I said. You know my father-

And where did *he* come from? he said. Or his father before him? Every man comes from nothing, in ways you don't think.

And in the same region, there were shepherds living in the fields, keeping a watch over their flock by night. And behold, a messenger of the Worker stood by them, and the glory of the Worker shone round about them, and they took fright at this awful terror. And suddenly with the messenger there came to be a horde of the æternal host, celebrating the sublime and singing glories to the sublime in the highest, and peace on earth within men who have pleased him.

Fear not, the messenger said to them, for behold, I bring you good news of what will be great joy for all people, for this day in the city of David, a saviour has been born to you who is anointed majesty. And this will be a sign to you: you will find the babe swaddled and lying in a trough.

And it came to be, as the messengers had departed from them into Æternity, the shepherds said one to another, Let us go now, even as far as Bethlehem, and see this thing that has come to pass, which the Worker has made known to us.

And they came with haste, to find Mary and Joseph, and the babe lying in a trough. And when they had seen it, the shepherds returned, celebrating and honouring the sublime for all the things that they had seen and heard, just as it had been told to them.

8

When eight days were accomplished for the circumcising of the child, his name was called Joshua, as he was so named by the messenger before he was conceived in the womb. And when the days of Mary's purification according to the law of Moses were accomplished, his parents brought him to Jerusalem, to offer a sacrifice in line with that which is written in the law of the Worker—a pair of turtledoves, or two young pigeons—and to present him to the Worker, as it is also written, *Every firstborn male shall be called holy to the Worker*. And behold, in Jerusalem there was a man whose name was Simeon; and this man was just and dedicated, waiting for the consolation of Israel. The sacred inspiration was on him, and it was revealed to him by the sacred inspiration that he should not see death before he had seen the Worker's anointed. So when the parents brought in the child Joshua, to do for him after the custom of the law, the inspiration led him into the temple. Then he took the babe up in his arms, and blessed the sublime, in the forecourt of the temple of the Worker where the messenger was slain.

Master, he said, let your slave go in peace now, in accordance with your word, for mine eyes have seen the glory of your people Israel, your salvation, which you have made ready in the sight of all people.

I break for a cup of coffee, click the kettle on to boil, spoon granules into a mug, think of you at your christening, lover of the sublime, the promise in any new life born into a history of horrors, all your faggot forefathers slaughtered for sexual sedition. Baptised into blood libel, raised in the ranks of anti-abortionists and opponents of gay marriage, you want your crypto-evangelist campaign to save invisible children from a warlord leader of the Lord's Resistance Army, and see no irony in your own attempts to infiltrate schools, recruit the innocent. Such promise squandered.

And Joseph and his mother were astonished at those things which were said of the babe; and Simeon blessed them.

Behold, he said to Mary his mother. This child is set down so many in Israel may fall and rise again; and as a sign which will be denied—aye, even as a sword shall pierce through your own soul also—that the thoughts of many hearts may be revealed.

And there was a prophetess, one Anna, the daughter of Phanuel of the tribe of Aser. She was of a great age, having outlived her husband seven years from her marriage, and was now a widow of about fourscore and four years who never left the temple, but rather served the sublime, night and day, with prayer and fasting. Entering in that instant, she likewise gave thanks to the Worker, speaking of him to all those who kept vigil for emancipation in Jerusalem. Then was fulfilled that which was spoken by Jeremiah the prophet, saying, *In Rama there was a voice heard, of lamentation, weeping, and great mourning, Rachel weeping for her children, inconsolable because they are no more.*

And when they had performed all things according to the law of the Worker, the family returned into Galilee, to their own city Nazareth.

Three thousand children of Israel executed by Archelous, Joshua's true father among them, and in a priest's vision and a widow's voice, the weeping of Rachel became the cries of a babe anointed to inherit as last survivor of his father's kin.

The Salt of the Earth

9

And the child grew and strengthened in inspiration, filled with wisdom, with the grace of the sublime upon him.

And his family journeyed to Jerusalem each year for the Passover feast. So when he was twelve years old, they went up to Jerusalem after the custom of the feast of unleavened bread. But when they had fulfilled the days, as they returned, the child Joshua lagged behind in Jerusalem, and went to the mount of Olives, though Mary and Joseph knew not of it. They, supposing him to have been in the company, went a full day's journey before they sought him among their family and friends, and when they found him not, they turned back again to Jerusalem, seeking him.

And early in the morning Joshua came again into the temple.

I imagine him standing in the forecourt of the temple, watching the slaughter of unblemished Pascha lambs and kids kept separate since the 10th of Nisan. Imagine him thinking of three thousand Pharisees, the blood of the innocent shed by Archelous. The conception of a messiah is memetic, not miraculous, a moment rippling the imagination to an interference pattern, ideas kaleidoscoping into sudden resolution, an accident of satori, inspiration.

I imagine you speared by such inspiration in your madness, after the backlash began with articles decrying your campaign as latter day colonialism, questioning the sources and spending of your charity's funds, unearthing the agenda of covert evangelism, tracing the ties to certain preachers, certain politicians, the proud planners of a bill to kill every faggot that a nation's force could catch. A force that might well learn a transferable trick or two from a hundred US military advisors. Did the *shaitan*—the *accuser*—show his face to you then, give you *gnosis* in the mirror, a vision of extermination?

And it came to pass, that after three days Mary and Joseph found him in the forecourt of the temple, sitting in the midst of the teachers, both hearing them, and challenging them.

Had you had known what it means to say, *I will have mercy and not sacrifice*, Joshua was saying, you would not have condemned the guiltless.

And all who heard him were astonished at his wisdom and answers, but the Select heard all these things, and they scoffed at him.

You are those, Joshua said to them, who declare yourselves upstanding in the sight of men. But the sublime knows your hearts, and those most reverend among men are, to a woman who was a widow, detestable in the sight of the sublime. For the realm of Zion has become like leaven which a woman took and hid in three measures of meal, till the whole was leavened. And she made risen loaves with it.

A poor widow, he thought, who couldn't afford to burn leaven or waste bread leavened by accident, even before the cost of the unblemished lamb. Her firstborn son had watched her cry as little Joseph—Joses, they called him—not knowing what else to say, asked the traditional question:

On all other nights, we eat either unleavened or leavened bread, but tonight we eat only unleavened bread?

You are the salt of the earth, said Joshua to the teachers. Salt is good; for every sacrifice must be cured with salt, as each of us must be cured with fire. But if the salt has lost his savour, how will it be cured? It is fit for neither the soil nor the shitheap, only to be thrown out, to be trodden under the feet of men.

And they were outraged by him.

10

When the everyman comes in his glory, Joshua said, all his holy messengers with him, he will sit upon the throne of his honour. All nations will be gathered before him, and he will sort them one from another, as a shepherd divides his sheep from his goats. He will set the sheep on his right hand, but the goats on the left.

———

He stood there, he told me, remembering their Passover lamb, Joses's tears at its slaughter, the blood daubed on the door; and Joshua's explanation only made it worse, Joses confusing Pharaohs and Pharisees, frantic that Death was coming for the firstborn, that their sickly sacrifice might not sate an angel sent by Herod.

Joshua hushed him, held his hand, but somewhere in teasing Joses's muddle apart, he felt... a dark mirror rippling, scattered images. Three thousand lambs, one firstborn son, the blood of innocents. Tribute and terror in place of justice.

I had the strangest thought, he told me, that Egypt is everywhere. That we never truly left.

———

So Joshua spoke his parable:

Then the craftsman shall say to those on his right hand, Come, you blessed of my father, inherit the realm made ready for you from the foundation of the world. For I was hungry, and you fed me; I was thirsty, and you gave me drink; I was a stranger, and you sheltered me; I was naked, and you clothed me; I was sick, and you visited me; I was in prison, and you came to me.

Master, the upright shall answer, when did we see you hungry and feed you? Or thirsty and give you drink? When did we see you a stranger and shelter you? Or naked and clothe you? When did we see you sick or in prison and come to you?

I tell you truly, the craftsman shall answer, in so far as you have done this for the least of my brethren, you have done it for me.

Then he shall say to those on the left hand, Go, you cursed of my father, into the incineration of history made ready for the slanderer and his messengers. For I was hungry and you gave me no meat; I was thirsty and you gave me no drink; I was a stranger and you would not take me in; I was naked and you would not clothe me; I was sick and you would not visit me; I was in prison and you would not come to me.

Master, the wicked shall answer him, when did we see you hungry, or thirsty, or a stranger, or naked, or sick, or in prison, and did not tend to you?

I tell you truly, he shall answer, in so far as you have not done this for the least of my brethren, you have not done it for me.

I put the scalpel down for a moment, my hand trembling. In my vision of you, lover of the sublime, bare feet slapping sidewalk as you pace, screaming at thoughts too horrible to suffer sanely, flailing hands on wrists as limp as the sassiest flamer, I can't help but pity and rage. How long did you rot in terror of being cast out, refused sustenance, shelter, solace; and every day of that fear a step closer to exactly this state, stripped down to wretchedness?

He never really cursed the wicked, you know. It's the belief that blocks care, the belief that deserves the reckoning.

And these last, said Joshua, shall go into the chastisement of history, but the upright into the life of ages.

11

And the clerks and Select brought to him a woman taken in adultery, and when they had set her in the midst, they questioned him.

Little rabbi, they said, this woman was taken in adultery, in the very act. Now, Moses in the law decreed to us that such should be stoned. But what say you?

This they said to test, that they might accuse him. But Joshua stooped down, and with his finger wrote on the ground, as though he did not hear them until, as they continued asking, he finally lifted himself up and spoke.

He among you who has never stumbled, he said, let him cast the first stone.

And again he stooped down, and wrote on the ground.

———

I imagine his finger tracing strange sigils: a snake; a stick; a bump: the word *sin*, lover of the sublime, the word that has replaced the *flaws* of *hamartia* and the *stumbling blocks* of *skandalon*, becoming the first stone cast in these seasons of the Gentiles, and a stumbling block of itself.

He was never one for the ethics of purity, Joshua, for your rhetoric of stained souls; it was always error, imbalance, accident. I still remember him saying so in no uncertain terms, lover of the sublime, to your Church's very own stumbling block of a rock-for-brains blockhead, for spouting pious bullshit about women's... you know... *issues*, how the unclean didn't belong among us. I remember Simon staring at one specific woman as he spoke, actually, one with a tale not unlike that of this harlot in the temple. But we'll come to that, lover of the sublime. Have patience.

———

And those who heard him, being convicted by their own conscience, went out one by one, beginning at the eldest, even to the last. And Joshua was left alone, with the woman standing in the midst.

Then he raised himself up and saw none but the woman.

Woman, he said to her, where are your accusers? Has no man condemned you?

She said, No man, Teacher.

And Joshua said to her, Nor do I condemn you. Go, and stumble no more, lest a worse thing come to you.

———

He turned, saw Joses holding his mother's hand, his father's double in looks as well as name. Joseph's favourite, though he'd loved his wife's son as his own, with a heart of quiet warmth when he returned from his travels to gather his family into his arms, or when he adjusted the stonemason's chisel in Joshua's hand, ruffled his hair, said he would make a great *tekton* one day. And with a sword of fire for a tongue at those who threw stones at the bastard, called him *setukhi! setukhi!*

Silent one.

It was the third Passover without this just man who refused to turn away a fiancée taken with another man's child, this itinerant stonemason who'd been as much a father to him as the martyred hero of the stories his mother told. It was the loss that had made him linger in the temple, gazing at the lintel, before he turned to find his family disappeared in the throng.

Teach me about this stone which the builders rejected, Joshua had asked him once, It is the cornerstone?

And Joseph had told him the story of Hillel the Elder, highest authority among the Pharisees, who was challenged to stand on one foot and explain the law.

Whatever is hateful to you, Hillel had said, do not do to your friend. That is the whole Torah; the rest is the explanation—go study it.

Joshua had laughed.

12

When Mary and Joses saw him, they were confounded.

Son, his mother said, why have you dealt with us so? Behold, your brother and I have sought for you in sorrow.

Why is it that you sought me? he said. Did you not know that I must be about my father's business? A vine was planted separate from the father, and since it is not established it will be pulled up by its roots and destroyed.

Which father was he talking of, do you think, lover of the sublime? The martyr or the mason, the warrior or the worker? The insurgent dragged before Herod, slain so a traitor tetrarch could wear Roman purple, slain for a challenge to his kingly claim? Or the itinerant who travelled town to town, building congregation houses—synagogues, churches, call them what you will—a craftsman struggling to put food upon his family's table? Both? Neither?

Whose business is that vine?

One madman to another—because let's face it, whether this testament is taken as prophecy or postmodernism, most readers will likely think me as lost in lunacy as you—don't we both know that vine is the business of every generation, this one, the one before, and so on back to Eden's fig leaves and wormy apples? Æternity rooted in the Earth, a realm of Zion spreading runners through existence, tendrils latched to reality, the æternal is your business and mine, lover of the sublime, and our fathers' before us. There's no one else whose business it might be.

And he spoke a parable to them:

A certain winemaker had a fig tree planted in his vineyard, he said, and he came seeking fruit on it one year and found none. And he came seeking fruit on it the next, and still found none. And he came seeking fruit on it a third year, and still there was none. So he turned to the keeper of his vineyard.

Behold, he said, these three years I come seeking fruit on this fig tree, and find none. Put the axe to the trunk and cut it down, and uproot it, and cast it in the fire. Why burden the ground with it?

Master, the keeper said to him, blessed are those who have not seen and yet have trusted. Let it alone this year also, and I will dig manure in around it. If it bears fruit, fine. If not, then after that you should cut it down.

I raise a red pen to Joshua's prophecy of *the son of man* coming in his glory, scribble in a translation of the common idiom for humanity, for the common man: *the everyman*. Wouldn't want the credulous imagining the egg in his mother's womb fertilised by the seed of *all humanity*, some Deus von Frankenstein grave-robbing the ages to assemble a perfect set of chromosomes. If you can happily claim that material inherited from a deity so anthropomorphised as to have a genome, lover of the sublime, I don't think my concerns are unwarranted.

I scrawl the word *apple* above *fig*, but with a question mark. Step back. Maybe I should use medlars throughout, I think wryly. They're at their best just a little rotten—bletted, they call it. Mortality gives the taste more tang.

And Joshua went down with them, came to Nazareth, and was obedient to them. And they understood not the saying which he spoke to them, but his mother kept all these sayings in her heart. And Joshua increased in wisdom and stature, and in the good graces of the sublime and man.

Crying in the Wilderness

13

Then, in the fifteenth year of the reign of Tiberius Caesar, with Pontius Pilate governor of Judaea, with Herod Antipas tetrarch of Galilee, with his brother Philip tetrarch of Ituraea and the region of Trachonitis, with Lysanias the tetrarch of Abilene, and with Annas and Caiaphas the high priests, the word of the sublime came to John the Baptist, son of Zechariah, in the wilderness of Judaea.

It was 27 CE or so, and the Romans ruled in Judaea, while in Galilee Herod had followed Herod had followed Herod. Four miles from Nazareth, the city of Sepphoris, razed for an insurrection that a martyr might have died in, its inhabitants sold as slaves, had been rebuilt by Antipas in a building project that a mason father might have worked on. In another project, on the south-western shore of the sea, on the site of ancient Rakkat, Antipas had raised his capital Tiberias over a cemetery and, when his citizens refused to settle such an unclean place, colonised it with the poor and with the dispossessed—foreigners, forced migrants, freed slaves. But in the south, Joshua had heard, in Judaea:

There was a man sent from the sublime, whose name was John. The same came as a witness, to testify of the enlightenment, that through him all men might trust. He was not that enlightenment, but was sent to testify of its light. And he came into all the country about Jordan, preaching the baptism of a changed heart for the remission of faults:

In the beginning was the word, he said, and the word was with the sublime, and the word was sublime. This word was with the sublime in the beginning, all things were made by this, and not a thing that was made was made without this. And the word was made flesh, and dwelt among us, and we beheld his honour, the honour as of the only begotten of the father, full of grace and truth. Life was in him, and that life was the enlightenment of men, and this light lit the darkness, but the darkness understood it not.

A beam of pink light slicing in through a Californian window. A glint of sunshine on a golden fish necklace worn by a delivery girl. The light that *this* aeon's John spoke of... even he didn't know what to make of a moment standing in a doorway when the whole world suddenly flooded with the numinous, or the whole series of voices and visions that followed in the weeks and months after. Over a decade, lover of the sublime, a speed-freak exegete wrestled the wild angel of his inspiration, struggling for a hypothesis that might hold more than a day. Lost his head, you might say.

He came to his own, and his own welcomed him not. But as many as welcomed him, to them he gave the power to become the scions of the sublime, to those who trust in his name, those who were not born of blood, nor of the will of the flesh, nor of the will of man, but of the sublime. He it was explained: none has ever seen the sublime, the only-begotten son who rests in the father's bosom. And I have seen and testified that this is the scion of the sublime, that we have all partaken of his fruition, taken grace for grace.

This was the true enlightenment, lighting every man who comes into the world: he is in the world, and through him the world comes to be, and the world knows him not.

14

And John wore a camel's hair robe with a leather belt around his waist, and his meat was locusts and wild honey that tasted like manna, like sweet cake cooked in oil; and Jerusalem, and all Judaea, and all the region around Jordan went out to him and were baptized of him in the river of Jordan, confessing their faults. But when he saw many of the Select and Righteous come to his baptism, he said to them, O generation of vipers, who has warned you to flee from the wrath to come?

———

A wild man preaching enlightenment, a cousin, the stories say. Although the stories don't add up, claiming conceptions for these cousins before the death of Herod the Great in 4 BCE, a birth for Joshua during the 6 CE census, a ten year gestation. But as we can allow that a parable is not history, we can shrug that the *mikveh* rite of immersion, the vows of impoverished abstinence, speak of an æternal cousin at least, a fellow Nazirite consecrated to the sublime, related in Æternity if not existence. There were the Essenes too, healers walking without a spare coin or coat from town to town, welcomed into the local Abba's home. As a second cousin by adoption come to Capernaum, where a Nazirite widow and her sons had found shelter with Cleopas.

A teacher around Jordan, he said, a baptist preaching revolution of the soul...

———

Bring forth the fruits fit for a changed heart, said John. For even now, the axe is put to the root of the trees, and every tree which does not bear good fruit will be hewn down and cast into the fire. Do not think to say within yourselves, But we have Abraham as our father! For I say to you that the sublime is able to raise up children to Abraham out of these very stones.

———

I remember the travellers on the road with us, on their way from Jerusalem to the Jordan. I remember them passing in and out of the way station of Qumran, as my father bartered and my brother stood solemnly behind him, learning, while I, an idle child, threw stones at some stray potshards lying a distance off in the dust, every now and then looking over my shoulder, just old enough for curiosity at the passing companies of ascetics walking the road together for safety from bandits, no servants for protection. At the thought of a wild man berating complacence.

What shall we do then? all the people asked him.

Whoever has two coats, he answered, let him give to him with none. Whoever has meat, let him do likewise.

Then taxmen also came to be baptized, and said to him, Teacher, what shall we do?

And he said to them, Tax no more than that which is appointed you.

The soldiers likewise demanded of him, saying, And what shall we do?

Neither do violence nor show the fig to any man, he said to them, and be content with your wages.

Fist closed, thumb-tip jutting between index and impudent fingers, these days the fig is a gesture suggestive of the cunt, obscene to some, a charm to others. I've heard this image linked to the modern notion of the *sukophantes* as groveler—the posture of an orifice offered like a dog in heat—but in truth, at the time, a fig-shower was a slanderer. It's only happy coincidence that John's injunction becomes an Aristotelian mean between brutality and obsequity, dominance and submission, expressed as earthily as the soldiers he was addressing.

15

And this is the record of John, when the Judaeans sent priests and Levites from Jerusalem to ask him who he was, while all the people were in expectation, and all men mused in their hearts of John, whether he were the anointed, or not: he confessed, denied not but confessed, I am not the anointed.

And those who were sent were of the Select, and they asked him, What then? Are you Elijah?

And he said, I am not.

Are you that prophet?

And he answered, No.

Who are you? they said then. That we may give an answer to those who sent us, what say you of yourself?

He said, I am the voice of one crying in the wilderness, Make ready the road of the Worker! Make straight the pathways as the prophet Isaiah said. Rethink! For the realm of Zion is to hand. Behold, I send my messenger in your sight, to make ready the paths before you. Every valley shall be filled in, every hill and mountain shall be levelled, every crooked track made straight, every rugged track made smooth; and all flesh shall witness the salvation of the sublime. After me, there comes one mightier than I, whose lace I am not fit to stoop and loosen, whose sandals I am not fit to bear.

Patch one old piece of cloth to another, a 6 CE nativity to a 27 CE coming forth of John. You likely imagine Joshua in his thirties, lover of the sublime, from one comment in a garble of texts that lost even the taste of wild honey, lost that poetic scrap of the taxman's gospel, the gospel of the Hebrews, thrown away in the recuperation of his teachings by apologists for Empire. What's left says thirty-something here, a three year mission there.

He was twenty one years yearning when he heard John's roar from the quiet wilds, prophesying to make it so: *one mightier than I.*

Why do you baptise then, they asked him, if you are not that anointed, nor Elijah, neither that prophet?

I baptise with water, John answered them, but among you there stands one you do not know. He is the one coming after me whose lace I am not worthy to unloose, he whose winnowing fork is in his hand; and he will completely cleanse his own threshing floor; and he will gather his own wheat into the garner but burn up his own chaff with insatiable fire. I have indeed baptised you with water, but he shall baptize you with fire and with the sacred inspiration itself.

I scroll an online article, read of an apology from the Church of Latter-Day Saints. It seems Simon Weisenthal's parents, murdered in the Holocaust, have been given a posthumous baptism by proxy by some errant chapter, against explicit orders to cease such insults. Some corn-bred Mormon twink of perfect teeth and bright-eyed faith like yours, lover of the sublime, has stood in for them in the ritual, hallelujah, because it would be too horrible, after all that concentration camp nastiness, if the poor souls burned in Hell just for being Jews. I feel baptised by fire, alright.

And John preached many more things to the people in his exhortations. These things were done in Bethabara beyond Jordan, where John was baptizing, before Herod Antipas the tetrarch, being chastised by him for marrying Herodias, his brother Philip's wife, and for all the wickedness which Herod had done, added on top of all of it, this too: that he shut up John in prison.

16

In those days, when all the people were being baptized, it came to pass that Joshua came from Nazareth of Galilee to be baptized by him, for he was troubled in inspiration. But John refused him.

I need baptized by you, John said, and you come to me?

Allow it to be so for now, said Joshua. This way is fitting for us to fulfil all the sublime conventions.

———————

I am a Nazirite, Joshua had declared—enough to make it true. And for the set time he had chosen he drank no wine or liquor, ate no grape or raisin, neither cut his hair nor came close to a corpse or crypt. Now the time was fulfilled and only the *mikveh* remained to end his vow, and the sacrifices that troubled his inspiration: the immolated lamb; the ewe in atonement; the ram for peace.

———————

Then John relented. And when Joshua was baptized, instantly he went up out of the water, and behold, the heavens opened up to him, and he saw sublime inspiration descending like a dove, alighting on him. And a great light shone around him, and fire filled the water. And lo, a voice from Æternity, saying:

This is my beloved son, in whom I am well pleased.

———————

On his back in the river, he opened his eyes to rippling light, John looming over him, numinous, hands pressing his shoulders down, matted locks shaking like a mane as he ranted sacred poetry muted by the water; and then Joshua was breaking the surface, gasping breath for lungs fit to burst, and above him John cried out: This is my beloved son!

———————

The next day John saw Joshua coming to him.

Behold the word of the sublime, he said, who takes away the failings of the world. This is he of whom I said, A man comes after me who is ahead of me because he was before me.

———————

And for a second, he told me, Joshua heard Aramaic *'imera* rather than Hebrew *'imerah... lamb* instead of *word*. As wild man John in his camel hair robe pointed a bony finger at the young Nazirite, cried out his claim, it almost seemed a gesture of accusation: behold, the lamb of the sublime.

Then John bore witness, saying, I saw the inspiration descend from the heavens like a dove and abide upon him. I knew him not, but came baptizing with water so he should be made apparent to Israel, and he who sent me said to me, The one on whom you see the inspiration descend and abide, this is the one who baptises with the sacred inspiration. For the law was given by Moses, but grace and truth came from Joshua anointed.

Again, the next day, John stood with two of his students.

Behold the word of the sublime! he said, looking on Joshua as he walked.

And the two students heard him, and followed Joshua.

Joshua turned, saw them following.

What do you seek? he said to them.

They said, Rabbi—which is, being translated, teacher—where do you dwell?

Come and see, he said.

They came and saw where he dwelt, and stayed with him that day, for it was about the tenth hour.

One of the two who heard John speak and followed was Andrew, Simon the Rock's brother. Quickly, he found his own brother Simon.

We have found the *messias*, he said to him. The anointed!

And Andrew brought him to Joshua, and Joshua beheld him.

You are Simon bar-Jonah, he said. You shall be called *Cephas*—which is, being translated, the Rock.

17

And full of the sacred inspiration, Joshua returned from Jordan, and was led by the inspiration into the wilderness, into forty days of testing by the accuser. And in those days he ate nothing.

It is day five of my own fast, lover of the sublime, though mine is less an ascetic's restraint than an artist's abandonment, doors locked and curtains drawn, phone unhooked and buzzer ignored, sealed in my urban wilderness of a tenement flat, foregoing food and sleep beyond absolute necessity, as I throw myself into this testament in seven parts, six chapters each part, four verses each chapter, six hundred words each verse. At a chapter a day, my own testing will last forty two days. Insane? The inspiration led me here as it led Joshua from Jordan, mad on mushrooms.

And the accuser said to Joshua, If you are the scion of the sublime, command this stone that it be turned to bread.

Joshua turned, saw the face of John gazing at him fiercely, John sitting upon a rock.

It is written, Joshua answered him, Man shall not live by bread alone, but by each word from the mouth of the sublime.

Ask, and you shall receive, he said to Joshua, that your joy may be full. For every scribe who is studied in the realm of Zion is like a householder who brings forth from his riches things both old and new, but no man drunk on vintage wine desires the new straight off, for he says the vintage is better.

Then he spoke a parable, saying, The realm of Zion is like a craftsman who arranged a marriage for his son, and sent forth messengers to tell the guests he had invited to the wedding, but they would not come. He sent forth other messengers then.

Tell those who are invited, he said, Behold, I have prepared my feast! My oxen and fatlings have been butchered. Everything is ready. Come to the marriage.

Yet each alike began to make excuses. For many are called but few are chosen.

I have bought a piece of ground, the first said. I must go to keep guard on it.

I have bought five yoke of oxen, another said. I must go to try them.

I have bought a house, another said, and they ask me for a day. I shall not have time.

I have bought a village, another said. I go to collect the rent. I shall not be able to come.

I have money with merchants, said another. They are coming to me in the evening for instructions.

I have just married a wife, another said. And I must stay at her side. I ask you to consider me excused.

The wedding is ready, he said to his messengers then, but those who were invited were not worthy. Go out quickly into the streets and lanes of the city, and bring in the poor, the blind, the crippled, the maimed.

Master, his messengers said, it has been done as you directed, but there is still room.

Go out into the highways and hedges, said the craftsman to his messengers then. Exhort them to come in, so my house may be filled. For I say to you that none of those men who were invited shall taste of my banquet. The buyers and the merchants shall not enter the places of my father.

So those messengers went out into the highways, and gathered together all that they could find, both bad and good: and the wedding was furnished with guests, and the oxen and fatlings served.

18

hen the accuser took him up into an exceeding high mountain, and showed	him all the kingdoms of the world in a moment of time, and the glory of them.

Laptop on and wifi-enabled, wired up to the wall-hung flatscreen TV around which I reconstruct this gospel, the internet is my window to the world, all the kingdoms of the world in a moment of time. The particular moment I see the power and glory in plays now on YouTube: footage of a campus policeman strolling along a line of seated students, casually pepper-spraying their faces. Riot-geared blackshirt, he comes straight from some schizoid dystopia of this aeon's Californian Baptist, John the Bugfuck, John of Paranoia; the cop's name, Pike, even echoes that pulp prophet's inspiration.

All this power I will give you, and the glory, he said to Joshua. For that is delivered to me, and	I give it to whoever I will. If you will therefore adore me, all will be yours.

And as he turned back from the vista, it was Joseph now beside him, the craftsman father dead over a dozen years now. And all Joshua wanted was for it to be so, for the power to bring him back, which nothing in the kingdoms of the world could do.

It is written, Joshua said to him, You shall worship the Worker,	your divinity, and him alone you shall serve.

Joseph laid his chisel down gently, folded his arms, every motion heart-wrenchingly familiar.

And if you have not been loyal with that which is another man's, he said to Joshua, who will give you that which is your own? If you have not been loyal with the wealth of the wicked, who will commit to your trust the true riches? For the realm of Zion is like a merchant man seeking precious pearls who has found one priceless pearl and sells all that he owns to buy it. The realm of Zion is like treasure hid in a field, treasure which a man keeps hidden when he has found it, but for joy of it goes and sells everything he owns to buy that field.

And he spoke a parable, saying, There was a certain rich merchant who had a steward; and that steward was accused by others that he had squandered his goods, so he called him.

Why do I hear this of you? he said. Give an account of your stewardship, for you may not be steward long.

Then the steward said within himself, What shall I do if my master takes the stewardship away from me? I cannot dig. I am ashamed to beg. I know what I must do, so when I am put out of the stewardship, they may take me into their homes.

So he called every one of his master's debtors to him, and said to the first, How much do you owe my master?

A hundred measures of oil, he said.

Take your bill, the steward said, and sit down quickly, and write fifty.

Then he said to another, And how much do you owe?

A hundred measures of wheat, he said.

Take your bill, the steward said, and write fourscore.

And his master commended the unjust steward, because he had done wisely, for the children of this aeon are wiser with their own than the children of light. I say to you, with the wealth of the wicked, make friends for yourself, so when you fail they may welcome you into the homes of ages. You cannot serve the sublime and wealth.

19

Then the accuser took him up into the holy city, set him on a pinnacle of the temple

If you are the scion of the sublime, he said to him, cast yourself down, for it is written, He shall charge his messengers to keep you, and in their hands they shall bear you up, lest at any time your foot stumble over a rock.

I stand at the edge of a precipice, an aeon that may end with a step out into blue sky faith, a plummet to destruction. I savoured the rhapsody of Rapture jokes on Twitter, lover of the sublime, the scathing satire and whimsy at a Californian radio prophet's Doomsday deadline come and gone not once but twice. But month by month, state after state, I've seen abortion law remade, an effigy of whoredom rising among you who would burn Babylon, build Gilead in its place. You'd have us all put ourselves in the hands of angels, lover of the sublime.

Get you behind me, accuser, Joshua said. Again, it is written, you shall not test the Worker, your divinity.

And Joseph became a stranger and a mirror, a lost brother at once recognised and unknown, a father never known. And was Joshua recognised in return? he wondered.

No man knows the son but the father, he said to Joshua. Neither does any man know the father, save the son, and whoever the son will reveal him to. For the realm is like a man who had in his field a treasure about which he did not know, and he died and left it to his son, who also did not know, who inherited that field and leased it. The man who leased it came to plough, found the treasure. And he began to lend money at interest to whoever he chose.

And he spoke a parable, saying, There was a certain rich nobleman who was clothed in purple and fine linen, and dined magnificently every day. And there was a certain beggar named Eleazar, who lay at his gate, yearning to be fed with the crumbs falling from the rich nobleman's table, covered in sores that only dogs licked clean. And it came to pass that the beggar died and was carried by the messengers into Abraham's bosom. And the rich nobleman went and hanged himself, died and was buried, and in Gehenna he lifted up his eyes, being in torments, and saw Abraham far off, with Eleazar in his bosom.

Father Abraham, he cried, have mercy on me and send Eleazar that he may dip the tip of his finger in water and cool my tongue; for I am tormented in this flame.

But Abraham said, Remember, son, that in your life you had your joys and Eleazar his sorrows, and now there is a great gulf fixed between us and you, so where he is comforted and you are tormented, any who would pass from here to you cannot. Nor can they pass to us, any who would come from there.

I pray you therefore, father Abraham, he said then, that you would send him to my father's house, to my five brothers, so he may testify to them, lest they also come into this place of torment.

They have Moses and the prophets, Abraham said to him. Let them hear them.

No, father Abraham, he said. But if one went to them from the dead, they would change their hearts.

If they do not hear Moses and the prophets, he said, neither will they be persuaded though a man rose from the dead.

20

At that time Joshua answered and said, All things are delivered to me from my father. I thank you, O father, Worker of Æternity and Earth, because you have hidden these things from the wise and prudent, but have revealed them to babes; even so, father, for to do so seemed good in your sight.

He only knew then what he'd always already known, he told me, just knew it in a way that made it fresh as living water, the way it is to eat fruit all your life, to grow up peeling oranges, sucking on them, juice dribbling down your chin, chewing the pulp and swallowing, to do this so often it is simply eating; and then one day, suddenly you focus on the taste and the more you do, the more the savour takes your breath away—no, *fills* you with breath—the scent, the sweetness. A recognitive cascade, a recognition of recognition.

And he said to Joshua, Son, you are ever with me, and all that I have is yours. My son, in all the prophets I was waiting for you, that you should come and I might rest in you. For you are my rest, and all mine are yours, and yours are mine. You are my first begotten son who prevails forever. He who seeks will find, and he who finds will be troubled. But he who is troubled will prevail and he who prevails will find peace.

No assumption of authority, no collaboration with power and glory, no surrender to securities of faith; these can only be at the expense of justice, mercy, wisdom. I was twenty one myself when he told me of meeting this æternal sum of selves you curse as daimon, twelve when that meeting was unfolding. And in the caprice of destiny, as he was being tested, I was arguing with teachers about the nature of his accuser.

We didn't conflate all emblems of antagonism as you do, you must understand, lover of the sublime. There was the serpent in the garden, the adversary of Job, the pagan overlord, the fallen Nephilim, the king of Babylon as Morningstar, and all of this still seeping through the cracks in exegesis to gather deep underground as the fiend of all fiends, your Lucifer. So, as a twelve year old, I argued with my teachers that Job's accuser must be the one true messenger of the sublime. Since to revere the sublime in human form is idolatry, only a messenger displaying his blasphemy, opponent to an idol of majesty, could be truly enacting the sublime's impetus—which it is blasphemy to slander with imagery of human volition.

And when the accuser had ended all the testing, he departed from him for a season, and Joshua was with the wild beasts, and hungry, but behold, messengers came and tended to him.

And Joshua returned in the power of the inspiration into Galilee, preaching the gospel of the realm of the sublime, and saying, The time is fulfilled. Rethink, for the realm of Zion is to hand. And there went out a fame of him through all the region round about.

So now I set out to retrace his footsteps from my shabby home at the end of the aeon he began, two thousand years between now and then, two millennia and the slenderest veil of progress. My living room a geniza in Qumran, the policeman Pike a centurion in Jerusalem, your Gilead my Rome... I rise from my Jordan, lover of the sublime, set out through the wilds of words.

Walk with me.

The Parable of the Parable

21

And leaving Nazareth, he came and dwelt in Capernaum, a city of Galilee, which is upon the sea coast, in the borders of Zabulon and Nephthalim, that it might be fulfilled as was spoken by Isaiah the prophet, saying, *The land of Zabulon, and the land of Nephthalim, by the way of the sea, beyond Jordan, Galilee of the Gentiles; the people who lived in darkness saw great light; and for those who lived in the land of the shadow of death, a light has dawned.*

He returned to Capernaum. Always he returned to Capernaum, and every time he came into the city he recalled his first sight of it as a young lad, running to the brow of the hill with Joses and his new brother James, racing, leaving Cleopas and Mary behind, Jude riding piggyback on his father, Symon cradled in his mother's arms. Cresting the hill to see their new home. And there it sprawled out before them, low and simple, no fortifications, just the single-storey homes of basalt blocks and thatch, stretched along the shore, all courtyards and cobblestones and sand, and all gardened green with palms and figs trees, a fertile spring of a city, framed in the cerulean vault of sky and curve of harbour.

And Joshua, walking by the sea of Galilee, saw two brothers, Simon and Andrew, casting a net into the sea, both being fishers.

Joses was as wary with the two as he was with James, at first, hanging back. Joshua was quiet, still that *silent one* inside. It was James who skimmed a pebble across the water, strode over to greet the two boys on the beach, having decided that they were to be friends, Simon who thrust out a hand to shake, each as resolute as the other, little generals meeting to plan a joint strategy. Simon who followed Andrew down to the Jordan. Simon who came back the same stolid fisher. Simon who stood now from his net, to greet the prophet of Galilee, Andrew rising too now.

Walk with me, Joshua said to them, and I will make you fishers of men.

And at once they left their nets, and followed him.

And going on from there, he saw another two brothers, Jacob and John, in a boat with Zebedee their father, mending their nets; and he called them. And at once they left their father Zebedee in the boat with his hired workers, followed him. And great mobs were gathered together to him.

The Sons of Thunder, as he called them, were there when he told me this, much later, when Capernaum was almost as much a home to me as it was to him, when I myself felt that I was always, would always be, returning to this simple Galilean fishing village. We walked on the beach. Ahead of us John slapped Jacob on his arm, pointed at a boat dragged up onto the pebbled shore. They lived up to their nickname, thundering joy at the sight. I didn't understand. Simon's boat, Joshua explained. In a way, this was where it all began.

And it came to pass, that, as the people pressed upon him to hear the word of the sublime, he stood by the sea of Galilee, and saw two boats standing by the lake. And he entered into one of the boats, which was Simon's, and sat, and asked him that he would thrust out a little from the land. And he sat down, and taught the people out of the boat, as the whole mob stood on the shore.

22

And he spoke a parable to them: The ground of a certain rich man yielded in abundance, he said. And the man thought within himself, saying, What shall I do, seeing as I have no room to store all my fruits? I will do this, he decided: I will pull down my barns, and build larger ones; and I will store all my fruits and my produce there. And I will say to my soul then, Soul, you have much produce laid up for many years now. Take your ease. Eat, drink, and be merry.

But the sublime said to him, You fool, your soul shall be required of you this very night. Then whose shall all that produce be? So is he who hoards his riches for himself, and is not rich in the sublime.

———

The water was calm at the side of the shallow boat, only a slight breeze rippling the surface, close enough to touch with fingertips; he barely needed the hand steadying himself on the mast as he stood, the cedar warming in the morning sun. Along its thirty foot length of patched scrapwood held together with mortise and tenon joints, Andrew and Simon sat fore and aft, their oars shipped, listening. The sail was furled, white canvas.

———

What shall we liken the realm of the sublime to? he said. With what parallel shall we compare it? The realm of Zion is like a net that is cast into the sea, to gather from every kind; and when it is full, you draw to shore, and sit down, gather the good into vessels but cast the bad away.

———

How do you know the difference? I asked, and he paused his reminiscence, slapped my shoulder, smiling.

If you know there *is* a difference, he said, that's a start. When I told that parable back then, I spent the next hour dealing with outrage at the very notion. How could a prophet of all people, the Baptist's anointed of all people, even *suggest* that the bounty of wisdom drawn from the sublime be treated with such dishonour? You should've heard Simon: *You'd pick and choose from it!*

I laughed at his mock indignation, his wink at the *harrumph* behind us.

Now when he had left speaking, he said to Simon, Launch out into the deep, and let down your nets for a haul.

Rabbi, Simon said to him, we have worked all the night, and taken nothing. Still, at your word, I will let down the net.

They rowed out into the lake, Joshua taking an aft oar from Simon, bending his back to the labour till sweat trickled his skin. A shoal of bream flashed as hidden silver below, in a glimmer, a glance. Joshua turned to Simon, who was already reaching for the net.

And when they had done this, they caught such a great mass of fish, their net broke. And they signalled to their partners, the sons of Zebedee, who were in the other boat, that they should come and help them. And they came, and filled both the boats, so that they sank under them. When Simon the Rock saw it, he was astonished at the bounty of fish which they had taken, as too were Jacob and John, and all who were with them.

And Simon fell down at Joshua's knees, saying, Depart from me; for I am an unworthy man, O Teacher.

Fear not, Joshua said to Simon, from this moment on you shall catch men.

And when they had brought their boats to land, they abandoned all, and followed him.

23

And he taught them many things by parables, and said to them in his teachings, Behold, a sower went forth to sow. And when he sowed, some seeds fell by the wayside, and the birds came and devoured them. Some fell where it was rocky, where they had not much earth, and they quickly showed their sprouts, because they had no depth of earth, but when the sun rose, they were scorched and withered away because they had no roots. And some fell among thorns, and the thorns sprouted and strangled them. But others fell into good ground, and bore fruit, some thirtyfold, some sixtyfold, some a hundredfold.

———

A seed of a moment: I scrambled up behind him, from stony beach into ryegrass of a fallow field sparse with sheep and goats. This much I'd heard before, so as he spoke, my hand and attention drifted off to brush the heads of a tall-stalked clump, and I remember how a Galilean breeze blew cool and sudden through me, made me shiver, which made him turn, which snapped my gaze back just as he finished speaking and... and I was sure he'd just said *machair*, a word I'd never heard before but somehow knew meant field. Another chill shivered my spine.

———

Now when he had ended all his sayings in the audience of the people, he entered into Capernaum, and Joshua sent the mob away, and went into the house.

———

It was Joses who heard his call and came first, grabbing him in wild joy, a crushing embrace oblivious to the haul of fish burdening Joshua's arms, the laughing protests of Thomas! Thomas! Before *the Rock* or *the Sons of Thunder* who followed him into his home, Joses was the first to get a nickname given with affection, rooted in a recognition of who you were. Joses the *twin*, the *Thomas*, double of his father, shadow of his brother.

He was grown now, a man. Even Jude and Symon, as they clamoured him with the *heart* and *fervour* of adolescence that made them Thaddaeus and Zelotes, even they were stripling tall. It hardly seemed that long since he'd left to follow John, but forty days in the sort of tale told by a man like Joshua or those who walked with him must be understood as... somewhat symbolic.

He had been gone for years, and his return was welcome, his welcome warm.

And his students came to him, saying, Why do you speak to them in parables?

I tell my mysteries to those who are worthy of my mysteries, he said. Who has ears to hear, let him hear. To you it is given to know the mysteries of the realm of Zion, but to them it is not. So I speak to them in parables, because seeing they see not, and hearing they hear not, nor do they understand. And in them is fulfilled the prophecy of Isaiah, who said, *By hearing you shall hear, and shall not understand; and seeing you shall see, and shall not perceive. For this people's heart is fattened, and their ears hardly hear, and their eyes are shut; otherwise they might experience with their eyes and ears, and understand with their heart, and might turn around, and I would heal them.* But blessed are your eyes, for they see, and your ears, for they hear.

For I tell you for sure that many prophets and kings have desired to see those things which you see, and have not seen them, and to hear those things which you hear, and have not heard them.

24

Hear you therefore the parable of the sower, he said.

They sat around him, all keen to know of Jordan, what he had seen, what he had learned. I imagine his eyes shone as he talked, lover of the sublime—they usually did, all the more when he was trying to explain why he couldn't explain the sacred inspiration that filled him, not in plain terms, why it could only be told in parables, the poetry of the prophet unpacked as far as it can go.

———

The sower sows the word. When any one hears the word of the realm, and understands it not, then something wicked comes, snatching away that which was sown in his heart. This is the seed sown by the wayside. Then the seed sown where it is rocky, the same is he who hears the word, and takes it straightaway with joy, but with no root in himself, endures only briefly. Then when tribulation or persecution arise because of the word, at once he stumbles over the block. And the others being sown among the thorns are those who hear the word, but the worries of the aeon, the fraudulence of riches, and the desires for things all choke the word, and it becomes unfruitful.

But some, like seed sown on good soil, hear the word and understand it; and it bears fruit and brings forth a crop, maybe a hundredfold, maybe sixty, maybe thirty.

Do you not understand this parable? And how then will you understand all parables?

And he said to them, Take heed what you hear, and more shall be given to you who hear. For he that has, to him shall be given; and he who has not, from him shall be taken even what he has.

The same day Joshua went out of the house and sat by the sea's shore.

———

He slipped away from his own reunion, left Andrew and the Sons of Thunder spilling tall-tale gossip from Bethsaida, Thomas listening with scepticism signalled in his folded arms, the Rock and James—James the Zadokite, James the Just, as Joshua called him—laughing over wine-cups filled to the brim, hearty Jude and zealous Symon rough-and-tumbling on the floor, Mary and Cleopas watching over it all. He wanted a little time alone just to settle back into Capernaum, he said, and as he told me, gazing back toward the shore where he'd sat that day, I understood.

So is the realm of the sublime, he said, as if a man should cast seed into the ground, should sleep and rise, night and day, and the seed should spring and sprout up, he knows not how. For the earth brings forth fruit of herself, first the shoot, then the ear, and after that the ripe grain in the ear.

The ephemeral sprouted to æternal.

Then when the fruit is brought forth, at once he puts in the sickle, because the harvest is come.

With many such parables he spoke the word to them, as they were able to hear it. He did not speak to them without a parable, though when they were alone, he expounded all things to his students. All these things spoke Joshua to the mob in parables, that it might be fulfilled which was spoken by the prophet, saying, *I will open my mouth in parables; I will utter things which have been kept secret from the foundation.*

For there is nothing hid which shall not be made apparent. Neither was any thing kept secret, but that it should be brought to light.

Capernaum

And Whose Son?

1

The following day Joshua would go forth into Galilee, and find Philip, and say to him, Walk with me.

Now Philip was of Bethsaida, the city of Andrew and Simon. And Philip found Nathanael bar-Tolmay of Cana in Galilee.

We have found him, he said, he of whom the prophets wrote, and Moses in the law—Joshua of Nazareth, the son of Joseph.

Can any good thing come from Nazareth? said Nathanael to him.

Come and see, Philip said to him.

Joshua saw Nathanael coming to him, and said of him, Behold, an Israelite indeed, with no deceit in him!

Where do you know me from? Nathanael said to him.

Before Philip called you, Joshua answered, I saw you when you were under the fig tree.

Rabbi, Nathanael said to him, you are the scion of the sublime. You are the King of Israel.

And Joshua said to him, For sure, I tell you, hereafter you shall see Æternity open, the messengers of the sublime ascending and descending upon the everyman.

Maybe you imagine, lover of the sublime, a miracle of omniscience here, sparking this sudden zeal. Was Nathaniel hidden under the leaves? Was the tree itself hidden? In Nathaniel's orchard? His childhood? *I saw you earlier*, hardly seems a remark to instantly convert a sceptic. The truth is, Nathaniel was often *under the fig tree*—studying the Torah, as the idiom means. So he knew the words of Zechariah, not the priest of this story but the inspirational father of John.

He knew Zechariah's prophecy, *I will remove the failings of the land in a single day. In that day each of you will invite your neighbour to sit under your vine and fig tree*, a promise made by a sublime messenger in the prophet's vision of the high priest Joshua in rags, tried by the accuser and acquitted, stripped naked and clad in new finery. A promise that he and his fellows were only prototypes of things to come- *a ne-tser* or *branch*, to be sent from the root of David. Then the messenger showed that Joshua a stone with seven eyes, a lampstand with seven lights.

And now here stood a Joshua of Nazareth, the Nazirite, the ne-tser, flanked by Simon and Andrew, Jacob and John, Philip and... Nathaniel understood the invitation that was being made, laughed and flourished his hand in a theatrical bow, proclaimed the anointed with the same *yeah, right!* tone that he scoffed him.

And so this magnificent seven were called, the menorah of the new aeon.

Joshua said, [amused, wry, knowing,] Because I said to you, I saw you under the fig tree, you trust? You shall see greater things than these. If you become my students and hear my words, these stones shall tend to you. For you have five trees in the orchard which do not move in summer or in winter, and their leaves do not fall. He who knows them shall not taste of death.

You know, I said, that would have been the year after...

Walking the streets of Capernaum, he'd run a hand along a rough wall, beckoned ahead; this was where Nathaniel joined the cause with a sarcastic joke, he'd told me, fleshing out his tale at my intrigued *Go on*. I swallowed now, thought of my sister pulling me from bitter argument with my father, my grief scorning his Pharisaic lies of afterlife, his cursing me for a Sadducee. While Joshua was promising the life of ages to Nathaniel, all I could taste was death.

I know, he said. Your brother.

2

And the third day there was a marriage in Cana of Galilee, and Joshua's mother was there, and Joshua was called, with his brothers and students, to the marriage.

And Nathaniel nodded at James and Joses, Jude and Symon.

The two olive trees that flanked the lampstand in Zechariah's vision? he said. And the two golden pipes pouring out oil? All we need now is a flying scroll.

———

And Joshua put forth a parable to those who were invited, when he marked how they chose out the places of honour.

When you are invited by any man to a wedding, he said, do not sit at the top table, lest a more distinguished man than you be invited, and he who invited you both comes and says to you, Give this man your place, and you begin with shame to take the lowest table. Rather when you are invited, go and sit down in the lowest table, so when he who invited you comes, he may say, Friend, go up higher. Then you shall have respect in the presence of those who sit at supper with you. For he who adores himself shall be denigrated; and he who denigrates himself shall be adored.

But the steward of the feast, when he came in to see the guests, saw there only a man who wore no wedding garment.

Friend, he said to Joshua, how did you get in without a wedding garment?

And Joshua was speechless.

———

I laughed as he told me this. Even restoring the punchline lost to another parable, the gospel story does little justice to his wit. You must imagine his friends flocked round him, nodding as he held court, the gravitas in his sermon suddenly punctured as, lesson expounded, wisdom dispensed, he moved to take a lowly seat, only for a steward to try and shoo the sophomore sage out as a beggar. I laughed as he aped his own flummox.

I can't imagine you speechless, I said.

Sometimes, he smiled wryly, humility is a lesson even the humble have to learn.

———

Still, when they wanted wine, Mary said to him, They have no wine.

Woman, said Joshua to her, what have I to do with you? My hour is not yet come.

———

Just perform the sacrifices, they'd said, end the Nazirite vow, and drink! No sacrifice, he said. No innocent blood.

———

His mother said to the waiters, Whatever he says to you, do it.

And six waterpots of stone were sitting there, according to the custom of purification, each holding twenty to thirty gallons.

———

And he wondered, Is a marriage feast about the ceremony or the celebration?

———

Fill the waterpots with water, Joshua said. And they filled them to the brim.

Now draw some out, he said, and take it to the steward of the feast.

So they took it, and when the steward had tasted the water that was made wine, not knowing where it came from—although the waiters who drew the water knew—he called the bridegroom.

Every man, he said, sets forth the good wine at the start, and then the poorer wine when men have drunk well. But you have held the good wine back till now.

No man drunk on vintage wine, said Joshua, desires the new straight off. For he insists the vintage is better.

This beginning of miracles Joshua did in Cana of Galilee, and manifested forth his glory; and his students believed in him. After this he went down to Capernaum, he and his mother and his brothers and students, and they continued there a few days.

3

And they went into Capernaum, and at once on the Sabbath day he entered into the congregation house and taught. And they were astonished at his teachings, for he taught them as one who had authority, not as the clerks.

Is circumcision of benefit or not? his students said to him.

Were it of benefit, he said to them, their father would beget them on their mother circumcised. But the true circumcision in inspiration has proven altogether practical.

Would you have us fast? his students asked him. And how shall we pray? Shall we give alms? And what rules shall we observe in eating?

Do not lie, Joshua said, and that which you hate, do not do: if you fast, you will beget a vice for yourselves; if you pray, you will be condemned; if you give alms, you will do a wrong to your inspirations.

And one of the company said to him, Rabbi, speak to my brother, that he divide our inheritance with me.

Man, Joshua said to him, who made me a judge or a divider over you?

He turned to his students and said to them, I am not a divider, am I?

I imagine Thomas in the audience, the look on his face as his older brother shrugs off circumcision as worthless, waves away every rite and rule for pious living, refuses point blank to arbitrate over those he's just told, to all intents and purposes, *do what thou wilt*, and then asks with utter disingenuity, I don't come across as divisive, do I? I wish I'd been there to see it. I wish Nathaniel had been there too, actually. You can be sure he would have had a sharp response.

And there was in their congregation house a man with a fouled inspiration; and he cried out with a loud voice, saying, Let us alone; what have we to do with you, you Joshua the Nazirite? Are you come to destroy us? I know you who you are—the holy one of the sublime.

And Joshua rebuked him, saying, Hold your peace, and come out of him.

And when the fouled inspiration had shaken him and shrieked, it came out, hurt him no more. And they were all amazed, insomuch that they questioned among themselves.

What a word is this? they said. What new teachings are these? For with authority and power he directs even the fouled inspirations, and they obey him.

By what authority do you do these things? they said. And who gave you this authority?

I will ask you one thing too, said Joshua, and if you'll tell me this, then likewise I will tell you by what authority I do these things. The baptism of John, from where was it? From Æternity, or of men?

And they reasoned with themselves, If we shall say, From Æternity; he will say to us, Why did you not trust him then? But if we shall say, Of men; all the people will stone us, for they are persuaded that John is a prophet.

We cannot tell, they answered Joshua.

And he said, Neither do I tell you by what authority I do these things.

Come, his students said then, let us pray today and fast.

What is my failing then, said Joshua, or in what way have I been vanquished? But when the bridegroom comes forth from the bridal chamber, then let them fast and pray.

The stones had tended to Nathaniel at his wedding, after all, the carved jars bringing forth wine that once was water. Even he should be convinced now.

4

And forthwith, when they were come out of the congregation house, they entered into the home of Simon and Andrew, with Jacob and John. But Simon's mother-in-law lay sick of a great fever, and they entreated him for her. So he came and took her by the hand, and lifted her up. And immediately the fever left her, and she tended to them.

She doted on him, Zebedee's wife, his aunt Salome, the midwife who vouched for Mary's virginity, that her sister's little *setukhi* must be a miracle. Unlike Joses, Joshua had held back the tears when her new husband took her away from Nazareth to Capernaum; when Mary's new husband Cleopas brought them all here too though, everyone's tears flowed at the reunion.

It was James who introduced Simon to the Sons of Thunder... and their sister, of course. I remember his rich laugh once, deep in the night and deep into the wine, as he recalled how shy she suddenly became with this brawny fisherman's lad from Bethsaida. How awkward Simon became in response, and how the clumsiest of courtships offered them all no end of amusement. Oh, and Simon the Rock in his wedding day best; there was a sight! And everyone laughed, but I remember the laughter slowly going quiet then, how I looked to Joshua for guidance, saw him lay his hand on Simon's.

I don't know how she died, Simon's wife—that was one of the few times ever that they talked about her—but I always felt she was the true indissoluble bond between them all, even in her absence. Especially in her absence.

Who are you, O man? Salome said. And whose son? You have sat on my couch, and eaten from my table.

I am he who is from the one, Joshua said to her. To me was given of the things of my father.

I am your student, Salome said.

Then I say, said Joshua, where there is division it will be filled with darkness, but where there is unity it will be filled with light. Blessed is he who was before he came into being.

To think I knew you when you were a twinkle in your father's eye, Salome said to him in words of the time and place. Her little Joshua who sang so sweetly from the Torah, returned from John a teacher and healer, a prophet. She'd made him that before he was even born, he said.

And when one of those who sat at supper with him heard these things, he said, Blessed is he who shall eat bread in the realm of the sublime.

Then said Joshua to he who invited him, When you make a dinner or a supper, do not call your friends, nor your brethren, neither your kinsmen, nor your rich neighbours, lest they invite you in return, and a repayment be made. But when you make a feast, call the poor, the maimed, the lame, the blind. Then you shall be blessed, for they cannot repay you, but you shall be repaid in the restoration of the just.

And at evenfall, as the sun set, they brought to him all who were diseased, and who were daimon-driven. And all the city was gathered together at the door, and he laid his hands on every one of them, and healed them. And daimons also came out of many, crying out, and saying, You are the anointed, the scion of the sublime. And he rebuked them, not allowing them to speak, for they knew that he was the anointed.

By Your Patience

5

And in the morning, rising up a good while before dawn, he went out and departed into a place in the quiet wilds, and prayed there.

He took me there once to see the sunrise, out past the congregation house, north of town, through the pastures around the seven springs, to a low hill dotted with palm trees and olives; we arrived just as the grey world's silhouette trees began to take form.

We're here, he said as we crested the hill.

Where?

Look.

The curve of the north-east shore sweeping off to our left, we sat, gazing out across the Sea of Galilee and watching the gloaming turn to golds and reds and pinks of dawn above the far-hilled horizon of the Gergesenes.

And Simon and those who were with him followed after him.

All men are searching for you, they said to him when they'd found him.

And he put forth another parable to them.

The realm of Zion is like a farmer, he said, who sowed good seed in his field. But while he slept, his enemy came and sowed ryegrass among the wheat, and went his way. So when the blade sprouted, as it ripened to fruition, the ryegrass also appeared.

So the farmhands of the householder came and said to him, Sir, did you not sow good seed in your field? Where did the ryegrass come from then?

An enemy has done this, he said.

Would you then that we go and gather them up? said the farmhands.

No, he said, lest while you gather up the ryegrass, you root up the wheat with it also. Let both grow together until the harvest, and in the time of harvest I will tell the reapers to gather the ryegrass together first, and bind it in bundles to burn, but gather the wheat into my barn.

And the students came and said to him, Explain to us the parable of the ryegrass of the field.

He said, He who sows the good seed is the everyman; the field is the world; the good seed are the offspring of the realm; but the weeds are the offspring of strife; the enemy who sowed them is the slanderer; the harvest is the culmination of this aeon; and the reapers are the messengers. As therefore the ryegrass is gathered and burned in the fire, so it shall be in the culmination of this aeon. I am come to send fire on the earth, and how I wish it were already kindled. I have a baptism to be baptized with, and how I am on the rack until it be accomplished.

For the everyman shall come in the honour of his father with the holy messengers, and then he shall reward each man according to his works. And he shall send his messengers with a great sound of a trumpet, and they shall gather together his successors from the four winds, from one end of the heavens to the other. They shall gather out of his realm all stumbling blocks and causes of iniquity, cast them into a furnace of fire. Then shall the upright shine forth as the sun in the realm of their father.

Have you understood all these things? said Joshua.

It's as if he saw even then how his word might be warped, from *aeon's culmination* to *world's end*, that the revolution of the soul he preached, humanity assuming its true glory, might become a bloody pogrom on *people* designated weeds, a holocaust on the field itself. You *understand?* he said.

Yes, Teacher, they said.

6

The harvest truly is plenteous, he said to his students then, but the labourers are few. Pray to the master of the harvest therefore, that he will send forth labourers into his harvest.

And John answered him, saying, Rabbi, we saw one casting out daimons in your name, but he does not follow us, so we forbid him, because he does not follow us.

Maybe it was not simply the next morning. Maybe it was days, weeks, months later, or longer, and Joshua had been carrying out his mission quietly in Capernaum, sowing the seeds of his teachings within his students, letting them grow. Sowing the seeds of trust in the community at large too, with his actions: healing the sick and casting daimons out, drawing out and dissecting with his words those fouled-up complexes of inspirations we still call personal demons, those monsters of the psyche that turn us rabid when confronted by a man who calls them what they are. And he tried, he said to me, he *tried* to tell his patients not to make him their new daimon in the guise of deity. For months in Capernaum, as they came to him, he said, as his seed spread wild until one who didn't follow him could heal. And his students bristled at this, as if they had the right.

Do not forbid him, Joshua said. There is no man who does a miracle in my name who can speak ill of me lightly. He who is not against us is for us. But what do you think? A certain winemaker had two sons. And he came to the first, and said, Son, go work today in my vineyard. And he answered, I go, sir; but went not. And he came to the second, and said likewise. He answered, I will not; but afterward he had a change of heart and went. Which of the two did the will of his father?

The last, they said to him.

So, he said to them, many that are first shall be last, and the last shall be first.

Simon was the first of the twelve, the last still to come, back then. Simon was the first of all Joshua's students down the centuries since those early days in Capernaum I can only reconstruct from weft of writings, warp of memories, calling on sacred inspiration to work through me, unravel gospel or glimpse of sunlight, rewind twine and knit it all into this weaving of words. I was the last of the twelve, first of his heirs, as you, lover of the sublime, are the last who may, I hope, be first, if you will only open your mind.

And it came to pass, that when Joshua had finished these parables, they brought to him one who was deaf and had an impediment in his speech, and they begged him to put his hand upon him. And he took him aside from the mob, and put his fingers into his ears, and he spit, and touched his tongue. And looking up to the heavens, he sighed, said to him, *Ephphatha*, that is, *Be opened.*

And at once his ears were opened, and the string of his tongue was loosed, and he spoke sense. And Joshua charged them that they should tell no man, but the more he charged them, so much the more a great deal they published it, and were beyond measure astonished, saying, He has done all things well. He makes both the deaf hear and the mute speak.

He who has ears, let him hear, I might say.

7

And it came to pass on a certain day, as he was teaching, that there were some of the Select and teachers of the law sitting by, and it was noised that he was in the house. And at once many were gathered together, insomuch that there was no room to welcome them, no, not so much as about the door. And he preached the word to them, and the power of the teacher was present to heal them.

They crammed the courtyard's cobbled floor, squeezed in around earthen furnace, basalt mills for grinding grain and pressing olives, perched on the stone steps up to the roof. Imagine Mary tutting in a doorway, hustling Jude and Symon out to grab clay pots and plates, amphorae and lamps from underfoot, take them into the surrounding cells of the clan's commune of a home, for safekeeping. Imagine Thomas muttering to his brother James in one doorway, Zebedee and Cleopas looking on bemused from another, Sons of Thunder playing doormen for the cell where Simon and Andrew brought the sick to Joshua.

And behold, they brought to him a man stricken by the palsy, lying on a bed which was borne by four. And they sought means to bring him in, to lay him before Joshua, so when they could not come near him for the press, they went up onto the rooftop, and let him down through the tiling with his bed into the midst before Joshua.

He was a good man, Joshua told me, the love and loyalty of his friends a silent witness to his worth, their sheer bloody-minded will to help him a testimony in sweat that the falling block of stone which left him paralysed was fate at its most unjust; and there he lay apologising to his friends for all their troubles.

And Joshua seeing their trust said to the man stricken by the palsy, Son, be of good cheer, [and he pointed at the man's friends as he said,] your failings are forgiven.

You understand, lover of the sublime, why your word *sin* is so wrong for the *hamartia* Joshua remitted, absolved, *dissolved?* A flaw, a failing, an error, a disability. Even the word *forgiveness* botches what he said to the man as he knelt down and took his hand: that he had *nothing* to feel guilt for; that his friends felt no burden in their care.

But the clerks and the Select began to reason with their hearts, saying, Why does this man speak blasphemies? Who can forgive failings but the sublime only?

Did he say, *I* who am the hand of the sublime, forgive your crime, now cleanse the stain upon your soul of having suffered bad luck? If this is your belief, you *are* the clerks and the Select.

And immediately when Joshua realised in his inspiration that they so reasoned within themselves, he said to them, Why do you think ill in your hearts? Is it easier to say to the sick of the palsy, Your failings are forgiven, or to say, Arise, and walk? But so you may know that the everyman has power on earth to forgive failings—and then he said to the sick of the palsy—Arise, take up your bed, and go to your house.

Molotov of metaphysical anarcho-socialism thrown, the everyman stood.

And he arose, and departed to his house. And when the mob saw it, they marvelled, and they honoured the sublime which had given such power to men, saying, We never saw it in this fashion. We have seen strange things today.

8

And a certain centurion's slave, who was dear to him, was sick of the palsy, grievously tormented, ready to die. And when he heard of Joshua, he sent the Jewish elders to him, begging that he would come and heal his slave. When they came to Joshua, they begged him at once, saying that he was worthy for whom Joshua should do this—for he loves our nation and has built us a congregation house.

I will come and heal him, Joshua said and went with them.

Out of the house, into the cul-de-sac it nestled at the end of, a few turns through the side-streets, and they were out of Capernaum's warren of alleys, onto the main street running south to north, from the lakeside to that congregation house. The elders led the way, he thought, like lackeys sent to fetch him.

But when he was now not far from the house, the centurion sent friends to say, Master, do not trouble yourself, for I am not worthy that you should enter under my roof, for which reason I neither thought myself worthy to come to you. Rather, say in a word, and my slave shall be healed, for I too am a man set under authority, having soldiers under me, and I say to one, Go! and he goes, and to another, Come! and he comes, and to my slave, Do it! and he does it.

Setting the text in place, I bristle at this first smear of blight, recall the rather different dismissal Joshua recounted: Don't trouble yourself, the centurion's message said. My slave is hardly worth your hassle. And with your power, surely you can just command it, no?

When Joshua heard this, he was shocked and turned himself about, spoke to the people who followed him.

I have never found such mighty faith, he said, no, not in Israel.

His voice was low, holocaust in his eyes.

Many shall come from east and west, he said, north and south, claim seats with Abraham, Isaac, Jacob, all the prophets, in the realm of Zion itself, while the children of the realm shall be cast out into outer darkness, and they shall fall by the edge of the sword, and shall be led away captive into all nations. There shall be weeping and gnashing of teeth, when you shall see yourselves thrust out. You shall be hated by all nations because of my name, and Jerusalem shall be trodden down by the Gentiles, until the seasons of the Gentiles be fulfilled.

Imagine a clenched fist.

But this Æternity will pass away, and the one beyond it will pass away. By your patience, win your souls. I will have mercy and not sacrifice.

Go your way, Joshua said, and as you have trusted, so let it be done to you.

And those who were sent, returning to the house, found the slave who had been sick healed in the self-same hour.

Let us go into the next towns that I may preach there too, said Joshua to his students, for this is why I am sent.

And he departed from there. Then Joshua went about all the cities and villages, teaching in their congregation houses, preaching the gospel of the realm, healing every sickness and every disease among the people. And at once his fame began spreading to every corner of the country around Galilee, and the people sought him, and came to him, and stayed him, that he should not depart from them. And he healed many who were sick of diverse diseases.

To Preach Deliverance

9

And he came to Nazareth, where he had been brought up. And, as was his habit, he went into the congregation house on the Sabbath day, and stood to read, the book of the prophet Isaiah delivered to him. And when he had opened the book, he found the place where it was written, *The inspiration of the Worker is upon me, because he has anointed me to preach the gospel to the poor; he has sent me to heal the broken-hearted, to preach deliverance to the captives, and recovering of sight to the blind, to set at liberty those who are bruised, to proclaim the propitious year of the Worker.*

And he closed the book, gave it again to the attendant, and sat down. The eyes of all those who were in the congregation house were fastened on him. All bore him witness, shocked at the gracious words which sprang from his mouth.

Is this not Joseph's son, they said, the craftsman's son—except it be for fornication? From where has this man this wisdom, these mighty works? Is his mother not called Mary? And his brethren, James and Joses, Jude and Symon? And his sisters, are they not all with us? From where then has this man all these things?

In Nazareth, he knew, Mary would always be, at best, the fornicator who gave herself to her fiancé before the wedding night, at worst, the adulterer who gave herself to another man as that fiancé slept. In Nazareth, he knew, he would always be the *setukhi* of unknown father, a son of shame to stay silenced. In the congregation that whispered disapproval as he read, he'd have seen boys who once spat at him, threw rocks, shouted *whore* at his mother, boys now grown to men in body but still brats of ignorance and spite in their stunted souls.

This day this scripture is fulfilled in your ears, he began to say.

But they were outraged by him, and he marvelled at their distrust and could do no mighty work there, save that he laid his hands upon a few sick folk and healed them.

You will surely say to me this proverb, he said, Physician, heal yourself; whatever we have heard done in Capernaum, do here in your country also. But I tell you truly, in the days of Elijah, when the heavens were shut up three years and six months, when great famine was throughout all the land, there were many widows in Israel; but Elijah was sent to none of them, save to Sarepta, a city of Sidon, to a woman who was a widow. And many lepers were in Israel in the time of Eliseus the prophet; but none of them was cleansed, saving Naaman the Syrian.

For sure, I tell you, he said, no prophet is accepted in his own country. A prophet is not without honour, but in his own country, among his own kin, in his own house. A physician cannot heal those who know him. But anyone who would be ashamed of me and of my words in this disloyal and delinquent generation, of him also would the everyman be ashamed.

And all those in the congregation house, when they heard these things, were filled with fury, rose up and thrust him out of the city, led him to the brow of the hill their city was built on so they might hurl him down headlong. But passing through the midst of them, he went his way, and came down to Capernaum, and taught them on the Sabbath days.

10

Now it came to pass on a certain day, when the evenfall was come, that he went into a boat with his students.

Let us go over to the other side of the lake, he said to them.

And if any man would tend to me, let him walk with me, and where I am, there also shall my attendant be. If any man would tend to me, my father will honour him.

With his spreading fame, the flocking of followers had begun. From a small coterie of kith and kin, now when he set out they would come to him by the score, to fawn their faith in his power and glory, pressing gruff Simon and the Sons of Thunder for an audience. At his side, sharp-tongued Nathaniel would make some droll comment at the honour of a prophet among those who *didn't* know him; he'd shake his head and wave the supplicant in. He set out at evenfall, hoping the late hour would whittle down the numbers, but still they came, gathered at the shore.

———

And a certain clerk came and said to him, Rabbi, I will walk with you wherever you go.

The foxes have holes, and the birds of the air have nests, Joshua said, but the everyman has nowhere to lay his head.

Teacher, I will walk with you, another said, but let me first go bid farewell to those who are at home at my house.

No man who looks back after putting his hand to the plough, Joshua said, is fit for the realm of the sublime.

Then another of his students said, Teacher, first let me go and bury my father.

Walk with me, said Joshua, and let the dead bury their dead.

———

I can imagine it, him turning a raised eyebrow on rash declarations, warning that even the Baptist couldn't smooth the path he was on; shaking his head at shallow caveats, dismissing the hobbyist revolutionaries; holding the gaze of those naively sure that *their* sacred priorities were inviolable, calmly taking a hammer to those idols. Imagine it? I experienced it; I was every one of those would-be followers when I came to him.

Let the dead bury the dead. Once a Nazirite sworn to bury any corpse they find even though the vow deems them soiled for touching it, he'd walked out into the quiet wilds, and he invited company, but that invitation was to walk *with* him, not follow. Followers were discouraged best he could.

———

So when he had sent away the mob, they took him just as he was, in the boat. And there were also with him other little boats. And they launched forth. But as they sailed he fell asleep, and there came down a great storm of wind on the lake. And the waves beat into the boat, and they were filled with water, and were in peril.

And he was in the back part of the boat, asleep on a pillow, when they awoke him

Rabbi, they said to him, do you not care that we perish? Teacher, save us! We perish!

Why are you fearful, he said to them, O you of little trust?

Then he arose, and scolded the winds and said to the sea, Peace, be still. And the wind ceased, and there was a great calm. And the men marvelled, saying, What manner of man is this, that even the winds and the sea obey him! And they came over to the other side of the sea, into the country of the Gadarenes, which is over against Galilee.

11

And when he was arrived at the other side, he came out of the boat into the country of the Gergesenes, and at once there met him out of the tombs a man with a fouled inspiration, exceeding fierce, who had his dwelling among the tombs so that no man might pass by that way. And no man could tame him or bind him, no, not with chains, for he had often been bound with fetters and chains, and the chains had been torn apart by him, and the fetters broken in pieces. And always, night and day, he was in the mountains, and in the tombs, crying and cutting himself with stones.

A foreign land of Gentiles, a murderous madman rattling his broken chains among the dead. How much of this actually happened? How much is just another of your parables? I asked as we sat in the house in Capernaum, Joshua telling the tale, his scribe setting it down for posterity.

All of it, said Joshua.

But when he saw Joshua from afar, the man ran and supplicated to him, crying with a loud voice, for Joshua said to him, Come out of this man, you fouled inspirations.

What have I to do with you, Joshua? he said. You son of the most high spirit! Are you come here to torment us before the time? I adjure you by the sublime that you torment me not.

What is your name? Joshua asked him.

My name is Legion, he answered, for we are many.

I glanced across the room at Thomas, saw my own worry in his nervous shuffle at a naming so bold. In my heart, I heard the rattle of swords instead of chains.

And he begged Joshua earnestly that he would not direct them to go out into the abyss. And nearby towards the mountains, there was a great herd of about two thousand swine feeding, so all the daimons pleaded with him.

Send us into the swine, they said, that we may enter into them.

And forthwith Joshua gave them leave, and the fouled inspirations went out, and entered into the swine, and the herd stampeded down a steep bank into the sea and were drowned in the waters. And those who fed the swine fled, and told it in the city and in the country. And behold, the whole city came out to see what was done, to find the man, out of whom the daimons were departed, sitting at the feet of Joshua, clothed and in his right mind. And those who had seen it told them how he who was driven by the daimons was healed, and about the swine as well. Then all the crowds of the country of the Gadarenes round about begged him to depart out of their coasts, for they were taken with great fear.

Let the swine of the Gentiles be driven to destruction by this spectre of the Legion, not us, not the Jews. It's hardly a surprise that his sedition inspired fear. I'm more surprised the tale survived the hands of Roman apologists.

So he went up into the boat, to return. And when he was come into the boat, he who had been driven by the daimons implored him that he might be with him. But Joshua did not allow him.

Go home to your friends, he said, and tell them all the Worker has done for you, how he was merciful.

And he departed, and began to publish in Decapolis what great things Joshua had done for him, and all men did marvel.

12

And when Joshua was passed over again by boat to the other side, many people gladly gathered to him, for they were all waiting for him. And he went forth and saw a great mob, and was moved with compassion toward them, because they were as sheep without a shepherd. And he went forth again by the sea side, all the mob came to him, and he taught them. And they were astonished at his teachings, for his word was with power.

And after some days, again he entered into Capernaum, and as he passed by, he saw a taxman named Matthew bar-Alphaeus, sitting at the tax booth.

All we need now is a flying scroll, Nathanael had said wryly.

Which, Joshua knew, in Zechariah's vision was twenty cubits by ten, size of the antechamber of the tabernacle of the ark, the holy place before the veil. A scripture as new outer shrine to the holy of holies then.

When he was arguing in the temple, you understand, lover of the sublime, it was because of Zechariah. From the earliest days he sat under the fig tree, he'd been drawn to that lurid messianic prophecy of a Joshua dressed in rags, felt it tremble the heart of a shy setukhi his widowed mother could barely feed let alone clothe. Every stone flung at his back, every insult spat in his face, he thought of a messiah in rags. And so when he returned to Capernaum, he built that vision around him, the lampstand's seven branches, two trees, two pipes.

A flying scroll sent out across the land to curse thieves on the one side, perjurers on the other. And if a man was to embody that as his scribe, who better than a taxman turned, a swindler with a foot on each side of the line, literate in Aramaic and Greek?

Joshua stopped at the tax-booth, looked at the man who'd one day write the lost gospel of the Hebrews—not the gospel named for him, but the original of which only such scraps as the taste of wild honey have survived the seasons of the Gentiles. In the collage of confusions that remains, lover of the sublime, James and Jude are also sons of Alphaeus. Siblings? You might wonder if Matthew's cheeks burned under Joshua's gaze as a firstborn black sheep of the family, a wealthy traitor bleeding Galilee for Rome.

———

Walk with me, Joshua said to him.

And he arose, left everything and followed him.

And Matthew made him a great feast in his own house, and those who collected the two drachma tax came to the Rock.

Does your teacher not pay the two drachma tax? they said.

Yes, he said.

But when he was come into the house, Joshua prevented him, saying, What are you thinking, Simon? Of whom do the kings of the earth take custom or head-tax? Of their own sons or those of strangers?

Of strangers, the Rock said to him.

Then the sons are exempt, Joshua said to him. Still, lest we should outrage them, go down to the sea and cast a line in. Take up the first fish that comes up, and when you have opened his mouth, you shall find a shekel. Take it, and give to them for me and you.

And it came to pass, as Joshua sat at meat in Matthew's house, behold, a great company of taxmen and delinquents came and sat down with him and his students.

And all the taxmen and delinquents drew near to him for to hear him.

Mercy and Not Sacrifice

13

And when the Select saw it, they murmured against his students, Why does your rabbi eat with taxmen and delinquents?

But when Joshua heard that, he said to them, Those who are whole have no need of the physician, only those who are sick. I am come to call not the upstanding but the delinquents to a change of heart. For the everyman is come to seek and to save that which was lost.

It was Simon who told him on his return with the shekel, bent down to whisper in his ear that the Select had accosted him outside, outraged that the young rabbi consorted with *that sort*. It wasn't just a matter of propriety though, but of politics, for that faction who gave three thousand lives to the blade of Herod. They bristled that Joshua ate with *collaborators*, profiteers of the Occupation. So he gave Simon a nod, excused himself, went to the door to talk.

And he spoke this parable to them, saying, The realm is like a shepherd who had a hundred sheep. One of them, the largest, went astray. He left the ninety-nine and sought after the one till he found it. When he had laboured, he said to the sheep, I love you more than the ninety-nine.

In the courtyard behind him, he heard the hubbub of feasting criminals and collaborators fall to a low murmur now, a spattering of oblivious chatterers shushed one by one. He heard Matthew's clipped voice, curt as he snapped a name, cut off a fellow taxman in full flow, dropped to a hissed apology and appeal. Outside, the Select—the ones you know as Pharisees—stood sullen and judgemental.

What man of you, he said, having a hundred sheep, if he loses one, does not leave the ninety-nine in the wilderness and go after that which is lost until he find it? And when he has found it, he lays it on his shoulders, rejoicing. And when he comes home, he calls together his friends and neighbours, saying to them, Rejoice with me, for I have found my sheep which was lost. I say to you that likewise joy shall be in Æternity over one delinquent who rethinks, more than over ninety-nine just men, who need no change of heart.

He was aware of Matthew standing at his back now, the room behind him gone quiet. Somehow he knew of the lump in black sheep Matthew's throat, he told me, and I don't doubt him.

For sure, Joshua said to them, I tell you that the taxmen and the harlots go into the realm of the sublime before you. For John came to you in the way of rectitude, and the taxmen and the harlots trusted him, but you, when you had seen it, had no change of heart afterward, that you might trust him.

With the word *harlots* he was back in the temple, twelve years old and fierce, defending the woman caught in adultery, *every* woman caught in adultery. Defending everyone.

And how can you behold the mote that is in your brother's eye, he said, but not consider the beam that is in your own eye? How can you say to your brother, Let me pull the mote out of your eye; and behold, a beam is in your own eye? You hypocrite, first cast out the beam from your own eye, and then you shall see clearly to cast out the mote from your brother's eye. Love your brother as your soul; keep him as the apple of your eye.

14

A certain man had two sons, he said. And the younger of them said to his father, Father, give me the portion of goods that falls to me. So he divided his living between them. And not many days after, the younger son gathered all together, and took his journey into a far country, and wasted his substance with riotous living there. And when he had spent all, there arose a mighty famine in that land; and he began to be in want. So he went and bonded himself to a citizen of that country, and was sent by him into his fields to feed swine. But he yearned to fill his belly with the husks that the swine were eating and no man was giving to him.

When he came to himself, he said, How many hired workers of my father's have a surfeit of loaves while I perish with hunger? I will arise and go to my father, and will say to him, Father, I have been delinquent against Æternity and in your sight, and am no longer worthy to be called your son; make me as one of your hired workers. So he arose, and came to his father. But when he was yet a great way off, his father saw him, and had compassion, ran and fell on his neck, and kissed him.

Father, the son said, I have been delinquent against Æternity, and in your sight, and am no longer worthy to be called your son.

But the father said to his slaves, Bring forth the best robe, and put it on him. Put a ring on his hand and shoes on his feet. Bring the fatted calf here and kill it. And let us eat and be merry! For this son of mine was dead, and is alive again; he was lost, and is found.

And they began to be merry. Now his elder son was in the field, and as he came and drew near to the house, he heard music and dancing. And he called one of the children, and asked what these things meant.

Your brother is returned, said the child, and your father has killed the fatted calf, because he has received him safe and sound.

And he was angry, and would not go in. Therefore his father came out, and begged him.

Behold, he said to his father, these many years I serve you, never at any time did I ignore your decree, and yet you never gave me even a kid that I might make merry with my friends. But as soon as this son of yours was come, who has devoured your living with harlots, you have killed for him the fatted calf.

Son, he said to him, you are ever with me, and all that I have is yours. It was fitting that we should make merry, and be glad, for this brother of yours was dead and is alive again, was lost and is found.

I remember the first night Matthew showed me the gospel he was building, this the first page of it, the first parable. It was the beginning of the story for him, of course, the first parable he heard, but it was also the most personal. He read it out by lamplight in Tabor, *sang* it as the scripture is still sung in the synagogues today, as the sacred inspiration *should* be sung. At the end, his voice caught a little, not at a promise of forgiveness but at a plea: to see nothing, lover of the sublime, nothing to forgive.

15

And all the people who heard him, being baptized with the baptism of John, even the taxmen, respected the sublime. But the Select and lawyers rejected the counsel of the sublime against themselves, being not baptized of him.

I would note, lover of the sublime, that the Pharisees of the history rewritten by generations of agendas, were hardly some shadow-puppet of ossified Judaism as cast from your pulpits. These were the people who gave us Hillel with his Golden Rule. It is because the word has been bleached of that heritage, redyed scarlet and purple as an expedient cipher, that I abandon it for naked flesh. If you would have a masque, let us strip the actors bare, dance them on a stage beyond time. Let us have Joshua stand at the door of a crack den in Capernaum, lighting a cigarette as he faces the Cardinals, the Calvinists, the Christian self-Elect, *the Select.*

And they said to him, Why do the students of John fast often, and make prayers, and likewise the students of the Select, but yours eat and drink?

When I saw the news break on the internet, followed the links to YouTube, saw you stripped and whipped into the street by your fouled inspiration, I saw Capernaum through a crack in the world, a man driven by daimons. I heard the Pharisees who raised you spouting abstinence and devotion, abstinence and devotion. I heard Joshua's voice within me spurning such desolate ritual, singing sacred inspirations of the bread of flesh, libations of wine for the temple of the body. I saw a rift in the veil of two millennia to be ripped open, Æternity revealed. I heard this:

And the teacher said, John the Baptist came neither eating bread nor drinking wine, and you say, He has a daimon. The everyman is come eating and drinking, and you say, Behold a gluttonous man and a swiller of wine, a friend of taxmen and delinquents! If you fast not from the world, you will not find the realm; if you do not keep the Sabbath as Sabbath, you will not see the father! But wisdom is proven by her children.

And the heady scent of cannabis filled the room behind him, wafted out through the door where Joshua stood in his pastor's black, shorn of the dog collar, facing the gathered priests and reverends of the small town, a preacher who'd renounced all that they understood as piety, it seemed, even as he gathered his congregation to a den of iniquity. They drank laudanum, strychnine, ayahuasca, snorted speed and coke and smack, dropped acid, ecstasy, ketamine—and were doing so now under the roof of Matthew the drug dealer. Joshua saw the disgust in their eyes.

And he spoke this parable to certain who trusted in themselves that they were upstanding and despised others: Two men went up into the temple to pray, one being a televangelist, and the other a taxman.

The televangelist stood and prayed thus with himself, God, I thank you, that I am not as other men are—extortioners, unjust, adulterers, or even as this taxman. I fast twice in the week. I give tithes of all I own.

And the taxman, standing afar off, would not so much as lift up his eyes to the heavens, but beat upon his breast, saying, God, be merciful to me a delinquent.

I tell you, this man went down to his house justified, not the other. Now go you and learn what it means to say, I will have mercy and not sacrifice.

16

While he spoke these things, behold, there came one of the lords of the congregation house, Jairus, for he had one daughter only, about twelve years of age, who lay dying. And when he saw Joshua, he fell at his feet and pleaded desperately, My little daughter lies at the point of death. I pray you, come lay your hands on her, that she may be healed, and she shall live.

So Joshua arose and followed him, And his students and many others followed, thronging him.

He hurried after the minister, down a sidewalk lit by halogen streetlamps, littered with trash, to one side walls graffitied with anti-Roman slogans, to the other kerb-crawling cars. An overdose, Jairus babbled, but he had no idea what she'd taken, no idea what to do.

What's her name? asked Joshua.

Sophia.

Then behold, a woman suffering a haemorrhage for twelve years, who had endured much from the hands of many physicians, spent all she had, and was not helped, only grew worse—having heard of Joshua, she came in the crowd behind, and touched the hem of his garment, thinking, If I may but touch his garment, I shall be whole.

At once the flow of her blood was dried up, and she felt in her body that her affliction was healed. But Joshua, realising that power had gone from him, turned himself about in the crowd.

Who touched my clothes? he said, and looked around to see who had done this thing.

When all denied, the Rock said, You see the mob thronging you and you ask, Who touched me?

A square of pimps and prostitutes, a statue of Caesar crowned with a traffic cone.

But the woman fearing, trembling, knowing what was done in her, came and fell down before him, told him all the truth.

Daughter, be of good comfort, he said. Your trust has made you whole. Go in peace, and be cured of your affliction.

And the woman was made whole from that hour.

What's your name? asked Joshua.

Sophia.

While he yet spoke, there came some from Jairus's home.

Your daughter is dead, they said. Why should you trouble the rabbi any further?

As soon as Joshua heard the word that was spoken, he said to Jairus, Don't be afraid, only trust and she shall be made whole. And he suffered no man to come with him, save the Rock, and the sons of Zebedee. And when Joshua came into the lord's house, he saw minstrels and people making a tumult, and those who wept and wailed greatly.

Why do you weep and make this ado? he said. Give way, for the girl is not dead, only sleeping.

And they laughed him to scorn. But when he had put them all out, he took the father and the mother of the girl, and those who were with him, entered in where the girl was lying. He suffered no man to go in, save the girl's father and mother, Simon, Jacob and John.

And he took the girl by the hand, said to her, *Talitha cumi*; which is, interpreted, Girl, arise. And her breath came again, and she arose at once, and walked.

Walk, he said hauling her arm over his shoulder, hefting her weight. Walk with me, Sophia, walk. And through the night, to the dawn, she walked.

And Joshua directed to give her food to eat, and all were taken aback with profound astonishment, so that while he charged them strictly that no man should know it, the fame went abroad into all that land.

Master of the Sabbath

17

And the students of John told him of all these things. And John called two of his students to him and sent them to Joshua, saying, Are you he that should come? Or do we look for another? When the men were come to him, they said, John the Baptist has sent us to you, saying, Are you he that should come? Or do we look for another?

And in that same hour Joshua cured many of their infirmities and plagues, and their inspirations of strife, and to many who were blind he gave sight.

The house he showed them into was harmonic chaos, students and patients coming and going, a melancholic being tended in the corner as he waited to see the teacher, a visitor from the chapter in Chorazin arriving without baggage, in patched clothes and shoes worn through at the sole. They were living communally by then, as the Essenes, their property shared, eschewing trade within themselves in favour of exchange, everything distributed—from each according to ability, to each according to need. John's students saw the visitor slipping on the new sandals given as they were called to the fifth hour meal, where the difference from the Essene way suddenly became marked in the free flow of wine and laughter. They did not partake, of course, uneasy with this schism from John's asceticism. But they could not deny the life reborn in the melancholic's face as he gazed up at the sunlight in Capernaum. They stood in the street outside the door.

Go your way, Joshua said to them, and tell John what things you have seen and heard. The blind receive their sight, and the lame walk, the lepers are cleansed, and the deaf hear, the dead are raised up, and the poor are preached to. And blessed is he, anyone who shall not be outraged by me.

And as Joshua departed from there, two blind men followed him, crying.

You son of David, they said, have mercy on us.

And when he was come into the house, the blind men came to him.

Do you trust that I am able to do this? Joshua said to them.

Yes, Teacher, they said to him.

And Joshua said to them, To what shall I liken the men of this generation then? What are they like? They are like children sitting in the marketplace, and calling one to another, and saying, We have piped at you, and you have not danced; we have mourned at you, and you have not wept. Though the days will come when the bridegroom shall be taken from them, and they shall fast then, can the children of the bridechamber mourn as long as the bridegroom is with them?

Then he touched their eyes, saying, According to your trust, let it be done to you.

The commune he showed them out of was harmonic chaos, hippies and addicts coming and going, an alcoholic being guided in the corner through an acid trip confrontation with his demons—with no fear in facing them though. Instead, the man smiled in wonder of understanding as Thomas held his hand, talked him through fields of wheat to the quiet wilds of his soul, wearing the faces of friends and family as required, transforming accusation to advocacy.

The methods are... unorthodox, said the elder of the two therapists from Johns Hopkins.

But they're proven, said Joshua.

And their eyes were opened, and Joshua strictly charged them, saying, See that no man know it. But they, when they were departed, spread abroad his fame in all that country.

18

And when the messengers of John were departed, he began to speak to the people concerning John. And all the people came to him; and he sat down, and taught them.

He sat up on a reception desk of scuffed wood, names and obscenities gouged into its surface or inked in black marker, red pen or white-out, alcove of wooden cubby holes behind him. The foyer was long-since stripped of wallpaper and wainscot, walls of crumbling plaster spray-painted as anarchic as the desk, whatever furniture might have dwelt here sold or stolen, replaced with ragged armchairs and sofas down front, and up back, at the bar, the trestle tables they served the destitute from. Crouched at a coffee table under him, Matthew clicked *record* on his cassette-player.

What did you go out into the wilderness to see? said Joshua. A reed shaken with the wind? But what did you go out to see? A man clothed in soft garments? Behold, those who are gorgeously apparelled live in palatial luxury. But what did you go out to see? A prophet? Aye, I say to you, and much more than a prophet. For all the prophets and the law prophesied only until the time of John. And if you will welcome it, this is Elijah himself, who was to come. This is he of whom it is written, Behold, I send my messenger before your face, who shall make ready your path before you.

The truth of prophecy, John had taught him, is that the poetry born of the sacred inspiration is the beauty of the sublime at large in the world, entering the hearts of men, exiting from their mouths to find its way via the ears into the hearts of as many as will hear it. The truth of prophecy is that the right phrasing, the right image—John himself as a man walking before the anointed, making ready his path—is a symbolic key that may unlock a door within, unloose what is always already there and thereby make it so.

For I say to you, said Joshua, among those who are born of women there is not a greater prophet than John the Baptist, but he who is least in the realm of the sublime is greater than he. For as the father has life in himself, so he has given to the son to have life in himself, and has given him authority to execute judgement also, because he is the everyman. The father judges no man, but has delegated all judgement to the son, that all men should honour the son, even as they honour the father.

And he looked out the window of the abandoned hotel on Capernaum's Main Street, now transformed by his squatting *cultists*, as they were considered, to halfway house, soup kitchen, needle exchange, looked out at the picket line of the pious waving placards in his name, not even knowing who it was within. He looked at the reverend holding the sign calling for repentance—not release from shame but bondage in it—and prayed that this fluid future might not be. The End of the World is Nigh, another sign said.

And if any man hear my words, he said, and trust not, I judge him not, for I came not to judge the world, but to save the world. He who rejects me and welcomes not my words has one who judges him: at the end of all days, the very words I have spoken will judge him: I will have mercy and not sacrifice.

19

And it came to pass that he went through the corn fields on the Sabbath day, and his students were hungry and began to pluck the ears of corn and to eat. But when the Select saw it, they said to him, Behold, your students do that which is not lawful on the Sabbath day.

———

And the *Fisher of Men* swayed on the bleak Atlantic swell as Simon and Andrew wound the fore and aft hawsers round their bollards, as Jacob worked the crane, as John guided the swaying haul now lowering towards the dock, as Joshua stood on the Hebridean harbour of Capernaum, the kirk elders around him.

———

Have you never read what David did, he said to them, when he had need and was hungry, he and those who were with him? How he went into the house of the sublime in the days of Abiathar the high priest, and ate the showbread—which is not lawful to eat except for the priests—and gave also to those who were with him? Or have you not read in the law how on the Sabbath days the priests in the temple profane the Sabbath but are blameless? And I say to you that in this place there is one greater than the temple.

———

If you'd been there, if I'd been there, lover of the sublime, we might have risen to uproar with the elders of the kirk, thinking he talked of himself, both of us born into our time and place, souls seeded and shaped by upbringing. There's no guarantee we'd see beyond an upstart individualist spouting blasphemy. As he turned and stalked away, his students following after him, we might have stood on the harbour, raging as Hebridean seas. Let us follow him now then, out of this aeon and back to his own, asking who is greater than the temple, who?

———

And when he was departed from there, he went into the congregation house and taught. And behold, there was a man who had his hand withered, who came to Joshua, saying, I was a mason, earning a living with my hands. I beg you, Joshua, restore my health to me, so I do not need to beg for my food in shame.

And the clerks and Select watched him, whether he would heal on the Sabbath day.

And they asked him, Is it lawful to heal on the Sabbath days? that they might accuse him.

But he knew their thoughts, and said to the man who had the withered hand, Rise up, and stand forth in the midst. And he arose and stood forth.

What man shall there be among you, Joshua said to them, that shall have one sheep, and if it falls into a pit on the Sabbath day, he would not lay hold on it, and lift it out? How much then is a man better than a sheep? For this reason then, is it not lawful to do good on the Sabbath days? I will ask you one thing, Is it lawful on the Sabbath days to do good, or to do ill? To save life, or to destroy it?

But they held their peace.

And he said to them, The Sabbath was made for man, and not man for the Sabbath. Therefore the everyman is master also of the Sabbath.

And when he had looked round about on them with anger, being grieved for the hardness of their hearts, he said to the man, Stretch forth your hand. And he did so, and his hand was restored whole as the other.

20

And the lord of the congregation house answered with indignation because Joshua had healed on the Sabbath day.

There are six days in which men ought to work, he said to the people, so come in during them and be healed, but not on the Sabbath day.

Moses gave circumcision to you, the teacher answered him, though not on account of Moses himself, but of the fathers; so on the Sabbath day you circumcise a man. If a man receives circumcision on the Sabbath day that the law of Moses should not be broken, are you angry at me because I have made a man fully whole on the Sabbath day? You hypocrite, does each one of you on the Sabbath not loose his ox or his ass from the stall, lead him away to watering?

And behold, there was a woman who had an inspiration of infirmity eighteen years, and was bowed together, and could in no way straighten herself. When Joshua saw her, he called her to him.

Woman, he said, you are loosed from your infirmity.

And he laid his hands on her, and immediately she was made straight, and honoured the sublime.

And should this woman, he said, being a daughter of Abraham whom the accuser has bound, behold, these eighteen years, not be loosed from this bond on the Sabbath day? Judge not according to the appearance, but judge upstanding judgement.

And when he had said these things, all his adversaries were ashamed, and all the people rejoiced for all the marvellous things that were done by him. But when Joshua knew it, he withdrew himself from there, and great mobs followed him, and he healed them all, and charged them that they should not make him known.

But it came to pass, when he was in a certain city, there came a leper to him who, seeing Joshua, fell on his face, begging him and saying to him, If you will it, you can make me clean.

And Joshua, moved with compassion, put forth his hand, touched him, and said to him, I will it, be clean. Now you are clean through the word which I have spoken to you.

And as soon as he had spoken, at once the leprosy departed from him, and he was cleansed.

And elsewhere, lover of the sublime, as you now lie in some hospital bed, taken naked from the streets, hustled away by the police for pounding sidewalk with your fists, for masturbating, for shame, handed over to the doctors, I too was sick to self-destruction, in rebellion against the earth under my feet and devilled by desire. The streets and bed of madness were one room, the police and doctors one face in a mirror, but I needed him as much as you do now, needed a Capernaum I'd never even heard of, a Capernaum you might someday know.

And he withdrew himself into the wilderness and prayed, and they came to him from every quarter.

The Eye of the Needle

21

But when the Select heard it, they said, This fellow does not cast out daimons but by Beelzebub the lord of the daimons.

And the clerks, who came down from Jerusalem, said, He has Beelzebub, and by the lord of the daimons he casts out daimons.

And Joshua knew their thoughts.

Outside, the dome of the Church of St. Dionysus was eggshell blue with lemon yellow stars, nestled among the sandstone townscape, jumbled rooftops of red tile, all hallowed golden with late afternoon sun, under the perfectly empty vault of a heaven darkening to azure; and the bells of Capernaum rang Compline. As he turned back to the bishop sitting in his study of oak bookcases and leatherbound tomes, Joshua knew he should choose his words carefully.

How can the accuser cast out the accuser? he said to them. How can anyone enter into the house of the mighty, and spoil his goods, unless he bind the mighty first? Unless, when the mightier than the mighty shall come upon him, after overcoming him, he takes from him all his armour that he trusted in, and divides his spoils. And then when this mighty, fully armed, guards the house of himself, his goods are in peace.

Somewhere on his shelves there was an ABC, one might say, of Albigensians, Bogomils, Cathars that John had given him, the teachings of gnosis at the heart of his own metaphysics, and enough to condemn him to the stake. Teachings he had moved on from, of course, knowing that the material world was no trap for angelic souls, that there *were* no angels, only fleshly messengers as much sent to the realm as from it—something his students throughout history consistently failed to understand. That the accuser cannot cast himself out, only return to Capernaum, always to Capernaum, to seat himself again in his house usurped by the lesser mighty, overcoming as the inspiration of dialectic followed through to integrity. This was the true wisdom of the Pharisaic Judaism that became Rabbinic, this Oral Torah as an ongoing process of analysis and argument the very opposite of ossified dogma. To bind this power of wisdom into an idol of scapegoat diabolism, this was the true stumbling block.

If a realm is divided against itself, he said, that realm cannot stand. If a house is divided against itself, that house cannot stand. And if the accuser rise up against himself, and is divided, how shall his realm stand then?

And elsewhere, elsewhen, I rose from my bed in a house divided, dressed myself and headed out past hollow rooms absent an elder brother and a younger sister, to join my father and the servants in the courtyard with the donkeys packed for the journey. I said little to his impatient questions and directives, five years of argument burned down to formalities of dutiful honour. I hated him. I loved him. I did as I was told. My elder sister managed to wrest a weak smile from me with a kiss on the cheek, then we were off.

So, if I cast out daimons by Beelzebub, said Joshua, by whom do your children cast them out? But if I cast out daimons with the finger of the sublime, then the realm of the sublime is come upon you. So I say to you, he who is against you is for you, and he who is far from you will draw near tomorrow. And all manner of delinquency and blasphemy shall be forgiven to men: but the blasphemy against the sacred inspiration shall not be forgiven to men.

22

And it came to pass the day after that he went into a city called Nain, at the foot of Mount Tabor, the hill of the teacher, and many of his students went with him, and many people who were come out of every town of Galilee, and Judaea, and Jerusalem.

So I was in Nain on business with my father when I first saw him, along to learn the family trade as *garibo*: literally, *potter* or *jar merchant*, practically, owning a pottery factory down by the Dead Sea, running the trade and distribution out of Bethany for its proximity to Jerusalem. Imagine a Victorian industrialist, a 21st century CEO; we were in Nain to make the sort of deal made with a handshake at the country club now. And I, let off the leash, had slipped away into the market when the escalating fervour of the crowd drew me to Joshua's arrival. They thronged him such that I could barely glimpse his face—no anaemic anorexic hippy Gentile, but a Galilean, hair trimmed to a curly tousle, a swart Bob Dylan with beard, eyes intense on the crowd. I was... captivated.

And he spoke a parable to them, saying, The everyman is as a man taking a far journey, who left his house, and directed the gatekeeper to watch it, and he gave authority to his slaves, and set each man to his work. After a long time the master returned, but now when he came nigh to the gate of the city, behold, there was a dead man carried out, the only son of his mother, and she was a widow, and many people of the city were with her.

And when the master saw her, he had compassion on her, and said to her, Weep not.

And he came and touched the bier, and those who carried him stood still.

Young man, he said. I say to you, Arise.

And he who was dead sat up, and began to speak. And the master delivered him to his mother.

And there came a fear on all, and they honoured the sublime, saying, A great prophet is risen up among us; and, The sublime has visited his people. And this rumour of him went forth throughout all Judaea and the surrounding region.

I imagine you halt as you read this, lover of the sublime. But the raising of the widow's son in Nain, you say, that was a miracle, not a parable. He didn't just tell the story to a crowd in a market place; he brought the boy back from the dead before their eyes. As if there is a difference. Believe what you will; as he said, it only really matters that you understand. Believe what you will; all I can say is how it happened for me, that I watched him conjure the dead alive again in words.

On what day will the rest of the dead come into being? his students said. And on what day will the new world come?

That which you await has come, he said to them, but you know it not. For the father loves the son, shows him all things he does himself, and he will show him greater works than these, that you may marvel. For as the father raises up the dead, and quickens them, even so the son quickens whom he will, for whatever things he does, these also does the son likewise. The father has not left me alone. He who sent me is with me, for I always do those things that please him.

23

And when he was gone forth on his way, there came a young man of Judaea running, and kneeled to him.

Good rabbi, he asked, what shall I do that I may inherit the life of ages?

I heard the promise of Æternity in his tale. I recognised the source in Elijah raising the widow's son on his visit to Nain, taking the dead youth from her embrace, carrying him up into a loft to lay him on a bed, to lay down upon him, bring life back into the corpse. The very phrasing—*delivered him to his mother*—was identical. And as I watched him tell it, I was one of those who knew a true prophet was among us, overflowing with life, passionate for the enlightenment of us all.

Still, as I said, I was as rash, as shallow, as naive as any of his dilettante devotees. I really thought his parable a call to those seeking everlasting life. How could I not? For all my arguments with my tutors, my father, for all the accuser in me struggling to articulate doubt, I was steeped in a heritage of the sublime thundering majesty in a voice from the heavens, of his realm as a kingdom from which he ruled, of bodies sleeping in the grave until he called them forth. I wasn't some Sadducee denying resurrection, denying the immortality of the soul itself. For all my grief-embittered denials, when Joshua's words breathed the sacred inspiration into my heart, I didn't understand the very truth I recognised as something I'd always known. So I came to him in faith, another supplicant to power and glory.

I looked up at him from my knees with utter infatuation.

Why do you call me good? Joshua said, I can do nothing of my own self. There is none good but one, the sublime. But if you will enter into life, keep the decrees.

Which? he said.

You shall do no murder, Joshua said, You shall not commit adultery, You shall not steal, You shall not perjure, Honour your father and mother, Love your neighbour as yourself.

All these things I have kept from my youth up, said the young man. What do I still lack?

I stood, keen as a pup, barely bothering to note such obvious requirements—because of course one loved one's neighbour as oneself, it was only natural, all life deserving empathy. But what else?

Then Joshua beholding him loved him.

If you will be perfect, he said, go sell all you have, give to the poor, and take your treasure in heaven. For what shall it profit a man, if he gain the whole world, and lose his own soul? What shall a man trade in exchange for his soul?

___

That bluntness cut me down but then... he leaned in to speak quietly.

___

He who would find his life must lose it, he said, and he who would lose his life for my sake shall find it. The heavens shall be rolled up and the earth before your face, and he who lives in the living one shall neither see death nor fear. For sure, I tell you, if a man keep my teachings, he shall never see death; but first he must suffer many things, and be rejected of this generation. But he who endures to the end shall be saved.

___

The sudden unfathomable intimacy.

___

He who shall find himself, he said, of him the world is not worthy. But when the young man heard that saying, he went away sorrowful, for he had great possessions.

24

And Joshua looked around, said to his students, How hardly shall those with riches enter into the realm of the sublime!

___

I shrank back into the crowd, cheeks burning, so shaken I wasn't even sure what I felt. The way he'd leaned in to speak only to me, his eyes holding mine with a look as tender as it was intense. Those eyes had flicked up and down as his words stripped all my finery, crumbled it to dust blown from his hand—What shall a man trade in exchange for his soul?—but in that moment, the petty embarrassment of privilege exposed was itself speared and splayed open, a far deeper desire laid bare. And touched gently.

He was still talking.

———

And the students were astonished at his words.

But Joshua answered again, Children, how hard is it for those who trust in riches to enter into the realm of the sublime! It is easier for a rope to go through the eye of a needle, than for a rich man to enter into the realm of the sublime. It is not possible for a man to ride two horses or draw two bows, and it is not possible for a man to serve two masters: for he will either hate the one, and love the other, or else he will be dedicated to the one, and disdainful of the other.

———

His gaze turned and stayed on me even as I backed away, bumping an amphora sat down between a merchant's feet, stumbling.

———

Teacher, Teacher, said one to him then, are there few that are saved?

Not every one who says to me, he said, Teacher, Teacher, shall enter into the realm of Zion, only he who does the will of my father who is in Æternity.

———

It happened the moment he said the word Æternity, a moment of time suddenly deep instead of long, infinitely deep, echoing. New meanings resounded in the word. Within me a rope unravelled, threaded the needle.

———

When his students heard it, they were astonished out of measure, saying, Who then can be saved?

And Joshua beheld them, said, With men this is impossible; but with the sublime all things are possible. Come to me, all you that labour and are heavy laden, and I will give you rest. Take my yoke upon you, and learn of me, and you shall find rest to your souls. For my yoke is easy, and my burden is light; for I am meek and lowly in heart.

Behold, the Rock said to him then, we have forsaken all to follow you. What shall we have therefore?

The student is not above his teacher, Joshua said, but every one who is fulfilled shall be as his teacher. As I hear, I judge; and my judgement is just, because I seek not my own will, but the will of the father who has sent me.

―――――――

And again his eyes found me in the throng. *Walk with me.*

―――――――

He who loves his father or mother more than me is not worthy of me, he said. He who loves his son or daughter more than me is not worthy of me. But every one who has forsaken houses or lands, brothers or sisters, father or mother, wife or children, for my name's sake, shall receive a hundredfold, and shall inherit the life of ages. For there are many first who shall be last, and they shall become a unity. I shall choose you, one out of a thousand, and two out of ten thousand.

And they shall stand as a unity.

Tabor

The Sword in the Wall

1

And Joshua withdrew himself with his students to the Sea of Galilee, and he spoke to his students, that a small boat should wait on him because of the mob, lest they should throng him, those who came to hear him and to be healed of their diseases. For he had healed as many as had afflictions, in such numbers that they pressed upon him to touch him. And when they saw him, those with fouled inspirations fell down before him and cried, saying, You are the scion of the sublime. And a great mob followed him from Galilee, Judaea, Jerusalem, Idumaea, and from beyond Jordan; and those around Tyre and Sidon came to him also, when they had heard what great things he did.

And he charged them strictly that they should not make him known, but the mob gathered again so that they could not so much as eat bread.

I didn't follow him to Capernaum, was still not wholly sure whether I'd been dismissed or called. Instead, I wandered the streets of Nain until my father found me, returned to Bethany with him, oblivious of his lashing tongue. I resumed studies that meant nothing to me now, or everything. I sat under the fig tree thinking of Nain, trying to retrace the potshards of notions—the everyman's return, the dead made quick, his father's will—that had somehow locked together for me and become whole in an instant, a recognition of recognition. I couldn't hope to understand it fully then though. It took me forty days to decide I needed to return to Nain.

In Capernaum, so he told me, Joshua himself was no less shaken.

And when his friends heard of it, they went out to lay hold on | him, for they said, He is beside himself.

It was the question, he said: *What do I still lack?* At first, for all the rich naif's privilege begging stripped by his tongue, he was charmed by its innocence. Then as he spoke, he found himself answering on another level, asking and answering himself. And a key turned, a door opened, and he saw... a whole lot more of how things might play out. It took him forty days to decide he needed to return to Nain.

And he went up into a mountain, and called to him those he wanted, | and they came to him.

I slipped out of bed in the pre-dawn dark, pulled on a pair of brown bell bottom cords, a beige cowboy shirt, leather sandals and an afghan coat. No watch, no jewellery, just the roll of bills I dug from the pawn shop slips crammed in the top drawer of my dresser. I hadn't hocked everything, but I had enough to feel wary at the station, peel the bills off in my pocket for the early morning Greyhound headed north out of Bethany, flickering golden sunrise through palm trees on my face as I sat staring out the window.
 I found them on the slopes of Mount Tabor, resting.

And he ordained twelve, that they should be with him, that he might send them forth to preach the realm of the sublime and heal the sick: Simon the Rock and his brother Andrew; and Jacob and John bene-Rama, who are the Sons of Thunder; and Philip, | and Nathanael bar-Tolmay; and Matthew the taxman; and James the Just, and Thomas, and Jude who is called the Hearty, and Symon the Zealous; and the young Judaean, the son of Simeon of Kerioth, who also betrayed him.

Our young Judaean, he said.

2

nd they went into a house. And he said to them: Behold, I send you forth as sheep in the midst of wolves; so be wise as serpents, harmless as doves. Carry neither gold, nor silver, nor brass in your purses, nor scrip for your journey, neither two coats, nor shoes, nor staves. Heal the sick, cleanse the lepers, raise the dead, cast out daimons. Freely you have received, freely give.

The room in the Nain chapter house was quiet, cleared for us. Supper done, we still lounged in the horseshoe of cushions, each leaning on his left arm, angled, overlapping like the scales of a fish. In the place of honour at his right hand as the last to join his inner circle—Come closer, beside me, he'd said as I took the furthest setting—I blushed at the darting gazes of eleven Galileans all wondering at this stranger in their midst, lowered my eyes. It wasn't as if I could even lock my gaze on him as he talked, shut out the attention; my head so close to his chest I could have leant back into it, felt his warmth, the beat of his heart, I could only look back over my shoulder for so long, like a dog sat between his master's legs, looking round, back and up, before the crick in my neck became too much.

Do not go into the roads of the Gentiles, he said, and do not enter into any city of the Samaritans, but go rather to the lost sheep of the house of Israel, saluting no man by the way. Do not go from house to house, but in whichever city or town you enter, enquire who in it is worthy, and abide there till you leave. When you come into a house, salute it, and into whatever house you enter, first say, Peace be to this house. And if the son of peace be there, your peace shall rest upon it. If not, it shall turn back upon you. And stay in that same house, eating and drinking whatever they set before you, for the labourer is worthy of his hire.

Peace, he said. I twisted round to take the joint from Joshua, copying his thumb and forefinger grip as I touched it warily to my lips, tried a shallow toke, and coughed. Laughter. I wrinkled my nose at the strange smell: spring meadows; stale farts; *both* somehow. And under it the musk of unwashed Galilean, rank, rich, riveting. The smell of Joshua behind me.

We sprawled in a circle, on rugs and throws, in an old schoolbus gutted and trimmed to psychedelic sanctuary from the hullaballoo of the festival outside. Passing the joint to Thomas, I listened as our guru called us to Æternity.

And as you go, preach, saying, The realm of Zion is to hand. He who welcomes you welcomes me, and he who welcomes me welcomes he who sent me. He who welcomes a prophet in the name of a prophet shall win a prophet's reward, and he who welcomes an upstanding man in the name of an upstanding man shall win an upstanding man's reward. Anyone who therefore shall embrace me before men, before my æternal father, I will embrace him also. But anyone who shall spurn me before men, before my æternal father, I will spurn him too.

So, wherever does not welcome you, nor hear your words, go your ways out into the streets of the same, and when you depart out of that house or city, shake the dust off your feet.

3

But beware of men, for they will deliver you up to the councils, for likewise they harried the prophets who were before you. And they will scourge you in their congregation houses, and you shall be brought before governors and kings for my sake, to give testimony to them and the Gentiles. If they have called the master of the house Beelzebub, how much more shall they call those of his household? He who shall know his father and his mother shall be called the son of a harlot. And you shall be betrayed both by parents, and brethren, and kinsfolks, and friends, and some of you they shall cause to be put to death. If they have kept my teachings, they will keep yours also, but if they have abused me, they will abuse you too. All these things will they do to you for my name's sake, because they do not know he who sent me.

———

Every so often, I'd look at the Rock or Andrew, down at the lowest settings, the feet of the horseshoe arrangement, but they were the most intimidating, in truth, his closest confidantes, first to be called and so... *Galilean.* A beardless boy of the Judaean upper classes faced with a Galilean fisherman like Simon, accent broad as his shoulders, you understand, I might as well have been some Etonian schoolboy among Glasgow's shipyard workers. So, the passing glances in curiosity, the *relentless* peer from Thomas—hardly unfounded with Joshua talking outright sedition now, set on active recruitment, and me there, a Sanhedrin member's son at his side. Their palpable puzzlement as to *who I even was* was enough to keep me... profoundly interested in the cushion I was leaning on, shall we say.

So, I could barely focus on Joshua's words, the mission he was setting out for the other ten. He wanted his scribe at his side, of course, and he had... other plans for me, it seemed, so Matthew and I were to stay with him while the others went out to the lost sheep of Israel, preached dissent, preached that the realm was there to be taken. To be taken back.

———

But when they deliver you up, he said, take no thought for how or what you shall speak, for what you shall speak shall be given you in that same hour. For it is not you that speaks, but the inspiration of your father which speaks in you, and I will give you a mouth and wisdom, which all your adversaries shall be unable to repudiate or resist. Blessed are you when men revile you, and harry you, and falsely accuse you of all wickedness, for my sake. Rejoice, and be exceeding glad, for great is your reward in Æternity. And when they harry you in this city, flee into another, for I tell you for sure, you shall not have gone through all the cities of Israel before the everyman is come.

I thought of the Roman guards moving down the Greyhound, checking visas, as we sat at the border, how the panic had risen in my breast, wondering what I'd say if my father had reported me, if my travel papers so close to expiry raised suspicions, if my clothes and hair marked me out, if they wanted to know where all the cash came from. I was so close to Galilee, to *him*, but if I couldn't get out of Occupied Judaea... I didn't know what I'd do.

A cursory glance at my documents though, and... and here I was, in the heart of revolution.

4

Do not fear those who kill the body, he said, but cannot kill the soul. Are two sparrows not sold for a farthing? And yet not one of them shall fall on the ground without your father. But the very hairs of your head are all numbered; you are of more value than many sparrows, so do not fear. Do not fear them, for there is nothing covered that shall not be revealed, nothing hid that shall not be known. What I tell you in darkness, speak in light, and what you hear in the ear, preach upon the housetops.

But I will forewarn you who you should fear.

I turned to him as he gave that warning, saw the guarded look in his eyes that he got, I would come to realise, whenever he knew a parable was taking him close to an edge, where a sheep might all too easily stumble and fall, be lost. At the time I thought maybe it was just the marijuana fug, a fuddle of projected meaning, menace. I'd heard maryjane made you paranoid, gave you The Fear.

Fear, he said, he who has power to cast into Gehenna after he has killed. Fear he who is able to destroy both soul and body in Gehenna. Aye, I say to you, fear him. He was a murderer from the beginning, and abode not in the truth, because there is no truth in him, that abomination of desolation spoken of by Daniel the prophet.

And I noted Matthew, on his other side, stop writing for a second, look up in shock at the word *murderer*. Wait, what? Of course the lord and judge of all our souls was to be feared, but had Joshua just called him a murderer, said there was no truth in him? And then the casual reference to Daniel's *abomination* came, and the scribe's brow unfurrowed. Ah, so Joshua meant to fear the Gehenna awaiting idolaters, fear the Roman overlord raised up as deity, Baal Shamem. For a second...

But I imagine you protesting, lover of the sublime, citing redacted scriptures of submission or perdition, insisting he *did* threaten us to fear. Yes, you say, tremble before Baal Shamem! Or to translate the Hebrew, *Lord of Heaven*. As you should know by now, lover of the sublime, that's the sort of thinking will cast a soul into Gehenna while the body is still very much alive.

I took another joint as it came my way, from Matthew this time, sucked down a toke, turned to Joshua.

Do not think that I have come to send peace on earth, he said. I come not to send peace, but a sword. For from this moment on there shall be five in one house divided, three against two, two against three. For I am come to set a man at odds with his father, daughter against mother, daughter in law against mother in law. And a man's foes shall be those of his own household. And the brother shall deliver up the brother to death, and the father the child. And children shall rise up against their parents, and cause them to be put to death.

His fingers brushing mine as he took the joint, an electric touch.

————————

The realm of the father, he said, is like a man who wanted to kill a great man. He drew the sword in his house and drove it into the wall, that he might know his hand was strong. And from that time he sought opportunity to betray him.

Then he slew the great man.

5

And it came to pass in those days, that he went out to Mount Tabor to pray, and continued all night in prayer to the sublime. And when it was day, he called his students to him, and he came down with them and stood upon the plain with the company of his students, amid a great mob of people out of all Judaea and Jerusalem, and from the sea coast of Tyre and Sidon. And those who were vexed with fouled inspirations came, and they were healed. And the whole mob sought to touch him, for power went out of him and healed them all.

And seeing the mob, he went up into a mountain, and his students came to him, and when he was set, he opened his mouth and taught them, saying:

No man sews a piece of new cloth on an old garment, else the new piece that patched it shrinks from the old, and the rent is made worse. But truly I say, do not think I am come to destroy the law or the prophets. I am not come to destroy, but to fulfil.

The beat and thrum of distant music carried up from the festival fields below, from the bands on stages, buskers among the tents and tipis, troubadours in patchwork motley and paisley pattern dancing through the mob. In this setting I conjure, most would imagine Joshua on stage for his speech, a break from healings and blessings to take the mic, address the masses. That turning point in Tabor wasn't a sermon though. It was a manifesto.

The morning sun was warm on us as he set out his pathway to a new aeon, fresh as the mountain air.

No man puts new wine into old wineskins, he said, else the new wine will burst the wineskins, the wine will spill, and the wineskins will perish. Rather new wine must be put into new wineskins, so both are preserved. But truly I say, not one speck or stroke shall in any way be taken from the law until all is fulfilled, until Æternity and Earth pass.

———

The twelve of us sat on the summit, at the end of a long trail up through woodlands to the ash and stone emplacement of the beacon fires lit to mark new months and feast days, signals to the earth we looked out on now, seeing how far that fire could shine—to the mountains of Samaria in the south, to Gilead in the east, all down the Jezreel Valley to Mount Carmel and the Mediterranean in the west, and to the north, beyond Upper Galilee, to Mount Hermon itself.

———

The law and the prophets were until John, he said, and since that time it is the realm of the sublime that is preached, every man driven into it. But truly I say, while anyone who shall do and teach one of these least decrees shall be called the greatest in the realm of Zion, anyone who shall break them, and teach others to do so, the same shall be called the least in the realm of Zion. I tell you that unless your rectitude shall exceed the rectitude of the clerks and the Select, you shall in no way enter into the realm. For wide is the gate and broad is the road that leads to desolation, and there are many who go in that way; and tight is the gate and narrow is the road which leads to life, and there are few who find it. You, enter in at the tight gate.

6

You have heard that it was said by those of the past, You shall not kill, that anyone who kills without a cause shall be in danger of the judgment. But I tell you that anyone who is angry with his brother shall be in danger of the judgment, anyone who says to his brother, You good-for-nothing! shall be in danger of the council, and anyone who says, You fool!

shall be in danger of Gehenna's fire. So, if you bring your gift to the altar, and remember there that your brother has anything against you, leave your gift there before the altar and go your way. You must be reconciled to your brother before you come and offer your gift.

I watched Matthew the taxman scribbling furiously, doing his best to keep up, thought of the parable of the prodigal he'd sung to me the previous night. As Joshua held his vigil, I'd sat outside the house in Nain, sat under the stars looking up at the dark hulk of the hill, the Milky Way. Inside, the others slept but I found Matthew writing by lamplight. What are you working on? I asked, and he showed me. I told you how his voice caught at the end, how it spoke to this taxman traitor returned to the fold. He cleared his throat when he was done, only then noticed me.

What's the matter? he said.

I shook my head. It was too personal.

As Joshua talked of Gehenna's fire then, I thought of the ire of the black sheep's righteous brother, the burning rancour that destroys a soul. If the sublime was a father to Joshua, to me he was always a brother, a twin gone to the wastes, leaving his other half with his sisters, suffering that fire. Not a fatherly judge at all, you understand, but a sibling and an unruly one at that, an Esau of the quiet wilds to the everyman forever nipping at his heels, wearing his clothes, stealing his realm, wrestling with his proxy. It's hard to deal with accusations made by an absence, to reconcile with a grave.

Judge not, said Joshua, and you shall not be judged; condemn not, and you shall not be condemned; forgive, and you shall be forgiven. Give, and it shall be given to you, in good measure—pressed down, shaken together, running over—poured into your lap. For you yourself shall be judged with what judgement you judge; and with the same measure that you dispense, it shall be measured to you in return.

We sat as children before a storyteller today, so I'd managed to hide myself away behind the others, out of their attention and largely blocked from his, peering out between James and Thomas.

While you are on the road to the magistrate with an accuser then, he said, settle with him lest he deliver you to the judge, the judge deliver you to the guard, and you are cast into prison. For sure, I tell you, you shall by no means come out from there till you have paid to the last copper.

When you talk of the sublime as your father, I said to Joshua once, sometimes I think you don't know your own teachings.

How so? he laughed.

You teach that the word made flesh was with the sublime in the beginning, I said, but the son can only come after the father. Shouldn't you say he is your brother?

He'll always be a father to me, Joshua said.

That was our one stumbling block, I think now.

7

You have heard that it was said by those of the past, You shall not commit adultery. But I tell you that anyone who looks on a woman to lust after her has committed adultery with her already in his heart. And if your right eye offend you, pluck it out, and cast it from you, for it is better for you that one part should perish than that your whole body should be cast into Gehenna. And if your right foot or hand offend you, cut it off, and cast it from you, for it is better for you to enter into life lame or maimed than that your whole body should be cast into Gehenna. Take heed, and beware of covetousness: for a man's life does not consist in the abundance of the things which he possesses.

Before his vigil, as we sat outside the log cabin, chugging beer and sharing a joint, I told him of my kid sister's husband and his best man who went all crazy stalker, till one night... it seemed to come out of nowhere, like he just flipped, though later the police found photos of her all over his apartment. Anyway, she got away but her husband... I looked up at the stars, the aircraft warning lights blinking high up on Mount Tabor.

She hasn't been the same since, I said.

He who has the bride is the bridegroom, he said, but the friend of the bridegroom, who stands and hears him, rejoices greatly at the bridegroom's voice: Because of this my own joy is fulfilled, he says, and if it were not so, I would have told you. In my father's house are many mansions; I go to prepare a place for you, for if I go and prepare a place for you, you have not chosen me, but I have chosen you, and ordained you, that you should go and bring forth fruit, and that your fruit should remain, that whatsoever you shall ask of the father in my name, he may give it you.

He talked of the ideal world where my sister's stalker would have been happy that she'd found love with his friend, happy for them both, but I hedged: it wasn't as simple as that; they'd had a thing together; she thought it was all her fault; and our father...

Whether you fancy it or father it, he said, a woman's body is still hers. He doesn't own her.

Try *disown*, I said.

And you think he'd do the same to you.

What do you mean?

I looked at the ground between my feet, knowing exactly what he meant.

He who has ears, he said, let him hear: Let your light so shine before men that they may see your good works, and honour your æternal father. No man, when he has lit a lamp, puts it in a secret place or under a bushel; rather he sets it on a lampstand that those who come in may see the light; and it gives light to all that are in the house.

The light of the body is the eye. If your eye should be clear then, your whole body shall be full of light. If your whole body is full of light then, having no part dark, the whole shall be full of light, as when the bright shining of a candle gives you light. But if your eye should be fouled, your whole body shall be full of darkness. If therefore the light that is in you be darkness, how great is that darkness!

8

He glowed as he spoke now, haloed in morning sunlight turned to streaming and shimmer as the anokhi mushrooms kicked in. I felt a judder in my spine, a strange quiver suffusing bone and muscle, like the comfortable ache that isn't an ache, when you lie in bed after some sickness, as the vestiges of fever seep away, the bouts of burning and freezing dissolved to a paradox in which you're simultaneously warm and cool, sore and snug, and feel so utterly fleshly in every inch of your body.

The whole world rippled with energy, and myself in it, and Joshua.

Again, you have heard that it has been said by those of the past, You shall not perjure yourself, but make good on your oaths to the Worker. But I say to you, swear not at all: neither by Æternity, for it is the sublime's throne; nor by the Earth, for it is his footstool; nor by Jerusalem, for it is the city of the great worker; nor by your head, because you cannot make one hair white or black. But let your communication be, Aye, aye; No, no; for whatever is more than these comes of strife.

And from the jury box, the twelve of us watched him take his right hand off the bible, lower the other as he stepped down off the witness stand, waving the clerks away, turning to face us, palms open at his side as he offered simply his word, the everyman as witness.

You have heard that it has been said, An eye for an eye, and a tooth for a tooth. But I say to you that you should not fight strife, but rather if anyone shall smite you on your right cheek, turn to him the other also. And if any man will sue you at the law, and take away your coat, let him have your cloak also. And if anyone shall force you to go a mile, go with him two.

And in the dock in orange jumpsuit, shackles, he gazed impassive as a centurion took each arm, led him away toward the prison of the pacifist, the everyman as defendant.

You have heard that it has been said, You shall love your neighbour, and hate your enemy. But I say to you, Love your enemies, bless those who curse you, do good to those who hate you, and pray for those who harry you, that you may be the children of your father. For he makes his sun rise over the good and over the wicked, and sends rain on the just and on the unjust.

He rose from the prosecutor's desk, the everyman as accuser of accusers.

For if you love those who love you, what reward have you? Even the taxmen do this, do they not? And if you salute your brothers only, what more do you do than others? Even the taxmen do this, do they not? So be fulfilled, even as your father is fulfilled. If you have money, do not lend at interest; if you lend to them of whom you hope to receive, what thanks have you? For delinquents also lend to delinquents, to receive as much in return. But give to him from whom you will not receive it back, and your reward shall be great: you shall be the children of the highest, for he is kind to the unthankful and to the wicked. So be merciful, as your father also is merciful.

A city that is set on a hill cannot be hid, and fortified it cannot fall.

What Will You Do?

9

Sell what you have and give alms. Amass for yourselves not treasures upon Earth, where moth and rust do corrupt, and where thieves break in and steal, but rather in Æternity, where neither moth nor rust do corrupt, nor worm destroy, and where thieves can neither break in nor steal. For where your treasure is, there your heart will be too.

Shouldn't they sell it, he'd said, and give the money to the poor?

The priest had smiled uncomfortably at this odd twelve year old—I'm not lost, he'd said, I just wanted to stay a little longer—his eyes on the statue of Laocoön and his sons being strangled by serpents, ineffably beautiful for a scene of torture, even with the ravages of time that had taken one son's arm, another's hand. Visitors to the Vatican Museum, the priest explained patiently, undoubtedly funded more good works than the sale of a single artefact.

Shouldn't you sell them *all*? Joshua had said.

And when you give your alms, do not sound a trumpet before you, as the hypocrites do in the congregation houses and the streets, that they may have the glory of men. For sure, I tell you, they have their reward, but woe to you who are rich! for you have received your consolation. Take heed that you do not give your alms before men, to be seen by them, otherwise you have no reward from your æternal father. When you give alms, do not let your left hand know what your right hand does, that your alms may be in secret; and your father who sees in secret shall reward you openly.

Joshua had wandered off from his mother and brother. Tagging onto a tour group, he'd seen the lavish wonders of the basilica's vast interior, the supreme artistry of the Sistine Chapel. He'd strolled the museum courtyard, hands behind his back like some miniature art critic, studying sculptures in their alcoves with precocious gravity. It was all beautiful, but all the while he'd thought of his mother scrimping coins for the collection every Sunday Mass, stuffing notes in a biscuit tin for The Pilgrimage, and struggling to pay the gas man who threatened to put in a card-operated meter.

And when you fast, do not be, as the hypocrites, of a sad countenance, for they contort their faces that they may display their fasting to men. For sure, I tell you, they have their reward, but woe to you who are sated! for you shall hunger. You, when you fast, anoint your head and wash your face, so that to men you do not seem to fast, only secretly to your father; and your father, who sees in secret, shall reward you openly.

And when you pray, you shall not be as the hypocrites are, for they love to pray standing in the congregation houses and in the corners of the streets, that they may be seen by men. For sure, I tell you, they have their reward, but woe to you who laugh now! for you shall mourn and weep. You, enter into your closet when you pray, and when you have shut your door, pray to your hidden father; and your father who sees in secret shall reward you openly.

William Blake, he'd declared with the unblinking assurance of a twelve year old with a Fact, said the Laocoön was actually God with his sons, Satan and Adam.

Satan was not God's son, said the priest.

Aren't we all? he'd said.

Well, figuratively, the priest had said, not literally.

What's *literally*? he'd said.

10

Woe to you, when all men shall speak well of you! for so did their fathers to the false prophets. Beware of false prophets, who come to you in sheep's clothing but inwardly they are ravening wolves. You shall know them by their fruits.

***

He'd read to near enough the whole village, friends and family and neighbours all crammed into the wee community hall, filling plastic chairs unstacked from the sides until it was standing room only at the back. Everyone wanted to hear Capernaum's favourite son, just back from studying under the Makar himself, Galilee's poet laureate. So he'd stood up on the stage, opened his chapbook on the lectern, pressed the pages flat, then looked up and out at the audience, staring fierce at the minister who stood in the doorway. He'd watched the man's sour face get redder with every line.

***

Do men gather grapes from thorns, or figs from camel-thistles? Such do not yield fruit. Even so, each good tree yields good fruit, while each rotten tree yields wicked fruit, by which you shall know them, for every tree is known by his own fruit. A good tree cannot yield wicked fruit, neither can a rotten tree yield good fruit. Either make the tree good, and his fruit good, or else let the tree rot and his fruit rot. For the tree is known by his fruit, and every tree that does not yield good fruit will be cut down and cast into the fire.

***

He'd dripped a single drop of water into his island malt from the jug, raised the glass to his nose for a sniff, a sip. Sláinte! said Andrew, and all seven crowded into the snug had joined the toast. Through the wee glass-panelled window at his side, Joshua had looked out on a few scattered sheep grazing on the machair, wondered if anyone got the pun on makar in the poem he'd read. The *makar*, the poet, the imagination as fertile field, *machair*. Burning ryegrass and poison apple trees as Calvinism rooted up and put to the torch, consigned to the fire of ages. Simon would take it literally of course, a threat of damnation.

Why then do you call me, Teacher, Teacher, he said, but not do the things which I say? Whoever comes to me, and hears my teachings, and does them, I will show you what he is like: he is like a wise man who built a house, and dug deep, and laid the foundation on a rock; and when the flood arose, the stream beat violently upon that house, but could not shake it, for it was founded upon a rock. But he who hears and does not is like a foolish man who built a house without a foundation upon the sand, against which the river smashed in violence, and at once it fell; and the ruin of that house was great. Not every one who says to me, Teacher, Teacher, shall enter into the realm of Zion, only he who does the will of my æternal father.

And up on Ben Tabor now, I shivered in my sodden afghan coat, the cold wind scouring my flesh as cruelly as it scoured the rock, envied the Galileans their Arran sweaters and anoraks—or envied the common sense of men knowing better than to hike up a hill in corduroy flares and sandals, no matter how warm the sun in the streets of Nain. I watched Joshua as he turned his gaze from James—a house, he said—to Simon— *founded upon a rock.*

11

Is the life not more than meat, the body more than garment? Behold the birds of the air, for they do not sow, nor do they reap, nor gather into barns, yet your æternal father feeds them. Are you not much more than they? Fear not, little flock, for it is your father's good joy to give you the realm. And why do you take thought for clothing? Do not be anxious from morning to evening, evening to morning, about what you shall wear.

———

I'd arrived in Nain with only the clothes on my back, alone and nervous as I stepped down from the Greyhound, seeing no Romans in the terminal, but crew-cut National Guardsmen, townsfolk frowning at the other freaks arriving, gathering out on the high street, dancing around me, a ring of girls in flared jeans and beads—*come on*—and we'd clambered up on the back of a pick-up, laughed at wind through our hands, jumped down, the girls skipping and twirling away into fields of men and women stripped to their skin, body-painted with flowers. I'd arrived.

———

Consider the lilies of the field, how they grow: they do not toil, nor do they spin. And yet I say to you that even Solomon in all his glory was not arrayed like one of these. Wherefore, if the sublime so clothe the grass of the field, which exists today and is cast into the furnace tomorrow, shall he not clothe you all the more, O you of little trust?

———

All I have and more, I'd said when I found him sitting on the slopes of Mount Tabor. I'd thrown the bag of money down at his feet, everything I owned sold for the coffers of the revolution. And more? he'd said, curious. I had suddenly... rethought my zeal then, mumbled of how all I'd sold was to be mine *someday* if it wasn't quite mine already. Beside him, Symon the Zealous had picked up the money-bag, babbled excitedly of the amount within. James had taken it from his hands, Joshua from his.

I didn't tell you to give it to *us*, he'd said. And tossed it back for me to catch.

———

So take no thought, saying, What will we eat? or, What will we drink? or, How will we be clothed? For your æternal father knows you have need of all these things—all these things the Gentiles prize.

Which of you can add one hour to his life by worrying? Take no thought for the morrow, for the morrow shall take care of its own; the strife of today is enough for today.

———

I'd thought he was rebuffing me for the second time, thought I was wrong to ever have imagined his gaze a call, fancied it in pure desire. How *could* he want me? But then he smiled. Our little unjust steward, he said. Keep the purse for all.

———

Rather seek the realm of the sublime, he said, and all these things shall be added to you. He who seeks, let him not cease seeking until he finds. Only ask, and it shall be given you; seek, and you shall find; knock, and it shall be opened to you: What woman having ten pieces of silver, if she loses one, does not light a candle, sweep the house, search diligently till she find it? And when she has found it, she calls her friends and her neighbours together, saying, Rejoice with me; for I have found the piece I had lost.

———

And now, high on Mount Tabor, he smiled at me.

12

Ask: *What do I still lack?* he said. Ask, and you shall receive. For which of you shall have a friend, and shall go to him at midnight, and say to him, Friend, lend me three loaves, for a friend of mine is come to me in his travels, and I have nothing to set before him? And if he from within shall answer and say, Trouble me not; the door is now shut, and my children are with me in bed; I cannot rise and give you? I say to you, if he will not rise and give you just because you are his friend, yet because of your brazen doggedness he will rise and give you everything you need.

———

He'd reached up from his slouch on the grass, as I stood there looking at the roll of bills, registering his action, his words and—I'd snapped out of it, stuffed the money in my pocket and grabbed his hand, gave a haul that helped him to his feet and ended in a handshake, an arm around my shoulder gathering me into the inner circle, to a confusion of introductions that were hearty and curious and wary, and all of them awkward on my part. Even now, up on Tabor, I couldn't quite believe a welcome so easy.

———

When you come in the light, he said, what will you do? What man is there among you who will give his son a stone if he asks for bread? Or if he asks for a fish, will give him a serpent? Or if he asks for an egg, will offer him a scorpion? If you then, being base, know how to give good gifts to your children, how much more shall your æternal father give good gifts to those who ask him? Blessed are they who hunger that they may fill the belly of him who desires. So then, do not turn away from he who would borrow from you, but give to every man who asks of you; and of he who takes away your goods do not demand them back.

———

And high on Mount Tabor, we listened in wonder as he gave us his manifesto founded not on temptation but on trust, lover of the sublime, not on some notion that all men are wicked, soiled with sin, but on a trust that all are just and only stumble blindly, weakly, lazily. As everyman, as accuser, we always already know by the knocking on the door what we should be doing. The details of it, as Hillel said, are only explanation.

———

Blessed are the merciful, he said, for they shall obtain mercy.

Blessed are they who mourn, for they shall be comforted.

Blessed are they who thirst for virtue, for they shall be filled.

Blessed are the meek, for they shall inherit the earth.

Blessed are the poor, for theirs is the realm of Zion.

Blessed are the pure in heart, for they shall see the sublime.

Blessed are the peacemakers, for they shall be called the children of the sublime.

Blessed are those who are harried for virtue's sake, for theirs is the realm of Zion.

When you come in the light, what will you do? Do you not perceive it yet, nor understand?

You are the light of the world. Take my yoke upon you, and learn of me, and you shall find rest to your souls. For my yoke is easy, and my burden is light: do to others as you would have men do to you—for this is the law and the prophets!

13

And he departed from there, and came close to the sea of Galilee. And it came to pass, that, as he was praying in a certain spot, when he finished, one of his students said to him, Teacher, teach us to pray, as John also taught his students.

We were on our way back to Capernaum, close by Tiberias. James and Joses had left us, Jude and Symon the Zealous too, headed south for Judaea. The rest of us, we came to him after another of his many vigils, deep in concentration out on a hilltop clearing. I followed his gaze east toward the dawn, and Herod's capital down on the coast.

By then I knew a little of his past, either from Matthew's writings or his own mouth. I wondered what he thought as he looked out toward the palace built high on the acropolis, the cemetery city. I wonder now if he thought of Herod the Great and his two sons, Archelous and Antipas, the slaughterer and the sympathiser who sold us all to Rome.

I think Blake was wrong about the Laocoön, you know. When I look at that statue, I see the serpents sent by wisdom herself, strangling a priest of Troy, priest of an idol Ilium's exiles would raise up with a little speck or stroke of ink here and there to turn the yod and vau of IHVH into those of IOVS, your Jehovah only Jove with a little *eh?* of ignorance and *ah!* of wonder spliced in.

As he rose to return to camp with us, it was Simon who asked if he would teach us his prayers just as he taught us his parables, for surely the Worker sublime would be pleased by his poetry. Not since David's psalms, Solomon's Song of Songs... Joshua smiled, started downhill toward trees and brush woven with creeping honeysuckle.

And he said to them, When you pray, do not prattle hollow rote as the Gentiles do, for they think that they shall be heard for their effusive gushing. So do not be like them, you, for your father knows what things you have need of before you ask him. You, pray in this manner then:

Father, may your name be hallowed. May your realm come, with your will being done on Earth as it is in Æternity. Give us tomorrow's bread today: forgive us our delinquencies, since we forgive those delinquent with us. And do not lead us into trials, but deliver us from strife.

There was no power and glory in the original, lover of the sublime, no fawning unction. We understood that. We didn't quite understand what he meant by tomorrow's bread, but we would soon learn.

And when you stand praying, if you have anything against anyone, forgive it. For if you forgive men their misdeeds, your æternal father will also forgive you, but if you do not forgive men their misdeeds, neither will your father forgive your misdeeds.

We came down through trees into meadows, crested a low rise and the camp sprawled before us, fields of souls.

And he said to them, You, come away into a place in the quiet wilds, and rest yourselves a while.

For there were many coming and going, and they had no leisure so much as to eat. And he took them, and went aside privately by boat over the sea of Galilee, into a place in the quiet wilds, in the territory of the city called Bethsaida. And when the people had heard of this, they followed him on foot out of the cities.

14

When the day was now far spent, his students came to him.

This is a place in the quiet wilds, they said, and the hour is well passed. Send the mob away, that they may go into the country round about, into the villages, and buy themselves bread, for they have nothing to eat.

You, he said, give them to eat.

Shall we go and buy two hundred denarii's worth of bread, Philip answered him, and give them to eat?

How many loaves have you? he said. Go and see.

And one of his students, Andrew, Simon's brother, saw the student whom Joshua loved following, and turning about, said to him, There is a lad here, who has five barley loaves, and two small fishes, but what are they among so many?

So I was carrying an armful of bread, a sceptic might say, a miracle not of magic, not of some cornucopic conjuring trick, but rather the miracle of a privileged little prince of Judaea walking into the sunlight. But I come not to destroy your faith, lover of the sublime, but to fulfil it. So if you would keep our parable a tale of marvels, you can imagine him reaching into the fishes' mouths to bring out a talent from each. If his simple student could draw out a shekel from a single fish to keep the Romans fat, do you not think the teacher himself could draw out six thousand's worth from two, to keep a hungry mob of Israel's children from starvation? So I brought to him the loaves and fishes.

And Joshua directed them to make all sit down by companies upon the green grass. And they sat down in ranks, by hundreds and by fifties. And when he had taken the five loaves and the two fishes, he looked up to the heavens, and blessed, broke the loaves, and gave them to his students to set before them. And he divided the two fishes among them all. And they all ate.

I tore the last of the bread in two, a hunk for myself, a hunk for him, set them both on plates and shuffled round with one in each hand for the fish he was still portioning out. He took one and handed it back laden, set the other down beside him. Plate in my lap, I picked a scrap of bread off, looked at him.

Go on, he said. Eat.

You'll get nothing at this rate, I said.

He waved a hand. I dipped the scrap in olive oil.

Here, I said.

He opened his mouth for me to pop it in, smiled, turned back to serve Philip.

And when they were full, he said to his students, Gather up the scraps that remain, that nothing be lost.

So they gathered them together, and filled twelve baskets with the scraps of the five barley loaves, which remained over and above to those who had eaten. And those who ate of the loaves were about five thousand men, beside women and children. Then those men, when they had seen the miracle that Joshua did, said, Of a truth, this is that prophet who should come into the world.

When Joshua therefore realised they would come and take him by force to make him a king, at once he urged his students to get into a boat, and to go before him to the shores of Capernaum, while he sent the mobs away. And when he had sent the mobs away, he went up into a mountain apart to pray, and was there alone.

15

And when evenfall was now come, his students went down to the sea, and entered into a boat, went over the sea toward Capernaum. And it was dark now, and Joshua was not come to them; the boat was in the midst of the sea, and he alone on the land. And he saw them toiling in rowing, about twenty-five to thirty furlongs in the midst of the sea, for the wind was against them. And about the fourth watch of the night he came to them, walking upon the sea, and would have passed by them.

I woke bleary from my sleep to Matthew's insistent shaking, in the midst of a storm. Was it our turn at the oar again? Already? I rubbed my eyes with blistered hands, felt the ache of a back unused to labour, only glad that the weak muscles of a taxman scribe and a lad were somewhat made up for by Jacob and John. But Simon and Andrew, Philip and Nathanael had set their oars down not to pass them on to us. Instead, they stared out into the dark behind me, back the way we'd come. And I turned and saw the shape in the distance, carried on the wind and waves themselves.

And when the students saw him walking on the sea, they were frantic, saying, It is a ghost! and they cried out in fear, for they did not consider the miracle of the loaves, for their hearts were hardened.

I could say that I saw the sea itself freeze beneath his feet, a whirlwind holding him in the air, but really... I wasn't sure quite what I saw at all. It was as if the distance of darkness between us and him was, in an instant, made a firmament around him, but a firmament that rippled, shattered, tore out of his way with every step, as if he walked through space and time itself, the laws of nature opening up to let him pass. We were in uproar.

But at once Joshua spoke to them, saying, Be of good cheer. It is me. Be not afraid.

Teacher, Simon the Rock answered him, if it is you, bid me come to you on the water.

And he said, Come.

And when Simon the Rock was come down out of the boat, he walked on the water, to go to Joshua. But when he saw the wind blustering, he was afraid, and beginning to sink, he cried, saying, Teacher, save me. And immediately Joshua stretched forth his hand, and caught him, and said to him, O you of little trust, why did you doubt?

And when they were come into the boat, the wind ceased. Then those who were in the boat came and adored him, saying, Of a truth you are the scion of the sublime.

———

I held back, the adoration in my heart too frightening now. For such a man?

———

And when they were gone over, they came into the land of Gennesaret, and drew to the shore. And when they were come out of the boat, at once they knew him, and they sent out into all that country round about, and began to carry about in beds those who were sick to where they heard he was, and brought to him all who were diseased. And wherever he entered, into villages, or cities, or country, they laid the sick in the streets, and begged him that they might touch if it were but the hem of his garment, and as many as touched him were made whole.

16

And Joshua went up into a mountain, and sat down there.

———

I followed him up the hill in the half-light, unsure why he'd asked me to come with him and with other things to brood on besides. Skirting Tiberias by sea had brought us halfway between Magdala and Capernaum, and now I thought of my younger sister and her troubles. How long it was since I'd seen her. How maybe I belonged with her.

Joshua took a seat facing west, beckoned me to join him.

We watched the sunrise in a silence I yearned to break but couldn't, though I knew every moment of it was an offer to listen, until eventually, with daylight, the camp below came alive.

And great mobs came to him, having with them those who were lame, blind, mute, maimed, and many others, and cast themselves down at Joshua's feet; and he healed them, insomuch that the mob wondered when they saw the lame walk and the blind see, the mute speak and the maimed made whole; and he began to teach them many things; and they honoured the spirit of Israel.

I'd only seen a fraction of his following in Nain and thought it a mob—and a *mob*, I admit, not a *multitude* or a *mass* but rather a *mob*, collapsing all into a collective entity shaded with everything that word implies to those who see the everyman as base and bestial. A multitude simply mills, throngs. Mobs gather and grow, grow restless and riot, loot and lynch. Mobs bay for blood, cry out for crucifixions... while their poor governors only try to keep the peace, of course. I use the word here that perhaps you might understand how, as we came close to Capernaum and I saw the crowds of Nain multiply to tenfold in this crucible of his fame, to a camp so vast and lit by scattered lamps at night I might have thought the heavens' very stars all fallen, when I saw the way Joshua tended to this host of hosts, for me... it slowly changed the very meaning of a word like *mob*.

In those days the mob being very great, and having nothing to eat, Joshua called his students to him.

I have compassion on the mob, he said, because they have been with me three days now, and have nothing to eat. And I will not send them away fasting, lest they faint on the road, for many of them came from afar.

From where should we have so much bread in the wilderness, his students said, as to fill so great a mob?

It didn't occur to John that Joshua had answered this only a day before. Nathanael didn't offer an acerbic quip at the folly of the question. Philip didn't pipe up that maybe another magic trick was due. We looked at the mob and wondered how so many could be fed.

———

How many loaves have you? Joshua said to them.

Seven, said the Judaean, and a few little fishes.

And Joshua directed the mob to sit down on the ground. He took the seven loaves and the fishes, gave thanks, broke them, and gave to his students to set before them, and they set them before the people. And they all ate and were filled, and they gathered up seven baskets full of the broken food that was left. And those who ate were four thousand men, beside women and children. And he sent them away.

———

You're not counting the women and children? I asked over Matthew's shoulder. There were so many.

The Inspiration Quickens

17

The day after, other boats came from Tiberias, and when they drew close to where the people had eaten bread after the teacher had given thanks, they saw that Joshua was no longer there, nor were his students. So those who had stayed on the other shore took to their boats with them, and all came to Capernaum, seeking for Joshua. But many realised there had been no boats on the other shore save the one his students had entered into, and they had seen that Joshua did not go with his students into the boat, but that his students had gone away alone. So when they had found him on the other side of the sea, they said to him, Rabbi, when did you come here?

He didn't answer, knew they wouldn't believe him. The surface of the sea freezing beneath his feet in the sudden squall, or the winds howling to his hands to hold him, or reality parting to let him step through time, walk in another layer of existence where the cosmos follows only the rules of grammar, where if it has been told it has been done. Call it history or call it myth. Call it the realm.

For sure, I tell you, Joshua said, you seek me not because you saw the miracles, but because you ate of the loaves and were filled. Do not toil for the food which perishes, but for the food which endures to the life of ages, which the everyman shall give to you, for the father, the sublime, has sealed him.

Ye ken how ye tell a false prophet, eh? I heard Nathaniel's quiet aside to Philip.

He took a last draw on his cigarette, looked down as if to check for sure it was dead, then back at Philip.

He gi'es ye a straight answer, he said.

A slap on the arm in response. Still, Philip chuckled. Nathaniel grinned as he flicked the butt away, bouncing it off the *Fisher of Men*'s hull, to tumble down between boat and jetty. I smiled myself, and Nathaniel caught it, winked. Down on the dock, Joshua stood in a crowd of Galileans.

———

What shall we do, they said, that we might work the works of the sublime?

This is the work of the sublime, said Joshua, that you trust in him whom he has sent. It is written in the prophets, *And they shall all be taught of the sublime.* So, every man who has heard and has learned of the father, come to me.

———

I sat on a bollard of Capernaum harbour, watching him talk, hands jammed in my pockets, an adolescent runaway in awe of something I had really only just glimpsed in a man walking on water. The rules of material reality set aside. The realm of Zion revealed.

———

But no man can come to me, he said, unless he is drawn by the father who has sent me. This is why, I say to you, you have seen me and still do not trust.

What sign do you show then, they said, that we may see and trust you? What do you work? Our fathers ate manna in the desert, as it is written, *He gave them bread from Æternity to eat.*

For sure, I tell you, Joshua said, Moses did not give you that bread from Æternity, but my father gives you the true bread from Æternity, for the bread of the sublime is he who comes forth from Æternity, and gives life to the world.

Teacher, they said, give us this bread from now.

18

And he went into the congregation house and taught:

Not in the kirk itself, of course, which would hardly be proper for this lay preacher, but in the community hall attached to it, which Suffragettes might have one week, the Women's Guild the next. We sat on fold-out metal chairs set neatly in rows upon the dusty wooden floorboards. Over my shoulder: the notice board beside the double-doors, poster for the Hogmanay Party tacked to it. Ahead: the upright piano sitting over in the top-left corner of the room, and the uncurtained stage. I watched him pace that stage where each year, no doubt, children acted out nativity plays to celebrate the miracle of his bastard birth. He came to Capernaum as a teenager himself, I knew, but I could imagine Simon as a wean up there, cast as booming angel or beefy innkeeper.

I imagine Simon reading this, puzzling at this shifting frame of reference. Parables or prophecy, poetry or prose, I'd say. Just listen.

I am the bread of life, said Joshua. He who comes to me shall never hunger, and he who trusts in me shall never thirst. All that the father gives shall come to me, and he who comes to me I will in no way cast out. For I came forth from Æternity not to do my own will but the will of he who sent me. And this is the father's will:

From the back of the hall, I watched them shuffle in their seats. Arms folded and heads turned to whisper. Standing down by the piano, Simon and Andrew had their heads together, gesticulations speaking their worry—a beckoning toward the stage, an arm gripped, a shake of head.

That I should lose *nothing* of all that he has given, said Joshua, that *everyone* who sees the son and trusts in him, may have the life of ages.

My heart caught as he looked straight at me, put the slightest stress on *nothing*, on *everyone*. I swallowed, realised he'd paused, and I'd stopped breathing, and we were as locked together across the crowd as that moment in the market in Nain.

They murmured at him then because he said, I am the bread which came forth from Æternity.

Is this not Joshua, they said, the son of Joseph, whose father and mother we know? How is it then that he said, I came forth from Æternity?

I didn't even notice the crowd until Joshua raised his hands to quiet it.

Do not murmur among yourselves, said Joshua. Your fathers ate manna in the wilderness and are dead. This is the living bread which comes forth from Æternity, that a man may eat of and not taste death. And the bread that I will give is my flesh, which I will give for the life of the world.

They therefore strove among themselves, saying, How can this man give us his flesh to eat?

For sure, I tell you, Joshua said to them, unless the flesh of the everyman become your nourishment, and his blood become your replenishment, you have no life in you. But whoever trusts in me, and savours and swallows my flesh and blood, has the life of ages. For my flesh is meat indeed, and my blood is drink indeed. He who eats my flesh and drinks my blood dwells in me, and I in him. As the living father has sent me, and I live by the father, so he who consumes me, even he shall live by me.

Parable or prophecy, promise or perception.

19

These things he said in the congregation house, as he taught in Capernaum. Many of his students therefore, when they had heard this, said, This is a hard teaching. Who can hear it?

They followed at his heels as he walked out of the community hall, a turmoil of mutterings at his sermon. Was he seriously claiming to have been sent by the sublime? Was he really saying we should feast on him to gain everlasting life? I heard Nathanael's dry tone: Have ye been watching yon vampire flicks, man?

When Joshua knew in himself that his students murmured at it, he said, Does this offend you? Then what if you shall see the everyman rise up to where he was before? It is the inspiration quickens; the flesh profits nothing. The words that I speak to you, they are inspiration. *They* are life.

The words themselves, the life of ages, epochs, aeons. I stood at the door of the hall, jostled out in the crowd, oblivious to Jacob and John shouldering by me to join the mass of locals clamouring alarm at wild notions of cannibal immortality, human manna from the skies.

As long as I am in the world, he said, I am the light of the world.

For pity's sake, said someone, d'ye ken what you're saying, man!

I felt queasy in my certainty he did. Suddenly, I did perceive, did understand, what he'd said to us at the height of that mushroom trip vision on Mount Tabor, of the light of the world, of a body full of that light, of a light not to be hidden. Or I was halfway there, at least, with a sense of just how far his manifesto reached. I knew what he was saying even if I didn't know the truth of it, not in my heart, not yet.

He broke free of the bedlam, raised his hands to try and quell the crowd again.

But there are some of you who do not trust, he said.

For Joshua knew from the beginning who they were that did not trust, and who should betray him.

This is why, he said, I told you that no man can come to me unless it is given to him by my father.

Matthew brushed by me, rolling up his transcript scroll of Joshua's teachings, stuffing it inside his jacket. *And the heavens shall be rolled up,* I thought, *and put away.* Joshua stood framed by the churchyard gates now, the crowd spread out over the gravel path and on the grass, among the gravestones. He seemed to reach for the words.

Those who are dead are not alive, he said, and those who live shall never taste death.

There is no taste to grave dust on a lifeless tongue, I thought.

From that time many of his students went back, and walked no more with him.

Many are called, said Joshua to his students, but few are chosen. Have I not chosen you, though one of you is a slanderer? Will you also leave?

Teacher, said Simon then, to who would we go? You have the words of the life of ages.

———

If we only understood them.

———

As they went out, behold, a mute man driven by a daimon was brought to him. And when the daimon was cast out, the mute spoke. And the mob marvelled, saying, Such was never seen in Israel.

But the Select said, He casts out daimons through the lord of daimons.

———

And I looked back as we left, at the minister standing at the kirk door, glowering.

20

And he left them, and entering into the boat again departed to the other side. Now the students had not remembered to take bread, neither did they have more than one loaf in the boat with them.

And he charged them, saying, Take heed, beware of the leaven of the Select and of the Righteous.

And they reasoned among themselves, saying, It is because we have no bread.

And when Joshua knew it, he said to them, Why do you reason so—because you have no bread? Do you not perceive it yet, nor understand? Have you still your hardened hearts? Having eyes, do you not see? And having ears, do you not hear? Do you not remember? When I broke the five loaves among five thousand, how many baskets full of fragments did you gather up?

Twelve, they said to him.

And when the seven among four thousand, how many baskets full of fragments did you gather up?

Seven, they said to him.

A dozen messengers of the life of ages. Seven lights on a lampstand. You know, I said to him once, when someone doesn't understand a metaphor, a more abstruse one as an explanation doesn't really help. He brushed his hand through the tall grass as we walked. Once you get it, he said, it's hard to see how others *can't*.

In the days when you were eating what is dead, he said, you made it life. And why do you not understand? Because the Select and the clerks have taken the keys of knowledge; they have hidden them. They did not go in, and those who wanted to go in they kept out. Woe to them, the Select! For they are like a dog sleeping in the manger of the cattle, for he neither eats, nor does he let the cattle eat.

From the headland we could see across the firth, look down on the whole town, harbour to kirk, the old hotel turned hostel, even in his absence walled by protesters with placards. From here we could see all the rough-hewn beauty of Capernaum, and the grim housing estates beyond, which alone created need enough for that first chapter house of the movement, even before the dispossessed of the realm started coming from all of Galilee and beyond.

And when Joshua had finished these sayings, again he entered Capernaum, then he began to berate the cities where most of his mighty works were done, because they had no change of heart.

Woe to you, Chorazin! he said, Woe to you, Bethsaida! For if the mighty works, which were done in you, had been done in Tyre and Sidon, they would have changed their hearts long ago. But I tell you, it shall be more tolerable for Tyre and Sidon at the day of judgement, than for you. And you, Capernaum, who are exalted to Æternity, shall be brought down to Gehenna, for if the mighty works, which have been done in you, had been done in Sodom, it would remain until this day. But I tell you, it shall be more tolerable for the land of Sodom and Gomorrah in the day of judgement than for you.

———

Muffled sounds of the Sunday Service droned from the kirk, rote incantations of the Lord's Prayer.

———

Then they understood how that he bade them not beware of the leaven of bread, but of the doctrine of the Select and of the Righteous, which is hypocrisy.

———

I walked with him to the hostel, feeling a liar in my heart for my silence as I thought of Sodom unfallen.

The Outside of the Cup

21

Then certain of the clerks and the Select came to him from Jerusalem. And when they saw some of his students eat bread with defiled—that is to say, with unwashed—hands, they found fault. For the Select, and all the Jewish people holding the tradition of the elders, do not eat unless they wash their hands often. When they come from the market, they do not eat unless they wash, and there are many other things they have received to hold, as the washing of cups and pots, of bronze vessels and of tables.

Why do your students break the tradition of the elders, the Select and clerks asked, not washing hands when they eat bread?

Imagine, lover of the sublime: a Capernaum in the Bible Belt; a jamboree for the whole town, a fair, churches and Rotary Club organising games and contests, a grand picnic; we freaks from the commune on the edge of town rolling in with no less food for the feast than others; a visiting reverend famed from TV jeremiads, bowing to unctuous exhortations, rising in modest pride to say grace. As others clasped their hands, we reached for food. Slick in his scripture salesman's piety, the reverend reined in his pique to paternal condescension: please, why such insult to our maker?

Why do you too break decrees of the sublime by your tradition? Joshua answered. Moses said, *Honour your father and mother,* and said, *He who curses father or mother, let him die the death.* But you say that whoever does not honour his father or his mother, whoever says to them, What you would have gained from me is *qorban,* dedicated to the sublime, he shall be free. And you allow him to do no more for them, making the word of the sublime of | no effect through your tradition, which you have delivered.

———

I paused with a hunk of home-made bread halfway to my mouth then, as he rose, tore off a crust with my teeth, relished the chew of it in my mouth as I relished the way Joshua stood, fiery as I'd never seen him.

———

You hypocrites, he said, well did Isaiah prophesy of you, saying, *This people draw near to me with their mouth, and honour me with* | *their lips, but their heart is far from me, but in vain they do worship me, teaching for doctrines the decrees of men.*

———

He pointed at a child sat at her mother's side. You'd teach her to be thankless to the parents who provide for her, he said, and call her show of clasped hands grace.

———

Now you Select make clean the outside of the cup and platter, the teacher said, but your inward part is full of ravening and wickedness. You fools, didn't he who made | that which is outside also make what is within? But rather, give offerings of such things as you have, and behold, all things are clean to you.

———

The reverend's knuckles paled as he gripped the table edge.

———

Woe to you, clerks and Select, hypocrites! for you are like to whited sepulchres, which indeed seem beautiful on the outside, but within are full | of dead men's bones, of all pollution. Even so you too seem outwardly upright to men, but within are full of hypocrisy and iniquity.

Full well you scorn decrees of the sublime, he said, so you may hold to the tradition of men—the washing of pots and cups, and all the other suchlike things you do.

He'd forged his manifesto up on Tabor, it seemed. Now the revolution was begun.

22

Then one of the lawyers answered.

Rabbi, he said, saying thus you reproach us also.

Woe to you also, he said, you lawyers! For you laden men with burdens grievous to be borne, and you yourselves do not touch the burdens with one of your fingers.

And on Fox News, the night before, the reverend from Jerusalem, in his patronising tone, explained he did not hate the sinner, just the sin, how those with *these sorts of desires* were blessed to have a greater testing, greater trials that only made the victory over them a greater glory to—I walked out of the room, lit up a cigarette with shaking hand. I'd been in Capernaum a week now, been so readily adopted into the clan, I thought I was home. Mary and Salome vying to mother me, I was happy, accepted, just needed to find the right time. Then suddenly reality had spat in my face.

Woe to you, lawyers! For you shut up the realm of Zion against men and have taken away the key of knowledge. You did not enter in yourselves, and you hindered those who were entering in.

And on Fox News, the night before, the reverend spoke on of marriage as a sacred institution that simply couldn't be opened up to include such unions—and I felt Joshua's hand on my arm. Was I alright? And I told him of the reverend's so-called therapy, of the friends I'd had in Jerusalem who'd been sent away for treatment, close friends. And it wasn't right, and I knew my father was just like theirs, so if I was like that, if I was like that... And then I stopped.

So I never told anyone, I said.

Woe to you! For you build the sepulchres of the prophets, and garnish the sepulchres of the virtuous, and say, If we had been in the days of our fathers, we would not have been partakers with them in the blood of the prophets. Truly you bear witness that you are the sons of those who killed the prophets.

And on Fox News, the night before, the reverend solemnly condemned all hate crimes, lamented tragic suicides—and Joshua led me back to stand before the TV screen, whispered a few words into my ears, and I saw the earth rolled back before my eyes. I saw the Roman features of Justinian blaming famine, earthquake, pestilence on the sinners, Valentinian ordering public immolation of the sinners, Constantius declaring unions born in love a crime, a sin.

I saw the world as he did.

The Empire never ended, Joshua said.

Therefore the wisdom of the sublime said also, Behold, I send to you prophets, and wise men, and scribes, and some of them you shall kill and crucify; and some of them you shall scourge in your congregation houses, and harry them from city to city, that upon you may come all the virtuous blood shed on the earth, from the blood of virtuous Abel to the blood of Zechariah, son of Johoiada, whom you slew between the temple and the altar.

For sure, I tell you, it shall be required of this generation. Fill up the measure of your fathers then. You serpents, you generation of vipers, how can you escape the sentence of Gehenna?

And as he said these things, the clerks and the Select began to urge him vehemently, provoking him to speak of many things, lying in wait for him, seeking to catch something from his mouth that they might accuse him.

But the realm endures, said Joshua.

23

And he called the mob. Hear, and understand, he said to them. It is not that which goes into the mouth defiles a man, but that which comes out of the mouth—this defiles a man. There is nothing from without a man that can defile him entering into him, but the things which come out of him, those are what defile the man. The clerks and the Select sit in Moses' seat: All and anything they bid you observe therefore, observe and do, but you...? Do not after their works, for they say and do not. For all their works they do to be seen by men: they make broad their amulets of faith; and they enlarge the borders of their garments; and they love the uppermost rooms at feasts, and the chief seats in the congregation houses, and greetings in the markets, and to be called by men, Reverend, Reverend.

Capernaum, 31 CE. I looked at the Pharisee's cup, saw a shining grail. I looked at his phylactery, saw a crucifix. I looked at the things of this aeon and saw the aeon to come, the seasons of the Gentiles. It didn't really make sense to me, lover of the sublime. It was fractured and flickering. *I* was fractured and flickering, shattered through Æternity and seeing aspects of it from all the disconnected shards of me, unable to piece it all together. I had to forget the grail to understand the cup, not understand the crucifix to see the phylactery. And most of all, most of all, I had to erase the seasons of the Gentiles from my mind simply to remain sane.

Then in the audience of all the people he said to his students, Beware of the clerks, who desire to walk in long robes, and love greetings in the markets, and the highest seats in the congregation houses, and the chief rooms at feasts, who devour widows' houses, and for a show make long prayers: these shall receive greater condemnation.

The fire in that *devour widows' houses* was audible, a passion not bitter but fierce, born of the poverty Mary had lived through before Cleopas. I remember noting that, holding on to it as the very dirt of this aeon. This solid detail of the evicted widow, a widow the gossips reviled as fornicator. I thought of her in the courtyard of the little house in Capernaum, at the basalt grain mill.

And when he was entered into the house from the people, his students came and said, You know that the Select were offended after they heard this saying? But he answered, Every plant which my æternal father has not planted shall be rooted up. Leave them alone: they are blind leaders of the blind. Can the blind lead the blind? Shall they not both fall into the ditch?

I sat silent, baptised by fire, changed forever.

Declare to us this parable, said the Rock.

Are you too still without understanding? said Joshua. Do you not yet grasp that whatever enters in at the mouth goes into the belly, is expelled into the sewer? But those things which pour out of the mouth come forth from the heart and they defile the man. For from within, out of the heart of men, pour vicious thoughts—murders, betrayals, infidelities, thefts, perjuries, envies, malice, deceit, prurience, callousness, blasphemy, pride, folly. All these vicious things come from within and defile the man, but to eat with unwashed hands does not defile a man.

If you had only stood on Tabor, lover of the sublime, perhaps you might understand.

24

And at once he entered into a boat with his students, and came into the coasts of Magdala, and the sister of that youth whom Joshua loved was there, and Joshua cast out many daimons, and did not suffer the daimons to speak because they knew him. And the Select came to him, testing him.

Is it lawful, they asked, for a man to put away his wife for every cause?

Have you not read, he said, that he who made us at the beginning made us male and female, and said, *For this cause shall a man leave father and mother, and cleave to his wife, and they two shall be one flesh?* Wherefore they are no more two, but one flesh. What the sublime has joined together then, let man not put asunder.

If you had only stood on Tabor, you might imagine him speaking for the wife here, the wife an Antipas might discard simply to have another, the fiancée that a Joseph would not dismiss for any stumbling. For the sister we found in a madhouse in Magdala, Mary, medicated to a shell of herself for a history that isn't what you think and isn't any of your business.

Why did Moses decree to give a writ of divorce then, they said, to put her away, except it be for fornication?

Moses allowed you to dismiss your wives because of the hardness of your hearts, he said, but from the beginning it was not so. To whom little is forgiven, the same loves little. And I say to you, whoever shall dismiss his wife to marry another commits adultery, and whoever marries her who is dismissed commits adultery.

If you had only stood on Tabor, you might hear him speaking simply of laws of the day, made *by* men *for* men, to accommodate their whims; of partnership turned to property that can be scrapped or sold, concessions made to cold indifference.

In the house his students asked him again of the same matter. If this is the case with a man and his wife, they said, it is not good to marry.

He shrugged at the tragic loss of privilege, then winked at me.

All men cannot accept this saying, he said, save those to whom it is given. For there are some unbreeding men who were so born from their mother's womb, and some who were made so by men, and some who have made themselves so for the realm of Zion's sake. He who is able to accept it, let him accept it.

If you had only stood on Tabor, you would not bluster that it wasn't queers he meant were born this way, that he spoke only of genitals in his talk of eunuchs born so from the womb... or for the realm's sake your priests and monks would take a blade to celibate balls.

There are many standing at the door, said Joshua, but the solitary are those who shall enter the bridal chamber, that the scripture might be fulfilled, *And he stretched himself upon the young man three times, and cried to the Worker, and said: O Worker my deity, I pray you, let this young man's soul come back into him; and the Worker hearkened to the voice of Elijah; and the soul of the young man came back into him, and he revived.*

But they understood not what notions these were that he spoke to them, save the son of perdition.

If you would only stand on Tabor, lover of the sublime. You can still hear his echo there.

Sychar

I See Men as Trees

1

It is the nineteenth day of my wilderness trials. Three weeks of barely eating, barely sleeping, working on this testament. But there is no alternative, lover of the sublime; I have walked as Joshua into the dark tomorrow where I fail. Today, every day, I see that hostel in Capernaum burned down for an abortion clinic, whores like my sister stoned with shame and shamed with sticks, faggots like her brother tortured to lies and madness. Tomorrow, I see cunt's choice and queer's nature stripped from us in Gilead, Uganda and Æternity. Walk with me, and I'll show you its roots in yesterday.

After this there was a feast, and Joshua went up to Jerusalem. Now there is at Jerusalem by the sheep market a pool, having five porticos, which is called in the Hebrew tongue Bethesda. In these lay a great mass of impotent folk, blind, halt, or withered.

Reconstructing Matthew's bastardised account the best I can, I read on, how patients waited for the rippling of the water, *for a messenger went down at a certain season into the pool, and stirred the water; whoever then stepped in first after the stirring of the water was made whole of any disease he had.* Really? So, an asclepeion founded by the Roman garrison of Antonia Fortress, tolerated as beyond the city walls at least, becomes a hallowed site of hoodoo healings?

And a certain man was there, who'd suffered an ailment thirty eight years. When Joshua saw him lie, and knew that he'd been in that state a long time now, he asked, Would you be made whole?

Sir, the man answered, I have no man to put me into the pool when the water is stirred, but while I am coming, another steps down before me.

Rise, said Joshua, take up your bed and walk.

A fairytale, and a redundant one at that, derivative...

And at once the man was made whole, and took up his bed, and walked. But that day was the Sabbath, so:

It is the Sabbath day, said the Select to he who was cured. It is not lawful for you to carry your bed.

... a veritable clip show of his exploits...

He who made me whole, the man said, told me to take up my bed and walk.

They asked him then, What man is it who said to you, Take up your bed, and walk?

But he who was healed did not know who it was, for Joshua had hurried himself away, a mob being in that place. But afterward Joshua found him in the temple.

... meandering inchoately, back and forth, but this, but that...

Behold, he said to him, you are made whole. Stumble no more.

And the man departed, and told the Select that it was Joshua who had made him whole. And for this reason the Select harried Joshua, since he had done these things on the Sabbath day.

... I'd simply prune away this piffle, lover of the sublime, but one line is true...

———

My father is still working, so I work, said Joshua. I must work the works of him that sent me, while it is day. The night comes, when no man can work.

———

As for the rest...?

———

Then they took up stones to cast at him, because he had not only broken the Sabbath but said also that the sublime was his father, making himself equal with the sublime; but Joshua hid himself, and went out of the temple, going through the midst of them, and so passed by.

———

Truth is, we came into Jerusalem unnoticed.

2

And it was at Jerusalem the feast of the dedication, and it was winter.

———

And white marble gleamed before us as we came in the Sheep Gate in the north-east corner of the complex, Herod's temple rising up out of the vast bazaar that was the Court of Gentiles, chaos walled in stone, a square-boxed sprawl of stalls of souvenirs and sacrifices, sellers of food, changers of money. To our left, the great colonnade of the Portico of Solomon ran down the east wall, with its gate out to Gethsemane. Behind us, to our right, the seventy cubit tower of the Antonio Fortress stood as Empire's sentinel. But it was the temple itself that seized the eye, the steps rising beyond the low wall of the *soreg* Gentiles couldn't pass, the great square-turreted walls around its courts, and the massive vault of the holy of holies. Foundations started late in 20 BCE and forty six years in the building that temple was, by Herod after Herod after Herod; I saw it grow through my childhood, completed early in 27 CE, when I was turning twelve, the year John cried out in the wilderness and his voice was heard all the way in Galilee. I was no longer twelve.

———

And Joshua walked in the temple in the Portico of Solomon, and as he passed by, he saw a man who was blind from his birth.

Rabbi, who was delinquent, his students asked him, this man or his parents, that he was born blind?

Neither has this man been delinquent nor his parents, Joshua said.

———

There were many walking there that day who were born blind, I might say, but it was neither their fault nor their parents. When the Empire takes a man's power, it takes their responsibility with it. That is its strategy.

———

There were present at that season some who asked him of the Galileans whose blood Pilate had mingled with their sacrifices.

Do you imagine, said Joshua, that those Galileans were delinquents over all the Galileans because they suffered such things? I tell you, no, but, except we rethink, we shall all likewise perish. Or those eighteen, upon whom the tower in Siloam fell and slew them, do you think that they were delinquents over all men dwelling in Jerusalem? I tell you, no, but, except we rethink, we shall all likewise perish.

———

He spoke of an earthquake in Siloam, a hurricane in New Orleans. At his side, I watched the crowd for scowling Select who'd grudge his challenge to the party line: these disasters as sublime justice for a city's sin. He spoke of Galileans slaughtered with their sheep and I looked to my sister on his other side, eyes peering into the throng, scouring it for Roman faces, Gentile informants for the Occupation who'd bleed us, salt us, burn us in a holocaust, and say we deserved it just for saying we didn't. Both of us watching also for a particular familiar face.

———

When he had spoken thus, he took the blind man by the hand, and led him out of the town. And he spat on the ground, made clay of the spittle, and anointed the eyes of the blind man with the clay. After that he put his hands again upon his eyes, and made him look up, and said to him, Go, wash in the pool of Siloam—which is by interpretation, sent. He went his way therefore and washed, and he was restored, saw every man clearly.

And he looked up and said, I see men as trees, walking.

3

So the neighbours, and those who had seen the man before, when he was blind, wondered, was this not he who sat and begged? And some said it was him, others said he was like him, but he said, I am he.

———

Imagine a chance meeting with old friends from Bethany, my home town so close to Jerusalem. Imagine questions as to where this prodigal had been, what on earth was he doing with those Galileans. Imagine talk turning to politics with the recklessness of one whose baptism by fire left him... hot-headed, one might say. Had Joshua's Magdalene been there, she might have gently persuaded me to prudence, but I'd known Caleb from childhood, he'd been like a brother to me even before I lost my own, and I knew exactly why he'd chosen the priesthood over marriage. I remembered watching workmen toil on Herod's temple with him, Roman troops marching through the streets. I thought I could make him see the light.

So they said to him, How were your eyes opened?

A man called Joshua, he said, made clay and anointed my eyes, and said to me, Go to the pool of Siloam and wash. And I went and washed, and I got my sight.

Where is he? they said to him.

Imagine an undertone in that voice, a shift in the air of old camaraderies recaptured. A shift in time, and I saw a little badge pinned to Caleb's lapel, an axe with sticks bound round its shaft.

I do not know, he said.

They brought the man who had been blind before to the Select then.

And outside the forecourt with its colonnades in marble, I found myself faced now with black-cassocked priests who talked of a Lateran Treaty with those carrying the fascii, a tissue of security bought from Il Duce Pontius Pilate with a promise of neutrality. Imagine the nails of my hands digging into my palms, frustration, remonstration: if they thought such accommodation would last with these murderous Romans, they saw nothing. But, no. If he comes from Galilee, said one, he'll be all too used to a rocking boat.

And the Select also asked him how he had received his sight.

He put clay upon my eyes, he said. I washed and see now.

How can a man who is a delinquent do such miracles? others said.

And there was a division among them.

What say you of him, they said to the blind man again, since he has opened your eyes?

He is a prophet, he said.

But the Select did not believe concerning him, that he had been blind and given his sight, until they called the parents of he who had received his sight.

His voice, clipped, snapping my name. I turned with dread, years falling away.

Is this your son, they asked them, who you say was born blind? How then does he now see?

We know this is our son, his parents said, and that he was born blind. But we do not know by what means he now sees. And we do not know who has opened his eyes. He is of age. Ask him. He shall speak for himself.

These words spoke his parents, because they feared the Select, for the Select had agreed already that if any man confessed that he was the anointed he should be put out of the congregation house. For this reason then his parents said, He is of age. Ask him.

Imagine a curt tone, ice-cold with disavowal. *Fear* is not the word, trust me.

4

Then again they called the man who was blind.

Give the sublime the praise, they said. We know that this man is a delinquent.

Whether he is a delinquent or not, he said, I do not know. One thing I know: where I was blind, now I see.

And it was the Sabbath day when Joshua made the clay, and opened his eyes.

This man is not of the sublime, some of the Select said therefore, since he does not keep the Sabbath day.

What did he to you? they said to him again. How did he open your eyes?

I have told you already, he said, and you did not hear. Why would you hear it again? Will you also be his students?

My voice rose with my hackles: I know the only thing that matters, that I see things now exactly as they are. How many times do I have to tell you before you listen? I cut my rant off as a pair of centurions passed by, officers in grey uniforms with peaked caps. For a second, I saw something in my father's face, a subtle set of jaw I knew only too well, then he was nodding a polite greeting, they were moving on, and I was rounding on him with upflung arms: Why even ask if you don't want to learn?

Then they reviled him.

You are his student, they said, but we are Moses' students. We know that the sublime spoke to Moses. As for this fellow, we know nothing of where he comes from.

Why herein is a marvellous thing, the man said, that you know nothing of where he comes from, and yet he has opened my eyes. Don't we know that the sublime does not hear delinquents? But if any man is a devotee of the sublime, and does his will, him he hears. Since this aeon began it is unheard of that any man opened the eyes of one who was born blind. If this man were not of the sublime, he could do nothing.

You were altogether born in delinquency, they said, and you would teach us?

And they cast him out.

And I stood as cold and white as the marble of the basilica, as the Select turned and stalked away, the word excommunicated carved into my heart. Until then, even with the glimpses given me by Joshua, I'd still believed there was hope. If I could only make them see the true face of the Empire, I'd thought, that there are no treaties with the fascii, only trainloads of Gypsies and Jews, sodomites and socialists. And who did they think would be next? But as I turned to my father, all I saw in his eyes was a look of shame that told me... I was all those things to him now, a black sheep gone to the goats. To vagabonds, apostates, libertines, revolutionaries.

Go, he said.

Joshua heard that they had cast him out; and when he had found him, he said to him, Do you trust in the scion of the sublime?

Who is he, Teacher, he said, that I might trust in him?

And Joshua said to him, You have both seen him, and it is he who talks with you.

Teacher, he said, I trust.

And he adored him.

And sobbed in his embrace.

For judgement I am come into this world, said Joshua, that those who do not see may see, that those who see may be made blind, and that the works of the sublime should be made manifest in him.

Your House is Left Desolate

5

And Joshua went throughout every city and village, preaching and showing the glad tidings of the realm of the sublime, and the twelve were with him, and certain women, who had been healed of infirmities and inspirations of strife: Mary called Magdalene, out of whom went seven daimons; and Joanna the wife of Chuza, Herod's steward; and Susanna; and many others, who ministered to him of their substance. And there followed him that certain young man, that it might be fulfilled: *He who would find his life must lose it, and he who will lose his life for my sake shall find it.*

A squat in Chorazin, an abandoned military complex, everything from barracks to bath-house, turned to a whole community. Mary and I leaned out on the rail of a slim balcony in a block that once housed soldier's families. We smoked and talked of Joshua, who lay asleep inside. I talked of glimpses of futures I didn't understand, wasn't sure I wanted to.

You know, I said, I can see them arguing over whether you were his beard or his bitch.

She laughed.

And what will they say about you?

I don't know, I said. Not sure I want to.

And there went great mobs with him, and he taught in their congregation houses, being honoured by all. And while he yet talked to the people, there came then his brothers and his mother, desiring to speak with him.

Then one said to him, Behold, your mother and your brothers stand beyond, desiring to speak with you.

But he said to him that told him, Who is my mother? And who are my brothers? And he stretched forth his hand toward his students, and said, Behold my mother and my brothers! For whoever shall do the will of my æternal father, the same is my brother, and sister, and mother. And when you have seen your brother, you have seen the Worker.

He caught my eye as I sat with Mary, listening but brooding, my sister's hand on my knee.

And it came to pass, as he spoke these things, a certain woman of the company lifted up her voice, and said to him, Blessed is the womb that bore you and the breasts which you have sucked.

But he said, Aye rather, blessed are those who hear the word of the sublime and keep it. For there shall be days when you will say, Blessed is that womb which has not conceived and those breasts which have not given suck.

And he turned, and said to them, If any man come to me, and hate not his father, and mother, and wife, and children, and brethren, and sisters, aye, and his own life also, he cannot be my student. For which of you, intending to build a tower, does not sit down first and count the cost, whether he has enough to finish it? Lest haply, after he has laid the foundation, and is not able to finish it, all who behold it begin to mock him, saying, This man began to build, and was not able to finish. Or what king, going to make war against another king, does not sit not down first and consult whether he will be able with ten thousand to meet he who comes against him with twenty thousand? Or else, while the other is yet a great way off, he sends an embassy, and desires conditions of peace. So likewise, whoever he might be among you who does not forsake all that he has, he cannot be my student.

6

And it came to pass, when Joshua had made an end of directing his twelve students, he departed from there to teach and preach in their cities. He departed from Galilee, and came with his students into the coasts of Judaea by the farther side of Jordan, and there he tarried with them and baptized.

So this is where it all began, said Mary.

In the tri-state area where Decapolis and Perea bordered North Judaea—or Samaria if you went by the handmade road-signs raised by locals uninclined to admit rule from Jerusalem let alone Rome. A river little more than a creek winding through the valley, fed by streams sparkling in from the green mountains either side, running down by Bethabara to the east, Aenon to the west. At the old schoolbus's wheel, Joshua led our small convoy of trailers and pick-ups off the dirt track into a fallow field.

This is it, he said.

And great mobs followed him, and he healed them there, and, as he was wont, he taught them again. After these things the teacher appointed another seventy also, began to send them forth by two and two, giving them power to heal sicknesses and to cast out daimons, directing them that they should take nothing for their journey. And they went forth to preach everywhere, saying, The realm of Zion is to hand, the teacher working with them, and confirming the word with signs following.

From the first five chapter houses set up by the ten, now there were forty scattered through Galilee and Judaea. Missions, hospitals, charities, schools. In Bethsaida, shipyard workers home from World War I learned to read and write from a schoolteacher turned activist. In Chorazin, a gay poet staged puppet shows for the people while writing the seditious plays he would be shot for. In Nain, a black actor and singer sought out miners starving from a hunger march, gave them food. We were everywhere, but still they came to us in Jordan, to him, to Joshua. In Jordan, a wild-eyed prophet popped another upper, tapped out a message on his typewriter: *The Empire never ended.*

And John also was baptizing in Aenon near to Salem, because there was much water there. And they came and were baptized, for John was not yet cast into prison. Then there arose a question between some of John's students and the Select about purifying. And they came to John.

Rabbi, they said, he who was with you beyond Jordan, to whom you bore witness, behold, the same baptizes, and all men come to him. He testifies what he has seen and heard, but no man welcomes his testimony.

A man can welcome nothing, said John, except it be given him from Æternity. Still, the father loves the son, and has given all things into his hand. He who does not trust in the son shall not see life; rather the wrath of the sublime remains on him. But he who trusts in the son has the life of ages, for this man whom the sublime has sent speaks the words of the sublime, for the sublime gives the inspiration to him without limit. He who has welcomed his testimony has set his seal to it that the sublime is true.

You yourselves bear me witness, that I said I am not the anointed but that I am sent before him. He who is of the earth is earthly, and speaks of the earth; he who comes from Æternity is beyond all. He must increase, and I must decrease.

7

And there was a certain man of the Select, a lord of the Judaeans, known as *the victory of the people*. The same came to Joshua by night.

In my shock to see him again, for an instant I felt panic, shame, anger. Yearning? I don't know what I felt, standing there at the door of the schoolbus. Then my eyes locked on his, fierce in the certainty of love that lay asleep behind me. And he looked old, old and tired. I thought of asking him how Martha was, but knew it would come out as an accusation. How was the pottery business? How was the Sanhedrin? How was Jerusalem under the Romans? All of it would come out as a challenge.

This Joshua of yours, he said, I want to speak to him.

I stepped back and waved him to come in, to follow me, to Joshua.

Rabbi, he said, we know that you are a teacher come from the sublime, for no man can do these miracles that you do, except the sublime be with him. Teach us concerning the place where you are, for it is necessary for us to seek after it.

His voice was a logician's, his gaze a lawyer's: if miracles, then the sublime; if the sublime, then... in your own words, tell us of it. I wondered what he really expected to learn, why he was here. Outside, off at the edge of the camp's light, I could just make out his parked car, silhouettes of two men standing beside it.

For sure, I tell you, Joshua said, that except a man be born again, he cannot see the realm of the sublime.

How can a man be born when he is of age? he asked. Can he enter his mother's womb a second time, and be born?

The weight in his voice, it *sounded* like regret.

———

For sure, I tell you, Joshua answered, that except a man be born of water and the inspiration, he cannot enter into the realm of the sublime. Do not marvel that I said to you, you must be born again. The wind blows where it wishes, and you hear the sound but cannot tell where it comes from, where it goes; just so is every man who is reborn of the inspiration. That which is born of the flesh is flesh, and that which is born of the inspiration is inspiration.

How can these things be? he said.

———

How *is* Jerusalem under the Romans? I thought.

———

Are you a teacher of Israel, said Joshua, and do not know these things? For sure, I tell you, we speak only what we know, testify only what we've seen, but you do not welcome our testimony. If I have told you earthly things, and you do not trust, how will you trust when I tell you of aeternal things? That no man has ascended up to Æternity save he who has descended from it? That as Moses lifted up the serpent in the wilderness, even so must the everyman be lifted up? That the sublime so loved the world that he gave to it his only begotten son, Adam, who was the son of the sublime? That anyone who trusts in him should not perish but have the life of ages?

———

A hand on my arm now—Mary beside me.

———

Behold, your house is left desolate to you, said Joshua. For sure, I tell you, you shall not see me until the time comes when you say, Blessed is he who comes in the name of the Worker.

8

The same day there came certain of the Select. Get you out, they said to him. Depart from here, for Herod will kill you.

The newspaper on the breakfast table spoke of Herod's forces moving against these Red hordes threatening law and order, civilisation itself. Spoke of insurgent zealots and sicarii quelled here, anarchists and communists arrested there. Warned of civil war. The younger of the two priests leaned across, hands gesturing his plea.

If they even knew we were here, he said. The church sides with the state.

The militia, I spat. Herod is no more the rightful ruler of –

Joshua stopped me with a hand on mine, laid flat on the table now as I stood from my seat. He shook his head at me, looked at this young man of the Select, the older priest sat at his side, my father beside him.

Go you, and tell that fox, he said, Behold, I cast out daimons, I do cures today and tomorrow, and the third day I shall be perfected. Still, I must walk today, tomorrow, the day after, for it cannot be that a prophet perish out of Jerusalem.

He rose from the table, paced to the window, rested a hand either side of the frame, a silhouette against the light. Mary slipped to his side, hand soft on his arm as she studied a father who glowered straight ahead, at me. He had disdained her presence on his arrival, ignored her through our talk, barked of more pressing matters when I snapped for him to look at his own daughter. But I saw a weakness now in him, a power in her, that she could stand *here* or *here* in the room, and it was he whose gaze turned from her defiance. But I wondered, if he knew as much of me as of her, would he even be here?

Joshua's words were barely audible, a murmur:

O Jerusalem, which kills the prophets, and stones those who are sent to you. How often I would have gathered your children together, as a hen gathers her brood under her wings, and you would not.

He turned back to the room, a touch of the wild Baptist in his resolve now.

This is why my father loves me, he said, because I lay down my life that I might take it again. No man takes it from me, but I lay it down of myself, have power to lay it down of myself. And I have power to take it again. I have received this decree from my father.

There was a division therefore again among the Select for these sayings.

He has a daimon and is mad, said many. Why do you hear him?

The old priest scowled as he hobbled out beside my father, his mutter voicing the majority, I knew. The younger caught my gaze from the door. I wondered just how few he spoke for.

These are not the words of one who has a daimon, said others.

Can a daimon open the eyes of the blind? said one.

And my father turned from the old priest, peered back at me as at a stranger.

Persuade him, he said.

When the teacher therefore knew how the Select had heard that he made and baptized more students than John—though Joshua himself baptized not, only his students— he left Judaea, departed again for Galilee. Then from that day forth they took counsel together for to put him to death, and sought to slay him, and Joshua therefore walked no more openly among the Judaeans.

9

After these things Joshua walked in Galilee, for he would not walk in Judea, because the Select sought to kill him. He went from there to a country near the wilderness, into a city called Ephraim, continued there with his students. And his fame spread through all Syria, and they brought to him all sick people who were taken with diverse diseases and torments, those who were driven by daimons, those who were insane, and those who had the palsy, and he healed them that it might be fulfilled which was spoken by Isaiah the prophet, saying, *Himself took our infirmities, and bore our sicknesses.*

He looks tired, I said.

I know, said Mary. I know.

Joshua sat in the back of the bus with Matthew, flicking through manuscript pages, writing notes in the margins, circling this here, scoring that out there—or underlining. I couldn't tell looking in the mirror over the wheel, where I sat steering us past a disused factory nestled among trees, onto the high street of the tiny mountain town. A general store with a porch and a bench outside. The high street seemed like most all there was to Ephraim, actually.

I glanced up in the mirror again.

I'll drive for a while, said Mary. Go on.

And he must needs go through Samaria, so he came to a city of Samaria which is called Sychar, near to the parcel of ground that Jacob gave to his son Joseph.

I remember a passing caravan out of Gilead as we waited in Joseph's Field, Mary browsing their spices and balms, haggling for labdanum. I thought of Joseph betrayed by his brothers, sold to a caravan of Ishmaelites for twenty pieces of silver near here, his coloured coat daubed with goat's blood to prove his death; of Ishmael, Isaac's elder brother, the slave girl's son, wild mule of a man, cast out on his brother's birth to fend for himself, a child archer in the desert; of hairy Esau, Jacob's elder brother, *Israel's* elder brother, the goatskin worn to steal his birthright.

What are you thinking? Joshua asked.

I don't know, I shrugged. Brothers. Scapegoats. Connections. I can't put my finger on it.

And the messengers gathered themselves together to Joshua, told him all things, what they had done, what they had taught. And the seventy returned again joyful, saying, Teacher, even the daimons are subject to us through your name.

And looking up to the heavens, he sighed.

And they saw a Samaritan carrying a lamb, going into Judaea.

Why does he carry the lamb? said Joshua to his students.

That he may kill it and eat it, they said.

So long as it is alive he will not eat it, he said, but only if he kill it and it become a corpse.

Otherwise he would not be able to do so, they said.

You also, he said, seek for yourselves a resting place within, lest you become a corpse and be eaten. Blessed is the lion eaten by the man, for the lion becomes man. Cursed is the man eaten by the lion, and the man become lion.

Have you understood all these things? said Joshua.

Yes, Teacher, they said.

I beheld the accuser fall as lightning from the heavens, he said. Behold, I give to you power to tread on serpents and scorpions, and over all the power of the enemy; and nothing shall by any means hurt you. Still, do not rejoice in this, that the inspirations are subject to you, but rather rejoice because your names are written in Æternity.

10

Now Jacob's well was there. Joshua therefore, being wearied with his journey, sat thus on the well, for his students were gone away to the city to buy meat. And it was about the sixth hour, when there came a woman of Samaria to draw water, a certain centurion's slave.

Would you give me to drink? Joshua asked her.

Then the woman of Samaria said to him, How is it that you, being a Jew, ask drink of me, a woman of Samaria? For the Jews have no dealings with the Samaritans.

He shrugged, gave a little smile. I leaned forward across the table, nudged Matthew's elbow, nodded at the strange exchange.

If you knew the gift of the sublime, Joshua answered her, and who it is that said to you, Give me to drink, you would have asked of him, and he would have given you living water.

Matthew angled round, arm up on the back of the red faux leather booth to watch Joshua at the bar—like most of the clientele now, all but those focused on Mary, haggling with the bikers at the table down front, the only one of us who remotely fitted in.

Sir, the woman said, you have nothing to draw with, and the well is deep. From where then have you that living water? Are you greater than our father Jacob, who gave us the well, drank from it himself, with his children and cattle?

Whoever drinks of this water shall thirst again, said Joshua, but whoever drinks of the water I give him shall never thirst, but rather the water I give him shall be a well of water in him springing up into the life of ages.

They all stared at me when we entered. Even Matthew, with his history among Capernaum's criminal fraternity, looked out of place in a Samaritan roadhouse. But it was Joshua they watched now, this Galilean freak trying to charm the waitress into a trade, liquor for *logos.*

Sir, the woman said, give me this water, that I will not thirst, neither come here to draw.

Go, call your husband, Joshua said, and come here.

I have no husband, the woman answered.

You have said well, I have no husband, said Joshua. For you have had five husbands, and he whom you now have is not your husband. In that you spoke truly.

And in Joseph's field, I watched from the shade of a fig tree, took the orange offered by Matthew with a distracted thanks as I listened in curiosity. He meant the people of Babylon, Cuthah, Avva, Hamath, and Sepharvaim, of course, brought by the king of Assyria to settle here, displace the Israelites. And now Rome, of course—because a slave's owner is not a wife's husband... for all the husbands who might disagree, behave as if this were the case, then as now.

Sir, I perceive that you are a prophet, the woman said. But our fathers worshipped on this mountain, and you say that the place where men should worship is in Jerusalem.

She waved a hand to the south, in the direction of Mount Gerizim where the Samaritans had their temple—and Jerusalem beyond, where we had ours.

Woman, trust me, said Joshua, the hour comes when you shall worship the father neither in this mountain nor at Jerusalem. You know not what you worship.

I know that the messiah comes, the woman said, he who is called the anointed. When he is come, he will tell us all things.

I who speak to you am he, said Joshua.

11

And upon this came his students, and marvelled that he talked with the woman.

I heard a shout, turned to see Jude the Hearty and Symon the Zealous running in, the Rock and others behind them laden with supplies, working their way through the camp that sprawled around the well, grown over the hours of arrivals who'd poured in from the chapter houses of Galilee and Judaea and all around the Jordan, the atmosphere growing to that of some great wedding feast, a joyous clamour with each reunion of friends and family who had not seen each other for years. I escaped a roaring bear hug from James now, only to find Thomas embracing me as if I were his own best friend and sister's bridegroom. I grinned nervously as we broke the hug, as he turned to notice the Samaritan woman Joshua had been speaking with. What was going on? And then Joshua broke the news that had worried me all the way here, knowing what this assembly was all about: he sought to reach out, talk with the Samaritans.

We know what we worship, they said, for salvation is of the chosen.

I thought Thomas would be the one to doubt, but it was the Rock who planted his heels into the ground, showed a side of him I'd never seen before. Had Joshua not said in Nain we were to avoid their cities?

Would he just abandon his own principles? For *Samaritans*? Worse than Gentiles. Half-breeds. A people polluted to a travesty of Israelites. As Joshua raised his hands to calm them all, call for quiet, Mary drew the Samaritan woman back from the throng, whispered not to worry.

———

And he spoke a parable to them:

The realm of Zion is like a householder, said Joshua, who went out early in the morning to hire labourers into his vineyard. And when he had agreed with the labourers for a denarius a day, he sent them into his vineyard. And around the third hour, he went out and saw others standing idle in the marketplace.

You also, he said, go into the vineyard, and I will give you whatever is fair.

So they went their way. Again around the sixth and ninth hours, he went out and did likewise. And finally around the eleventh hour he went out, found others still standing idle.

Why do you stand idle here all day? he said.

Because no man has hired us, they said.

You also then, he said, go into the vineyard, and whatever is fair, that you shall receive.

So when evenfall was come, the master of the vineyard said to his steward, Call the labourers, and give them their hire, beginning from the last to the first.

So when those who were hired about the eleventh hour came, they received a denarius per man. But when the first came, they supposed that they should have received more, yet they too received a denarius per man. When they had taken it then, they murmured against the master of the house.

These last have worked but one hour, they said, and you have made them equal to us, we who have borne the burden and heat of the day.

Friend, I do you no wrong, he answered one of them. Did you not agree with me for a denarius? Take what is yours, and go your way. I will give to this last, even as to you. Is it not lawful for me to do what I will with my own? Is your eye wicked, because I am good?

12

The woman left her waterpot then, and went her way into the city.

Come, see a man who told me everything I ever did, she said to the men. Is this not the anointed?

Then they went out of the city and came to him. And many of the Samaritans of that city believed in him for the saying of the woman, who testified, He told me all that I ever did. So when the Samaritans were come to him, they begged him that he would stay with them a while, so he waited there two days. And many more believed because of his own word.

Now we believe, they said to the woman, not because of your saying but because we have heard him ourselves and know that this is indeed the anointed, the saviour of the world.

You really think this can work? said Thomas.

We'd wandered out of the camp for a little peace, to catch up, reminisce on old times. Now we sat on a rock up on a hill, looking down on the tents and scattered fires. He was wary as ever, but I had to admit, Joshua's expansion of the movement left me more than a little worried too. Still...

The model should scale up, I said.

From each according to ability, to each according to need, a distributed cooperative spreading through the land, trade without profit, credit without interest. If the children of Israel couldn't mint our own money, we would dispense with the Roman coin. If we couldn't fight their legions, we could fight their taxes, the whole system.

But the Samaritans? said Thomas.

There was a time, I reminded him, when you would have said, But a Judaean?

In the meanwhile his students prayed him, saying, Rabbi, eat.

But he said to them, I have meat to eat that you know not of.

So the students said one to another, Has any man brought him anything to eat?

My meat is to do the will of he who sent me, said Joshua, to finish his work. Do not say, There are still four months before the harvest, are there not? Behold, I say to you, lift up your eyes, look on the fields, for they are already white to harvest. And he who reaps receives wages and gathers fruit to the life of ages, so both he who sows and he who reaps may rejoice together. Thus is that saying true, *One sows, and another reaps.* I sent you to reap that which you bestowed no labour on. Other men laboured, and we are all entered into their labours.

And after the Samaritans? said Thomas. Who next? The Syrians? The Greeks? The *Romans*?

The scornful dismissal was in my mouth when—the world lurched, aeons ripping round me, pivoting with me torn in its wake through horrors I'd seen in Capernaum years past, mind opened for a second of Æternity, a week of echoes and reflections afterwards. And now... now I was on the ground.

What happened? Thomas was saying.

I couldn't tell him. Before, the wisps of memory dissipated as a dream. Now there was nothing, only a sickening sense of everything having changed, changed utterly.

For the hour comes, said Joshua, *now is*, when the true devotees shall adore the father in inspiration and in truth, for the father seeks such to adore him. The sublime is an inspiration, and those who adore him must adore him in inspiration and in truth.

And Joshua went out from there, and came into his own country; and his students followed him.

Are You Too of Galilee

13

Then the feast of tabernacles was at hand.

Depart from here, his brothers said to him therefore. Go into Judaea, that your students also may see the works that you do. For there is no man who does anything in secret, but he seeks himself to be known openly. If you do these things, show yourself to the world.

He'd said the harvest was here, and now here was the harvest, Symon the Zealous pointed out, the festival itself. We were strong in Galilee, consolidating in Judaea. Even across Samaria, the movement was taking hold, burgeoning. It was time to take it to Jerusalem itself. We had word that Pilate had seized temple money to build an aqueduct into the city. Worse, he threatened to restore the gold shields he'd once raised in the forecourt, his *gift to Herod to celebrate the grand work's completion*, glorious with Caesar's effigy. If ever the city was ripe for insurrection it was now.

My time is not yet come, Joshua said then, but your time is already here. The world cannot hate you, but me it hates, because I testify of it, that its works are wicked. You go up to this feast. I will not go up yet to this feast, for my time is not yet full come. Why do you seek to kill me?

For Herod himself had sent forth and laid hold on John, and bound him in prison.

You have a daimon, his brothers scoffed, for neither did his brethren believe him. Who seeks to kill you?

And somewhere, a Roman hand dips stylus in black ink, and scrawls the *Jews* in every spare inch of the parchment.

When he had said these words to them Joshua remained still in | Galilee. But when his brethren were gone up...

I coaxed him. We had word from my father too, that if his children were to be performing the rites as required of any Jew, they would be welcome under his roof. And their sister would be glad to see them.

Them, I said to Mary.

Then Joshua too went up to the feast, not openly but as | it were in secret.

The whole city was green with the leaves of *hadar*, palm and willow, green with the *sukkot* filling every corner of the city—streets and courtyards, rooftops, camps beyond the walls, anywhere a tabernacle could be built. Walls and porches were co-opted, swallowed in the foliage, the whole city now a maze of narrow verdant alleyways, abuzz with festival. Passing this *sukkah* or that, I looked in and saw the fruits of harvest decorating them, the seven species—wheat and barley, grape and pomegranate, fig and olive and date. So, slowly, we made our way to the Court of the Gentiles, the men on their carpets busy as ever changing Roman lucre for Tyrian shekels. With a cut for themselves, of course, and a cut for Rome, watching from Antonia Fortress. We squeezed our way into the crowd gathered in the courtyard of the Temple, waiting for Herod to come forth, to read piously from the Torah. It was the tradition.

Then the Select sought him at the feast, and said, Where is he? And there was much murmuring among the people concerning him, for some said he was a good | man but others said, no, rather he deceived the people.

Still, no man spoke openly of him for fear of –

And somewhere, a Roman hand dips stylus in black ink, and scrawls *the Jews*, as if every man who felt that fear were not a Jew.

14

Now about the midst of the feast Joshua went up into the temple, and taught.

He read from the book of the Speaker, son of David, king in Jerusalem. He stood in the shadow of a white marble folly and sang of the vanity of great projects, houses built and vineyards planted, gardens, parks and lakes to nourish them. And as I listened to him, I thought of how the house in Bethany loomed vast with significance in my imagination as we travelled the road, seemed suddenly quite small when it came into sight, dissolved to nothing when Martha came running out to greet us.

And the people marvelled, saying, How does this man know letters, having never learned?

I have done one work, Joshua answered them, and you all marvel. My teachings are not mine, but those of he who sent me. If any man would do his will, he should know of these teachings, whether they are of the sublime, or whether I speak of myself. He who speaks of himself seeks his own glory, but he who seeks the honour of the one who sent him, that man is true, and there is no vice in him.

He sang of slaves and servants, herds and flocks, silver and gold, the utter vacuity of all such grandeur, all glory, a song that might be Solomon's or Sartre's, how the wise and foolish end the same way, how their toil and play have the same end, all grand narratives returned to dust, just as our bones. And as I listened, I thought of the quiet walk with Mary up to the Mount of Olives, to visit the graves of our mother and brother, of gathering stones that had tumbled from the mounds, gently setting them back in place.

Then some of them from Jerusalem said, Is this not he whom they seek to kill? But behold, he speaks boldly and they say nothing to him. Do the lords know for sure that this is the very anointed? Surely we know where this man comes from, but when the anointed comes, no man will know where he is from?

And Joshua cried out in the temple as he taught:

You know me, he said. Yes, and you know where I am from. I am not come of myself though, and he who sent me is true, and you know him not. But I know him, for I am from him, and he has sent me.

He sang how the dead know nothing, no reward, their names forgotten with their loves and hates, their jealousies long gone, no part again in anything that happens under the sun. As I listened, I thought of his insurgent father, nameless, graveless, erased.

And many of the people believed in him.

When the anointed comes, they said, will he do more miracles than those this man has done?

Who knows, he sang with scorn, if souls of humans float into the sky, if souls of beasts sink into the earth? Who knows? So eat! And drink!

Yet a little while am I with you, said Joshua to them then, and then I go to he who sent me. You shall seek me, and shall not find me, and where I am, there you cannot come.

Where will he go, that we shall not find him? they said among themselves then. Will he go to the dispersed among the Gentiles? What manner of saying is this that he said, You shall seek me, and shall not find me, and where I am, there you cannot come?

15

In the last day, that great day of the feast, Joshua stood and cried out.

We had met his brothers with blessings that the judgement for the new year, sealed on Yom Kippur, delivered today, would be a good one. We had carried the Arba Minim—the date palm frond and bough of myrtle, willow branch and citron fruit—and walked our seven circuits of the temple with the crowd. We had sung hosannas for Abraham, for Isaac, and for Jacob, hosannas for Moses, for Aaron and for Joseph, hosannas for David. The priests had sung the liturgies. They'd called as the voice of Elijah heralding, called for the coming of the messiah. And then Joshua stood and cried out.

If any man thirst, he said, let him come to me, and drink. He who trusts in me, as the scripture has said, out of his belly shall flow rivers of living water.

He spoke this of the inspiration which those who trust in him should receive—for the sacred inspiration was not yet given, because Joshua was not yet honoured. So, many of the people, when they heard this saying, said, Of a truth this is a prophet. Others said, This is the anointed, and this is why mighty works manifest themselves in him. But some said, Shall the anointed come from Galilee? Has the scripture not said that the anointed comes from the seed of David, out of the town of Bethlehem where David was? So there was a division among the people because of him.

I watched the princes of my nation scorn the whole idea of a prophet out of Galilee, a peasant *anointed*. Some fisherman from the provinces? The very thought of it! I swallowed the bile in my throat though; it was the others that mattered. Not those jumping to proclaim him David's heir, bootstrapping belief with rationalisations that he *must* have come from Bethlehem somewhere along the way. No, rather I marked the ones who listened, disregarded accent and anointment and just listened. The ones who said, Whatever, this is a prophet.

Those were the ones we wanted for the movement.

———

And the Select heard that the people murmured such things concerning him, and the Select and the chief priests sent officers to take him. And some of them would have taken him, but no man laid hands on him, so the officers returned to the chief priests and Select.

Why have you not brought him? said the Select.

No man ever spoke like this man, the officers answered.

Are you too deceived? the Select answered them. Have any of the lords or the Select believed in him? But this people who do not know the law are cursed!

Then one of them, he who came to Joshua by night, the one known as *victory of the people* spoke.

Does our law judge any man before it hears him and knows what he does? he said. Did Moses not give you the law, and yet none of you keeps the law?

Are you too of Galilee? they said. Search and look, for no prophet rises out of Galilee.

And every man went to his house.

So they sought again to take Joshua, but he escaped out of their hand, because his hour was not yet come, and went away again beyond Jordan into the place where John at first baptized, and there he abode. And many resorted to him, saying that John did no miracle, but all the things that John spoke of this man were true. And many believed in him there.

16

Now Herod the tetrarch heard of all that was done by him, and he was disturbed, and desired to see him because it was said by some that John was risen from the dead, by some that Elijah had appeared, and by others that one of the old prophets was risen again.

And Herod said, I have beheaded John, so who is this I hear such things of?

For Herod himself had bound John in prison for Herodias' sake, his brother Philip's wife, for he had married her, and John had said to Herod, It is not lawful for you to have your brother's wife. Have you not read, he said, that he who made them at the beginning made them male and female, and said, *For this cause shall a man leave father and mother, and shall cleave to his wife: and they two shall be one flesh? Wherefore they are no more two, but one flesh.* What the sublime has joined together then, let no man put asunder.

In the field up on the Jordan, between Bethabara and Aenon, before Sychar we'd heard the news on an old TV running off the gas-powered generator, Mary calling Joshua and I to come quick, John had been arrested. Old news footage played of his protests in the capital. One sign held by two men: *DIVORCE* with a tick, *GAY MARRIAGE* with a cross, a question mark underneath.

Therefore Herodias had a grudge against him, and would have killed him, but she could not, for Herod feared John, knowing that he was a just and holy man. When he would have put him to death, he feared the mob because they hailed him as a prophet, so he kept him close, and listened to him and was... pleasantly perplexed by what he heard.

They came for him with the euphemisms of the police state: protective custody; treatment; for his own safety; his condition. He woke in a room, a padded cell in a black iron prison. Across the table from him, a doctor flicked through a typewritten manuscript taken from his filing cabinet. Tell me about these visions and voices, he said. What does it mean, *The Empire never ended?* Behind a dark mirror, Herod listened to the madman rant.

But a convenient day came when Herod, on his birthday, made a feast for his lords and high captains, and the first of Galilee. And the daughter of the said Herodias came in, and danced, pleasing Herod and those who sat with him. So he promised her with an oath, Whatever you shall ask of me, I will give it you, to the half of my realm.

Instructed by her mother beforehand, she said, Bring me the head of John the Baptist on a platter.

The king bitterly regretted it. [*Regretted. Bitterly*]. But for his oath's sake, and for the sake of those who sat with him, he *could not* deny her. So at once the king sent for an executioner, commanded John's head to be brought. And the executioner went and beheaded John in the prison, brought his head on a platter; and he gave it to the girl, and the girl gave it to her mother.

And when his students heard of it, they came, they took his corpse, and they laid it in a tomb and went and told Joshua.

In the field up on the Jordan, we heard the news from a pair of activists who rolled up in a station wagon, ashen-faced. On the news, the word *gay* was now banned in Samaritan schools.

And Men Do Not See It

17

And from there Joshua arose, went into the coasts of Tyre and Sidon, and entered into a house, and would have no man know it.

We came into Tyre at dusk, strangers in a strange land, all of us wondering at the wisdom of this move. But we were far from Pilate in Jerusalem, far from Herod in Tiberias, and for a Roman province... well, the Empire's eye was turned to wine and women in these cities so safely Hellenised. It wasn't scrutinising a small party of some dozen or so coming through the gate—wedding guests, said Matthew to the centurions—wasn't watchful for some Galilean prophet causing trouble in Jerusalem. So we found ourselves in the safe house, home of a wine merchant healed in Galilee. Spacious even with so many guests, it reminded me of Bethany. I remember saying that to Mary, how it reminded me of home.

But he could not be hid, for a certain woman of Canaan, whose young daughter had a fouled inspiration, heard of him, and came out of the same coasts, fell at his feet and cried to him.

Have mercy on me, she said, O Master, you son of David.

The woman was a Greek, a Syrophoenician by nation, a certain centurion's slave, and she begged him that he would cast forth the daimon out of her daughter, but he answered her not a word.

Mary and I shared a wary look as he walked away, crouched at the hearth. We'd seen him pensive, gazing out at the camp before a vigil in the quiet wilds, or when men threw themselves at his feet. But never like this, at a plea for healing.

Then his students came and begged him, Send her away, for she cries after us.

I am not sent but to the lost sheep of the house of Israel, he said then. The rest are as men a king invited to a feast: they took his messengers and treated them with utmost spite, slaughtering them; and when the king heard of this, he was filled with fury, sent his armies out to destroy those murderers and light fires in their cities.

Do not go into any roads of the Gentiles, he'd said in Nain. The mission was only to the Jews, to heal the inequities and insanities, bring the nation together to stand against Rome, a movement to reclaim the realm.

But she came and supplicated to him, saying, Master, help me.

Let the children be filled first, said Joshua. It is not fit to take the children's bread and cast it to the dogs. Do not give that which is holy to the dogs, nor cast your pearls before swine lest they trample them under their feet, turn again and rend you.

Do not enter into any city of the Samaritans, he'd said. But in Sychar, after John's arrest, he'd reached out to them, knowing that the revolution needed us to put aside ancient enmities.

Yes, master, she answered. Still, the dogs under the table eat of the children's crumbs.

O woman, he said. Great is your trust. Let it be to you even as you will it. For this teaching, go your way; the daimon is gone out of your daughter.

And when she was come to her house, she found the demon gone out, and her daughter laid upon the bed.

I found him later, alone in the garden, weeping.

You couldn't refuse her, I said.

I realise now it was cold comfort set against two millennia of Gentiles murdering Jews. In his name.

18

And departing from the coasts of Tyre and Sidon, Joshua returned to the sea of Galilee, through the midst of the coasts of Decapolis. And it came to pass, when the people were gathered thick together, then one was brought to him, driven by a daimon, blind and mute, and he healed him, insomuch that the blind and mute both spoke and saw. And all the people were amazed, and said, Is this not the son of David?

What are you writing? I asked.

Matthew looked up from the scroll.

A genealogy, he said, tracing Joshua's descent from David... from Abraham, actually.

I imagine the look on my face would have given Thomas a run for his money. He took a sip from his wine, went back to writing. I poured a cup for myself.

The book of the generation of Joshua anointed, the son of David, the son of Abraham:

Abraham begat Isaac; and Isaac begat Jacob; and Jacob begat Judas and his brethren; and Judas begat Pharez and Zara of Thamar; and Pharez begat Hezron; and Hezron begat Ram; and Ram begat Amminadab; and Amminadab begat Nahshon; and Nahshon begat Salmon; and Salmon begat Boaz of Rachab; and Boaz begat Obed of Ruth; and Obed begat Jesse; and Jesse begat David the king.

I read over Matthew's shoulder, troubled at the idea of this unashamed *setukhi*, staunch defender of the illegitimate and dispossessed, self-professed *everyman*, conjuring a grand lineage for those who'd have their robes of purple, royal blood, heredity, the stuff of Herods. If they want you from the branch of David, I thought, tell them your humble birth is *exactly* what makes you the shepherd boy's scion.

David the king begat Solomon of her that had been the wife of Uriah; and Solomon begat Rehoboam; and Rehoboam begat Abijam; and Abijam begat Asa; and Asa begat Jehosaphat; and Jehosaphat begat Jehoram; and Jehoram begat Uzziah; and Uzziah begat Jotham; and Jotham begat Ahaz; and Ahaz begat Hezekiah; and Hezekiah begat Manasseh; and Manasseh begat Amon; and Amon begat Josiah; and Josiah begat Jeconiah and his brethren, about the time they were carried away to Babylon.

Why? I said.

So whoever reads it know his blood is Abraham's, said Matthew. So they remember he's a Jew.

Who does he expect to read it? I said.

Matthew shook his head.

And after they were brought to Babylon, Jeconiah begat Shealtiel; and Shealtiel begat Zerubbabel; and Zerubbabel begat Abiud; and Abiud begat Eliakim; and Eliakim begat Azor; and Azor begat Zadok; and Zadok begat Achim; and Achim begat Eliud; and Eliud begat Eleazar; and Eleazar begat Matthan; and Matthan begat Jacob; and Jacob begat Joseph the husband of Mary, of whom was born Joshua, who is called the anointed.

But Joseph wasn't his father, I said.

I know, he said. Think of it as... figurative heritage.

So all the generations from Abraham to David are fourteen generations, and from David until the carrying away into Babylon are fourteen generations, and from the carrying away into Babylon to the anointed are fourteen generations.

You missed one, I said. That last group is only thirteen. Unless you're counting the marriage to Mary as some strange sideways generation, that last group is one short.

Matthew took another sip of his wine, pinched the bridge of his nose with thumb and forefinger.

Joshua wanted an error, he said, a deliberate self-contradiction so readers *have* to question it, something that just doesn't make sense.

A whole generation lost, I said, between the captivity and the anointed. I suppose that should do it.

19

Then certain of the clerks and the Select answered, saying, Rabbi, we would see a sign from you. And others, testing him, sought of him a sign from Æternity.

And he sighed deeply in his breath, said, Why does this generation seek after a sign?

They stood at the wrought iron gates, the minister, clerk of session and kirk elders, blocking the path up to Capernaum's little church and community hall. A wall of accusations and challenges, outrage at his blasphemy, but Joshua met their wrath with calm. Galileans themselves, and they couldn't believe in a prophet out of Galilee. Born among fishermen and farmers, and they couldn't believe a child of their ilk anointed. Quick to denounce any hint of the miraculous as black magic, and they wanted some wonder to prove his power. A sign?

When it is evening, he answered, you say it will be fair weather, for the sky is red. And in the morning, you say it will be foul weather today, for the sky is red and lowering. When you see a cloud rise out of the west, at once you say there is a shower coming, and so it is. And when you see the south wind blow, you say there will be heat, and it comes to pass. You hypocrites, you can discern the face of the sky and of the earth, but can you not discern the signs of the times?

He pressed his way through, not aggressive but resolute, and we hurried after, Matthew with the paper, myself with the hammer and nail, nervous. If Joshua was cool, I carried all his tension in my gut, a gnawing angst that had been growing since Sychar, a sense of the stitch in my memory weakening, a fold in time straining to unwarp. The Samaritans, the Greek woman, the genealogy... I sensed a road narrowing to a tight gate.

A wicked and disloyal generation seeks after a sign, he said, and there shall be no sign given to it save the sign of the prophet Jonah. For as Jonah was three days and nights in the whale's belly, so shall the everyman be three days and three nights in the heart of the earth. And as Jonah was a sign to the Ninevites, so too shall the everyman be to this generation.

The men of Nineveh shall rise in judgement with this generation and condemn it, because they changed their hearts at the preaching of Jonah, and behold, one greater than Jonah is here. The queen of the south, shall rise up in the judgement with this generation and condemn it, for Sheba came from the uttermost parts of the earth to hear the wisdom of Solomon, and behold, one greater than Solomon is here.

At the kirk doors, he stopped, held out his hand for the paper, the nail, the hammer. Over their cries, he shouted back:

As it was in the days of Noah, so shall it be in the days of the everyman. They ate, they drank, they married wives, were given in marriage, until the day that Noah entered into the ark, and the flood came, and destroyed them all. So it was too in the days of Lot. They ate and drank, bought and sold, planted and built. But the same day that Lot went out of Sodom it rained fire and brimstone from the heavens, destroyed them all. Remember Lot's wife.

———

A single hammer blow. He turned.

———

He who is not with me is against me, and he who does not gather with me scatters abroad.

20

And he said to them, When the fouled inspiration is gone out of a man, it walks through quiet wilds, seeking rest. And finding none, it says, I will return to my house where I came out from. And when it comes, it finds it swept and garnished. Then it goes, and gathers to it seven other inspirations more wicked than itself, and they enter in, and dwell there. And the last state of that man is worse than the first, because they said, He has a fouled inspiration.

———

And then it happened. Time tore around the minister as he stalked towards us up the gravel path, Calvinist with one step, cardinal with the other, a Pharisee by the time he stood before us. As Joshua had opened my eyes when I cursed a reverend on Fox News, as I'd seen a grail in a cup, a crucifix in a phylactory, now I saw this member of the Select as Joshua did: a man born again and baptised, exorcised and confessed, cleansed time and again, and driven by worse daimons than ever. Reality from a dozen angles of time at once was still too much to grasp, a shattered hologram of shards that whirled, I think now, precisely because it had to be unknown; otherwise, I might have murdered the two of us there and then. But I was stable in it. Joshua looked at me, and I knew he knew.

Even so shall it be to this wicked generation also, he said. Even so shall it be in the day when the everyman is revealed. I tell you, in that night there shall be two men in one bed; the one shall be taken, and the other left. Two women shall be grinding together; the one shall be taken, and the other left. Two men shall be in the field; the one shall be taken, and the other left.

No doubt you find it hard to believe, lover of the sublime, that I walked with him through centuries, millennia, through a realm under the skin of time itself. Then don't. Cling while you still can to your banal little neverafter of a line that never ends; dream your soul a clockwork monkey marching forever. Someday you will roll over in bed and see yourself asleep beside you, and be gone.

O generation of vipers, how can you, being wicked, speak good things? A good man yields that which is good out of the good treasure of his heart; and a wicked man yields that which is wicked out of the wicked wealth of his heart: for his mouth speaks from the heart's abundance. But I say to you, that every idle word that men shall speak, they shall have to account for in the day of judgement. For by your words you shall be justified, and by your words you shall be condemned.

What will they say of you, lover of the sublime, when your tale has been told two thousand years?

And when the Select demanded of him when the realm of the sublime should come, he answered. The realm of the sublime comes not with observation, he said. Neither shall they say, Look here! or, Look there! for behold, it is spread out upon the earth and men do not see it. The realm of the sublime is within you.

———

The paper nailed to the door fluttered in the breeze. No Lutheran declaration, inscribed on it was only a single simple phrase: The realm is to hand.

———

Therefore the Select sought all the more to kill him.

Steadfast for Jerusalem

21

And when Joshua came into the coasts of Caesarea Philippi, he questioned his students.

Who do men say that I am? he said.

Some say you are John the Baptist, they said, some say Elijah, and others Jeremiah or one of the prophets.

But who do *you* say that I am? he asked.

You are the anointed, said Simon the Rock, the son of the living spirit.

You are blessed, Simon bar-Jonah, said Joshua, for flesh and blood has not revealed it to you, but my æternal father.

I sat peeling an orange, remembering Capernaum, remembering the televangelist of another aeon, how I'd trembled with rage until Joshua whispered a few words in my ear, how suddenly it had all collided—the stonings of one aeon, the ex-gay therapy of another, the fear and shame in both. I didn't say who he was *to me*; words were inadequate.

On what day will you be revealed to us? his students said. On what day shall we see you?

When you unclothe yourselves and are not ashamed, Joshua said, and take your garments and lay them beneath your feet like little children, and tread upon them. Then you shall see the son of the living one, naked man to naked man, and you shall not fear.

He'd shown me these... costumes of aeons, and for a moment it all made sense. For a few days, I'd held onto that understanding of time's depths, before it dissipated. But now as I looked back into my own memory, on the porch of a log cabin in Nain, I sipped from a beercan and lay it down as a gourd. The trappings of time were shucked and I saw simply... myself, sitting there beside him.

———

Then he charged his students that they should tell no man that he was Joshua the anointed. From that time forth Joshua began to reveal to his students how he must go to Jerusalem, and be rejected of the elders and chief priests and clerks, killed and raised again the third day.

———

And made a figurehead of all he fought, I brooded. The whirling of fragments still refused to resolve, not least because every single thing as simple as a beercan sparked a cascade of related memories, sucked me instantly into the self of that time and place. But one thing was clear: that the very movement he founded to fight the Empire became it, in blood.

———

Then the Rock took him, began to rebuke him.

Be it far from you, Teacher, he said. This shall not happen to you.

But when Joshua had turned about and looked on his students, he rebuked the Rock.

You are a stumbling block to me, he said, for you savour not the things that are of the sublime, only those that are of men.

———

His jaw clenched as he glanced at me.

———

I say also to you that you are the Rock, and upon this rock I will build a church, he said. I will yield to you the keys of the realm of Æternity, and whatever you bind on Earth shall be bound in Æternity, and whatever you unleash on earth shall be unleashed in Æternity, and the gates of Gehenna shall not overcome it.

Later, as the others slept, I lay in his embrace, looking up at the stars.
   Why? I whispered. Two thousand years of... you can't want that.
   It's already happened, he said. All we can do is keep fighting.
   I don't understand, I said. I can't handle all this.
   A gentle squeeze.
   Not yet, he said.

22

And it came to pass, when the days of his ascension were fulfilled, he set his face steadfast for Jerusalem. And as they were on the road going up to Jerusalem, Joshua went before them, and as they followed, they were amazed and they were afraid. And again he took the twelve students apart on the way, and began to tell them what things should happen to him. And he spoke this saying openly, and how it is written of the everyman, that he must suffer many things, and be set at nothing.

Behold, he said, we go up to Jerusalem; and the everyman shall be betrayed to the chief priests and to the clerks, and they shall deliver him to the Gentiles. They shall scorn him, and scourge him, and spit upon him, and they shall condemn him and kill him, and the third day he shall rise again.

I walked in silence. How many times had I heard him say, I will have mercy and not sacrifice? And delivered to the Gentiles, just what would he become? What have you made of him, lover of the sublime? One Lamb, and how many scapegoats?
   Don't crash us, said Mary.
   My attention snapped back to the road, to headlights on tarmac at night, the rhythm of white lines pulsing past, the flash of cat's eyes sliding sideways as the bus drifted out of lane. I steered us back on course, looked up at Mary.

Sorry.

Pull over. I'll drive.

It's OK.

You're wrecked. You need rest.

So I eased us over to the side of the road, to a stop, let her take the wheel, and headed back to Joshua, took the joint he offered with a smile before turning back to Matthew's latest pages.

Then the mother of Zebedee's children came to him with her sons, Jacob and John, adoring him and desiring a certain thing.

What do you wish? he asked her.

Grant that my two sons may sit in your realm, she said, one on your right hand, the other on the left.

You do not know what you ask, said Joshua. Are you able to drink from the cup I shall drink from, to be baptized with the baptism I am baptized with?

We are able, they said.

You shall indeed drink of my cup, he said, and be baptized with the baptism that I am baptized with, but to sit on my right hand and on my left is not mine to give, but it shall be given by my father to them for whom it is prepared.

And when the ten heard it, they were moved with indignation against the two brethren. And there was an argument among them over which should be deemed the greatest.

But Joshua called them to him.

You know that the lords of the Gentiles exercise dominion over them, he said, and those who are mighty exercise authority upon them. But it shall not be so among you. Rather whoever would be great among you, let him be your attendant, and whoever would be chief among you shall be slave of all. For which is mightier, he who sits at supper, or he who serves? Is it not he who sits at supper? But I am among you as he who serves. For the everyman came not to be tended to, but to tend. And behold, there are least which shall be most, and there are highest who shall be lowest. If any man desire to be leader, the same must be follower of all, and attendant of all.

23

And he came to Capernaum, and there were little children brought to him, that he should put his hands on them, and pray; and being in the house, the students scolded those who brought them. But when Joshua saw it, he was much displeased.

Suffer the little children to come to me, he said. Forbid them not, for of such is the realm of the sublime.

And he asked, What was it that you disputed among yourselves on the way?

But they held their peace, for along the road they had bickered among themselves as to who should be the greatest. So he sat down, and called the twelve. And Joshua saw some infants at the breast. He took them up in his arms, put his hands on them, and blessed them. Then he took a child, set him in the midst of them.

The *Fisher of Men* already docked in the harbour as we drove past, the hostel was a bustle of life when we entered it, the others already arrived, the trestle tables dragged forward from the wall, turned longways to cram as many chairs around as possible, Philip and Nathaniel carting plates through from the kitchen.

Children everywhere, the babe in Salome's arms whose forehead Joshua kissed –

These little ones at the breast, he said to his students, are like those who enter into the realm. Whoever shall humble himself as this little child, that one is greatest in the realm of Zion. Take heed that you do not disdain one of these little ones, for I say to you, in Æternity their messengers ever behold the face of my æternal father. So, they shall be your judges. The man aged in his days will not hesitate to ask a little child of seven days about the place of life, and he shall live.

– the nipper he scooped up from a flailing giggling run, set on the table with a scruff of hair –

———

And when he had taken the child in his arms, he said, Whoever welcomes one such little child in my name welcomes me; and whoever welcomes me, welcomes not me, but him that sent me. For the everyman is come to save that which was lost. It is not the will of your æternal father that one of these little ones should perish. So, whoever gives you a cup of water to drink in my name simply because you belong to the anointed, for sure, I tell you, he shall not lose his reward. Whoever gives one of these little ones a cup of cold water to drink simply in the name of a student, for sure, I tell you, he shall not lose his reward. He who has ears, let him hear—*they have their reward.*

———

– the toddler he hoisted up, as he took his seat, to dandle on his knee.

———

But whoever becomes a stumbling block to one of these little ones who trust in me, it were better for him that a millstone were hanged about his neck, that he were drowned in the depth of the sea. Woe to the world for its stumbling blocks! With certainty, the stumbling blocks will come, but woe to that man by whom the stumbling block arrives!

If we are as children then, they said, shall we enter the realm?

Whoever shall *not* welcome the realm of the sublime as a little child, he said, shall in no way enter. For sure, I tell you, unless you are turned around and become as little children, you shall not enter into the realm of Zion.

24

And after six days, he took with him Simon the Rock and Jacob and John, and brought them up into a high mountain apart, to that mountain where Joshua had appointed them, to pray, and as he prayed, was transfigured before them. And the fashion of his countenance was altered, his face shone as the sun, and his garments became glistering and shining, beyond white as snow, so as no fuller on earth could whiten them. And, behold, there appeared to them Moses and Elijah talking with him, who appeared in glory, and spoke of his death which he should accomplish at Jerusalem.

They had built a church on Mount Tabor, over the ruins of the Byzantine and Crusader churches that had risen and fallen, part of the Franciscan monastery complex, all blond stone and red tile roof, that nestled among the trees upon the summit. Flagstones of irregular shape but smooth beneath our feet led to a pillared arch before the entrance, bell-towers on either side with chapels dedicated to Moses and Elijah. Inside the marble arches of the high vault caught the August afternoon sunlight that streamed in and, just for a short while, bounced off a glass plate set into the floor to illuminate the gold mosaic above the altar, make it gleam with glory. The saviour floated in the air, draped in white raiment, haloed, hands raised as to bask in adoration.

And the Rock and those who were with him were heavy with sleep, but while they were awake, they saw his glory, and the two men who stood with him. And while he yet spoke, behold, a bright cloud overshadowed them, and lo, a voice out of the cloud:

This is my beloved Son, it said, in whom I am well pleased. Hear you him.

The voice of the tourist guide reverberated as a choir, the same words spoken in language after language after language.

When the students heard it, they fell on their faces, terrified, but Joshua came and touched them.

Arise, he said. Do not be afraid.

And when they had lifted up their eyes, and looked around, they saw no man any more, only Joshua with themselves.

And they stood on the summit of Mount Tabor, empty now but for the signal fire.

And it came to pass, as they departed, the Rock spoke to Joshua.

Rabbi, it is good for us to be here, he said. If you want, let us make here three tabernacles—one for you, and one for Moses, and one for Elijah.

For he knew not what to say, for they were sore afraid.

But as they came down from the mountain, Joshua charged them.

Tell the vision to no man, he said, until the everyman be risen again from the dead.

And they kept it close in those days, and told no man any of those things which they had seen, but questioned one with another what the rising from the dead should mean.

If you showed Simon more, I said later, if you showed him what you showed me...

Wouldn't it change it? he said. No.

We sat on the porch of the cabin, where I'd told him about Mary that first night. Cicadas chirped at fireflies.

No, he said. Simon would understand it the only way he could. The first time I saw a Jerusalem in an aeon of streetlights, looking down from the Mount of Olives at night... that orange glow... I thought I was seeing hell.

Isn't it? I said. Isn't that what we make it?

Not yet, he said.

Bethany

As a Mustard Seed

1

And they departed from there, and passed through Galilee. And he went through the cities and villages teaching, journeying toward Jerusalem. And as he entered into a certain village—[A certain village, a certain man, a certain centurion's servant... when you read such wording, lover of the sublime, you should hear the stress of ellipsis, the invitation to ask: in which village?]—there met him ten men who were lepers, who stood far off. And they lifted up their voices.

Joshua, they said, Rabbi, have mercy on us.

Because who else will? I muttered.

What? said Mary.

Never mind.

I stirred the pot on the iron range, a stew of bandages boiling to sterility, Mary beside me soaking lint swabs in carbolic acid solution. Behind us, Simon and the others moved among the sick, applying dressings as directed by Joshua, Thomas wrinkling his nose at a scent part perfume, part vinegar and rancid butter. We trusted in Joshua rather than Pasteur and Lister, but it was better, I suppose, than trusting in prayer, telling the wretched to scream a little quieter.

Go show yourselves to the priests, | said Joshua when he saw the ten.

Show them the efficacy of actual medicine.

And it came to pass, that, as they | went, they were cleansed.

We gathered in Shiloh, in a log-cabin church, in a tabernacle built for the ark of the covenant long before Herod's marble folly. We gathered in Shiloh, where men of the ten tribes seceded after Solomon's death once came to launch a surprise attack on the Union troops of one loyal tribe. Or something like that. We were camped on the long march for Jerusalem, unmoored in time, and I felt sicker than the ten leprous gangrenous wounded casualties lain on pallets and soiled blankets, sackcloth and wool, this one sobbing for his ma, that one moaning in delirium as students moved between the beds, mopping brows and brushing off the dust that crumbled down at the shudder of timbers, at the boom of cannons. Bonesaws and suffering. Black iron bars on the windows. I looked at it all and felt sick to my stomach, could barely keep my rations down, and it wasn't from the stench of rot.

You're starting to see it more now, aren't you? said Joshua. Æternity?

If this is Æternity, it's insane, I said.

And the HIV patients lesioned with Kaposi's Sarcoma rose from their hospice sickbeds, trudged past us on their way to the chapel, and as they passed Joshua reached out to them and they shimmered, became the angels of another aeon, dancers in white feather wings, half-naked and healthy, marching proud. Or something like that.

And one of the ten, when he saw that he was healed, turned back and with a loud voice honoured the sublime, and fell down on his face at his feet, giving him thanks. And he was a Samaritan.

Were there not ten cleansed? Joshua said. But where are the nine? O disloyal generation, how long shall I be with you? How long shall I suffer you? There are none found who returned to give honour to the sublime, save this stranger?

None who remember, I thought as the others walked on, oblivious of their restoration. The Samaritan touched Joshua's feet with fingers that had been stumps a moment before, kissed them with lips that had been eaten away until Joshua raised a hand and pulled a healthy body from Æternity into existence, adjusted not flesh but time.

Arise, Joshua said to him, go your way. Your trust has made you whole.

2

And it came to pass, as he went to Jerusalem, that he passed through the midst of Samaria, and sent messengers before his face. They went ahead, entered into a village of the Samaritans to make ready for him. But the villagers did not welcome him, because his face was as though he would go to Jerusalem.

The Peace March passed in rain and gloom down the empty streets of the mining town, cobbles underfoot slicked to a grey as dark as the rooftop slates, the soot-grimed walls. A sideburned statue, top hat under one arm, stared across our path at a cenotaph commemorating those we had survived. Lace curtains twitched. Doors closed.

And his students Jacob and John saw this.

Lord, they said, would you that we call down fire from the heavens to consume them, even as Elijah did?

But he turned and rebuked them.

Hear what the unjust judge said, that men should pray endlessly and never falter. Don't you know, he said, what manner of inspiration you're come from?

How many years with him? And still the Sons of Thunder lived up to their nickname, echoing mindless judgement from a sky in turmoil. It was in their blood, I thought: thunder at night drowning men's voices as Hebridean seas roil wild to drown their souls; thunder from a Presbyterian pulpit, rumbling reckoning in wintery eyes, brows furled as storm cloud; the thunder of war our banners denounced.

I was glad of the rain. It hid the tears in my eyes from Mary, hope of change dissolving to a taste of salt.

———

He spoke a parable to them to this end, saying, There was in a city a judge who neither feared the sublime nor respected man. And there was a widow in that city. She came to him, saying, Avenge me of my adversary. He would not for a while, but afterward he said to himself, Though I neither fear the sublime nor respect man, since this widow nags me, I'll avenge her, lest she weary me by her incessant coming.

And the teacher said, Though he can suffer patiently with those who lament day and night to him, shall the sublime not bring justice to his own successors? I tell you he'll make justice for them speedily. For the everyman is not come to destroy men's lives, but to save them.

And yet, he said, when the everyman comes, shall he find trust upon the earth?

———

We trudged through the godless rain toward a promise that seemed emptier by the step.

———

Increase our trust, the ambassadors said to the teacher.

For sure, I tell you, said Joshua, this generation shall not pass away till all is fulfilled. There are some standing here who shall not taste of death till they see the everyman coming in his realm.

He spoke of the Judaean, son of Simeon of Kerioth, being one of the twelve, for he it was who should betray him, but Joshua would not that any man should know it.

———

Not even me. Not yet.

So he taught his students, and told them to let these teachings sink down into their ears: for the everyman shall be delivered into the hands of men, and they shall kill him; and after he is killed, he shall rise the third day. They were exceeding sorry then, but they understood not this saying; it was hid from them, that they perceived it not, and they feared to ask him, all save the son of perdition.

And Joshua took him, went aside, and spoke to him three words.

3

And they went to another village. And when they beheld him, at once all the people were greatly amazed, and ran to him, saluted him. And when he came to his students, he saw a great mob around them, clerks questioning with them. When Joshua saw that the people came running together...

You'll come soon? I said as we approached.

Soon, he promised and sent me onward with a slap on the shoulder.

What question do you have with them? he asked the clerks.

Rabbi, one of the mob answered, I bring you my only son, who has a mute inspiration. Whenever it takes him, it tears him, and he foams and grinds his teeth, goes limp. I spoke to your students that they should cast him out, but they could not. This kind does not go out but by prayer and fasting.

Bring him to me, Joshua answered.

And they brought him to Joshua. And when he saw Joshua, at once the inspiration tore him, and he fell on the ground and wallowed, foaming.

I skirted the edge of the crowd, got a curious gaze from Thomas as I passed, said nothing.

How long since this came upon him? Joshua asked the boy's father.

From an infant, he said. Often it has cast him into the fire and the waters, to destroy him, but if there's anything you can do, have sympathy for us, help us.

If you can trust, said Joshua, all things are possible to he who trusts.

He looked at me as he spoke, across the gulf of the crowd between us.

You expect me to trust you, I'd said as he laid out his plans the night before, that without this grand show it would be worse. That it wouldn't be better just to do nothing than to become the Empire we're fighting. How can you ask me to trust you?

To trust *yourself*, he said. You can't trust the everyman unless you trust yourself.

Teacher, I trust, the father of the child cried out at once. Help my disbelief, he said through tears.

You deaf and mute inspiration, he said, I charge you, come out of him, he rebuked the foul inspiration. Enter into him no more.

And the inspiration cried, rent the boy sore, came out of him. Then the boy was as one dead, so that many said he had died. But Joshua took him by the hand, lifted him up, and he arose.

A last glance as the crowd swarmed in around him. I turned. Down by the congregation house, on the edge of town, Mary waited with the pack animals, ready for our journey ahead, to the safe house in Jericho and then on to our father's house in Bethany.

———

When Joshua was come into the house, his students asked him privately, Why could we not cast him out?

Because of your distrust, said Joshua.

The realm of Zion, he said, is like a grain of mustard seed which is less than all the seeds in the earth, but when it is sown, it grows up, and becomes greater than all herbs, and shoots out great branches, so all the birds of the air may lodge under its shadow. For I tell you truly, if you have trust as a grain of mustard seed, you shall say to this mountain, Remove from here to yonder place, and it shall remove. You might say to this sycamore tree, Be plucked up by the root, and be planted in the sea, and it will obey you. Nothing shall be impossible to you.

4

All things are possible to he who trusts, he said. I try to keep this in mind as I stare at the walls now papered with gospel scraps, edited and arrowed in blood-red ink, knowing how you'll see me, lover of the sublime, as a fool, a liar, a madman or all of the above. I look at the photograph of you posing with an assault rifle in Uganda, lobbying the world for a righteous nigger hunt while your friends lobby the nation for a crusade on faggots, and it's as hard for me to trust you as it is for you to trust me, I dare say. But I can't trust the everyman unless I trust you, so I hold to a kernel of hope, knowing that your folly, lies and madness are as human as mine, as any man's.

———

And they came to Jericho. Now a certain young man of Bethany was wasting.

———

All things are possible to he who trusts. I'd kept that in mind as I left Mary in Jericho, to walk the long road to Bethany alone, as I'd stood in my father's house, waved away the servants. As I sat in the garden, under the fig tree, fasting.

———

And the sister of that youth whom Joshua loved, his mother and Salome were there, but Joshua did not receive them. Therefore his sisters, Martha and Mary—who anointed the teacher with ointment and wiped his feet with her hair—sent to Joshua. Now Joshua loved Martha, and her sister and brother.

Teacher, they said, behold, he whom you love is wasting.

———

And in Bethany, I watched the bowl of fruit set out before me slowly rot, despairing the decay of faith even in him.

———

When Joshua heard that, he said, See that you are not troubled, for all these things must come to pass, but the end is not yet. This wasting is not to death, but for the honour of the sublime, that the scion of the sublime might be honoured through it. He who has known the world has found the body, and he who has found the body, the world is not worthy of him; so I will raise him up at the last day. Even so did my mother, the sacred inspiration, take me by one of my hairs, and carry me to the great mountain Tabor.

When Joshua heard that he whom he loved was wasting then, he endured two days still in the same place where he was, then after that he said to his students, Let us go into Judaea again.

Rabbi, said his students, the Judaeans sought to stone you of late, and you go there again?

Are there not twelve hours in the day? said Joshua. If any man walk in the day, he does not stumble, because he sees the light of this world. But if a man walk in the night, he stumbles, because there is no light in him.

He said these things, and after that:

Our friend sleeps, he said, but I go, that I may awake him out of sleep.

Teacher, his students said then, if he sleeps, he shall recover.

Now Joshua spoke of his death, but they thought now that he was speaking literally of sleep.

He is dead, said Joshua bluntly then. And I am glad for your sakes, for the sake of your trust, that I was not there. Nevertheless, let us go to him.

Then Thomas, who is called Didymus, spoke to his fellow students:

Let us also go, that we may die with him.

$\mathcal{A}$ $\mathcal{C}ry$ $\mathcal{M}ade$ at $\mathcal{M}idnight$

5

So Joshua entered and passed through Jericho. And behold, there was a rich man named Zacchaeus, chief among the taxmen, who yearned to see this Joshua, who he was, but could not for the throng because he was short in height. So he ran ahead, climbed up into a sycamore tree, knowing Joshua was to pass that way. And when Joshua came to that place, he looked up and saw the man.

Zacchaeus, he called up to him, make haste to come down, for today I must abide at your house.

Zacchaeus made haste to come down, and welcomed him joyously. When they saw it, everyone murmured, muttering that Joshua was gone to be guest with a man who was a delinquent.

Zacchaeus stood, said to the teacher, Look, Teacher, half of my goods I give to the poor. And if I have taken anything from any man by fraud, I return it to him fourfold.

This day is salvation come to this house, said Joshua, because he too is a son of Abraham.

In Bethany, under the fig tree, in the courtyard garden, I sat with my father's empty house around me, wondering if the whole movement was simply wrong, if the solution was only another iteration of the problem... *worse*. In shards of memory too sharp to grasp, I glimpsed black-cassocked priests signing treaties with the Empire, jackboots marching through Jewish streets, not salvation for the sons of Abraham but factories of death. I heard my father beg me to eat something; no fast should be this extreme. I clung to conviction.

He said he would come soon, I told him.

But as they heard these things, because Joshua was close to Jerusalem now, some thought that the realm of the sublime should appear at once, so he added and spoke a parable.

The realm of Zion shall be compared to ten virgins, he said, who took their lamps and went forth to the bridegroom's processional reception. Five of them were wise, and five were foolish. Those who were foolish took their lamps without oil with them, but the wise each took oil in their flasks along with the lamp of herself. While the bridegroom lingered, they all slumbered and slept.

Behold! a cry was made at midnight. The bridegroom comes! Go out to meet him.

Then all those virgins rose, each readying the lamp of herself.

The foolish said to the wise, Give us some of your oil, for our lamps are going out.

No, said the wise, not lest there be too little for us as well as you.

Instead? You, go to those who sell, and buy for yourselves.

But as they went to buy, the bridegroom came, so those who were ready went in with him to the wedding, and when the other virgins also came, later, the door was shut.

Master, Master, they said, open to us.

For sure, I tell you, he answered, I do not know you.

Watch therefore, Joshua said, for you know neither the day nor the hour when the everyman comes. When the master of the house has risen up and shut the door; when you have stood outside, and knocked at the door, saying, Master, Master, open to us; when he has answered you, I do not know where you have come from: then you shall begin to say, But we have dined and drunk with you, and you have taught in our streets.

I do not know where you have come from, he shall say, I tell you. Depart from me, you workers of iniquity.

6

So Joshua went out of Jericho with his students and a great number of people. And as he went, blind Bartimaeus, the son of Timaeus, sat by the roadside begging. Hearing the mob move past, he asked what it meant, and they told him that Joshua the Nazirite passed by.

Joshua, you son of David, he cried, have mercy on me!

Many charged him that he should hold his peace, but he cried out all the more:

You son of David, have mercy on me!

In Bethany, a bruise darkened on orange peel. The accuser came to me with my father's face, scorning me for a madman that I refused paternal mercy.

Then Joshua stood still, directed him to be called. So they called the blind man, telling him to be of good comfort—Rise, he calls you. And he rose, casting away his garment, and came to Joshua.

What will you that I should do to you? said Joshua.

Teacher, said the blind man, that I might receive my sight.

Go your way, said Joshua. Your trust has made you whole.

And immediately he received his sight, and followed Joshua on the road.

In Bethany, mould spread white around a blue-grey bruise more lurid now than dark. The accuser came to me with my brother's face, baffled as I rebuffed a lie of love defeating the grave.

And the Passover was at hand, and there were certain Greeks among those who came up to worship at the feast. The same came therefore to Philip, and entreated him.

Sir, they said, we would see Joshua.

So Philip came and told Andrew, and Andrew and Philip told Joshua.

Come, Joshua answered them, the hour is come in which the everyman should be honoured. The light will only stay with you a little while longer. Then I will draw all men to me if I am raised up from the earth.

This he said to signify by what death he would die.

In Bethany, a fetid citrus scent filled the garden. The accuser came to me with Joshua's face, wept that I wouldn't surrender to a pipe-dream of salvation. Didn't I love him?

We have heard from the law, the people said, that the anointed will remain for ever. How then can you say the everyman must be raised up? Who is this everyman?

While you have the light, trust in the light, said Joshua, that you may be the sons of light. Walk while you have the light, lest darkness come upon you, for he who walks in darkness does not know where he is going.

In Bethany, under the fig tree, all was rot. The accuser came to me with my own face, came from within as that one true messenger of the sublime always does, from a soul more human than even the Sadducees imagined, not just mortal but man-made.

And now my soul is troubled, said Joshua. What shall I say: Father, spare me from this hour? But for this very reason I came to this hour. Father, honour your name!

And while some of the bystanders who heard it said it thundered, others said a messenger spoke to him, that there came a voice from Æternity, saying, I have both honoured it and will honour it again.

This voice came not for me, said Joshua, but for your sakes. Now is the judgement of this world. Now shall the lord of this world be cast out.

In Bethany, under the fig tree: death.

These things spoke Joshua, and departed, and hid himself from them.

7

And when Joshua came to Bethany, he found that a certain woman whose brother had died was there, that he had lain in the grave four days already. For as soon as she heard that Joshua was coming, Martha went to meet him, though Mary sat still in the house. And coming, she prostrated herself before Joshua, saying, Son of David, have mercy on me.

Your brother shall rise again, said Joshua.

It was the same promise he'd given me before he sent me on ahead. It is the same promise I offer you, lover of the sublime, if you can understand it. Four days in the cold earth, dead flesh oiled to sweeten the scent of decomposition. Four days in the ICU, sleeping flesh tendriled by intubator, catheter, drips and electrodes. Four days under observation, sectioned and sedated for a suicide attempt or psychotic break. Four days in a garden, fucked out of your head on mushrooms and misery, identity dissolved to darkness and breath. There are a thousand ways to tell this story. Maybe now you've had your own long dark night of the soul, lover of the sublime, you'll see past the literal to an existential void.

Under the fig tree, the accuser came to me as he'd come to Joshua in the desert, the sacred inspiration as a death rattle, the sublime as mortality's dream of meaning. In the knowledge that Joshua was sent from nothing, from unbearable irremediable *nothing*, I died.

I know that he shall rise again in the revival at the last day, said Martha.

I am the revival and the life, Joshua said to her. He who trusts in me, though he were dead, yet he shall live. And anyone who lives and trusts in me shall never taste of death. Do you believe this?

Death has no taste. No sight, no sound, no taste. Not even the scent of a rotting orange. You will never know it, lover of the sublime, because it leaves no you to do the knowing.

Aye, Teacher, she said to him. I believe that you are the anointed, the scion of the sublime, who should come into the world.

And when she had said so, she went her way, and called Mary her sister secretly, saying, The rabbi is come, and calls for you.

As soon as she heard that, Mary rose quickly, and came to him. Now Bethany was close to Jerusalem, about fifteen furlongs off, so many of the Select had come to Martha and Mary, to comfort them concerning their brother. And the Select who were with her in the house to comfort her, when they saw Mary, that she rose up hastily and went out, they followed her, saying, She goes to the grave to weep there.

And Joshua was not yet come into the town, but was in that place where Martha met him.

When Mary came to where Joshua was and saw him then, she fell down at his feet. So, as Joshua saw her weeping and those who came with her also weeping, he groaned in the inspiration, was troubled.

Teacher, she said, if you had been here my brother would not have died. But I know that even now whatever you will ask of the sublime, the sublime will give it to you.

Where have you laid him? Joshua said.

Teacher, she said to him, come and see.

Then those who were with her rebuked her, but Joshua, being angered, went off with her. And they came into Bethany, into the garden where the tomb was.

Joshua wept.

8

ehold, said the Select then, how he loved him! Couldn't this man who opened the eyes of the blind, said some, also have kept this youth from dying?

So Joshua groaning again in himself came to the grave, which was a cave, and a stone lay upon it.

Inside, in the tomb of all I'd once believed in, I lay lacklust and laughless, steeped in fragrant decay and shrouded, a life stilled to the cold of vacuum, a light dulled to the dark of endings in crypt or coffin, coma or catatonia. This is the best I can say. Story cannot tell of such extinction. It cannot conjure my brother, Joshua's father or Simon's wife out of absences too painful to outline in more than elliptical references, passing comments, sad jokes around a hearth years down the line. Always already collapsing into the figurative and fantastic, narrative abhorring such a vacuum of purpose, story can seldom enter the garden let alone walk up to the grave itself, lay a hand upon the door of this whited sepulchre.

Take the stone away, said Joshua.

Teacher, said Martha, by now he stinks, for he has been dead four days.

Did I not say to you, said Joshua, that you would see the glory of the sublime, if you should trust?

Then they rolled the stone away from the door of the tomb where the dead was laid, and Joshua lifted up his eyes.

Father, he said, I thank you that you've heard me. I knew that—you always hear me—but I say it for all these people who stand by, so they may trust that you have sent me.

There is no way to tell this story. Story cannot tell of Æternity's twin, of the negative space that begins where all else ends, of death. If poetry can barely point to it, what hope has prose written and revised to compromise by generations of cowards to conjure any more than Joshua standing on the threshold, talking to a dead father he carried in a tomb carved in his heart, in every breath he sighed up to the sky? I take my red pen to the Bible pages, scoring out a word here, adding another there, slashing and weaving an alternative clause structure, but still it's only a palimpsest of a second-hand record set down by a Matthew who wasn't there. There is only one use for words in the face of death—to scream a conjuring that tears and turns.

And when he had spoken thus, he cried out with a loud voice, | Eleazar, come forth!

An invocation that refuses absence, swears the identity of word and flesh in a name, a plea.

And at once a great cry was heard | from the tomb.

I have woken to my own roar in the madhouse, a cry made at midnight.

And going in where the youth was, Joshua stretched forth his reach, seized his hand and raised him. And he who was dead came forth, bound hand and foot with | graveclothes, his face wound round with a napkin.
    Loose him! Joshua said to them. Let him go!

As they unbuckled the straitjacket, all I saw was his gaze.

And the youth, looking upon Joshua, loved him, began to beg that he might be with him. And going out of the tomb they came into the house of the youth, for he was rich. And Joshua told him what to do, that after six days, in the evening, the youth should come to him, wearing a linen cloth over his naked body.

A Memorial of Her

9

And it was six days before the Passover when Joshua came to Bethany, where the young man lived who had been dead. And many of those who came with Mary and had seen the things which Joshua did now trusted in him, but some went their ways to the Select, told them what things he had done.

And a certain woman named Martha welcomed him into her house, the house of Simeon of Kerioth, the potter, one of the Select, who desired that he would eat with him. And Joshua went into his house, sat down to meat. There they made him a supper, and Martha served, and the beloved student who he raised from the dead was one of those who sat at the table with him. And many people of the Judaeans therefore knew that he was there, and they came not for Joshua's sake only, but that they might also see the young man whom he had raised from the dead.

And he had a sister called Mary also, who was a delinquent, who sat at Joshua's feet, and heard his word. Yet no man said, What do you seek? or, Why do you talk with her?

Let Mary go forth from among us, Simon the Rock said to them, for women are not worthy of the life.

Behold, said Joshua, I shall lead her, that I may make her male, in order that she also may become a living inspiration like you men. For every woman who makes herself male shall enter into the realm of Zion.

Really? said Mary. If I *make myself male*, then I'm worthy?

She clinked her cutlery down on her plate, turned to him with folded arms. For a second, I thought to interject some hand-waving that he meant *masculine*: assertive, empowered. I looked at her face and thought better of it. To her right, my left, at the foot of the table, Joshua wore no expression, an enigma.

The same is true, he said, for every man who *makes himself female.*

A marked look toward me, a cool gaze on Simon. As the Rock reddened, it wasn't hard to guess whose gruff words Joshua was echoing, and why.

Then Mary took an alabaster box of a pound of ointment of spikenard, very costly. She stood at Joshua's feet behind him weeping, and began to wash his feet with tears, to wipe them with the hairs of her head. She kissed his feet, anointed them with the ointment, and the house was filled with the odour of the ointment. But when one of his students saw it, he had indignation.

Then said the Judaean, the son of Simeon of Kerioth, who was to betray him, To what purpose is this waste? Why was this ointment not sold for three hundred denarii, and given to the poor?

This he said not because he was a thief, and had the bag, carrying what was put therein, but because he cared for the poor.

When Joshua understood it, he said, Why do you trouble the woman? For she has wrought a good work upon me. For you have the poor with you always, but you will not always have me. Let her alone. She has kept this for the day of my burying, and in so far as she has poured this ointment on my body, she did it for my burial. For sure, I tell you, wherever this gospel shall be preached in the whole world, this also shall be told there, what this woman has done, for a memorial of her.

10

But Martha was cumbered about much serving, and came to him.

Teacher, she said, do you not care that my sister has left me to serve alone? Bid her that she help me then.

Martha, Martha, Joshua answered her, you are full of cares and troubled over many things.

But one thing is needed, and Mary has chosen that good part, which shall not be taken away from her.

Still, when he who had invited him saw this, he spoke within himself.

This man, he said, if he were a prophet, would have known who and what manner of woman this is that touches him, for she is a delinquent.

He didn't have to speak his thoughts out loud for me to read between the lines of his polite conversation at the dinner table, the senator's gaze turned cold not on his bipolar faggot son but on his slut of a daughter for a change, while his chat with our... unorthodox therapist remained banal, empty as all etiquette. *R.D. Laing, indeed? I'm not familiar with him.* And so on. As Joshua talked of primal screams, the ontological insecurity of existing in the world for others, the validity of a patient's self-description as being dead, I could see my father thinking quackery and hogwash. As Mary's hand rested on Joshua's arm, while she talked of addiction to one drug cured in a single night with another, I could see him bristle with suspicion, knew he was imagining acid-fuelled orgies before pagan idols.

Silent, I sawed a chunk of fillet mignon off with my steak knife.

Simeon, Joshua said to him then, I have something to say to you.

Rabbi? he said. Say on.

There was a certain creditor who had two debtors, one owing five hundred denarii, and the other fifty. But when they had nothing to pay, he simply forgave them both. Tell me then, which of them would love him most?

I suppose, said Simeon, he to whom most was forgiven.

You judge right, said Joshua.

He paused to reach for his wine as my father did the same, the space between them, from the head of the table to the foot of it, filled less with centrepiece and platters, condiments and decanters, than with the clink and scrape of my silverware on china, as I was all too well aware of. Martha set the replenished water jug on the table and retook her seat, spread her napkin on her lap, ever the surrogate mother. Mary reached for the water, filed her own glass, then Joshua's.

And he turned to the woman, said to Simeon, You see this woman? I entered into your house, and you gave me no water for my feet; but she has washed my feet with tears, and wiped them with the hairs of her head. You gave me no kiss; but since the time I came in this woman has not ceased to kiss my feet. You did not anoint my head with ointment; but this woman has anointed my feet with ointment. So I say to you, her delinquencies, which are many, are forgiven, for she loved much. But he to whom little is forgiven, the same loves little.

Your trust has saved you, he said to the woman then. Go in peace.

And those who sat at meat with him began to say to themselves, Who is this who forgives delinquency also?

It's not for you or I, said my father, to condemn or acquit, only for he who will judge all.

The everyman, said Joshua.

Posterity, I thought.

11

And he began to speak to them by parables:

For sure, I tell you, he said, he who does not enter into the sheepfold by the door but climbs up some other way, the same is a thief and a robber, but he who enters in by the door is the shepherd of the sheep. The porter opens to him, and the sheep hear his voice as he calls his own by name and leads them out. And when he puts forth his own sheep, he goes before them, and the sheep walk with him for they know his voice. They will not walk with a stranger though, but will flee from him, for they do not know the voice of strangers.

———————

Behind him on the wall, from a small ellipse of sepia heritage, the top-hatted, mutton-chopped visage of my father's grandfather, great patriarch of the Iscariot family, industrialist born into poverty in provincial Kerioth, pulled up by his bootstraps to prosperity and prestige, to parliament itself as Whig MP for Bethphage and Bethany, gazed out over the scene: the deep crimson and gold fleur-de-lis wallpaper running round the dining room above the dado rail and wainscoting; the table fussy with manners made solid in forks for oyster, salad and dessert, knives for butter, fish and meat; the crimson curtains framing my father at the head of the table; Joshua facing him from the foot; Mary to Joshua's left, wiping a splash of water from the outside of his glass; myself across from Mary; some dozen Galileans sitting awkward in their seats between their teacher and their host; Martha to my father's right, where my mother once sat; the chair to his left, empty as always.

I held out my water glass in response to Mary's gestured offer, felt my cheeks flush with heat as the bandage on my wrist slid out from under sleeve.

———————

And the thief comes for nothing but to steal, said Joshua, to kill and to destroy. And he who is a hireling and not the shepherd, to whom those sheep are not his own... he sees the wolf coming, leaves the sheep and flees, and the wolf catches them, scatters the sheep. The hireling flees because he is an hireling and does not care for the sheep.

This parable spoke Joshua to them.

———————

I sat my glass down, slunk my hands under the table to tug my cuff back into place.

———————

Then Joshua said to them, For sure, I tell you, I am the door of the sheep. All who ever came before me were thieves and robbers, but the sheep did not hear them. I am the door. If any man enter in by me, he shall be saved, and shall go in and out, and find pasture. I am the good shepherd, and know my sheep, and am known by mine. As the father knows me, even so I know the father, and I lay down my life for the sheep. The good shepherd gives his life for the sheep.

***

And those of us, my father flared, who serve in the Sanhedrin, here in Jerusalem, with Pilate breathing down our necks, we're mere hirelings? While you dance naked in the quiet wilds of Jordan, Galilee, wherever, preaching revolution of the soul, we're not risking our lives every day? No, *you're* the good shepherd of the Jews?

***

And other sheep I have, said Joshua, which are not of this fold; them also I must bring, and they shall hear my voice, and there shall be one fold, and one shepherd.

12

On the morrow, when the students drew close to Jerusalem and arrived at Bethphage and Bethany, at the mount of Olives, then Joshua sent two students.

Go into the village over against you, he said, and at once you shall find an ass tied, and with her a colt no one has ever ridden. Loose the colt, and bring it to me. And if any man says anything to you, you shall say, The teacher has need of it. And at once he will send it.

All this was done that it might be fulfilled as was spoken by the prophet, saying, *You, tell the daughter of Sion: Behold, your king comes to you, sitting meekly upon an ass, a colt, an ass's foal.* At first his students did not understand these sayings, but when Joshua was honoured they remembered that these things were written of him, that they had done these things for him.

I stood out on the porch of peeling white paint and spring-green ivy, balanced Matthew's leatherbound journal on the balustrade and flicked to a clean page, Thomas and him leaning in as I sketched out the road to Bethphage—right fork down to the creek, across the covered bridge, and just follow this dirt track here. The scent of magnolias filled the morning air as they headed off, Matthew closing the journal flap, winding the leather cord around it, slipping it into his satchel. We could've sent a boy, I'd said, but Joshua wouldn't hear of it.

So the students went their way, and found the colt in a place where two roads met, out in the street, tied by a doorway. But as they were loosing the colt, its owners said, Why do you loose the colt?

They spoke just as Joshua had directed though, and the owners let them go.

And they brought the colt to Joshua, draped their garments over it, and he sat upon it. And a great mob spread their garments on the road, while others cut down branches from the trees, scattered them upon the road. So those who were with him when he called the young man from his grave, raised him from the dead, bore record—for this reason the people also greeted him, because they heard that he had done this miracle.

At times I felt as many eyes on me leading the colt as on him riding it. I glanced back once or twice, saw James the Just and Simon the Rock at the head of his students, his two generals, the latter watching with a face of Galilean stone.

Two futures, Joshua had told me as we sat on the porch swing the evening before. Right now, he said, you see only one pathway in Æternity. All you see is an unending Empire that could be the realm of the everyman, a prison of black iron that could be a garden of palm trees.

Could be, I'd said. Is *could be* worth the risk?

I... don't know.

And when he was come near, Joshua beheld the city, and wept over it, saying, If you had known, even you, at least in this your day, the things which belong to your peace! But now they're hidden from your eyes. For the days shall come upon you that your enemies shall dig a trench encircling you, besieging you on every side. And they shall lay you flat to the ground and your children within you. They shall not leave one stone in you upon another, because you did not know the time of your visitation.

Dried Up From the Roots

13

When they were come from Bethany, he was hungry. And seeing afar off a fig tree with leaves, he approached, if by chance he might find anything upon it, but when he came to it, he found nothing but leaves, for the time of figs was not yet.

And Joshua said to it, May no man eat fruit from you hereafter for ever.

And his students heard it.

And we went on, following a road that wound downhill through groves of olives, and beyond them graves of kings. Apple trees and topiaries and beyond them marble crypts watched over by angel statues in dove wings and drapery. Grass parkland of students playing frisbee and beyond them mausoleum follies in Mock Gothic. And the crowd lay down robes of linen and cotton, silk and satin. They whirled off hempen cloaks and army greatcoats, flourished ankle-length furs and quilted anoraks. So, where the dust of that time and place should have been kicked up under my feet and the foal's hooves, we trod our way down to Jerusalem over the garments of two millennia's worth of adoration.

And when he was come near, even now at the descent of the Mount of Olives, the mobs that went before and after began to rejoice, celebrating the sublime with a loud voice for all the mighty works that they had seen.

Hosanna to the son of David! they cried out. Blessed is he who comes in the name of the Worker! Blessed be the realm of our father David, which comes in the name of the Worker! Hosanna in the highest!

Did ye ken yer wee brother was royalty? said Nathaniel to James. Yer mother must be right proud.

James just laughed. Aye, well, he said, he's no the first setukhi and he'll no be the last. Away and ask your own mother; you be sure yer a son of Abraham yerself, before ye bother about him being a son of David.

As the Peace March entered the city gates to streets lined with crowds as crammed and excited as for a queen's silver jubilee, waving hats and banners, I tried to see us all in a world without kirks. Couldn't.

———

And when he was come into Jerusalem, the whole city was moved, saying, Who is this?

This is Joshua the Nazirite, said the mob, the prophet of Galilee.

Rabbi, some of the Select from among the mob said to him, rebuke your students.

I tell you, said Joshua, that if these should hold their peace, the very stones would at once cry out.

So the Select said among themselves, Do you perceive how you prevail nothing? Behold, the world has gone after him.

But for all that he had done so many miracles before them, still they did not trust in him, that the saying of Isaiah the prophet might be fulfilled, which he spoke, *Master, who has believed our report? and to whom has the arm of the Worker been revealed?* They could not trust then, because Isaiah said again, *He has blinded their eyes, and hardened their heart; that they should not see with their eyes, nor understand with their heart, and be turned around, and I should heal them.* These things said Isaiah, when he saw his glory, and spoke of him.

And yet, nevertheless, even among the lords there were also many who trusted in him, but who would not proclaim him lest they should be put out of the congregation house by the Select, who loved the praise of men more than the praise of the sublime.

———

14

And Joshua went into the temple, and found in the temple those who sold oxen and sheep and doves, and the changers of money sitting. And when he had looked round about upon all things, he made a scourge of small cords, and he drove them all out of the temple, and the sheep and the oxen, and poured out the changers' money, and overthrew the tables and the seats of those who sold doves, and would not suffer that any man should carry any vessel through the temple, saying, Take these things away. And he taught, saying to them, Is it not written, *My house shall be called of all nations the house of prayer?* But you have made it a den of thieves.

Imagine the oak doors of every kirk and chapel, lover of the sublime, splintering at his axe, shattering to his sledgehammer. Imagine the boot, the shoulder, the smashing open, iron handles cracking into plaster. Imagine racks of Focus On The Family flyers swept from the table in the vestibule, the table itself overturned. Imagine hymnbooks grabbed from hands as he stalks down the aisle, hurled through stained glass windows of warrior angels. Imagine a wooden collection bowl slapped up out of the hands that hold it, scattering coins and notes. Imagine a censer torn from an altar boy's grasp, swung as flail to take down candlesticks and flowers. Imagine a silk stole whipped from the neck of a priest fallen scrabbling backwards, wound around a hand and twisted to a locker-room towel whip. Imagine a congregation in panic, fumbling foxfurs and scarves, wedding hats and fedoras as they stumble into each other, flustered by the riot of queer punks pouring in through the doors, rushing among them as wild dogs, barking obscenity. Imagine pews heaved over. Imagine a Joshua in torn bleached denims and Doc Martens leaping up to grab a golden altarpiece of crucifixion, to heave it with a roar, to topple it finally and forever.

Imagine the man you paint as anodyne angel of the beatific, the banal, standing furious on the altar, unbuttoning fly to work his cock free and let loose a stream of piss on all the chattels of soul merchantry.

And he beheld them and said, Did you never read in the scriptures, *The stone which the builders rejected, the same is become the head of the corner: this is the Worker's doing, and it is marvellous in our eyes? Whoever shall fall upon that stone shall be broken; but whoever it shall fall on, it will grind him to dust.* So I say to you, The realm of the sublime shall be taken from you, given to a nation bringing forth the fruits thereof.

A shudder ran through me as I stood at the back of the cathedral with Mary and Matthew, looking on the wreckage of riot, Simon and Andrew, the Sons of Thunder pacing as lions, still wild-eyed and fierce in stance. Swept up in the moment, I felt the same defiance as fire in my blood. This was what it was for, what it was always leading to: taking back the realm. But standing also in Æternity, I felt that moment flicker between triumph and tragedy, fraught with the potential to establish exactly what it overthrew.

No, do not think for one second, lover of the sublime, that I will let this be a story of your Church's founding. It is a story of its end.

And his students remembered that it was written, *The zeal of your house has eaten me up.*

15

And Joshua said to them, A certain winemaker planted a vineyard, and set a hedge about it, dug a winepress, built a tower, and let it out to vine-growers, and went into a far country. And when the season of the fruit drew near, he sent a runner to the vine-growers, that he might receive from the vine-growers of the fruit of the vineyard. But they caught him and beat him, sent him away empty-handed. Perhaps they did not know him, his master said. So again he sent another runner to them, but they cast stones at him, wounded him in the head, and sent him away shamefully handled. Again he sent another, and him they killed, and many others, beating some, and killing some.

I won't list them all, lover of the sublime, all the messengers sent from the sublime as so many of them thought, sent from the accuser as so many of you thought, forged in the dialectic of souls and sent from nothing, nothing but the sacred inspiration, just as Joshua was before them. I won't list all the heretics sent by history, by humanity, to reclaim the fruit of the realm for the everyman.

I'll give you just one, Peter of Bruys, defrocked preacher of Dauphiné and Provence, who discarded all but these gospels I work with now; who disdained the Church with its bullshit of baptism as empty rite to sanctify an infant's unmade soul, preached no salvation without understanding; who taught that temples were pure vanity, the wealth in them a waste; who called for crosses to be broken and burned, cursed the veneration of an instrument of torture; who denied the sacramental grace of the Eucharist as magic trick; who derided all sacrifices, prayers and alms offered by the faithful living for the faithful dead, bribes of loyalty or coin elicited by the vineyard's keepers to buy loved ones a better afterlife.

Made halfway through these seasons of the Gentiles, at most his was a halfway claim, a move to take back for the everyman a debt half-understood. Still, he was murdered by an angry mob for his arrant heresy, for his audacity in echoing Joshua's simplest sentiments. The share of fruit claimed by this heretic or that all down the centuries of the seasons of the Gentiles is there to read in seven words: I will have mercy and not sacrifice.

So, having yet one son, his well-beloved, said Joshua, he sent him also last to them, saying, They will respect my son.

But when the vine-growers saw the son, they said to themselves, This is the heir. Come, let us kill him, and the inheritance shall be ours. And they took him, killed him, and cast him out of the vineyard.

What shall the master of the vineyard do then? He will come and destroy the vine-growers, will give the vineyard to others, who shall render him the fruits in their seasons.

When the chief priests and the clerks heard it, they said, Æternity forbid.

And the same hour they sought to lay hold on him, but feared the people: for they knew that he had spoken the parable against them. So they left him, and went their way, but they watched him, and sent forth spies, who should feign themselves simply men that they might take hold of his words, so that they might deliver him to the power and authority of the governor.

And when the eventide was come, Joshua went out to Bethany with the twelve, and he lodged there.

16

And in the morning, as they passed by, they saw the fig tree dried up from the roots.

And when the students saw it, they marvelled, saying, How soon is the fig tree withered away!

For sure, I tell you, Joshua answered, if you have trust and doubt not, you shall not only do this which is done to the fig tree, but also if you shall say to this mountain, You, be removed, and be cast into the sea, it shall be done.

And as we walked—just the small group of us today, on foot, all need for grandiose symbolism sated by yesterday's triumphal entry—he kicked a rock too small to even be a stumbling block, glanced back at Simon, and I thought I knew what mountain he was talking of. Jacob and John to either side, the Rock walked with the authority of years as leader as much as student, given trust instead of orders, travelling like the rest of the twelve, setting up and checking in on chapter houses on Joshua's behalf. And now, he'd seen Joshua transfigured on Tabor and been promised the keys of the realm. Under his rough-hewn propriety, I knew there was no real animus, just a Way Things Are, but now there was revelation in his giant's stride.

He's changed, I said quietly to Joshua.

I hoped it meant he could *still* change, and the future with him.

And all things whatsoever you shall ask in prayer, said Joshua, trusting, you shall receive.

And early in the morning, all the people came to him in the temple, for to hear him. And those who had been with him when he called the young man from his grave, and raised him from the dead, had borne witness, so people also came to meet him for this reason, because they heard that he had done this miracle.

A clatter of hobnail boots on marble echoed in the vaulted hush. I turned to see a boy in school uniform staring up at me, past him a bespectacled teacher over by his classmates, oblivious to the loss of a stray.

You were dead, the boy said.

It wasn't a question.

He who trusts in me, Joshua cried out, trusts not in me, but in he who sent me. And he who looks on me sees he who sent me. I am come a light into the world, that anyone who trusts in me should not dwell in darkness. For I have not spoken for myself. Rather the father who sent me gave me a decree, what I should say, what I should speak, and I know that his decree is the life of ages. Whatever I speak therefore, even as the father said to me, so I speak.

And the blind and the lame came to Joshua in the temple, and he healed them. But when the chief priests and clerks saw the wonderful things that he did, and the children crying in the temple, and saying, Hosanna to the son of David, they were sore displeased, and sought how they might destroy him, for they feared him, because all the people were astonished at his teachings.

Do you hear what these say? they said to him.

Aye, said Joshua. Have you never read, *Out of the mouth of babes and sucklings you have perfected praise?*

And in the day time he was teaching in the temple, and at night he went out, and abode in the mount that is called the Mount of Olives, among the tombs, the lamb of the sublime.

The Father Who Sent Me

17

And Joshua said to them all:

For the realm of Zion is as a nobleman travelling into a far country to receive a realm, who called his own slaves and gave them his funds, to each according to his ability, saying, Trade with these till I return. To one he gave five talents, and to another two, and to another one. And at once he took his journey.

But his subjects detested him, so they sent an embassy to say, We will not have this man to rule over us.

I sat in Sunday School, aged twelve and argumentative.

Wikipedia says it's a reference to Herod Archelous, I said.

You can't believe everything in Wikipedia, said the teacher gently.

He went to Rome, I insisted, to get the Emperor to make him king. But he was cruel, so the Pharisees went too, to say they didn't want him.

But it's really about the kingdom of heaven, isn't it? So how can the king be Herod? Just listen.

Meanwhile, he who had received the five talents went and traded with them, and made ten talents for each. And he who had received two made five for each. But he who had received one went and dug in the earth, hid his master's money in a sweat cloth.

After a long time the master of those slaves returned and reckoned with them. So he who had received five talents came and brought the other fifty, saying, Master, you delivered five talents to me. Behold, each talent has made ten more. He who had received two talents also came and said, Master, you delivered two talents to me. Behold, each talent has made five more.

Well done, you good and faithful slaves, said their master. He who is loyal with petty things is loyal also with great things, and he who is unjust with the petty is unjust also with the great. You have been faithful over a few things, so *you* I will make lord over ten cities, and *you* I will make lord over five cities. Enter into the joy of your master.

Then he who had received the one talent came and said, Master, I knew you that you are a hard man, reaping where you have not sown, gathering where you have not scattered. So I was afraid, and went and hid your talent in the earth. Behold, here you have what is yours.

You wicked and lazy slave, said his master, I will judge you by your own words. You knew that I reap where I have not sown, and gather where I have not scattered.

You ought to have put my money to the usurers then, so I would have received my own with interest at my return.

You, he said to those standing there, cast the unprofitable slave into outer darkness. Bind him hand and foot, and take him away, and cast him into outer darkness! There shall be weeping and gnashing of teeth! And take the city from him, and give it to he who has ten.

But master, they said, he has ten cities already!

And as for my enemies who did not want me to reign over them, said the king, bring them here and kill them in my presence! For more shall be given to everyone who has much, so he shall have abundance, but even that which he has shall be taken away from he who has little.

You see? said the teacher. It's about the reward for using what God has given you in his service.

Is not, I sulked.

18

So he taught daily in the temple.

And he told of how at the dawning of the day the unprofitable slave was slain, in the forecourt of the temple of the Worker, and the children of Israel knew not that he was slain. I watched the faces as he told his parable in which the master was no deity but a thinly-veiled Herod, in which the realm of Zion was ruled by a thief who plundered the fields that others worked, a slave-master who set his servants to profit by usury, a loan shark who tortured and dispossessed those who returned what was his without interest, a traitor who gave our cities to Rome, a murderer who had his enemies slaughtered before him. He told of the rich made richer and the poor made poorer, and the broken tenderness of Billie Holiday's lament stretched the veil between aeons so thin I could hear the radio of Occupied Judaea.

For from the days of John the Baptist until now, he said, the realm of Zion is abused, and the abusers conquer it by might. But know this, that if the master of the house had known what hour the thief would come, he would have watched, would not have suffered his house to be broken into.

I looked round the Court of Gentiles for faces of resistance in the crowd, saw only faces of worry on men in black cassocks, faces of fury on men in black shirts.

So the chief priests and the clerks and the elders of the people sought to destroy him, but could not find what they might do, for all the people were very attentive to hear him. But it came to pass, on one of those days, as he taught the people in the temple, preaching his gospel, that the chief priests and the clerks and the elders came upon him.

And when they were come, the chief priests said to Joshua, Rabbi, we know that you are true, and care for no man, for you disregard the person of men, teaching instead the way of the sublime in truth. Is it lawful to give tribute to Caesar, or not? Shall we give, or shall we not give?

But he, knowing their hypocrisy, said, Why do you test me? Bring me a penny, that I may see it.

And they brought it.

Whose is this image and superscription? he said.

Caesar's, they said.

Render to Caesar the things that are Caesar's, said Joshua to the chief priests, what belongs to the sublime give to the sublime, but what is mine give to me.

He flicked the coin back to them, spinning through the air.

Woe to you, clerks and Select, hypocrites! he said, for you pay tithes of mint and anise and cumin, and have discarded the burden of the law—justice, mercy, loyalty. It's these you should have done, not neglected. You blind guides, who strain at a gnat, and swallow a camel.

And Joshua sat over against the treasury, watched how the people cast money into the treasury. And many who were rich cast in much, but there came a certain poor widow, and she threw in two mites, which make a farthing.

He called his students to him.

For sure, I tell you, he said to them, that this poor widow has cast in more than all those who have cast into the treasury. For all those who were avaricious have cast in from their abundance, but she in her penury has cast in all the living that she had.

19

The clerks therefore said to him, Who are you?

Then Joshua spoke again to them, saying, Even the same that I said to you from the beginning. I am the light of the world. He who walks with me shall not walk in darkness, but shall have the light of life.

You bear record of yourself, the clerks said to him then. Your record is not true.

Imagine the YouTube footage linked on Twitter with an #OccupyHeaven hashtag. In the background: a line of students cross-legged on the ground in the Court of the Gentiles, arms linked; a crowd surrounding. A shaky cameraphone shows a phalanx of centurions in Kevlar, insectoid gasmask faces, guns for rubber bullets and tear gas canister. One fat fuck of a pig strolls down the line, pepper spraying teens: tears flow. In the foreground: Joshua arguing with the clerks, spokesman of the movement undaunted by their outrage. Who is he? Who does he think he is?

———

If I bear witness of myself, said Joshua, my witness is not true? But he who sent me is true, and I speak to the world those things I have heard from him. You must not have his word abiding in you, for the one he has sent, you do not trust him.

———

He was his father's son, the *son of man* as the idiom of the day would have it. Man as martyr or mason, as the voice of a wild man crying inspiration in the wilderness, or as the vision of a secret self testing inspiration in the desert. If you can't believe he was sent by humanity, history itself demanding that someone, anyone, *everyone* stand against the Empire, I pity your lack of trust in the only divinity there is. Do you really think so little of humanity that you can't imagine it fathering wisdom, justice and mercy? Fathering truth?

———

Also, it is written in your law, that the testimony of two men is true. Well, there is another who bears witness of me and I know that the testimony he witnesses of me is true. You sent to John, and he testified to the truth. The father himself, who has sent me, has borne witness of me. I am one who bears witness of myself, and the father who sent me bears witness of me.

———

You style him European on your crucifixes, lover of the sublime, long wavy locks and dainty beard. You might as well picture the Guy Fawkes mask of Anonymous. It would be closer to the truth of the everyman.

But I have greater witness than that of John, for the works which the father has given me to finish, the same works that I do, also bear witness of me, that the father has sent me. For sure, I tell you, the son can do nothing of himself, but what he sees the father do. When you have lifted up the everyman then you shall know that I am he, and that I do nothing of myself. I only speak these things as my father has taught me.

But I take no testimony from man, said Joshua to them. I say these things only that you might be saved. But now I go my way to him that sent me, and none of you ask me, Where do you go? Even if I bear record of myself, my record is still true; for I know where I came from and where I go, but you cannot tell where I come from, where I go.

You don't have the first idea.

20

Where then? the elders said to him. Where is this father of yours?

Search the scriptures, said Joshua, for in them you think you have the life of ages, and it is those who testify of me. If you trusted Moses, you would trust me, for he wrote of me. But if you do not trust his writings, even Moses, how will you trust my words? How can you trust, you who welcome honour from one another, but do not seek the honour that comes only from the sublime?

Maybe you'll see it yet, lover of the sublime, an interview on BBC News 24, CNN or Fox News, footage boxed and caption-cut to soundbites scrolling headlines of the Empire's war in Gaul, pundits and presidential candidates with fascii pins on their lapels just like the anchors haggling for the realm, and all the while that smile of the everyman, not serene but sly.

So I say to you that you shall die in your delinquency, he said, for if you do not trust that I am he, you shall die in your delinquency. I go my way, and you shall seek me, and shall die in your delinquency. Where I go, you cannot come.

Will he kill himself? said the elders then because he said, Where I go, you cannot come.

Maybe you'll see, as I have seen, Saint Paul the infiltrating agent of Empire, sent to harry Joshua's students, standing guard over the clothes of witnesses as Stephen was stoned, arriving in Damascus as a blind man seeking a healing from Ananias, carrying on his mission of destruction under guise of conversion, cover so deep you wonder if even he believes his own rhetoric. Maybe you'll see him spinning the "Mercy Not Sacrifice" slogans to a nodding Geraldo, fresh from his debriefing by King Felix in a Wall Street board room, competing for ratings with Beck and Limbaugh, ranting against adulterers and fornicators, sorcerers and dogs, celebrating salvations of blood ablution.

Maybe you'll see some unfamiliar face on the screen, some nobody with no grand tale of a miraculous enlightenment in being struck blind, no epistles to his name, just his integrity, calling out the Empire's snake in the grass for the poison in his every word, and you'll recognise the everyman come from nothing, from the void of the beyond.

You are from beneath, said Joshua. I am from above. You are of this world; I am not of this world. You judge after the flesh. I judge no man. And you will not come to me that you might have life. If another should come in his own name, *him* you would welcome. But I am come in my father's name, and you do not welcome me. If you had known me, you should have known my father also. But you have neither heard his voice at any time, nor seen his shape. You neither know me, nor my father. I know you though, that you have no love of the sublime in you. I have much to say and to judge of you.

Maybe one day you'll switch on the news, lover of the sublime, and see his face everywhere, his story everywhere, see his father in him, him in his father, all history's quick and dead.

Do not think I will accuse you to the father though, Joshua said to them. There is another who accuses you.

These words spoke Joshua in the treasury as he taught in the temple, and no man laid hands on him, for his hour was not yet come.

21

While the clerks were gathered together, Joshua asked them, What do you think of the anointed? Whose son is he?

———

He brushed the lapel of his white linen three-piece, sharp heyday Hollywood vision of a Southern civil rights attorney. Up on the stand, four witnesses for the prosecution cleared their throats, began, a barbershop quartet in vests of solemn black instead of candy-stripes, visors instead of boaters, sleeve garters.

———

The son of David, they said, being as was supposed the son of Joseph, son of Heli, son of Matthat, son of Levi, son of Melchi, son of Janna...

———

The voices echoed round the courtroom, one voice carrying on...

———

...son of Joseph, son of Mattathias, son of Amos, son of Naum, son of Esli, son of Nagge, son of Maath...

———

... as another split off, took a different track...

———

... son of Mattathias, son of | son of Joanna, son of Rhesa, son
Semei, son of Joseph, son of Juda, | of Zorobabel...

... the third another again...

... son of Salathiel, son of Neri, | of Cosam, son of Elmodam, son
son of Melchi, son of Addi, son | of Er...

... as too the fourth...

... son of Jose, son of Eliezer, son | of Levi, son of Simeon, son of
of Jorim, son of Matthat, son | Juda...

... monotone voices battling the clackety-clack of typewriter, stenograph,
cash register and abacus...

... son of Joseph, son of Jonan, | of Menan, son of Mattatha, son
son of Eliakim, son of Melea, son | of Nathan...

... a cacophony of lineage...

... son of David, son of Jesse, son | Salmon, son of Naasson, son of
of Obed, son of Booz, son of | Aminadab...

... this voice rising out of the rhythms, that one falling...

... son of Aram, son of Esrom, | of Jacob, son of Isaac, son of
son of Phares, son of Juda, son | Abraham...

... the whole droning fugue of heritage simplifying again...

... son of Thara, son of Nachor, | of Phalec, son of Heber, son of
son of Saruch, son of Ragau, son | Sala...

... as one refrain remerged with another...

... son of Cainan, son of Arphaxad, | Lamech, son of Methuselah, son
son of Shem, son of Noah, son of | of Enoch...

... until all four were intoning the same patriarchal origins...

... son of Jared, son of Mahaleleel, | of Seth, son of Adam...
son of Cainan, son of Enos, son |

... son of Adam... son of Adam... son of Adam... the echo faded.

Who was, said Joshua, the son of | the sublime.

Chaos erupted from the public gallery, tumult over the gavel-crack like a firework and *Order! Order!* of the magistrate in his wig and robes. Women in bonnets fainted. Apes unleashed by creationists screeched in mockery of evolution, threw shit. Half the crowd heard him claiming divinity for himself, casting himself as not just David's heir but the deity's. Half heard him dismissing it as irrelevance, inherited by all, casting David as only another name in a lineage stripped back to the first human, any son of man a son of the sublime. None heard the truth which was both and neither.

How can the clerks say that the anointed is the son of David? said Joshua. And David himself said by the sacred inspiration, in the book of Psalms, *The Worker said to my master, You, sit on my right hand, till I make your enemies your footstool.* David himself called him master then, so from where is he then called his son?

A clerk raised a bible, thumped it down on his desk to flick through pages. He held it up, splayed open, finger poking at black ink proof.
 Micah or Matthew? said Joshua.

22

But the elders answered, Do we not say well that you are a Samaritan and have a daimon?

And in the public gallery they rose, bespectacled men in toupées, corpulent as middle managers fed on bonuses, gaunt as corporate asset strippers starved of humanity, in pinstripe suits, checked slacks for the golf course, gold-buttoned blazers for the marina. I saw my father among them, harried by a business partner I remembered from youth, a partner who remembered me, pointed me out with an accusing finger as he asked, I imagine, what sort of son Simeon of Kerioth had raised to follow this daimon-driven mongrel.

———

I have no daimon, Joshua answered. I only honour my father and you insult me. And he who insults the son insults the father who sent him. But he who hears my word, trusts in he who sent me—he has the life of ages, shall not come into condemnation, but is passed from death to life.

———

Trust, he'd said to me before I left for Bethany.

How can you ask me to have faith? I said. After what you've shown me?

Not faith, he said. Faith is infidelity to wisdom, adultery of the soul. Trust isn't blind.

———

For sure, I tell you, he said, he who can glean the meaning of these words shall not taste of death. No, but the hour is coming when the dead shall hear the voice of the scion of the sublime. Do not marvel at this, but the hour is coming, now is, when all who are in the graves shall hear my voice. And those who hear shall live and shall come forth—those who have done good to the revival of life, and those who have done ill to the revival of judgement.

———

He'd tossed an orange for me to catch.

The fruit of every tree in Eden, he'd said. Wisdom and the life of ages.

———

Now we know you have a daimon, said the elders. Abraham is dead, the prophets are dead, yet you say, If a man keep my teachings, he shall never taste of death. Who do you imagine yourself? Are you greater even than our father Abraham, who is dead?

―――――――

You just have to understand that you're already dead, he'd said.

―――――――

If I honour myself, Joshua answered, my honour is nothing. There is another who seeks and judges; it is my father who honours me, of whom you say that he is your deity though you have never known him. Well, I know him and keep his teachings. I know him, and if I were to say I do not, then I should be a liar like you.

―――――――

Rotary Club officials, presidents and treasurers and secretaries, a scout leader with belly bulging over shorts. Elders rotting in their graves already. Among them, my father argued, gestured at me, at Joshua.

―――――――

Adam came into being from an immense power, an immense wealth, and yet he was not worthy of you, for if he had been worthy, he would not have tasted death. He who has ears, let him hear: *there is no life in you.*

―――――――

He was a Samaritan with a daimon, they shouted, a Jew with Commie sympathies, an atheist with a grudge.

―――――――

I desire no honour from men. I seek no glory for myself. But I tell you, your father Abraham rejoiced to see my day, and he saw it, and was glad. You are not yet fifty years old, the elders said, and have you seen Abraham?

For sure, I tell you, Joshua said, before Abraham was, I am.

23

As he spoke these words, many believed in him.

If you continue in my word, said Joshua to those who believed, then you are indeed my students, and you shall know the truth, and the truth shall make you free.

We are Abraham's seed, they answered, and were never in bondage to any man.

Thirty days into my testing in the wilderness now, I break for coffee and a cigarette. An #OccupyHeaven hashtag on Twitter says I'll get a break when this is all over. I click through to an article, set the embedded report to play.

Close-up on an interviewer, all sympathy and sincerity, furrowed brow and hand to chin, white hair and teeth of a talk show host:

So how can you say, you shall be | made free?

Cut to wide shot as the interviewer leans forward across the desk, pointing the sheaf of prompt cards in his hand toward Joshua on the sofa. Beyond the potted palm that guards the guest, the backdrop is skyline at night, stylised cityscape silhouette stamped with windows white as the moon.

For sure, I tell you, said Joshua, though you do not know it, anyone who is delinquent is the slave of delinquency.

Close-up on Joshua as his hand seems to grasp a thought in the air, to judge its weight, a man looking for just the right phrasing

---

Which of you, he says, having a slave ploughing or feeding livestock, would say to him by and by, when he is come from the field, Go and sit down to your food?

The host throws his hands up, mugging the zaniness of such a notion. The audience laughs as a studio assistant walks the wasteland between them and the TV cameras, holding up a LAUGH sign. I don't need the camera turned to see it, lover of the sublime, if you're wondering, not since Bethany.

Which of you would not rather say to him, Make ready wherewith I may dine, and dress yourself to serve me, till I have eaten and drunk; then you may eat and drink... afterward?

Joshua flicks his hand in mock hauteur.

And does he honour that slave because he did... the things that were commanded him?

Eyebrows raised in incredulity: Get real.

I think not.

The audience laughs again, eating it up. Cut to close-up on Joshua as he turns, finds the camera that's on him, stares into the lens, at you the viewer.

So likewise you, when you've done all that you are ordered, say, [a caricature of self-abasement taken to the grotesque:] We are unprofitable slaves; we have only done the duties we had to.

The audience is roaring at his wacky schtick before the meaning even sinks in; the studio assistant has the LAUGH sign up after all.

But while the slave will not dwell in the house forever, the son abides. So if the son shall make you free, you shall be free indeed.

The interviewer frowns confusion, wariness...

And some of the Select who were with him heard these words, said, Are we also blind?

If you were blind you would have no fault, said Joshua, but now you say, We see! so your fault remains. You are of your father and will do the lusts of your father. I know that you are Abraham's seed; but you seek to kill me because my word has no place in you. I speak what I have seen with my father, and you do what you have seen with your father.

... suspicion, hostility.

Abraham is our father, they said.

24

If you were Abraham's children, Joshua said, you would do the works of Abraham. But now you seek to kill me, a man who tells you the truth I've heard from the sublime. If I tell the truth, why do you not trust me? You do not trust me *because* I tell you the truth. Abraham did not do this; you do the deeds of your father.

We are not born of fornication, they said. We have one father, even the sublime.

———

On another channel, an arts review programme cuts to footage from the Panorama documentary: Joshua's clash with the Capernaum Baptists Church, the now-infamous scene outside the women's shelter where he stands against a mob of God Hates Sluts banner-wavers, thrusts a rock into their pastor's hand, dares him to take his best shot. The father's face is pure hate as Joshua steps back, arms spread wide: Throw it!

———

If the sublime were your father, said Joshua, you would love me, for I sprung forth and came from the sublime. I did not come of myself, but was sent by him.

———

As his voice on the documentary carries on, I remember a reverend father in the seminary citing the Church Fathers, a whole heritage of fathers begun with a Rock and a Roman infiltrator, outraged that, yes, I'm seriously suggesting that our saviour casting the sublime as a father was not just a metaphor but a bad metaphor. Not as bad as casting it king or judge, but in the same territory: abrogated autonomy; empathy and ethics sacrificed to might as right; an idol of authority modelled on human privilege and power. I couldn't imagine his æternal father as anything more than a figurative device. Worker and master, all one big metaphor.

I projected modern atheism on a culture without the notion, said the reverend father. It was unthinkable.

Are you sure? I said. The Sadducees rejected the mortality of the soul. The Gnostics rejected the creator as demiurge. Atheism's not that big a leap.

———

Why do you not understand my speech? Because you cannot hear my word? He who is of the sublime hears the words of the sublime. If you do not hear them, then you are not of the sublime. Which of you convicts me of delinquency? You do not know what you worship, in whom you trust. When he speaks a fiction, he speaks in his native tongue, for he is a fiction, and the father of fiction.

———

On the wall of scripture, I take my red pen to the last section of *Bethany*, edit *lies* to *fiction*, folding father and accuser into one another. One man's atheism, lover of the sublime. is another man's anarchist metaphysics.

———

Then the Select gathered round him, said, How long will you make us doubt? If you are the anointed, tell us plainly.

I told you, Joshua answered, and you did not trust. The works that I do in my father's name, they bear witness of me. But you do not trust because you are not of my sheep, as I said to you. My sheep hear my voice, and I know them, and they walk with me. I give the life of ages to them, and they shall never perish, neither shall any man pluck them from my hand. My father, who gave me them, is greater than all, and no man is able to pluck them from my father's hand. Take heed; he who hates me hates my father also. I and my father are one.

———

The everyman.

———

And the common people heard him gladly.

Gethsemane

Destroy This Temple

1

The same day there came to him those Righteous who say there is no resurrection.

Rabbi, they asked him, Moses said, If a man die without children, his brother must marry his wife and raise up seed to his brother. Now suppose there were seven brethren, and the first took a wife, and died leaving no seed. And the second took her, and also died leaving no seed. And the third likewise. All seven married her, indeed, and died leaving no seed. Finally, the woman herself also died. So... in this resurrection, when they rise, whose wife shall she be out of them all? For all seven had her as their wife.

You err, said Joshua, understanding neither scriptures nor the power of the sublime.

Question Time on BBC1: a pop scientist and a politicking journalist, two Righteous sat to one side of the dicky-bowed host, Joshua and a silently-fuming bishop to the other. Superstitious mumbo jumbo, they scoffed, with no place in the 20th century. Memes, sneered one. Pipe dreams, sneered the other. Who gets the widow in the afterlife, eh?

Just tell them, I thought. Tell them they're halfway there already. Tell them that if they only knew to read prophecy as poetry though, they'd hear the beat of the sublime in the bongo drums of Richard Feynman on a New Mexico mesa, know not to squander logic on a song.

For a second I thought he might, and I watched James and Simon, sat on the couch, studied them with eyes keen for trust and denial, keen for a cusp, a glimpse of a future where James remained sitting, weighing inspiration with impartiality, as Simon walked out in disgust.

Joshua shook his head.

The sons of this aeon marry, he said, and are given in marriage. But the sons of the revival, the scions of the sublime, those who are deemed worthy to attain revival from the dead, those who will achieve that aeon, they neither marry nor are given in marriage, but are as the messengers of the sublime in Æternity. He who has ears, let him hear.

In the Bethany commune that our father's house had become, Mary shooed a hugger-mugger of children from in front of the black-and-white set, twisted the hoop aerial round this way and that to tame the hiss. I watched from the doorway to the hall, wondering if in *any* aeon even the rationalists would understand Joshua's philosophy, his existential soul alchemy of Steiner and Sartre, Laing and Leary. Onscreen, the host pressed him to address the question.

As for the dead, said Joshua, that they rise, have you not read in the book of Moses how the sublime spoke to him from the bush, saying, I am the divinity of Abraham, the divinity of Isaac, the divinity of Jacob? He is not some deity of the dead, but of the living, for all his are alive. I am come that they might have life, that they might have it more richly.

I thought of endless death glimpsed in an acid vision, in a garden, a grave. Of Joshua's hand, his haloed face, my joy in rebirth.

Look upon the living one so long as you live, he said, that you may not die longing to see him, unable to see.

And when the mob heard this, they were astonished at his teaching.

Rabbi, certain of the scribes said, you have spoken well.

And they could not take hold of his words before the people, and they marvelled at his answer, and held their peace.

2

But when the Select heard that he had quieted the Righteous, they gathered together. And one of them, who was a lawyer, heard them reasoning and judged that Joshua had answered well. So he came to ask a question, testing him.

A cocktail party in Jerusalem's Hôtel de Ville, chatter echoing hollow under painted ceilings and chandeliers of the Salle des Fêtes, all watched over by grand posters of Herod Pétain and Herr Chancellor Tiberius. My father scowling at them as we enter, Mary on his arm, myself behind. Joshua beside me, awkward in the white tux borrowed from his young Judaean prince as David once borrowed Jonathan's regal finery. The young barrister sidles up to him through the crowd, champagne flute in hand.

Rabbi, he said, which is the prime decree in all the law? What must I do to inherit the life of ages?

What is written in the law? said Joshua. How do you read it?

Hear, O Israel! said the lawyer, the Worker, our spirit, is one master.

A clink of glasses as they drink to one master, to unity… sovereignty. I note the pause in the lawyer's toast, the injection of solemnity understated to subtext: the word emancipation hangs in the air, unspoken oath.

With all your heart and mind, said Joshua, all your intellect and muscle, love the Worker, your spirit. This is the first and greatest of decrees. And the second is equivalent: You shall love your neighbour as yourself. There is no decree greater than these. All the law and the prophets rest on these two decrees.

———

They drink to liberty, fraternity, equality. Heads turn, not a few with pursed lips, but enough with the slightest nod, the casual tilt of a glass raised for a coincidental sip.

———

Well, rabbi, said the lawyer, you have said the truth, for there is one deity only, none but him. And to love him with all the heart, with all the mind, with all the strength, and to love his neighbour as himself, is more than all the sacrifices, all the offerings burnt in their entirety.

And Joshua saw he answered wisely.

You are not far from the realm of the sublime, he said.

———

Even in the shadow of the Empire, I think, even here. I take a champagne flute from a passing waiter.

———

The lawyer wished to justify himself though.

But, he said, who is my neighbour?

A certain craftsman went down from Jerusalem to Jericho, said Joshua, and ran into thieves who stripped and beat him; and having set upon him, off they went, leaving the man half dead. By chance a certain priest came down that road, but when he saw the man, he passed by on the other side. Likewise a Levite, having reached this place, having glanced upon the man, he also passed by on the other side. But a certain Samaritan on a journey came to where he lay and, when he saw the man, felt sympathy, came to wrap his wounds, pouring on olive oil and wine. He set the man on his own beast of burden, brought him to an inn, and tended to him. And on the morrow when he left, he took out two denarii, gave them to the host.

Take care of him, he said, and if you spend more, anything whatever, I'll repay you when I return.

Now, which of these three, do you think, was neighbour to he who ran into the thieves?

He who showed mercy on him, said the lawyer.

Then said Joshua to him, Go, and do you likewise.

3

Then the Select took up stones again to stone him.

Jump-cut to the Court of Gentiles and a counter-protest of the Select in dog-collars of Protestant ministers, rosaries of Catholic priests, pectoral crosses of Anglicans, spitting fury from Solomon's Porch, while police in black and fluorescent yellow form a wall of riot shields in front, with more troops pushing in now to close off the Sheep Gate, kettle the marchers. From within the ranks of hundreds in Anonymous masks though, a projector renders the temple itself screen for a statement too offensive to be tolerated. From the ranks of the Select, rotten eggs fly through the air at that same bearded visage scaled up to monumental.

I squeeze through the crowd, aiming for Mary, zeroing in by the same scarlet hoody that disguises her, just as my purple hoody disguises me. A reach through the press of bodies gets fingertips to a shoulder.

Have you seen him? I shout.

Every one of us wears the mask. Any one of us could be him.

One Joshua shouts into a loudspeaker from the mob. Under the crackling reverb of distortion, there's a hint of Galilean accent, maybe, but it could be most any of the others as easily as it could be him, only the physique to narrow it down. Thomas?

I have shown you many good works from my father, Joshua said. For which of these do you stone me?

We do not stone you for good works, they said, but for blasphemy, because you are a man and make yourself the sublime.

Pixels flicker like cards held by a crowd in a stadium to form that face out of a thousand, flicker again to blackness and a message in white: THE REALM IS TO HAND.

———

Is it not written in your law, said Joshua, *I said, you are sublime?* For sure, he to whom the word of the sublime came called them sublime. If the scripture cannot be broken, how can you say then, of he whom the father has hallowed and sent into the world, that I blaspheme because I said, I am the scion of the sublime?

———

Flicker again through a montage of protests, marches, camps, to another message: THE EVERYMAN COMES.

———

If the works I do are not of my father, do not trust me. But if they are... if you will not trust me, trust the works, that you may know and trust that the father is in me, and I in him. After the glorious one has sent me against the nations that have plundered you—for whoever touches you touches the apple of his eye—I will surely raise my hand against them so that their slaves will plunder them.

———

Colosseum. Legions. Sieges. Sackings. THE EMPIRE NEVER ENDED

———

What sign will you show to us, the Select said to him then, seeing that you do these works?

———

Pogroms. Crusades. Inquisitions. Slavery. THE EMPIRE MUST END NOW.

Destroy this temple, Joshua said, and on the third day I will raise it up.

This temple was forty-six years in the building, they said, and you will raise it in three days?

I will return to Jerusalem with mercy, he said, and there my house will be rebuilt.

But he spoke of the temple of his body. So when he was risen from the dead, his students remembered that he had said this, and they believed the scripture, and the word which Joshua had said.

And the measuring line will be stretched out over Jerusalem.

Holocaust. I WILL HAVE MERCY AND NOT SACRIFICE.

4

Then Joshua went out, departing from the temple, and his students came to him, to show him the buildings of the temple, some speaking of this second temple, how it was adorned with goodly stones and gifts. Woe to you, you blind guides, he said, who say that an oath on the temple is nothing, but an oath on the gold of the temple is a debt! Who say that an oath on the altar is nothing, but an oath on the gift that sits upon it is guilt. You fools and blind! Which is greater, the gold or the temple that sanctifies the gold? Which is greater, the gift or the altar that sanctifies the gift? Whoever then swears by the altar, swears by it, and by all things upon it. And whoever swears by the temple, swears by it and by he who dwells within it.

I swear to God, he says. That's what you say. *As God is my witness.* Man, if he's your witness, I want him *in the room.*

He owns the stage of the Johnny Carson Show, working mic and audience.

———

And he who swears by Æternity itself, he said, swears by the throne of the sublime, and by he who sits upon it.

But he spoke of the temple of his body.

———

You know who is in the room? he says. My cock. Joshua Junior, Joshua Hallelujah Cock. You swear on your *cock* and *then* I'll trust you: I swear to cock, as cock is my witness, for the love of cock, may Cock Almighty strike me down!

A beat.

Of course, for the sisters in the audience, *cunt* is also acceptable.

The *technical difficulties* sign comes quick.

———

As for these things which you behold, he said, the days will come in which not one stone shall be left upon another, that shall not be thrown down. I will destroy this house, he said, and none shall be able to build it again.

———

And I stand here at the end of this aeon, watching him on YouTube clips, as Lenny Bruce, George Carlin, Bill Hicks, tear into the temple you've built, all the Select of the season of the Gentiles, for the power and glory of the Herods and Pilates you fear and obey.

———

Then, as they watch for those things which are coming, there shall be great earthquakes in diverse places, famines and pestilences. There shall be great signs from the heavens, fearful sights because the powers of the heavens shall be shaken: the sun shall be darkened, the moon not give her light, the stars fall from the skies. And upon the earth: the anguish of nations in chaos; the sea and the waves roaring.

———

Look at the stone that fell from the heavens, you say, how it has become the corner stone. But what if that stone should become a stumbling block, barracks and basilica? If the rock's inscription should be scoured away, how will the rock regain its truth? It is fit neither for the sacred altar nor the sepulchre, only to be thrown down, smashed, trodden under the feet of men.

I promise you, lover of the sublime, we will destroy this stumbling block, pave the way for every man who comes after us.

———

He who has ears, let him hear: All these are the beginning of sorrows, men's hearts failing them for fear. But when these things begin to come to pass, then look up, and lift up your heads at once; after the tribulation of those days your emancipation draws close.

———

And the Empire will end.

Culmination of the Aeon

5

Now when he was in Jerusalem at the Passover feast, many trusted in his name when they saw the miracles that he performed. But Joshua did not commit himself to them, because he knew all men, and did not need for any to testify of man, for he knew what was in man. So, as he sat upon the mount of Olives, the students came to him privately.

In sunlight dappled by leaves of olive trees, he sits, slicing an apple with a knife to share with Mary and I, as if restaging Eden might undo the curse on maiden's passion and serpent's wisdom. Lazed on the ground on the prop of an elbow, I lean back into his breast to take a slice from him, popped into my mouth by his hand, like an emperor fed a grape by his slave. I relish the juice of it. Looking down on the tents of the Occupy movement's secondary site, I want so desperately for this all to work.

Tell us, they said, when will these things be? And what will be the sign of your coming, and of the culmination of the aeon?

The thrum of police helicopters in the blue sky. I shade my eyes to peer up at strange locusts of Æternity. The Roman presence increases by the day, on the streets and in the air now. I think of Mary trying to placate my father, insisting that the movement is wedded to passive resistance, that nothing *we* do will lead to violence.

The days will come, said Joshua, when you shall yearn to see, if it were possible, one of the days of the everyman, but you shall not see it. Nation shall rise against nation, and kingdom against kingdom, and you shall hear of wars and rumours of wars in my name. When this gospel of the realm shall be preached in all the world for a testament to all nations, take heed that no man deceive you, for many shall come, saying, I am the anointed.

Matthew lounges against a tree, fidgets with his recorder. My gut churns at the knowledge of what those words will become, *have already* become.

Many false prophets shall rise. False messiahs and false prophets shall arise, and show great signs and wonders, insomuch that they will deceive the very successors. The sign of the everyman in Æternity shall appear, and then many shall be outraged, and betray one another, hate one another. The love of many shall cool because iniquity shall flourish. They shall see the everyman coming in the clouds of the heavens with grand glory and might, and shall deceive the masses; do not go after them.

But I've already seen him on the cross, banner of Empire, all of Christendom going after that transcendent travesty.

If any man shall say to you, Behold, the anointed is here! or there! do not believe it. If they say to you, Behold, he is in the desert! do not go forth. If they say to you, Behold, he is in the secret chambers! do not believe it. For as the lightning comes out of the east and shines even to the west, so too shall the coming of the everyman be.

Where, Teacher? they said.

In every church and chapel and cathedral, in every twelve year
old bastard, queer or just plain runt sat in a pew, the fire of sacred
inspiration in their heart stoked to smelting furnace at the insult of
empty repetitions droning.

Wherever the corpse is, he said, there will the vultures be gathered together.

6

So, when you see, he said, Jerusalem surrounded by armies and, standing in the holy place, that abomination of desolation spoken of by Daniel the prophet—Baal Shamem, the LORD of Heaven—then let those who are in Judaea flee into the mountains; and let those who are in the hills not go into the city; and let those who are in the midst of it get out.

Here is a prophecy fulfilled, lover of the sublime: a young boy kneels
before a minister for wine and wafer, shadowed by the golden crucifix
on which an Apollonian and Dionysian tragedy is tortured to sick
triumph; and beyond, above, a teraphim of the heart, a great grey-
bearded emperor upon his throne wears the face of Zeus, the sublime
itself blasphemed by two millennia's devotion to the face and fist of
might and violence. And every ancestor of the boy who kneels before it,
every child he might have been twenty centuries before, cursed for the
crime committed by that fist.

If you cast the sacred inspiration as some *father*, I hiss at Joshua as
we watch, you *know* Simon will take it literally.

And pray that your flight is not in the winter, for then there shall be great tribulation, such as was not since the beginning of the world to this time, no, nor ever shall be. For these are the days of vengeance, that all things which are written may be fulfilled. And except that for the sake of the successors, whom he has chosen, the Worker had shortened those days, no flesh should be saved.

Here is a prophecy fulfilled, lover of the sublime: that boy a young man now, in a soldier's uniform and fascii armband, modernity's centurion smashing his rifle-butt across a face, kicking a human beast back into the herd, shoving the huddled mob on through the winter grey of snow trodden into dust, toward the wooden goods-carriage of a train headed from Jerusalem to Armageddon and the ashen smoke of burning bones. Yellow stars, brown and blue, purple and pink triangles, for Samaritans and foreigners, heretics and homosexuals. We wear red for politicos, Joshua's stitched to the black of his tattered cassock.

Just show me the world where this doesn't happen, I beg him.

And woe to those who are with child, and to those who give suck, in those days! for there shall be great distress in the land, and wrath upon this people, in the name of the father, and of the son, and of the sacred inspiration. And then all the tribes of the earth shall mourn, and the end of the aeon shall come.

Here is a prophecy fulfilled, lover of the sublime: that young man now some bearded power-monger out of Pasolini's Salò, ripping a child from mother's breast, from mother's womb, to raise him on shit and rape, bring him before the altar of that abomination. From Joshua's Baal to Ginsberg's Moloch, these are the cycling seasons of the Gentiles, an eschaton that is always already with us. This is how it ends, lover of the sublime, the culmination of the aeon.

Give me something, I say, something to hope for...

But take heed: anyone who speaks a word against the everyman, it shall be forgiven him, but anyone who speaks against the sacred inspiration, it shall not be forgiven him, neither on the Sabbath day, nor in this aeon, nor in the aeon to come. For sure, I tell you, Æternity and Earth shall pass away, but my words shall not pass away.

7

Behold, I have foretold you all things, but of that day and hour no man knows, no, not the messengers of Æternity, but my father only. Take you heed, watch and pray. For you know not when the time is. For the everyman is as a craftsman taking a far journey, who left his house and directed the gatekeeper to watch, and he gave authority to his apprentices, and to every man his work. But when the master returned, he found them asleep.

Day 32. I don't know how long I've been awake now, working on coffee and nicotine. Better that than to have slept for two thousand years though, dreaming that you do his work by building the Empire.

Watch you therefore, and pray always, that you may be accounted worthy to escape all these things that shall come to pass, and to stand before the everyman. For if the wicked apprentice say in his heart, My master delays his coming, and shall begin to beat *his* apprentices, to eat and drink, and to be drunken, the master of that apprentice will come in a day when he is not watching for him, and at an hour when he is not aware, and will cut him in two, and will appoint him his portion with the hypocrites. For much shall be required of he to whom much is given; and to whom men have entrusted much, of him they will ask the more.

I tear a piece off a slice of factory-made bread, dribble red wine from a box into a glass. Mine is not some ascetic's fast, starvation of the flesh while the soul feasts to flab on fantasies of his body and blood.

Watch, lest coming suddenly he find you sleeping, for you do not know when the master of the house comes, at even, or at midnight, or at the cockcrowing, or in the morning. Blessed is that apprentice whom his master shall find watching when he comes. And if he shall come in the second watch, or come in the third watch, and find them so, blessed is that apprentice. Of a truth I say to you, that he will make him lord over all that he has. For sure, I tell you that he shall gird himself, and make them to sit down to meat, and will come forth and serve them.

With the curtains closed, I'm not sure what hour it is, but it doesn't matter. In Gethsemane, it's always night.

Watch, and let your loins be girded about, and your lights burning, and you yourselves like men who wait for their master, when he will return from the wedding, that when he comes and knocks, they may open to him at once. So that apprentice, who knew his master's will, and prepared not himself, neither did according to his will, shall be beaten with many stripes, while he who committed things worthy of stripes but did not know shall be beaten with few stripes. Be you therefore ready also, for the everyman comes at an hour when you think not.

Teacher, the Rock said then, do you speak this parable to us or even to all?

What do you think? said the teacher. Who is that loyal and wise steward whom his master shall make lord over his household, to give them their portion of meat in due season? Do you not perceive it yet, nor understand? And do you not remember?

He who is against you is for you, and he who is far from you will draw near tomorrow.

8

And he spoke a parable to them:

So the realm of Zion is compared to a certain king, who would take account of his slaves. When he had begun to reckon, one was brought to him who owed him ten thousand talents. But since he had nothing to pay with, his master directed him to be sold, and his wife, and children, all that he had, and payment to be made.

Kings and slaves, humans as chattels. I read a cardinal's open letter on the Telegraph website, the rhetoric of legalised slavery applied to gay marriage by a self-proclaimed servant. I think of this.

The slave therefore fell down, supplicated to him.

Master, he said, have patience with me, and I will pay you all.

The master of that slave was moved with compassion, and loosed him, forgiving him the debt.

The cardinal decries a tyranny of tolerance, a Son of Thunder who won't be told not to call down raining fire.

But that same slave went out and found one of the fellow slaves he commanded, who owed him an hundred denarii. He laid hands on him, took him by the throat, saying, Pay me what you owe.

His fellow slave fell down at his feet, begged him.

Have patience with me, he said, and I will pay you all.

The wicked slave would not though, but went and cast him into prison, till he should pay the debt. But when his fellow slaves saw what was done, they were very sorry, and came and told their master all that was done.

So the master, after he had called him, said, O you wicked

slave, I forgave you all that debt, because you asked me. Should you not also have had compassion on your fellow slave, even as I had pity on you?

The cardinal rails at the liberal dogma teachers will be forced to parrot, or be judged an intolerant bigot.

And the master was furious, and delivered him to the tormentors, till he should pay all that was due to him. So likewise shall my æternal father do also to you, if you do not forgive from your hearts every one his brother their trespasses.

No mercy for the merciless, I pin Joshua's judgement of judgement onto the wall of gospel, golden rule for every ethical retard who thinks himself a slave.

Then the Rock came to him, asking, Master, how often shall my brother be delinquent with me, and I forgive him? Until seven times?

Not until seven times, said Joshua, but until seventy times seven, I say to you. Moreover if your brother shall trespass against you, go and tell him his fault between you and him alone. If he shall hear you, you have gained your brother. But if he will not, then take with you one or two more, that in the mouth of two or three witnesses every word may be established. And if he shall refuse to hear them, tell it to the congregation, and if he refuse to hear the congregation, let him be to you as a Gentile and a taxman. But if he trespass against you seven times in a day, and turn again to you seven times in a day, saying, I rethink; you shall forgive him. And what I say to you I say to all.

And it came to pass, when Joshua had finished all these sayings, he spoke to his students.

You know that the feast of the Passover is in two days, he said, and the everyman is betrayed to be crucified.

Leaning on Joshua's Bosom

9

And in two days was the feast of the Passover, the feast of unleavened bread, and many went out of the country up to Jerusalem, to purify themselves before the Passover. Then the chief priests, and the clerks, and the elders of the people, assembled together.

———

A black Duesenberg rolls through a city of spotlit streets, armoured patrol cars, soldiers swivelling sights of mounted machine-guns; slows to a stop at a checkpoint, window winding down. Papers are exchanged, chauffeur to guard and back. Inside, my father fingers the brim of his fedora as the car moves on again. A few minutes more down boulevards of banners, and he's stepping out of the car, placing the hat on his head only to offer it, with white scarf and gloves, to the—*por favor, caballero*—servant at the door. The gentleman's club is full of cigar smoke and murmurs.

Pilate's patience is wearing thin; if the Sanhedrin will not deal with these troubles among their people, Rome will. And if Rome were to make this rebel a martyr, it has been made clear, all who might be galvanised by his blood on Roman hands would need dealt with too. All of them.

———

What do we do? they said. This man does many miracles. If we let him alone like this, all men will believe in him.

You know nothing at all, said one by name of Caiaphas. You have no idea how imperative it is for us that one man must die for the people, give his life a ransom for many, that the whole nation should not perish.

This he spoke not for himself, but being the high priest that same year, he foresaw that Joshua must die for the nation, and not for the nation alone but also that he should gather together in one the children of the sublime who were scattered abroad.

Heads turn to him, my father's among them, the words filling him with horror. He is no supporter of Herod, and this Joshua has the people's love... his own children's love. But for the Sanhedrin to refuse, force Pilate's hand... my father lived through Archelous's purge, three thousand Pharisees shot in the forecourt of a temple still under construction.

Then the Select were filled with madness and went out, held a council with the Herodians against Joshua, whether they should destroy him.

A drive across town to another grand edifice, the Roman Embassy, where another crowd of Jerusalem's rich and powerful gathers round a baby grand as Salome finishes a Piaf song, moves on to Billie Holiday, *God Bless the Child*. No awareness of irony is perceptible as she sings a black woman's lyrics of privilege and poverty. After, Pilate in white tux lights the cigarette in her holder, paints her a starlet of Hollywood screen or Broadway stage.

My father feels a general's handshake: at last he's come.

And the Herodians cried out, saying, If you let this man go, you are not Caesar's friend! Whoever makes himself a king speaks against Caesar, and the Romans shall come and take away both our place and nation.

Then they sought for Joshua, and spoke among themselves as they stood in the temple, What do you think, that he will not come to the feast? Now both the chief priests and the Select had given a decree, that, if any man knew where he were, he should show it, that they might take him. But they said, Not on the feast day, lest there be an uproar among the people. In the absence of the mob.

10

Then the first day of unleavened bread was coming, when the Passover must be killed. So Joshua sent the Rock and John, saying, Go and prepare us the Passover, that we may eat.

Where do you want that we prepare? they said.

Behold, he said, when you are entered into the city, a man shall meet you there, bearing a pitcher of water. Follow him into the house he enters, and say to the master of the house, The master would ask of you: Where is the guestchamber where I shall eat the Passover with my students? And he shall show you a large upper room furnished. Make ready there.

So they went and found as he had said to them, and they made ready for the Passover.

I was still making arrangements when he arrived, Mary and I as locals having sourced the venue least snooty as regards our Galilean comrades—and the least impressed by my father's name, by no small chance. And feel free to imagine me in my element ordering napkins folded just so, floral centrepieces right here, place-cards and party favours and what not. Feel free to picture me in full flounce when I felt a hand on my arm that made me turn, smile to see him.

It should all be ready for tomorrow, I told him.

He told me to call everyone together now.

Now before the feast of the Passover, when Joshua knew the hour was come that he should depart out of this world to the father, having loved his own who were in the world, he loved them to the end. And when the hour was come, he sat down, and his twelve ambassadors with him.

And Mary. I sat to one side of him, Mary to the other, his faggot and his whore—and his decision. I'd set Simon beside me; maybe if I reached out, I thought...I hoped...

I had hoped with all my heart, he said, to eat the coming Passover with you before I suffer.

So he took bread, gave thanks, and broke it, gave to them, saying, Take, eat: this is my body. For I say to you, I will eat no more of such until it is fulfilled in the realm of the sublime.

And he took the cup, gave thanks, and said, Take this, and divide it among yourselves; this is my blood of the new testament. For I say to you, I will not drink of the fruit of the vine until the realm of the sublime shall come.

I took the wine from his hand, sipped to his simple Nazarite vow: no Passover until Empire's end.

When Joshua had spoken thus, he was troubled in inspiration, and testified, and said, Now I tell you before it comes so that when it is come to pass, you may believe that I am he. For sure, I tell you, one of you who eats with me shall betray me. I do not speak of you all—I know who I have chosen— but that the scripture may be fulfilled, *He who eats bread with me has lifted up his heel against me.* Behold, the hand of he who betrays me is with me on the table. And truly the everyman goes, as it was determined, but woe to that man by whom he is betrayed.

Then the students looked one on another, worrying about who he spoke of. And they began to be sorrowful, and to say to him one by one, Is it I? and another said, Is it I?

11

Now leaning on Joshua's bosom there was one of his students, whom Joshua loved, carried up into Æternity and sat at the right hand of the sublime, that it might be fulfilled: *Let not your left hand know what your right hand does.*

So Simon the Rock beckoned to him, that he should ask who it would be, of whom he spoke.

He who was lying back in Joshua's breast then whispered to him, Teacher, who is it?

My name is stripped from your gospels, left only in the tale of my raising. Open your eyes and read that tale though, and you'll find my sisters begging Joshua to save *he whom he loved.* Open your eyes and read of the needle's eye, when Joshua first *looked at him and loved him.* Open your eyes and see who asked.

It is he, Joshua answered, to whom I shall give a sop, when I have dipped it.

And when he had dipped the sop, he gave it to him, the Judaean, the son of Simeon of Kerioth.

Open your eyes and read your rags of gospel, see the supper in Bethany after my raising, my sister anointing Joshua's feet in the house of Simeon the Pharisee, the potter, of Kerioth. Open your eyes and see who was answered.

What you do, said Joshua to the Judaean then, do quickly.

Now because the Judaean had the bag, some of them thought that Joshua had said to him, Buy those things that we have need of against the feast; or that he should give something to the poor. So no man at the table knew for what reason he spoke this to him.

Except for his beloved, lover of the sublime, who knew exactly what that sop meant, who would have answered the Rock's question, *everyone's* question, don't you think, were that sop given to *anyone other than himself?* Open your eyes and see Joshua's beloved not naming Joshua's betrayer for the only possible reason, the truth too terrible to voice.

And after the sop the accuser | entered into him.

Doubt entered into me, a shadow of self, refusing to believe it, hating him for the role he'd cast me in, but nausea churning in my gut as a thousand stained glass glimpses of Æternity, pulpit preachers and black leather books, swam through the air, clicked instant after instant into a vast mosaic.

He then having received the | it was night.
sop went out at once: and |

I stood at the window, looking out at the night. I don't know when I left the table. Maybe it was in another aeon entirely.

And the son of Simeon of Kerioth | the chief priests and captains, how
went his way, and communed with | he might betray him to them.

I stood at the window, looking at the reflection of a man who would be torn to scraps: a beloved leaning on his bosom here; a betrayer kissing him there; a dead man risen; a hanged man cursed. A boy carrying bread. A traitor haggling coins. A youth in white linen with all meaning lost. A symbol stamping hate into a word not even his name.

What will you give me if I deliver | covenanted with him for thirty
him to you? he said. | pieces of silver. And he sought
     And they were glad, and | opportunity to betray Joshua.

The red pen nearly rips the paper as I slash my sorrow through it, bitter, raging. A slice of scalpel, a little square of paper, two little words of truth. I slap it into place:

He wept.

12

And with supper ended, knowing that the father had given all things into his hands, that he was come from the sublime and went to the sublime, Joshua rose, laid aside his garments, took a towel, and wrapped himself in it. After that he poured water into a basin, began to wash the students' feet, and to wipe them with the towel he was wrapped in.

Then he came to Simon the Rock.

Teacher, said the Rock, do you wash my feet?

You do not understand what I do now, said Joshua, but you shall understand later.

You shall never wash my feet, said the Rock.

If I do not wash you, you have no place with me, said Joshua. You are clean, but not all.

For he knew who should betray him; this is why he said, you are not all clean.

I sat watching as he washed Simon's feet, told myself that I hadn't left, that the story was wrong because I hadn't left. This was the cusp of it. If I refused, he would order Simon, Simon would do it, he would argue but he'd do it, he'd be cursed for it, James would run the movement, and the seasons of the Gentiles would never happen, never happen.

Simon, said the teacher, behold, the accuser has desired to have you, that he may sift you as wheat, but I have prayed for you, that your trust not fail, that when you are turned around, you will strengthen your brethren.

He would do it, I told myself, and I'd know it wasn't truly a betrayal, I'd tell everyone it wasn't truly a betrayal, the only true betrayal would be mine in refusing.

Teacher, he said, I am ready to go with you, both into prison and to death.

I tell you, Rock, said Joshua, the cock shall not crow this day before you will have thrice denied that you know me.

Teacher, said Simon the Rock, not just my feet then, but my hands and my head as well.

He who is washed only needs to wash his feet, said Joshua, but is every bit clean.

His hands were gentle on my feet as they massaged the soles, worked between the toes. I leaned close enough to whisper that I couldn't do it, wouldn't.

It's already done, he said.

So after he had washed their feet, taken his garments, and sat down again, he said, Do you understand what I have done to you? You call me rabbi and teacher, and you speak well, for so I am. If I then, your teacher and rabbi, have washed your feet, you also ought to wash one another's feet. For I have given you an example, that you should do as I have done to you. For sure, I tell you, the student is not greater than his teacher, nor he that is sent greater than he that sent him. If you know these things, you are happy if you do them.

When I sent you without purse and scrip and shoes, he said, did you lack any thing?

Nothing, they said.

But now, he said to them then, he who has a purse, let him take it, and likewise his scrip. And he who has no sword, let him sell his garment, and buy one. For I say to you, that this which is written must yet be accomplished in me, *And he was reckoned among the transgressors*: for the things concerning me have an end.

Teacher, they said, behold, here are two swords.

It is enough, he said.

A Grain of Wheat

13

And when they had sung a hymn, they went out into the Mount of Olives.

We walked through groves and between graves, slowly as if he were looking for one he couldn't find—a warrior, a carpenter, a baptist? He turned at one point, back toward Jerusalem and the sunset beyond it, to the west.

You all shall be tripped because of me this night, said Joshua to them then, for it is written, *I will smite the shepherd, and the sheep of the flock shall be scattered abroad.* Behold, the hour comes, aye, is come even now, that you shall be scattered, each man to his own. He who does not love me will not keep my teachings, the word you hear, which is not mine but the father's who sent me.

Sunlight died in a fever of red and gold, faded to cold grey-blue of twilight.

The west, I thought. It wasn't just that the *kittim* would come from the west—*had* come to smash the sovereignty of our people, give us their governor and their puppet king with his temple stained with blood. It was that they'd drive our people ever westward, and in his name. They'd smash his body and they'd smash our nation with the temple that below gleamed golden in the sunset; they'd even twist Joshua's prophecy of its fall to a curse on the heart of our nation, twist our hatred of Herod's folly and the Roman coin in it to a hatred of the very source of his teachings.

They shall put you out of the congregation houses. Aye, the time comes when whoever kills you will think that he does a service to the sublime. And they will do these things to you because they have not known the father, nor me. If you were of the world, the world would love his own, but because you are not of the world, because I have chosen you out of the world, the world will hate you. If the world hate you, know that it hated me before it hated you.

It was that a man called Saul would be sent by Rome to liaise with local authorities, to persecute and imprison the seditious, oversee the first execution in a purge that would leave James the Just dead in prison and Simon the Rock in charge.

If I had not come and spoken to them, if I had not done among them the works which no other man did, they would have no failings. But now they have no cloak for their failings, so now they have seen and hated both me and my father. Still, this comes to pass, that the word might be fulfilled that is written in their law, *They hated me without a cause.*

It was that Saul would walk into a chapter house in Damascus one day, blinded by the light—as if occlusion was a miracle—and begin the long slow process of spinning Joshua's execution into a blood sacrifice, justifying countless others with his rhetoric of baseless hate.

Little children, yet a little while I am with you. Yet a little while, and the world sees me no more, though you will see me. I came forth from the father, and am come into the world; again, I leave the world, and go to the father. A little while, and you shall not see me; and again, a little while, and you shall see me. And as I said to the Select, so now I say to you, Where I go, you cannot come.

14

Then some of his students said among themselves, What is this that he said to us, A little while, and you shall not see me; and again, a little while, and you shall see me? So they said, What is this that he said, A little while? We cannot tell what he said.

Now Joshua knew that they longed to ask him, and said to them, Do you wonder among yourselves about what I said?

None of them saw how they walked from crypts carved into rock to weed-strewn graves with pebbles balanced on the headstones, to row upon row upon of identical markers stretching to the horizon, to a hatchwork of paths sloping down till they were swallowed in a forest of ash-grey monoliths. I saw it, and all his elliptical talk of a miraculous return meant little in the face of that grim memorial, built in another nation out of guilt for its final solution to the problem of our people.

Do not let your heart be troubled, neither let it be afraid because I go to the father. For sure, I tell you that the world shall rejoice while you weep and lament, and you shall be sorrowful, but your sorrow shall be turned into joy.

His fingertips brushed concrete, marble, limestone, grass as he led us through the garden cemeteries of an unborn aeon. Caught a stalk of ryegrass and plucked it idly. I would betray him, I thought, by not betraying him.

A woman has sorrow while she is in labour, he said, because her hour is come, but as soon as she is delivered of the child, she remembers the anguish no more, for joy that a child is born into the world. And you now therefore have sorrow, but I will see you again, and your heart shall rejoice, and no man will take your joy from you.

He stripped the leaves, lower to upper, outer to inner, till there was only the thin hard stalk topped by its alternating spikelets. I swore to myself I would abort this new aeon conceived in Sychar when he expanded the mission. If he could see hope here, a short labour and birth of joy under James, all I could see was a two thousand year breach birth, a womb cut open for a stillbirth. I'd be betraying us all to let that happen.

I will not leave you comfortless, he said. I will come to you, will come again and welcome you to myself, that where I am now, there you may also be. In the world you shall have tribulation, but be of good cheer; I have overcome the world.

One by one, he nipped off each spikelet with thumb and forefinger, crumbled it to the wind. All I could see was every Jew I'd be betraying if I obeyed him.

These things I have spoken to you, that you might have peace in me. I leave peace with you, give my peace to you—not as the world gives, but I give it to you. I have spoken these things to you while I am still here with you, have told you these things before they come to pass so that, when they come to pass, you might believe.

Westward, the sun set.

I have told you these things so that when the time shall come, you may remember that I told you of them. Hereafter I will not talk much with you, for the lord of this world comes, and has nothing in me.

Arise, let us go from here.

15

Teacher, said Simon the Rock, where do you go? Where I go, answered Joshua, you can not come with me now, because I go to my father. But you shall walk with me afterwards. I still have many things to say to you, but you cannot bear them now. These things I have spoken to you in proverbs, but the time comes when I shall speak to you in proverbs no more, but I shall show you plainly of the father.

Teacher, said the Rock, why can I not come with you now? I will lay down my life for your sake.

Will you lay down your life for my sake? said Joshua. But there shall not perish a hair of your head. For sure, I tell you, the cock shall not crow till you have denied me thrice. Let not your heart be troubled. You trust in the sublime; trust also in me. And you know where I go, and you know the way.

The Rock frowned, too simple ever to understand that he knew the way, always already knew it, as Joshua had been saying since Tabor. What father would give his son a scorpion if he asks for an egg? he'd said, and now he went to join the dead martyr and the dead mason that shaped that philosophy of ethics in empathy, innate and sublime. I felt the muscles in my jaw clench. What brother would risk betraying all his brothers out of trust in one?

Teacher, said Thomas, we do not know where you go, so how can we know the way?

I am the way, the truth, and the life, said Joshua. No man comes to the father, but by me. The words that I speak to you I speak not of myself, but rather the father who dwells in me, he does the works. Trust me that I am in the father, and the father in me, or else trust me for the very works' sake.

I heard the sacred inspiration in him, knew he had opened himself up to it so wholly he spoke *as* it, but he was still a man, not omniscient, not omnipotent, all his prophetic poetry born of questions. He paused, a hand on Thomas's arm, a gaze into doubtful eyes that might, of all of them, be most likely to glimpse the accuser within the anointed, the father within the son, the everyman...

Teacher, said Philip, show us the father, and it will suffice us.

Have I been so long a time with you, said Joshua, yet you have not known me, Philip? He who has seen me has seen the father, so how do you say then, Show us the father? Do you not trust that I am in the father, and the father in me? From this moment on, you know him and have seen him.

Teacher, said Jude, how is it that you will manifest yourself to us, and not to the world?

If a man love me, said Joshua, he will keep my words, and my father will love him, and we will come to him, make our abode within him.

... the everyman within every man.

We know that you will go from us, said Nathaniel. Who is he who shall be great over us?

In the place to which you come, said Joshua, you shall go to James the Just for whose sake Æternity and Earth came into being. But when you have become two, he said, what will you do?

He looked from James to Simon, from justice to stumbling block.

16

Days will come when you will seek after me, said Joshua, and you will not find me. But if you love me, keep my decrees, and I will pray the father, and he shall give you another advocate, that he may abide with you for ever, the very inspiration of truth. Though the world cannot welcome because it sees him not, neither knows him, you know him, for he dwells with you, and shall be in you.

One day I hope you'll know him, lover of the sublime. Not as some absentee father of stern visage, king and judge in the neverafter, but as an equal—living here and now on the earth; and dead and gone within it, inked into its history; and nascent as the future, waiting to be born— an equal, as the everyman can only be to every man and woman and child who ever lived, ever will. See him not even as the brother I hoped Joshua would see, but rather, echoing your epithet in this testament, the byname I've bestowed unpacking the *Theophilus* of Luke's gospel to its meaning, see the everyman as your beloved:

When the advocate comes, whom I will send to you from the beloved, the very inspiration of truth which bursts forth from the beloved, he shall testify of me. He will expose the world as regards delinquency, rectitude, judgement: delinquency, because they do not trust in me; rectitude, because I go to my beloved, and you see me no more; judgement, because the lord of this world is judged. I beheld the accuser fall as lightning from the heavens; and as long as I am in the world, I am the light of the world.

***

One day I hope you'll see him in the mirror.

***

These things I did not say to you at the beginning, because I was with you. But the advocate, which is the sacred inspiration, whom the beloved will send in my name, shall teach you all things, bring all things to your memory, whatever I have said to you. He will show you things to come, and in that day you shall ask me nothing. Rather when the inspiration of truth is come, he will guide you into all truth, for he shall not speak of himself, but whatever he shall hear, that shall he speak. He shall honour me, for he shall receive of mine and show it to you. All things that the beloved has are mine; this is why I say that he shall take of mine, and shall show it to you, that the world may know that we love the beloved, and as the beloved guides us, even so we do.

***

One day I hope you'll truly hear his words.

***

If you loved me, you would rejoice, because I said, I go to the beloved, for my beloved is greater than I. But because I have said these things to you, sorrow has filled your heart. Still, I tell you the truth: It is good for you that I go away, for if I do not go away, the advocate will not come to you, while if I leave, I will send him to you.

***

He let the stalk fall, held the last spikelet of the ryegrass in his hand, crumbled it. If he could change water to wine, I like to think, couldn't he change ryegrass to wheat?

For sure, I tell you, he said, except a grain of wheat fall on the ground and die, it lives alone; but if it die, it yields much fruit.

Before You Into Galilee

17

His students said to him, Behold, you speak plainly now, with no proverbs. Now we are sure that you know all things and need no man as inquirer. By this we believe that you came forth from the sublime.

Plain speech and a persuasive sense of confidence in one's own convictions. It's what two thousand years of false messiahs and false prophets have offered, lover of the sublime, the sop of simplicity and assurance so much more palatable than metaphor and caveat, whether soaked in wine or blood. Drag an ape up onto the witness stand to show a simplicity of common sense thought so absolute it doesn't even require words; flourish a hand for all to observe the absurdity of the evolutionist's claims. Better that than imagine Joshua walking the Mount of Olives, every tree around him fruited with the knowledge of good and evil, and fruited too with the life of ages, the realm of Zion everywhere, always already to hand.

Joshua answered them, Do you now believe? Now is the everyman honoured, and the sublime is honoured in him. And if the sublime is honoured in him, the sublime shall also honour him in itself.

Better to empty an idiom of all meaning, make of it a title—Son of Man—and slather glory on this idol as gold leaf than to try and walk with the man who wore those words the same way thousands now wear a rebel's mask and a name that speaks similarly of their identity with the masses. Better the crude certainties than the twisting path through graves and groves to a moonlit vista on Æternity coiled in existence like the energy locked in an atom.

———

For the sublime did not send his son into the world to condemn it, but that it might be saved through him. He who trusts in him is not condemned, but he who does not trust is condemned already, because he has not trusted in the name of the only begotten scion of the sublime, the everyman.

———

Better a wunderkind begotten of a tyrant deity's jizz than some bastard brat who might be any bastard brat from a province of a province of Empire, a prophet out of Galilee and for it, for the æternal Galilee, scion of the sublime because there is no human being on this eight billion year old lump of rock who *isn't.* Better the prince of a wicked judge than just the thrashing dialectic of the accuser at every door, fruit in hand, calling each of us to the æternal throne, not as martyr but as messenger, to deliver judgement on judgement itself.

———

But this is the condemnation: that light is come into the world, and men loved darkness rather than light, because their deeds were wicked. For every one who does ill hates the light, neither comes to the light, lest his deeds should be accused. But he who does truth comes to the light, that his deeds may be made manifest, that they are wrought in the sublime.

———

Day 35. I find it hard to put in words the agony of doubt I felt as I tried not to let the sacred inspiration in his voice seduce me out of trust and into faith, not in some deity in the sky scheming salvation, not in some infallible avatar sent down to earth to execute his plan, but simply in Joshua as a man who saw a possible world I was still blind to. I write it in the interstices between your gospel words of victory, my testament of defeat.

18

I am the true vine, and my beloved is the husbandman. Every branch in me that does not bear fruit he takes away, and every branch that bears fruit, he purges it, that it may yield more fruit. Abide in me, and I in you.

Because I live, you shall live also. As the branch cannot bear fruit of itself, except it abide in the vine, no more can you, except you abide in me. I am the vine, you are the branches.

We looked down on a Jerusalem lit in the dusk by the glow of lamps from windows, fires for warmth in the cool spring night here and there. I thought of death sweeping down through the city, indifferent to sacrifices and signs daubed in blood on door-frames, pruning and harvesting all the same, as Adam in the garden or Cain in the fields, with secateurs or scythe. No Passover story of Israelites in Egypt, not even the panicked imagining of an infant Thomas with angels sent by Herod, just the merciless and all-consuming locusts of Rome.

He who abides in me, and I in him, the same brings forth much fruit, for without me you can do nothing. If a man abide not in me, he is cast forth as a branch, and is withered, and men gather

them, cast them into the fire, and they are burned. Herein is my beloved honoured, that you bear much fruit, so you shall be my students.

He leaned against a tree—fig or apple, orange or olive, it hardly matters. I might hang myself in that tree, I thought, make myself a strange fruit indeed, and make that part of your story true even as I rewrote the rest of its ending. But if my truth could be buried in erasures and revisions, maybe it wouldn't matter. Maybe he'd turn to another, call on Mary or Thomas, my suicide only sealing my blame in that botched record. I swallowed, the taste in my dry mouth as rich as rot, acrid as venom.

From Adam to John the Baptist there is none born of woman who is higher than John the Baptist, so that his eyes will not be broken. But I have said, He among you who shall be as a little one shall know the realm and shall be higher than John, and you too shall testify, because you have been with me from the beginning. When you see him who was born not of woman, if you do anything I direct you, throw yourselves down upon your face and adore him. He is your beloved.

The taste of the sacred inspiration is bittersweet as love asking an unbearable action.

For sure, I tell you, whatever you shall ask the beloved that is in my name, he will give it you. Hitherto you have asked nothing in my name. At that day you shall ask in my name, and I say to you not that I will pray the beloved for you, for the beloved himself loves you, because you have loved me, and have trusted that I came out from the sublime. But whatever you shall ask that is in my name, that will I do, that the beloved may be honoured in the lover. If you shall ask anything that is in my name, I will do it. If you abide in me, and my words abide in you, you shall ask what you will, and it shall be done to you. Is it not written in your law, *I said, you are sublime?*

19

If you keep my decree, you shall abide in my love, even as I have kept my beloved's decree, and abide in his love. He who has my decrees, and keeps them, he it is who loves me. And he who loves me shall be loved by my beloved, and I will love him, and will manifest myself to him, and shall at once honour him.

When you know yourselves, then you shall be known, and you shall know that you are the lovers of the living beloved, with the honour which I had with you before this world began.

Simon sat upon a boulder, sharpening one of the swords. Beside him, Andrew held the other, a finger touched to its edge, running tentatively along it. In another aeon, they held guns, riflemen of some resistance, guerrillas in camouflage and red bandanas or black balaclavas. Matthew clicked a button on his *dictaphone* to eject the tape, flip it over, slide and snick it back in, hit record again. Joshua paused at the rumbling crunch of tires on dirt, a flash of headlights through trees at a turn—a Roman Army jeep patrolling the road between Bethany and Jerusalem.

Remember the word that I said to you: The student is not greater than his teacher. From this moment on I do not call you students; for the student does not know his teacher's works. Instead I call you friends. You are my friends, for all things I have heard from my beloved I have made known to you.

Jacob and John, the Sons of Thunder handed out masks to all in Joshua's image. My hand trembled as I took mine, as I wondered which of them he might turn to in my refusal, which I would condemn to my burden, whether they could bear it any more than I. I imagined him betrayed with despair turned to resentment, resentment to hate. I imagined him betrayed with a gob of spit in his face, a slap, a fist. I imagined him sent to his death with vicious fury, deserted by the beloved he trusted beyond all.

You have heard how I said to you, I go away, and come again to you. A new decree I give to you, that you love one another—that as I have loved you, you love one another also. As the beloved has loved me, so have I loved you. You, continue in my love. All men shall know by this that you are my students, if you have love one to another. This is my decree, that you love one another, as I have loved you. And no man has greater love than this, but that he lay his life down for his friends.

These words spoke Joshua, and lifted up his eyes to the heavens.

I give you back your father, his father, for these words of blessing, keep the beloved for myself.

Holy father, he said, I have manifested your name to the men you gave me from the world. As you have sent me into the world, even so have I sent them into the world. As I am not of the world, even so are they not of the world. I have given them your word, the words you gave me, and they have welcomed them, have trusted, have known that I was surely sent from you. I have given them your word, and they have kept it. Those that you gave me I have kept, and have loved them as you have loved me, and none of them is lost.

20

While I was with them in the world, I kept them in your name, and so the world has hated them. But now I am no more in the world, and these are in the world, and so I come to you, for they are yours again, and for their sakes I hallow myself, through your own name, that they too may be hallowed through the truth, that they may see my honour, which you have given me, that they may be one as we are, now they know that everything you have given me is of you.

He prayed to the moonlight, the wind in the olive trees, the sacred inspiration in all of it.

Keep those you have given me. I pray not for the world, but for those you have given me. I pray for them. Yours they were, and you gave them to me, so I pray not that you should take them out of the world, but that you should keep them from the strife. Nor do I pray for these alone, but also for those who shall trust in me through their word, that they may also be one in us, that they may all be one, as you, father, are in me and I in you.

He prayed to the sacred inspiration in all of us, accuser and advocate.

Father, I will that they also, whom you have given me, be with me where I am now. O upstanding father, the world has not known you, but I have known you, for you loved me before the foundation of the world. And I have declared your name to these who have known that you have sent me, and will declare it, that the love that you have loved me with may be in them, and I in them. And now I come to you, and these things I speak in the world, that they may have my joy fulfilled in themselves.

He prayed to the everyman he could only ever see as father. And I... I turned from him to walk back down from the Mount of Olives, to the house where the servants would be clearing the remnants of his last supper, to send word to my own father that the Sanhedrin need argue no longer, that Joshua would surrender willingly, to tell the men that they would know who they were looking for by the kiss of a young man clad in white linen, because Joshua was the man this Eleazar, son of Simeon of Kerioth, loved with all his heart, loved so much he could refuse him nothing.

Father, the hour is come. I have finished the work which you gave me to do, and I am honoured among them. I have made you honoured on the earth. And the honour which you gave me I have given them, that they may be one, even as we are one, I in them and you in me, that they may be made perfect in one, and that the world may know that you have sent me. And now, O father, honour me with your own self. Honour your son, that your son may honour you too, as you have given him power over all flesh, that he should give the life of ages to as many as you have given him. Now hallow them through your truth, for your word is truth, for this is the life of ages—that they may know you, the only true divinity.

And after I am risen again, I will go before you into Galilee.

<hr>

Take This Cup

21

And they came over the brook Cedron, where there was a garden, to a place called Gethsemane. And with Simon the Rock and the sons of Zebedee following, he became anguished, agitated.

My soul is past sorrowful, he said, even to death. Wait here, and watch for me.

And withdrawing from them a stone's throw or so, he kneeled down and prayed that this hour might pass from him, if it were possible.

Abba, he said, to you all things are possible. Father, take this cup away from me—yet not as I will, but as you do.

In the house, I held the cup of his last supper, still wet with wine. I set it down, began to undress.

And he came back, and found them sleeping. So he went away a second time, and prayed again.

O my father, he said, if this cup may not be taken away from me unless I drink it, let your will be done.

Naked, I took the shroud from my revival in Bethany, only six days past... and a deep forever. I draped one end over my left shoulder, wound the other round my waist, slung it back over the shoulder.

And when he returned, again he found them asleep, for their eyes were heavy.

Simon, do you sleep? he said. Could not you watch one hour? Watch you and pray, lest you enter into testing. The inspiration truly is willing, but the flesh is weak.

But they did not know how to answer him, so he left them, went away again, and prayed a third time, saying the same words. And being in an agony he prayed more earnestly, until his sweat was like great drops of blood falling down to the ground.

I set out for the Mount of Olives, for Gethsemane, for Joshua.

Because of the weak, I was weak, he said, because of the hungry I was hungry, and because of the thirsty I was thirsty. I stood in the midst of the world, and I appeared to them in flesh, Joshua the anointed whom you have sent. But I found them all drunk, found none among them thirsting, and my soul was afflicted for the everymen, for they are blind in their heart and do not see. For they came into the world empty, and they seek also to leave from the world empty. When they have thrown off their wine, then they will rethink, but for now they are drunk. And father, there are many about the well, but no one in the well.

And I came over the brook Cedron, where there was a garden, to a place called Gethsemane. I climbed up past Simon and the Sons of Thunder, to where he sat.

Then there appeared a messenger to him from Æternity, strengthening him. For in the evening the youth came to him, that student whom Joshua loved came, one of the twelve, wearing a linen cloth over his naked body.

Friend, Joshua said to him, where have you come from?

We have come from the light, he said.

With shaking voice.

And he stayed with him that night, for Joshua taught him the mystery of the realm of the sublime, naked man to naked man. And when they rose up from prayer and were come to his students, for sorrow, Joshua found them sleeping again.

Sleep on now, he said. Take your rest. Behold, the hour is at hand, and the everyman is betrayed into the hands of delinquents. Rise up, let us go. Behold, he who betrays me is at hand.

22

And at once, while he yet spoke, there came the chief priests and the clerks and the elders, and with them a great mass with swords and staves.

Pistols and machine-guns. Tasers and pepper-spray. Batons and riot shields. Alsatians and Dobermanns snarled and barked, strained on their leashes. Centurions poured in on from all sides, cutting off escape, shouting orders to comply, get down on the ground, on your knees, hands on your head. Black shirts and golden armour, blood-red armbands, rifle-butts in faces. The details do not matter, lover of the sublime. Every vial of wrath is a tear gas canister, every sword of fire a flamethrower in a jungle, a garden, Eden or Gethsemane. And every night for the last two thousand years, I walk out with Joshua among the forces of the Empire I have brought to this place, to seal the fate of one aeon and begin another.

And he who betrayed him had given them a token, saying, Whoever I shall kiss, that same is he. Take him, and lead him away safely.

And as soon as they were come, he went at once to him, and said, Rabbi, and he kissed him much.

My Judaean, Joshua said to him, you betray the everyman with a kiss?

His face in my hands, our foreheads touching, I begged him to tell me that he knew what he was doing, that all of this was not already written. Everything they would do to him, to us. I begged him to show me this other future he saw, to tell me that it wasn't just a world of James as leader after him, but a world of Joshua alive. Every night for the last two thousand years, I clasp his face in my hands, tears in my eyes, beg him to change this story, change this turning of the seasons. He kissed me back, told me it was mine to change.

Then they came, and laid hands on Joshua and took him. And so, knowing all things that should come upon him, Joshua said to them, Who do you seek?

Joshua the Nazirite, they answered him.

I am he, said Joshua.

And the moment he had said this, they staggered backward, falling to the ground.

You can imagine men struck down from where they stand by these three little words, lover of the sublime. Can you imagine a man struck out of time into Æternity. If not, if not...

Imagine me dead and in hell, reliving the betrayal over and over again, a ghost of a traitor you can't even begin to trust. Imagine me some madman of modernity, in a self-made asylum of a tenement flat somewhere, mundane personal history lost in gibbering delusion as he patches this tale together like some conspiracy nut weaving meaning out of coincidence, stitching it together with wild leaps. Imagine my whole voice nothing but pure conjuring, a figment, a fiction woven through a sacrilege of scripture recombined to blasphemy by whatever pulp pomo homo has his name set on the cover of the book you're reading. Imagine any simple and reassuring story that makes sense to you. But understand, lover of the sublime, that such details do not and will never matter.

———

Who do you seek? he asked them again.

And they said, Joshua the Nazirite.

Joshua answered, I have told you that I am he. So if you seek me, let these go their way, that the saying might be fulfilled, which he spoke, *I have lost none of those who you gave me.*

23

When they who were around him saw what would follow, they said to him, Teacher, shall we smite with the sword? And, behold, Simon the Rock stretched out his hand, and drew his sword, and struck a slave of the high priest's, and sliced off his right ear.

You go too far! said Joshua. Do you not think that if I prayed to my father now, he should at once put twelve legions of messengers at my hand? But how then should the scriptures be fulfilled, when it must be thus?

And he touched the slave Malchus's ear, and healed him.

Then said Joshua to him, Put your sword away again into its place, for all those who seize the sword shall be slain by the sword.

———

Except... it was James, who raised no blade that day, who was slain by the sword of Herod while Simon walked free from the black iron prison. James and Simon, Jerusalem and Rome. Two bishops and one sword. I've often wondered, lover of the sublime, if that other future Joshua saw turned on that moment, Simon the Rock dead by the sword and the movement in the hands of James the Just.

———

Then Joshua said to the chief priests, and captains of the temple, and the elders, who were come to him, Are you come out as against a thief, with swords and with staves to take me? When I was daily with you in the temple, you stretched forth no hands against me. But this is your hour, and the power of darkness, and the scriptures must be fulfilled.

And if the scriptures aren't fulfilled? If the one to die by the sword of Herod instead returns claiming miraculous release? A light that shone in his cell, shackles that fell from his wrist, iron gates that opened of themselves, guards who simply *watched* him pass with his magnificent escort? While James died by the blade meant for him?

I imagine what would have happened if Ananias and Sapphira had been brought before James instead of Simon, that husband and wife cursed to death for not surrendering all they owned to his church, his all too earthly kingdom of heaven. *The feet of the men who buried your husband are at the door, and they will carry you out also*, he said to the weeping woman. Every revolution has its Stalin, lover of the sublime, its man of steel or stone, and it's hard not to see Simon becoming ours with two executions as perfunctory as any ordered by a Pilate or Herod.

I imagine James giving merciful justice rather than brutal sanction, imagine Ananias coming to him with suspicions that this Roman agent turned convert was as blind as he ever had been, imagine James calling out the quisling, burning his epistles of pious hatred for whores and faggots, cleaving to Jerusalem and the Jews where Simon turned to Rome and the Gentiles.

I imagine Joshua risking all for a world where you, lover of the sublime, might have been born into a movement that toppled the Empire rather than one that became it.

And having forsaken him, all fled, and they seized that certain young man who followed, having a linen cloth cast about his naked body, so he left the linen cloth, to flee from them naked. Then the band and the captain and officers took Joshua, and led him away to Annas first, for he was father in law to Caiaphas, who was the high priest that same year. And Annas sent him bound to Caiaphas the high priest.

24

And the Rock followed afar off, with that other student, he whom Joshua loved. He stood outside the door, but that other student was known to the high priest, and went with Joshua into the high priest's palace, then came out, spoke to she who kept the door, brought in the Rock. Slaves and attendants stood there, who had made a fire of coals, for it was cold, and they warmed themselves; and the Rock stood with them, warming himself also. But as the Rock was beneath in the palace, one of the maids of the high priest came to him, and when she saw him warming himself, looked upon him earnestly.

You also were with Joshua the Nazirite, she said. Are you not also one of this man's students?

I am not, he denied. I neither know nor understand what you say.

He went out into the porch, but the maid who kept the door saw him again, began saying to bystanders, This is one of them.

Again he denied with an oath, Woman, I don't know him.

Then after about the space of one hour, one of the high priest's slaves, a kinsman of he whose ear the Rock cut off asked if he hadn't seen him in the garden with Joshua.

Surely you're one of them, he said, a Galilean. Your speech betrays you.

But he began to curse and swear, saying, I don't know this man you speak of.

Immediately the cock crew. And Simon the Rock remembered the promise Joshua had made to him, Before the cock crows twice, you shall deny me thrice. And he went out, wept bitterly.

Then, seeing that Joshua was condemned, the Judaean had a change of heart; he departed and brought again the thirty pieces of silver to the chief priests and elders who had betrayed him.

They offered me the money there, for my service. I had proven myself the upstanding citizen a young man of my status should be, measured up to my blood and upbringing, set the right example for other young princes swayed by sedition. My father would be proud, they said.

I have done evil, he said. I have betrayed the innocent blood.

What is that to us? they said. See to that yourself.

He cast down the pieces of silver in the temple, so it was fulfilled as was spoken by Zechariah the prophet: *And the Worker said to me, Throw it to the potter! the handsome price they valued me at. So I took the thirty pieces of silver, threw them to the potter at the house of the Worker. And he broke his second staff called Union, breaking the family bond,* so that they might deliver him to the power and authority of the governor. Then the chief priests discussed whether they should also put the young man to death, since many of the Judaeans went away and trusted in Joshua because of him.

Take me, I shouted. Do it. Let me die with him.

I would be the criminal at his side, I ranted at them, hung with a cross for my tree. It would fit; I'd stolen his heart, his life, murdered him. I screamed for my arrest until they dragged me away.

Then they took the silver pieces.

It is not lawful to put them into the treasury, they said, because it is the price of blood.

So they took counsel, to buy Simeon the potter's field with them, to bury foreigners in, and for this reason that field is called the field of blood to this day.

Golgotha

What Is Truth?

1

The high priest then asked Joshua of his students, his teachings.

Joshua in fetters, shoved to shuffle at gunpoint along fluorescent-lit corridors of ceiling tiles and endless black rubber flooring, into an interview room. The scraping bounce of a steel frame chair pulled back from a table. Sit, please. Passport scrutinised by a TSA guard. Questions about his tweets, support for Wikileaks, Anonymous, the Occupy Movement. *Destroy this temple?*

I spoke openly to the world, Joshua answered him, and have said nothing in secret. Always I taught in the congregation house, in the temple, where we ever resort. Why ask me? Ask those who heard me what I have said to them. Behold, they know what I said.

When he had spoken so, one of the guards who stood by struck Joshua with the palm of his hand.

Do you answer the high priest so? he said.

If I have spoken ill, said Joshua, testify of the vice. But if well, why do you strike me?

Joshua in orange jumpsuit and fetters, shoved to shuffle at gunpoint along windowless corridors of concrete and steel ducts, pushed stumbling and falling into a cell empty of all but the dark mirror on the wall, to wait alone. A click, a voice over the intercom: Turn to your left, please.

Now the chief priests, elders and all the council sought for witnesses against Joshua, to put him to death, but found none. For many bore false witness against him, but their testimonies did not hold together. At last, two false witnesses came forward to testify that this fellow said he was able to destroy the temple of the sublime and rebuild it in three days. Still their testimonies did not agree together either. So finally the high priest stood up in the midst.

Joshua in black hood, orange jumpsuit and fetters, shoved to shuffle blindly on, stumble steps, bump walls, until finally he's jostled to a stop, and the hood is ripped off, sudden blaze of daylight dissolving with his blinks to wood panelled chamber of rostrum ahead, amphitheatre seating behind. Above the rostrum, bronze fascii flank a flag of red, white and blue—red field, white circle, blue eagle—just as the centurions flank Joshua. Centre-stage on his throne, the speaker of the house of representatives, aged toad of a man, points a withered finger.

Do you answer nothing? he said. What is it these testify against you?

But Joshua held his peace, answered nothing.

Again the high priest asked him.

I adjure you by the living deity that you tell us, he said. Are you the anointed, the scion of the sublime?

If I tell you, said Joshua, you will not believe. And if I were to ask you, you would not answer me, nor let me go. Still, I say to you that hereafter you will see the everyman sitting on the right hand of power, coming in the clouds of the heavens. And anyone who does not take up his cross and follow me is not worthy of me. If anyone would come after me, he must deny himself, take up his cross and follow me.

Behind him, the house erupts at his insurrectionist call.

Are you then the scion of the sublime? they all said then.

You say this of me, said Joshua.

Then the high priest tore at his clothes.

He has spoken blasphemy! he said. What further need do we have of witnesses? Behold, now you have heard his blasphemy from his own mouth. What do you think?

He does deserve death, they answered.

2

When the morning was come, at once all the chief priests and elders of the people took counsel, and bound Joshua and carried him away. It was early, and they led him from Caiaphas to the hall of judgement, to deliver him to Pontius Pilate the governor, though they themselves did not go into the judgement hall, lest they should be defiled, but that they might eat the Passover.

Pilate in the makeup room, having forehead powdered, coiffure teased, an assistant announcing *one minute* as the tissue is whipped from his collar. He looks in the mirror with eagle eye, sees the face of an Empire occupying hearts and minds, the face of Vox Network's *Court of the People*: guilty or innocent, you decide; phone now to vote! He rises to stride through parting bustle, the assistant bouncing fingers: five; four; three; two; one. Onstage to fanfare, rapturous applause.

Pilate then went out to them, and said, Do you bring some charge against this man?

If he were not a criminal, they said, we would not have delivered him up to you.

And the chief priests accused him of many things.

We found this fellow claiming that he himself is the anointed king, they said.

Then you, said Pilate, take him and judge him by your law. I'm not some Jew, am I?

Contempt in the phrase *some Jew* prompts boos and hisses from the audience, catcalls as for a Wrestlemania heel. Everyone loves a good stage villain. He bangs his gavel, raises a hand for quiet, twirls it in disingenuous disinterest: *go on.* It's how they know he's fair and balanced, his disdain for all.

But that the saying of Joshua might be fulfilled, which he spoke, signifying what death he should die, they said, It is not lawful for us to put any man to death.

So Pilate entered into the judgement hall again, and Joshua stood before the governor.

As the ad break runs, the makeup lady powders shine on the bridge of his aquiline nose. He studies Joshua.

Do you not hear, said Pilate, how many things they witness against you? What *have* you done?

But Joshua answered him with not a word, so that the governor was most bemused.

So, Pilate asked him, are you this King of the Jews?

Do you say this thing of yourself, said Joshua, or did others tell you this of me?

You do not answer me? said Pilate. Do you not know I have power to crucify you and power to release you?

His threat unsheathes the steel of Empire.

You could have no power at all against me, said Joshua, were it not given you from above.

So he who has delivered me to you has the greater delinquency.

To the Jews, said Pilate. Your own nation and your chief priests have delivered you to *me*.

My realm is not of the world, said Joshua. If my realm were of the world, then my attendants would fight that I should not be delivered. But now my realm is not here.

You are a king then? said Pilate.

It's you who say I am a king, said Joshua. To this end I was born, and for this cause came I into the world, that I should testify to the truth. Everyone who is of the truth hears my voice.

———

But for the Empire which operates through symbols, lover of the sublime, from the fascii to the flag-pins, truth is only whatever trivial rearrangement of beliefs is imposed upon the mob. Pilate smiles coldly.

———

What is truth? he said.

3

And when he had said this, Pilate went out again to the chief priests.

———

He strides through the door in a flourish of ermine-lined red, a gleam of armour, gauntleted fist of the Holy Roman Empire. He looks the cassocked clergy up and down. They have already been told that Rome would really rather this Joshua die as a traitor to the Jews than as a martyr to them.

———

I find no crime in him at all, he said.

———

It has been made very clear that Rome will happily *assist* in the governance through the turbulent transition, but it is not here to *meddle*. No, Rome stands for *freedom*, Judaea its beacon of democracy in this barbaric region. If the Jews would have the privilege of civilisation, they must take the responsibility.

———

We have a law, the chief priests said, and by our law he ought to die, because he made himself the scion of the sublime.

So when Pilate heard that saying, he brought Joshua forth, and sat down in the judgement seat in a place that is called the Pavement, but in the Hebrew, *Gabbatha*. But when Pilate was set down on the judgement seat, his wife sent to him, saying, Have nothing to do with that just man, for I have suffered many things this day in a dream because of him. When Pilate therefore heard that saying, he was the more afraid.

———

At his desk in the Oval Office, the Emperor folds the note, hands it back, waves the intern away, an animatronic judder to his actor's grace—early-onset Alzheimer's. He doesn't share his wife's belief in oneiromancy, but a deeper fear of lost control gnaws at his gut. He lifts the phone, ignores the click of a tape starting to record as he sends his orders from on high.

———

And from that moment on Pilate sought to release Joshua, and went again into the judgement hall.

———

Louche predator in black leather overcoat, silver skull insignia on cap, Pilate, local officer in this provincial backwater, barely glances at the prisoner dragged in from the streets.

———

Where are you from? he said to Joshua.

But Joshua gave him no answer.

And the chief priests and clerks stood and fervently accused him. And they were the more fierce, saying, He stirs up the people, teaching throughout all Judaea, beginning from Galilee to this place, perverting the nation.

And forbidding to give tribute to Caesar, they said.

When Pilate heard of Galilee, he asked whether the man were a Galilean. And as soon as he knew that he belonged to Herod's jurisdiction, he sent him to Herod, who was himself also at Jerusalem at that time.

———

General Herod flicks through the CIA dossier, swats a fly at his fat neck.

———

And when Herod saw Joshua, he was beyond glad, for he'd been keen to see him for a long season, had heard so many things of him, *longed* to see some miracle done by him. Then he questioned with him in many words, but Joshua answered him nothing. And the men who held Joshua mocked him. And when they had blindfolded him, then they spat in his face, thrashed him. And others struck him with the palms of their hands.

Prophesy to us! they said. You, the anointed! Who was it struck you?

And Herod with his men of war set him at nothing, mocked him, arrayed him in a gorgeous robe, and sent him again to Pilate. And the same day Pilate and Herod were made friends together, for before they were at enmity between themselves.

4

Now at that feast the governor was wont to release a prisoner to the people, whoever they desired. And there was one known as bar-Abbas, the son of the father, who lay bound with those who had made insurrection. And Pilate knew that for envy they had delivered him also.

I lie weeping as I watch it play out in my concrete padded stone cell skull thrashing raw against iron manacles leather straps straitjacket visions circling seasons of the Gentile mob pouring river of blood libel voices through streets to marble white house temple cathedral echoing for centuries the lamentations of Rachel's children.

And when they were gathered together, Pilate said to them, Who would you rather I release to you? The son of the father or Joshua who is called the anointed? Which of these two would you have me release?

A face peers in through black iron bars, a key turns in a lock, a door opens and I'm dragged to the courtyard of Pilate's praetorium, thrown to the ground beside Joshua, under the shadow of Antonio Fortress. Red robe to my white, he looks at me through the eye that isn't swollen shut, reaches out, his hand struck down by a centurion's swagger stick.

And the chief priests and elders persuaded the people that they should ask for the son of the father and destroy Joshua, that Joshua must die for the nation, and not for the nation alone.

Away with this man, they all cried out at once. Release to us the son of the father.

A few hundred Jews fill the courtyard, beg to save an honoured elder's son.

What shall I do then, said Pilate, with Joshua who is called the anointed?

Beyond them, countless Christians fill Æternity, beg sacrifice to save their souls.

Let him be crucified, cried the Select, as a ransom for many.

Why, said the governor, what wrong has he done? You bring this man to me as one who perverts the people, and behold, having examined him before you, I find no crime in this man as regards those things you accuse him of. No, nor has Herod, for I sent you to him, and behold, to him nothing worthy of death is done. I will chastise and release him then.

But the Select cried out the more, saying, Let him be crucified, as a ransom for many.

Hands over my ears, I still hear it, Jews crying in sorrow, Christians crying in zeal.

When Pilate saw that he could not prevail, but that rather a tumult was made, he took water, and washed his hands before the crowd, saying, I am innocent of the blood of this just person, which is shed for many. See you to it.

We have an understanding?
My father, on his knees before him, nods a head bowed in defeat.

Then answered all the Select, and said, His blood be on us, and on our children. And Pilate, happy to satisfy the Select, released to them he who was cast into prison for sedition and murder, whom they had desired, and gave sentence that it should be as they required,

that the saying of Joshua might be fulfilled, which he spoke, *They shall deceive the very successors.*

And stumbling free into the crowd, half-carried by my father into the arms of Mary, I scream of robes washed white in blood of the lamb of whited sepulchres of outward beauty full of dead men's bones within full of all pollution from generation to generation until the seasons of the Gentiles be fulfilled.

5

Then the soldiers of the governor took Joshua into the common hall called the praetorium, gathered to him the whole band of soldiers. They stripped him, scourged him, put on him a scarlet robe. And the soldiers wove a crown of thorns, put it on his head, with a reed in his right hand: and they bent the knee before him, mocked him, and said, Hail, King of the Jews! So Pilate went forth again. And it was the preparation of the Passover, about the sixth hour...

Fanfare of trumpets, rapturous applause, and Pilate jogs out onto the stage to whoops and whistles, punches the air with the mic in one hand, a boxer's one-two, yeah—badaboom go the drums. Thank you! he preens, and slips slick into a stand-up intro to tonight's spectacular show, oh yes, and with such a special guest.

Behold, he said, I bring him forth to you, that you may know I find no fault in him.

The one and only, all on his lonely... please give it up for *Joshua*!

Then Joshua came forth, wearing the crown of thorns and the purple robe, and he delivered Joshua to their will.

Behold your king! he said to the Jews.

And oh, what fun as Pilate jigs: a contest for the king to judge! And centurions wheel the gallows on, a foal hung from it, body gaudy in stripes of a psychedelic zebra, mane and tail beaded in the colours of the rainbow, yes, it's the foal that Joshua rode into Jerusalem on, hogtied, strung upside down, braying in panic as the contestants enter now, a choir of blindfolded brats in confirmation suits, swinging Louisville Sluggers at the flesh piñata, cheered on with hallelujahs and amens.

And that was just the warm-up, Pilate crows as they sweep the carcass away, blood-baptised children grinning. Now! he shouts. The man of the hour, with the glory and power! Bring on the anointed!

And Joshua stands there, centre-stage.

And the soldiers spit upon him, took the reed, smote him on the head, saying, Crucify him, crucify him. And so when the chief priests and officers saw him, and the whole band of soldiers gathered round him, they cried out.

Shall I crucify your king? said Pilate.

The chief priests answered, We have no king but Caesar.

And Pilate said, Behold the man!

A geek in barbed wire crown, robe red with blood—his blood or of doves of sacred inspiration, snakes of wisdom decapitated with his teeth, spitting heads—Hypatia! Schwarz! Galileo! Bruno!—does it matter?

So then Pilate delivered him to the soldiers to be crucified. And they took the robe from him, put his own raiment on him, led him away to crucify him. And as they came out, they found a man of Cyrene, Simon by name, the father of Alexander and Rufus, who passed by coming out of the country, and they forced him to carry Joshua's cross.

And there followed him a great mob of the Jews, of men and women, who also bewailed and lamented him. But Joshua turning to them said, Daughters of Jerusalem, weep not for me but for yourselves, for your children. For, behold, the days are coming in which they shall say, Blessed are the barren, the wombs that never bore, the breasts that never gave suck. Then they shall begin to say to the mountains, Fall on us; and to the hills, Hide us. For if they do these things when the tree is green, what shall be done when it is dry?

6

And there were two others also led with him to be executed, criminals. And when they were come to the place called Calvary or Golgotha, that is to say, a place of skulls—after the head-tax of the Romans— they gave him vinegar mingled with gall to drink, but when he had tasted thereof, he would not drink. And they gave him wine mingled with myrrh to drink, but he took it not.

From the distance, I see him wave it away, heart breaking to know what he's doing, I think, staying true to his Nazirite vow of the last supper: no matzo bread, no four cups of wine, no taste of the Seder: no Passover till Empire's end. And no sedative poison to dull the pain, I think, no place for even a sham of mercy in this display of sacrifice stripped to its brutal truth of slaughter. And I know, I know, that this is his plan: that he abhors sacrifice so wholly, he goes to his death as undeniable demonstration of its unconscionable merciless iniquity.

And it was the third hour, and they crucified him. Then the two thieves, who had committed murder in the insurrection, were crucified with him, one on his right hand, the other on his left. So the scripture was fulfilled, which said, *And he was numbered with the lawless.*

Socrates and Sartre, Spartacus and Sade, rebels against unquestioned truth, they are all sedition as they spit, swear of what it is to be, to do, as soldiers in khakis and green berets fire nailguns through their wrists, set up pulleys and hoists, block and tackle, methodical as if they're raising flagpoles. All roads lead to Rome, they say. I see all of them lined with crucifixes.

———

Father, said Joshua then, I entrust | my inspiration into your hands.

———

Struggling, reaching from the crowd's grip, I weep for the everyman who is the future.

———

Father, forgive them, he said, for | they know not what they do.

———

Struggling, reaching from the crowd's grip, I weep for the everyman who is history.

———

And Mary Magdalene stood there by the cross of Joshua, and his mother, the wife of Cleophas, mother of James and Joses and Jude and Symon the Zealous. So when Joshua saw his mother, and the student whom he loved standing by, he said to his mother, Woman, behold your son! Then he said to the student, Behold | your mother! And from that hour that student took her to his own home, that it might be fulfilled as was spoken by Isaiah the prophet, saying, *Behold my child, whom I have chosen, my beloved, in whom my soul is well pleased. I will put my inspiration upon him, and he shall show judgement to the Gentiles.*

———

The Marys hold me back as I scream in the faces of those soldiers of Empire, swear to show them the judgement they exercise on us, to make them see. I will rip Paul from history. I will smash the Rock to sand. I will shove the truth down Pilate's throat.

Then the soldiers, when they had crucified Joshua, took his clothes and his coat, and made four piles of his clothes, a pile for each soldier. But the coat was without seam, woven from the top throughout, so they said among themselves, Let us not tear it, but cast lots for it, to decide whose it shall be. So, the soldiers did these things, that the scripture might be fulfilled, which said, They parted my raiment among them, and for my vesture they did cast lots.

7

And sitting down, they watched him there; and Pilate wrote a title, and put it on the cross, over his head.

A line in Greek inserted on a fresh scroll that will consign the Gospel of the Hebrews to the fires. A final signature on a concord of creeds that will condemn all splinter sects as heresies. A seal on an edict that confers unquestionable authority on the canon. A stamp on the travel papers, letters of marque, personal mandate from the Emperor himself, in the hand of one slick-suited salesman with a suitcase full of salvation, bound for the future. Crouched at the foot of the cross, Pilate lays the brush down, hands the paint-daubed board across the centuries to a faceless murderer in jackboots.

And the writing was *Joshua the Nazirite, King of the Jews*. And many of the Judaeans read this title, for the place where Joshua was crucified was close to the city, and it was written in Hebrew, and Greek, and Latin.

And in English, in German, in Russian, in French, every tongue of Christendom. It is painted on a board, inked on a vellum manuscript, printed on an iron-framed press, broadcast on the radio, transmitted to TV sets, spread over the internet, engrained into infant minds. Mycelia of the lie permeate every culture touched by your gospels, lover of the sublime, instil the image of Joshua as judge and master.

Do not write, The King of the Jews, the chief priests said to Pilate. But write, He said, I am King of the Jews.

And I'm shouting that he said, You say I am. But my words are lost in the baying of the mob, so only Mary hears me, and holds me, tries to calm her broken-minded brother even in her own grief. We are on our knees, both of us.

What I have written I have written, said Pilate. And no man was able to answer him a word, neither did any man dare ask him any more questions from that day forth.

And those among the clerks and elders who passed by reviled Joshua, shaking their heads.

I watch them come, from every year of the season of the Gentiles, in black suits, cassocks, robes, one glancing up to see a heretic on a pyre, another a sodomite on a stake. This one sees a blasphemer in the pillory, that one a traitor on the gallows.

Save yourself, they jeered, you who would destroy the temple and build it in three days. If you are the scion of the sublime, come down from the cross.

Likewise also the chief priests mocked him

He saved others, they said. He cannot save himself. If he is the King of Israel, let him come down from the cross now and we'll believe him. He trusted in the sublime. Let the sublime deliver him now, if the sublime will have him. After all, he said he was the scion of the sublime.

And one of the thieves who was crucified with him also cast the same in his teeth, railed on him, saying, If you are the anointed, save yourself and us.

But the other rebuked him, saying, Do not you fear the sublime, seeing you are in the same condemnation? And we at least receive the due reward of our deeds in justice, but this man has done nothing wrong.

Teacher, he said to Joshua then, remember me when you come into your realm.

For sure, I tell you, said Joshua, today you shall be with me in the orchard.

8

Now from the sixth hour to the ninth there was darkness over all the land until, around the ninth hour, Joshua cried with a loud voice, saying, *Eli, Eli, lama sabachthani?* which is to say, My deity, my deity, why have you forsaken me?

Some of those who stood there, when they heard that, said, This man calls for Elijah.

But kneeling there, I knew that if he truly called on any deity, that call could have no answer. Oh, I yearned for him so painfully I could dream a cry from on high, simple, reassuring: No, you are not forsaken. But as

I kneel there now again, I know such folly only proves one has yet to know the sacred inspiration, feel its loss, the breath crushed from your lungs, legs buckling in weakness of despair.

If he truly called on his deity. You know my name, lover of the sublime, not the curse you call me by, no more my name than Joses's was Thomas, but that which he raised me by in Bethany, the name he would shorten to soft endearment as we sat alone in the quiet wilds around Capernaum to watch a sunrise. Did the blood and swelling blind him now, that he did not know his Eleazar, his Eli, was so close? I cannot bear that thought, so I hear his question as a final lesson, an elicitation of understanding in answer as reminder: For love.

After this, knowing that all things were now accomplished that the scripture might be fulfilled, Joshua said, I thirst.

His voice was barely audible.

And there were many women there who had followed Joshua from Galilee, and many others who came up with him to Jerusalem, tending to him, among them Mary Magdalene, Mary his mother and of James and Joses, and Salome, the mother of Zebedee's children, who followed him even when he was in Galilee. So while the rest said, Leave it be, let us see whether Elijah will come to save him, the mob began to cry out, demanding that it should be as he had ever done for them. And there was set a vessel full of vinegar, so at once one of them ran and took a sponge, filled it with vinegar, put it upon a hyssop reed, and put it to his mouth to drink.

So when Joshua had taken the vinegar, he said, It is finished.

And he bowed his head, gave up the breath.

And, behold, the sun was darkened, and the veil of the temple tore in two from top to bottom; and the earth did quake, the rocks tore, and a lintel of the temple of immense size was broken. And the graves were opened. Many bodies of the saints which slept arose, came from the graves, and went into the holy city, appeared to many.

———

And for that moment, all Jerusalem saw itself as he did, an Æternity walked by men already dead.

———

Now when the centurion, and those who were with him watching Joshua, saw the earthquake and those things that were done, they feared greatly, saying, Truly this was the scion of the sublime.

———

The centurion looked down at the blood-stained robe he'd won, crouched down to touch that which had once touched him, mired now with glory, with the gore of miracles. And the murderer's eyes shone golden as salvation.

———

And the whole populace who gathered together to that sight after his revival, seeing the things which were done, beat their breasts and left. But all who knew him stood afar off, watching.

The Keeper of the Orchard

9

When the evenfall was come, because it was the preparation—the day before the Sabbath, that is—there came a rich man of Arimathaea, named Joseph, who was also Joshua's student, who also waited for the realm of the sublime, though secretly for fear of the Select. And he was a good man and just, an honourable member of the Sanhedrin, who had not consented to their decision and action. He went in boldly to Pilate, and begged the body of Joshua, that the bodies should not remain upon the cross on the Sabbath day. Because this Sabbath day was a holy day, he begged Pilate that their legs might be broken, that they might be taken away, and Pilate gave him leave.

He looks like a rat-faced bank manager, Joseph thinks, receding hairline and weak chin, beady eyes behind wire-frame spectacles, thin-trimmed moustache sealing the fate of a countenance that could only ever invoke words like prissy, petty, parsimonious. Pilate pushes the spectacles up his nose, takes the sheaf of procedural expedition warrants from Joseph's hands, flicks through them, stamping each in turn, hands them back without a word.

Then the soldiers came, and broke the legs of first one then the other who were crucified with him. But when they came to Joshua, and saw that he was dead already, they did not break his legs. But Pilate wondered if he were truly already dead, and calling the centurion to him, asked if he had been dead any length of time. So one of the soldiers pierced his side with a spear, and blood and water came out.

And he... he who saw it bears record—and this record is true, he knows that it is true—that you might trust. For these things were done, that the scripture should be fulfilled, *A bone of him shall not be broken.* And again another scripture said, *They shall look on him whom they pierced.*

Then when he knew it from the centurion, Pilate commanded the body to be delivered. And when Joseph had taken the body, he bought fine linen, took him down, and wrapped him in the clean linen cloth.

I brought it to him, draped between my arms, the shroud of my interment in a Bethany grave and my initiation in a Gethsemane grove, washed clean and yet... still I could swear there was a scent, the slightest scent of sweat and grass.

Now in the place where he was crucified there was a garden, and in the garden a new sepulchre, wherein man was never yet laid. And Mary Magdalene and Mary the mother of Joses, sitting over against the sepulchre, beheld where he was laid. And they went away, to prepare spices and ointments, and to rest the Sabbath day according to the decree, because of the Jewish preparation day, and since the sepulchre was close at hand they laid Joshua there. They took the body of Joshua, wound it in linen clothes with the spices, as is the manner of the Jews to bury, and laid it in Joseph's own new tomb, which he had hewn out in the rock. And there came also the Judaean who first came to Joshua by night, and brought a mixture of myrrh and aloes, about a hundred pound weight.

Mary's voice at the door of the crypt. I saw my father standing there, quiet. He would not come in. I rose to take the ointments, squeeze his arm in gratitude.

And he rolled a great stone to the door of the sepulchre, and departed.

10

Now the next day, that followed the day of the preparation, the chief priests and Select came together to Pilate, saying, Sir, we remember what that liar said, while he was yet alive: *After three days I will rise again.* Command then that the sepulchre be made secure until the third day, lest his students come by night, and steal him away, and say to the people that he is risen from the dead. That last lie should be worse than the first.

You may have your watch, Pilate said to them. Go your way. Make it as secure as you can.

So they went, and made the sepulchre secure, sealing the stone, and setting a watch.

And through the streets of Jerusalem, around Bethany and Bethphage, circling Golgotha and Gethsemane, the tanks of Empire rumbled on their rolling treads, and centurions with rifles slung over their shoulders swept their searchlights from the watchtower of the Antonio Fortress, beams white as bleached bone in moonlight scything brick walls, tarmac and cobblestones as the soaring, swooping vision of an angel of death. And somewhere in the curfewed night, a bishop closed the shutters of his window on crusaders, walked to the wireless on his study desk and turned the volume up on Salome's lilting *Kyrie Eleison*, let the waves of music wash away the sounds of marching feet and breaking glass outside.

But behold, there was a great earthquake, for the messenger of the Worker descended from the heavens, and came and rolled back the stone from the door, and sat upon it.

And out of the curfewed night, the sound of the blast brought shouting guards and barking dogs running through the gnarled olives to the crypt, the great iron door blown from its hinges, a figure on it crouched to gaze into the dark, but turning as they arrived, turning to let a flash grenade roll from his hand, a magnesium shockwave that left them blinking phosphene after-images of his mask greasepaint white in their flashlights, bearded and grinning.

His countenance was like lightning, and his raiment white as snow.

And by the time their vision cleared he was gone, only his message left in an abandoned mask.

And they went out quickly, fled from the sepulchre; for they trembled, were amazed. Neither said they anything to anyone, for they were afraid. But as they were going, behold, some of the watch came into the city, and showed to the chief priests all the things that were done. And when they were assembled with the elders, and had taken counsel, they gave much money to the soldiers.

You, they said, say that his students came by night, and stole him away while we slept. And if this come to the governor's ears, we will soothe him and keep you safe.

And for fear of him the keepers did shake, became as dead men, so they took the money and did as they were told, and this saying is commonly reported to this day.

A fiction answering a fiction answering a fiction.

The story isn't even over and already it's mutating, I say.

Hush, says Mary.

On the floor of the old bus, I lie half-buried in patchwork quilts and paisley throws, clutching a cushion for a pillow, for the smell of him on it. She sits with me, stroking my hair, as I try to tell her how there's already a story of him risen from the dead, a story of us stealing his corpse in response, this story in response to that.

Hush, she says. Hush.

11

Now when Joshua was risen early the first day of the week, he appeared first to Mary Magdalene, out of whom he had cast seven daimons. When the Sabbath was past, Mary Magdalene, and Mary the mother of James, and Salome had bought sweet spices, that they might come and anoint him. So, very early in the morning the first day of the week, they came to the sepulchre at the rising of the sun.

Who shall roll us away the stone from the door of the sepulchre? they said among themselves, for it was very great.

But when they looked, they saw that the stone was rolled away. Then Mary Magdalene ran, came to Simon the Rock, and to the other student, whom Joshua loved.

Who do you seek? they said. Woman, why do you weep?

Because they have taken away our teacher, she said, and I know not where they have laid him.

And when she had said this, she turned herself back, and the Rock therefore went forth, and that other student, and came to the sepulchre. They both ran together, but the other student outran the Rock, came first to the sepulchre. And stooping down, and looking in, he saw the linen clothes lying, but he did not go in.

I stood at the door of the desecrated tomb, looking in at the low stone shelf, back at Mary, back at the shelf, at the shape of linen laid upon it. I heard Simon mutter of hysteria, but Mary was right. He wasn't there.

Then Simon the Rock arrived behind him. And stooping down, he entered the sepulchre, and he beheld the linen clothes laid by themselves, and the napkin that was about his head, not lying with the linen clothes, but wrapped together in a place by itself. And then that other student, who came first to the sepulchre, and was seen by Simon, then as Mary stood outside the sepulchre weeping, then he also went in.

Inside, Simon touched the face shroud gently, traced a contour with such tenderness I couldn't believe he'd curse a fly. I walked to the other end, knelt down where toes should be wiggling ticklish as I washed between them. He wasn't there.

And he saw, and believed: *Because* | *I live, you shall live also.*

I saw that he was *here*, you understand.

And as Mary wept, she turned herself and crouched down, and looked into the sepulchre, and saw two messengers in white sitting, the one at the head and the other at the feet, where the body of Joshua had lain. But the Rock departed, wondering in himself at what had come to pass, for as yet they did not understand the scripture, that he must rise again from the dead. So it was Mary Magdalene and Joanna, and Mary the mother of James, and other women that were with them, who told these things to the apostles.

For entering into the sepulchre, they saw a young man sitting on the right side, clothed in a long white garment.

As I held the shroud, I saw that he was gone to nothing, to empty rags, and right here, right here.

And the fashion of his countenance was altered, his face did shine as the sun, and his raiment became | glistering, shining, beyond white as snow, so as no fuller on earth can whiten them.

I felt the everyman here with us, now.

And they were afraid. |

And I rose from the empty wrappings, turned to my sister.

And Joshua said to her, Woman, | why do you weep?

12

And she saw Joshua standing, but knew not that it was Joshua, imagining him to be only the keeper of the orchard. | Teacher, she said, if you have carried him off, tell me where you have laid him, and I will take him away.

I look around this room, this cell, concrete or padded, papered in his story, my own scribbled between the lines—psychosis or sacrilege to you, I'm sure, if not both. It is a sad sweet scene, this one, and not even so far from Matthew's heart-breaking original, the empty tomb, the one we loved among us unknown, but... it is time to unfold this grandest of parables to its truth.

Do you know where he is now? is what my sister asked me as I held her in my arms, gazing over her shoulder at the empty wrappings of linen and flesh. Had he told me last secrets of everlasting life, she wanted to know, left me the keys of the realm, showed me the gates to the orchard?

———

Do not fear, the messenger said to the women, for I know that you seek Joshua who was crucified. Why do you seek the living among the dead?

———

I stroked her hair, felt the silk of his smile running through my fingers. She wanted the Joshua we remembered, I said, the Joshua who lived and breathed. The neverafter was no place to look for such life.

———

Remember how he spoke to us when he was yet in Galilee, he said, saying the everyman must be delivered into the hands of delinquent men, be crucified, and rise again the third day. Behold the place where they laid him. He is not here, but is risen.

———

I wiped a tear from her eye, tasted my own, the salt of his laughter in lamplight. I remembered everything he said to us in Galilee. I remembered everything he said, sacred inspiration welling up in my heart, pouring from my mouth, and him sparkling in every drop of that living water. As Joshua spoke as the sacred inspiration, I spoke as Joshua.

———

Mary, said Joshua to her. He who has known the world has found the corpse, and he who has found the corpse, the world is not worthy of him. As long as we are in the world, we are the light of the world.

———

I cupped her face in my hands, raised it to lock her eyes with mine, that we should see him in each other.

And she said to him in Hebrew, Rabboni—which is to say, Teacher.

Then the women remembered Joshua's words, and they came and held him by the feet, adored him.

Do not touch me, said Joshua, for I am not yet ascended to my beloved. But go to my brethren, and tell them I ascend to my beloved and your beloved, to my spirit and your spirit. Go your way, tell the Rock and his students that he goes before you into Galilee.

I kissed her forehead, his mercy sweet on my lips.

You shall see him there, as he said to you.

And they returned from the sepulchre. And Mary Magdalene came and told the students she'd seen the teacher, that he'd spoken these things to her. She went and told all these things to the eleven, and to all the rest, those who had been with him, as they mourned and wept, but they, when they had heard that he was alive, and had been seen by her, did not believe, for her words seemed to them as idle tales.

13

Then the students went away again to their own home. And behold, that same day, two of them, Cleopas and James, went to a village called Emmaus, about sixty furlongs from Jerusalem. And they talked together of all these things which had happened. And it came to pass, that, while they talked together in debate, Joshua himself drew near, clothed in a long white garment, and went with them.

They were walking on the edge of the cobble-stoned road from Jerusalem to Sycaminum, seeking shade from the afternoon sun under the olive trees they passed, when I arrived to find them deep in conversation, deep in mutual consolation.

And behold, Joshua greeted them, saying, All hail.

But their eyes were seized that they should not know him.

I was surprised, at first, that they didn't recognise me, peered at me like we'd never met, but perhaps I was already dissolving into the interstices. Had I called them by name? Perhaps Cleopas would have looked up, seen the Judaean he thought hanged, or maybe James would have seen... that student Joshua loved... what was his name? But no.

You do not know me when you see me, lover of the sublime, so why should they? You see a rich young man begging the secret of everlasting life, a lad carrying bread, a beloved student leaning back in love's embrace, a dead man risen from the grave, a traitor with a bag of coins, even a naked youth half-glimpsed in flight, white linen sheet left in a soldier's grip.

Just as you look at me here in your scriptures and see this, look at me there in your scriptures and see that, so on the road to Emmaus, Cleopas and James saw only... a stranger on the road to Emmaus.

———

What manner of talks are these that you have with each other, he said to them, as you walk in sorrow?

And one of them, Cleopas, answered.

Are you only a stranger in Jerusalem, he said, not knowing the things which are come to pass there in these days?

———

He walked slow with age and sadness, James beside him keeping pace, a second staff for him to lean on. I turned as Cleopas paused under his burden.

———

What things? said Joshua.

To do with Joshua the Nazirite, they said, who was a prophet great in deed and word in the sight of the sublime and all the people; and how the chief priests and our lords delivered him to be condemned to death, and how the Romans have crucified him; and we trusted that it was he who should have emancipated Israel; and beside all this, today is the third day since these things were done; aye, and certain women also of our company shocked us; they were at the sepulchre early, and when they did not find his body there, they came to tell us, saying also that they'd seen a vision of messengers who claimed he was alive; and some of those who were with us went to the sepulchre, and found it even as the women had said, but they did not see him.

You are speaking of the dead, said Joshua then, and neglecting he who is alive before you. O fools, and slow of heart to trust all that the prophets have spoken.

And beginning at Moses, he expounded to them everything in all the scriptures of all the prophets, everything written about himself.

It was less pompous than it sounds.

Twenty-four prophets spoke in Israel, they said, and they all | speak in you.

14

And they drew nigh to the village where they were headed, and he made as | though he would have gone on further until they stopped him.

I close the car door softly, crick my back in a welcome stretch and turn, gaze out over the car roof and across the parking lot, toward the stream of trucks and pickups, thrumming Dopler pulses of noise, headlights on already mostly. A flick of a softpack to knock a smoke loose, a shift of rucksack slung over shoulder, and I start around the car for the road, the long road to Galilee. Feel a hand on my arm before I even turn to say my thanks and goodbye. Liver-spotted, frail but firm in its clasp. Cleopas smiles, sad and warm.

Stay with us a while, they said, for it is getting on to evening, and | the day is nearly done.

Behind them, the truck stop diner is a humble little pageantry of light in the dusk, and I'm hungry with a way to go, and it's a good moment in the tale for me, a good and right moment of the everyman, not a virgin birth or blind man made to see, just a kind hand and an offer of a meal to a young hitcher picked up by these passers-by. I smile at them, the old man and his son, Cleopas and James, and nod, slip the cigarette back into the pack and follow them inside.

So he went in to bide with them a while, saying, Bring a table and bread.

And it came to pass, as he sat at meat with them, he took bread, and blessed it, broke it and gave it to James the Just and said to him, My brother, eat your bread, for the everyman is risen from the dead.

And their eyes were opened, and they knew him, then the vision vanished, vanished from their sight.

An all too familiar motion in the breaking of bread, an echo of sentiment or voice in my words, and James is setting down his glass and Cleopas furrowing his brows in sudden recognition, both rising. James reaches across to take the Yankees baseball cap from my head, peer at my face. And there are tears in his eyes, the impossible joy of a dream in which some lost loved one is not dead after all, not really. I smile and nod as he drops the cap on the table, pick it up.

And then the moment is slipping past and I'm not Joshua, just his beloved student, and I'm not his beloved student, just a stranger picked up on the road to Emmaus, some young everyman they thought was someone else, just for a second, for a second already slipped from memory, leaving only the echo of its joy.

Then it's over and I stand at the door, awkward fumble for money refused, hands shaken, leave taken, glancing back at this facet of Æternity. Already gone. I let the door swing shut behind me and walk out across the asphalt of the parking lot, toward the edge of a road where moments like this might be scattered anywhere along the way, waiting for a passer-by to pull their car over to the verge, reach over and open the passenger door.

And they said one to another, Did our hearts not burn within us while he talked with us on the road and while he opened up the scriptures to us? Ought not the anointed to have suffered these things, and to enter into his glory?

15

And they rose up the same hour, returned to Jerusalem, and found the eleven gathered together, and those who were with them. And they told what things were done on the road, how Joshua was recognised by them through the breaking of bread. But Thomas, one of the twelve, called Didymus, was not with them when Joshua came.

So the other students said to him, We have seen the teacher. The teacher is risen indeed.

But he said, Unless I see the stamp of the nails in his hands, and put my finger into the stamp of the nails, thrust my hand into his side, I will not believe.

Then the same day at evening, being the first day of the week, when the doors were shut where the students were assembled for fear of the Select, as they thus spoke, Joshua himself stood in the midst of them. This was the third time now that Joshua showed himself to his students after he was risen from the dead.

You might imagine me doubling back on the road to Galilee, quietly following Cleopas and James, tapping a secret knock upon the door. Or you might imagine me just suddenly being there in James's laugh of wonder—Joshua's laugh—at the impossible meeting on that road. Both would be more true than the ghost conjured in gospel. I was *there*, you understand.

His students were within, Thomas with them, and then came Joshua and stood in the midst, appeared to the eleven as they sat at meat.

I paid the landlord and took a sip of my whisky, watched them for a moment as they sat in the snug of that little pub in Jerusalem, laughing wild as a wake should be, a wee slice of Galilee in Judaea, sealed so secure in its fraternity that right now there might be nothing beyond those doors, no Select, no Herod, no Empire. I took a breath to gather myself, himself, and walked across to them, glass in hand for the toast.

Peace be to you, he said.

And when they saw him, they adored him, but some doubted; they were terrified with fright, and supposed that they had seen a vision. He chided them for their hard hearts and distrust, because they had not trusted those who'd seen him after he was risen.

Why are you troubled? he said. And why do thoughts arise in your hearts? Do not distrust, but trust. Behold my hands and my feet, that it is I myself. Handle me, and see, for an inspiration has not flesh and bones, as you see me have.

And when he had thus spoken, he showed them his hands and his feet.

Bring your finger here, he said to Thomas, and study my hands. Bring your hand here, and thrust it into my side.

I held his hand to my side, Joshua's agony in the tremble of his fingers. And a sceptical frown became quizzical, questioning, searching, surprised.

My teacher, said Thomas. And... | my God.

Think of it more as expletive than honorific.

Thomas, said Joshua, because you have seen me, you have trusted.

Then the students were glad, when they saw the teacher. And while they still did not believe for joy, and wondered, he spoke to them:

Have you any food here?

And they gave him a scrap of broiled fish, and he took it, ate in their sight.

Peace be to you, said Joshua to them again.

And when he had said this, he breathed on them, saying, Welcome the sacred inspiration. Seek, and you shall find.

16

Then he opened their vision that they might grasp the scriptures.

Thus it is written, he said, thus it suited the anointed to suffer and rise from the dead the third day, that a change of heart and release from delinquency should be preached in his name among all nations, beginning at Jerusalem.

I knew even as I opened their vision—just a crack—that it might close again all too quickly. I saw Simon who would murder with his curse, James who would die in prison, all of it already written, and felt sick even as I breathed the inspiration into them. I saw it all. If there was something that could have been done then and there to change it all, that vision died on Golgotha. Even the everyman has his limits.

In my name they shall cast out daimons, speak with new tongues, take up serpents. If they drink any deadly thing, it shall not hurt them. They shall lay hands on the sick, and they shall recover.

I saw the exorcisms of epileptics, the glossalalia of hysterics, the snake-handling of maniacs. I saw doctors pleading with parents to let them treat a dying child, charlatans calling the desperate to their sideshow stages. As I opened their vision, I hoped they saw it too, but they were no more equipped to face it than I. I could see understanding on their faces, dying even as it was born.

You are witnesses of these things, you who have continued with me through my trials. Go then, you, and teach all nations, baptizing them. Go you into all the world, and preach the gospel to every creature, teaching them to observe any and all decrees I've given you, that all things may be fulfilled as were written in the law of Moses, in the prophets, and in the psalms, concerning me. I appoint to you a realm, as my beloved has appointed to me. As my beloved sent me, so I send you.

I spoke with grim resolve. I saw the word warping as it spread, the revolution co-opted into the very foundations of Empire, trust turned to faith, inspiration to ignorance, his whole philosophy twisted to the ultimate viral carrier for everything we opposed. I tried...

Preach as you go, saying, The realm of Zion is to hand! Preach as you go, saying, I will have mercy and not sacrifice! Preach as you go, saying, I have come to destroy sacrifices! And if you do not stop making sacrifices, the wrath of the sublime, the accuser, will never leave you. Call no man your father upon the earth, for only one is your father, and you are all brothers. Do not be called rabbi either, for only one is your teacher, the anointed.

I tried, but I saw it all, took comfort only in this vision: word as code, scraps of original broken function deep in the machinery; seeds of sacred inspiration spread via that viral strain, permeating the system's very core; fragments warped and buried, but waiting, waiting for the right trigger to reactivate them, recombine them, restore them to... a simple message, really.

He was a burning and shining light, he who is in Æternity, and you were willing for a season to rejoice in his light.

The word as a Trojan Horse, disseminated over this two millennia aeon, everywhere now, a sleeping giant.

———————

But behold, I am with you all the days, even to the culmination of | this aeon.

———————

Consider this the aeon culminated. Time to wake up, everyman.
   Yes, I mean you.

Raise Up the Stone

17

Tell us, the students said to Joshua, how our end shall be.

Have you resolved the beginning then, said Joshua, that you seek after the end? As the beginning is, so shall be the end.

And looking up to the heavens, he sighed:

He who knows all but fails to know himself lacks everything.

I slugged back the last of my whisky, chased it down with a sip from my pint. Mary's hand on my arm.

What do your students seem to you? Mary said to Joshua.

Like little children playing in a field which isn't theirs, said Joshua.

On the walls of salvaged scripture, I restore now the first fragments lost to Empire, purged even from Matthew's Gospel of the Hebrews, lost to apocryphal obscurity. The remnants of ever-dubious Thomas's cutting-room collation barely amount to a handful of aphoristic exchanges, but maybe, I think, there's just enough. There should be. As the wake wore on into the night, seeing a bleary Matthew fumble a tape into his machine, it was Thomas I found myself turning to.

You have to write this all down, I said. All of it.

Then he spoke to them a parable:

Behold the fig tree, he said. Behold *all* the trees. As their buds shoot forth, as you see now, you know of your own selves that summer is close at hand. But he who has ears, let him hear: A certain winemaker had a fig tree planted in his vineyard, and he came seeking fruit on it one year, found none. He came seeking fruit on it the next, but still found none, came seeking fruit on it a third year, and still there was none. So he turned to the keeper of his vineyard.

Behold, he said, these three years I come seeking fruit on this fig tree, find none. Put the axe to the trunk and cut it down, uproot it, cast it in the fire. Why burden the ground with it?

Master, said the keeper, blessed are those who have not seen, and yet have trusted. Let it alone this year too, and I will dig manure in around it. If it bears fruit, fine. If not, then after that you should cut it down.

Now I say, for sure, I tell you, you who have walked with me, such signs shall accompany *all* those who have faith. You also shall sit on thrones, twelve of them, judging the twelve tribes of Israel. But behold, I lay the promise of my father upon you, that whichever of any man's delinquencies you resolve, they will be resolved to them; but whichever of any man's delinquencies you retain, they will be retained.

———

I remember my hand gripping Thomas's arm, my focused gaze—*remember* this—as I promised the power and glory of our Pyrrhic victory, every student a saint in Heaven and no healings for the blind from healers blind themselves. So the time would come…

———

So when the owners of the field return, they will say, Yield up to us our field! The messengers will come to you, and the prophets, and they shall give you what belongs to you. In the regeneration when the everyman shall sit in the throne of his glory, you too then, give them everything that's in your grasp. Naked before them, you are to yield it up to them, give them back their field. Take heed. Ask yourselves: On what day will they come, take back what's theirs?

Only Thomas remembered. It's the loss of that question everywhere else which makes the answer *today*.

18

Who are you, his students said to him, that you should say these things to us?

We sit in the Bethsaida Bothy in Jerusalem, heavy wooden doors of the pub shut and bolted for a lock-in, landlord sitting now with the Sons of Thunder, sharing stories of back home. As I look around me, I see all the gilded halos of glory, all the great grey beards of might that the Empire will paint them with. And already it's begun. Every one of them glows more radiant than any stained glass, if they could only see it, but here they sit, echoing the same old question of every aeon's Select: who do you think you are?

You test the face of Æternity and Earth, he said. You do not know he who is before you, and you do not know not to test this moment. I am the light that is over them all. I am the all. The all has come forth from me, and the all has culminated in me.

I once asked Joshua that question, back before Gethsemane, before Bethany, before Sychar and Tabor even, not in outrage but in wonder at his audacity, at his talk of taking the realm back from the Select, giving it to everyone, to the part of everyone that it belonged to. Who do you think you are? I laughed. His eyes glinted with a wry smile it took me all my life with him to understand, lesson after lesson dismantling the folly of presumption until finally in a place of skulls I realised the truth of an everyman who could never truly be defeated, always already returning to take back the birthright of even some bastard boy from Nazareth.

Tell us who you are, they said to him, that we may trust in you.

From what I say to you, said Joshua, you do not understand who I am, but you have become as the Select. For they love the tree and hate its fruit, and love the fruit and hate its tree. You too, then, be watchful over against the world, lest at any time your hearts be *overloaded with debauchery and excess*, so that day comes upon you unawares. For it shall come as a stumbling block on all who dwell upon the face of the earth.

The sacred inspiration flows bitter from my mouth, laced with irony to verge on lashing: go on, build your Church! curse the world and the flesh! live in terror of temptation! I try to rein it in, tell myself they're not that yet—*we're* not that yet—but I hear the venom in my words.

Aye, bide your time in the city of Jerusalem. Teach the Gentiles until you be bestowed with power from on high, and sit on thrones judging the twelve tribes of Israel, in sackcloth and ashes. Gird up your loins with great strength, that the thieves may not find a way to come at you. The advantage for which you look they *will* find.

If there is no changing what's already written, it's some small comfort that this aeon *will* end.

I sigh and, as he would do, once again, I try.

These things I have spoken to you so my joy might remain in you, so your joy might be full, so you should not be upset: he who trusts and is baptized shall be saved, but he who does not trust shall be condemned. But *these* things I decree to you: that you love one another; you are sublime.

The only sublime there is.

19

And Joshua came to them, saying, These are the words I've spoken to you, while I was still with you. But some of those things you asked me about in those days, I did not tell you then. Now I wish to tell them, but you do not ask. Many times you've desired to hear these words I speak to you, and you have no-one else to hear them from.

Their eyes are wide. In the corner of the snug, I look past them at the panels of stained glass that run along the top of the bar, a lattice of diamonds.

All power is given to me in Æternity and Earth, he said. When you bring forth what is within you, that which you have will save you. And at that day you'll know that I am in my beloved, you in me, and I in you, and will leave me alone—though I am never alone, since the beloved is with me.

I want to tell them that the world is a matrix of such panels, light crystallised as hologram, big picture latent in each shard of a particle, the everyman only that integration on a human scale, each of us contained within the other. But even the mass unconscious is just the sacred inspiration finding a metaphor for itself, for what needs to be brought forth.

If you do not have that in yourselves, that which you do not have in you will destroy you. And then... woe to you, clerks and Select, hypocrites! for you will compass sea and land to make one proselyte, and when he is made, you will make him twofold more the child of Gehenna than yourselves, a light of revelation for the Gentiles. So likewise you, when you shall see all these things, know that it is near, even at the doors.

———

I rise from the table, the others rising with me. Outside, dogs bark in the night streets of occupied Jerusalem, and soldiers patrol with rifle or sword, and the weeping of centuries has only just begun. It will be a long time until the promised day, a whole aeon to let the seed germinate, the shoots take root, the wheat lost in the ryegrass until that next shift in Æternity's eternal revolution. I pause at the door, search for words that might be such seeds.

———

He who has become rich, let him become king. He who has power, let him deny. If those who lead you say to you, Behold, the realm is in the sky! then the birds will be in your sight. If they say to you, It is in the sea! then the fish will be in your sight. But the realm is within you and outside of you.

———

The problem is finding the right metaphor, I think.

———

He who has found the world and become rich, let him deny the world, the cares of this life. But if you do not know *yourselves*, then you are in poverty, you *are* poverty. When you know yourselves, then you shall be known, and you shall know that you are the lovers of the living beloved.

———

I open the door.

He who has ears, let him hear: If the flesh has come into being because of the inspiration, it is a marvel; but if the inspiration has come into being because of the body, it is a marvel of marvels. Indeed, I wonder at this, how this great wealth has taken root in this poverty.

Breath, lover of the sublime. Life. The only true miracle there is.

20

Teach us about this place you are now, said his students, for it's essential that we seek for it.

I stand in the doorway, looking back at them, and for a moment all the haloed glory of sainthood is just the golden glow of lamplight. There are no stained glass scarlets and purples in their robes, no celestial ceruleans or indigos of tempera frescos yet to come, only the earth tones of hide and hemp and unbleached linen. I almost feel that I could grasp Thomas by the hand, drag him across the threshold at my back, across the whole bloody, bawling newborn aeon, from *this* moment there in Jerusalem, to *this* moment here in Æternity, as I write. Almost. But for now I can only set them on the path.

The ideas are revealed to the man, he said, but the light in them is obscured by the idea of the light of the father. He shall be revealed, but his idea is obscured by his light. So I would give you that which eye has not seen, which ear has not heard, which hand has not touched, which has not entered into the heart of man. Except... when you see your reflection in a mirror, you rejoice, but when you see your ideas which came into being before you—which neither die nor are made manifest—how much will you bear?

They follow me out into the night of a city whose conqueror they'll marry. Halogen orange streetlights carve stone to rough beauty glowing solid in the night, man-made and wholly natural. I feel melancholy in leaving it, but it's time to go. I can't bear two thousand years in a Jerusalem mirroring our dreams with a Herod for God, his glory blinding us to his lies, lies blinding us to our own truths.

Blessed is he who shall stand in the beginning, he said. There is a light within a man of light, and it illuminates the whole world. But if it does not give light, there is darkness; so he shall know the end but shall never taste of death. This is the true enlightenment, lighting every man who comes into the world: you are in the world, and through you the world comes to be, and the world knows you not.

They follow me out through the gates, to the Mount of Olives, through its graves and groves. I turn back to the west for a last look, gaze down on a thousand cities folded into one, glowing as the embers of a hearth or a hell.

I have cast fire upon the world, and behold, I guard it until it is ablaze. He who is near to me is near the fire, and he who is far from me is far from the realm. Where there are three deities, they are without the sublime; where there is only one, I am with him. Split the wood, and I am there. Raise up the stone, and there you shall find me.

They follow me past a fruiting fig tree.

––––––

May there be a man of understanding among you.

And he led them out as far as to Bethany, lifted up his hands, blessed them. And after eight days, it came to pass, while he blessed them, he was parted from them. And arising from there, he returned to the Jordan's other side. And they adored him, returned to Jerusalem with great joy, were ever in the temple, blessing and celebrating the sublime.

But they understood not that he spoke to them of the beloved.

A Movement and a Rest

21

After these things the eleven students went away into Galilee, and there were together Simon the Rock, and Thomas the Twin, and Nathanael of Cana in Galilee, and the sons of Zebedee, and two other of his students, when Joshua showed himself again to them at the sea of Galilee. This is how it happened:

I am going fishing, Simon the Rock had said to them.

We will go with you too, they had said to him.

So they had gone forth at once, and entered into a boat.

That night they caught nothing. When the morning was come though, now, Joshua stood on the shore, though the students did not know that it was Joshua.

I lean on the iron rail that runs along the concrete jetty, cupping my hands to guard a Zippo flame, puff a roll-up into life. It's not too cold, a summer morning, but the wind is high, as it ever could be in Capernaum, whipping the flame to a roar before I turn to try and shelter it better, whipping my scarf. A city boy in hipster jeans, biker jacket, baker boy hat, I look like a hustler who pulled a trick on Amsterdam's docks, woke up by accident in Aberdeen. Still, the crew of the *Fisher of Men* don't cast me a second glance, busy winding ropes round bollards, shouting banter and backchat as they carry out tasks long learned to automation.

Friends, Joshua called to them, have you not caught any fish?

No, they answered him.

I skim a hand along the iron rail that runs—I turn, slide a little side-step through Æternity—up to the boat's prow, starboard side, flick my roll-up into the white spume that is cut and churned, turned by the steel hull slicing through the water. Silver flashes of a shoal of bream dart below in the darkness. I holler out for the men behind me, hand waving, pointing.

———

Cast your net on the right side of the boat, he said, and you shall find.

So they cast the net, and now were not able to draw it for the mass of fishes; so it was, in this way, that he showed himself.

———

I grab for the oar John drops to struggle with the net, catch it just as Thomas does too, and catch a grin flashed from him at our shared alarm. Then, as the two of us heave it into the low wooden boat, the Sons of Thunder busy with the haul, that's when his jaw drops. His mouth works as he stares at me, tries to articulate... something. All this time, I've been just a strange passer-by hired on for a short-handed boat and now... I wonder if he might see me as myself in this moment—hope that he might, it's been so long since I shared his company—but then he's calling excitedly to the other boat, to Simon and Andrew, Nathaniel and Philip. And they're rowing over, shouting back. Is it really?

———

So that student whom Joshua loved called to the Rock, It is the teacher.

———

Then I nod at a net that needs our hands, and we fall to it.

———

Man is like a wise fisherman, he said, who cast his net into the sea, drew it up full of small fish. Among them the wise fisherman found a good big fish. He threw down all the small fish into the sea, chose the big fish without trouble.

And none of the students dared ask him, Who are you? knowing it was the teacher.

22

Now when Simon the Rock heard that it was the teacher, he wrapped his coat around him, for he was stripped, and dived into the sea. And the other students came in a little boat, for they were not far from land, only two hundred cubits or so, dragging the net with fishes. As soon then as they were come to land, they saw a fire of coals there, and fish laid there upon it, and bread.

Bring some of the fish which you have caught now, Joshua said to them.

Simon the Rock went up, and drew the net to land full of great fishes, a hundred and fifty three. And for all that there were so many, yet the net was not broken.

I can't help but admire the gusto in him, here and now, this powerhouse of us all, as he heaves the catch to shore, the mass of flapping, slapping silver splaying out across the pebbles, the sheer heart of him as he backslaps and bearhugs in wonder. How? he wants to know. How?

Again, said Joshua, I say that if two of you agree on earth on anything that they would ask, it shall be done for them by my æternal beloved. For where two or three are gathered together in my name, I am there in the midst of them.

I see the momentary *huh* dissolve to *aha* as Simon parses my words, I dare say, to a message on the efficacy of prayer. Ah, Simon. In some aeon, I think, sooner or later, *eventually*, you'll get it. So I let him have his ideas, as simple fare as the fish we pick out of the catch to gut with the skills of Galilean fishermen and cook on a bonfire that lights up the beach at night, the aroma from the tinfoil parcels building as Nathaniel cracks open a beercan, hands it to me.

As I sip, I am glad as ever to be back in Capernaum, gladder still to return as a stranger passing through and become Joshua in their midst because that is how Thomas sees me.

Make a comparison to me, said Joshua to his students, and tell me what I seem to you.

An upstanding messenger, said Simon the Rock.

A wise man of understanding, said Matthew.

Rabbi, said Thomas, my mouth will in no way suffer that I say what you seem.

And I look on him, I think, as Joshua once looked on me. Whatever Joshua saw in this privileged Judaean naif, in Thomas I see the wariness that is fidelity to wisdom, the doubt that keeps him true to his soul.

I am not your teacher, Joshua said. He who drinks from my mouth becomes as me. Because you have drunk, you have become drunk from the bubbling spring which I have poured out. For sure, I tell you, he who trusts in me, the works that I do he shall do also, and he shall do greater works than these. I will become him, and the hidden thing shall be revealed to him.

And he took him, went aside, and spoke to him three words.

Now when Thomas came to his companions, they asked him, What did Joshua say to you?

If I tell you one of the words which he said to me, said Thomas, you will take up stones and throw them at me, and a fire will come out of the stones and burn you up.

Joshua came then, and took bread and gave them, and fish likewise.

Come and dine, he said.

23

lessed are those who have been tormented in their heart, said Joshua, for it is they who have known the beloved in truth. Blessed is the man who has suffered, for he has found his life. Wretched is the body which depends upon a corpse, and wretched is the soul which needs both. Woe to the flesh which needs the soul, and woe to the soul which needs the flesh.

Thomas, Æternity in his eyes, sits on the white sands of a Capernaum new to me, one leg tucked under him, the other drawn up to prop his chin. Blue jeans and ratty sneakers, a checked shirt with the sleeves ripped off, beaded necklace, he looks at home here, some beach bum of this aeon who might head off for India any day.

On the day when you were one, you became two, but when you make the two one, you shall become the everyman. If two make peace with one another in this house, they will say to the mountain, Be moved, and it will be moved. When you make the two one; when you turn the inside out and the outside in; when you make the top into the bottom; when you make a union of the male and female, so the male is not *masculine* and the female not *feminine*; when you make eyes in the place of an eye, a hand in place of a hand, a foot in place of a foot, an idea in place of an idea: then you shall enter the realm.

Thomas, the seed of Joshua in his heart, takes a sip of wine and gazes down into the plastic tumbler in his hand, looks back at me. I have no idea what he's thinking. All I know is that I look at him and see an Æternity with no Empire.

Blessed are the solitary and the successors. You shall find the realm, for you came forth from it and shall return to it again. If they ask, Where have you come from? tell them, We have come from the light, the place where the light came into being through itself alone, where it stood and revealed itself in its ideas. If they ask, Who are you? say, We are his sons and we are the successors of the living father. If they ask you, What is the sign of your father in you? tell them, It is a movement and a rest.

Thomas reaches for bread, brows furrowed, listening.

And when they had dined, Joshua said to Simon the Rock, Walk with me.

Truly I tell you, he said, When you were young, you dressed yourself, walked where you chose. But when you are old, you shall reach out your hands, and another will dress you in sackcloth and ashes, carry you where you would not go.

This he spoke, signifying by what death the Rock would honour the sublime. And he stretched forth his hand toward his students.

Simon bar-Jonah, said Joshua, do you love me more than these?

Yes, Teacher, said the Rock, You know I love you.

Tend my lambs, he said.

Simon bar-Jonah, Joshua said the second time, do you love me?

Yes, Teacher, said the Rock, You know I love you.

Watch my rams, he said.

Simon bar-Jonah, he said a third time, Do you love me?

And the Rock was piqued because he said the third time, Do you love me?

Teacher, he said, you know all things. You know I love you.

And Joshua said to him, Feed my sheep.

24

When he had spoken this, then Simon the Rock, turning about and following, saw the student loved by Joshua, who leaned on his breast at supper and who asked, Teacher, who is it will betray you?

This is the student who testifies of these things, who wrote them down, here in this testament that we all know is true. There are other things that Joshua did too, so many that if every one of them were to be set down in ink on paper, even the world itself could not contain the books that should be written, I imagine.

But there's at least one book that *must* be written, I think as I place the final pieces. Why? There is nothing hidden which shall not be made apparent, and neither was anything kept secret, but that it should be brought to light.

And so I write this, lover of the sublime. Here at the end of this aeon, I rebuild Matthew's truth devoured by Empire, patch in the scraps of Thomas's wisdom that survived the purge, weave through it all my own inspiration blossomed in another's flesh, as Joshua's in mine. From the beloved to the lover, I write this in the hope that you will read it and remember, walk with me in Galilee, in this moment, as Simon turns and sees the beloved student:

And seeing him, this man, the Rock asked of him, what would he do?

If I would have it that he stay a while, said Joshua, what is that to you? You, until I come, walk with me, that you may eat and drink at my table in my realm.

From that day on, this saying went abroad among the brethren, that this student should never die, though Joshua never said to the Rock, He shall not die, only, If I would have it that he stay a while, what is that to you?

I talk of Æternity, knowing that all Simon hears is forever. I show him myself, knowing that all he sees is a dead man risen to immortality. So I do not show him the horror he makes of that realm. It is too late to turn back the seasons of the Gentiles, too late to bring him to the kirk where a minister must have taught him his own tragedy, the murders of Ananias and Sapphira. Instead, I write this testament, the story latent in your mutant plague of a gospel bred from elisions and revisions, trusting in the everyman to wake and spread the word, rise to dismantle Empire, as I have risen from two thousand years, lover of the sublime, to call you not in the name of sacrifice but of mercy.

The realm is to hand, my everyman. Walk with me as I tell Simon how to find it:

Know what is in front of your face, Joshua said, and what is hidden from you shall be revealed to you, for all things are revealed before Æternity. The realm of the beloved is like a woman, carrying a jar full of meal and walking a long way. The jar handle broke; the meal poured out behind her on the road. She was unaware, knew not her loss, but when she came into her house, she put down the jar, found it empty.

But somewhere behind her, scattered all along the road, the realm of Zion lay, waiting to be found and returned by any passing everyman.

And Joshua, walking by the sea of Galilee, stooped down, and wrote on the ground.

Become passers-by, said Joshua.

Amen.

Hal Duncan is the award-winning author of VELLUM and INK, along with numerous short stories, poems, essays, and even a few musicals. Homophobic hatemail once dubbed him "THE.... Sodomite Hal Duncan!!" (sic), and you can find him revelling in that role online.

www.ingramcontent.com/pod-product-compliance
Lightning Source LLC
Chambersburg PA
CBHW051001210726
48287CB00004B/1323